RANSOM ISLAND

RANSOM ISLAND

A NOVEL BY MILES ARCENEAUX

Ransom Island

This book is a work of fiction.
Names, characters, places, and incidents are either products of the authors' imaginations or are used fictitiously.
Any resemblance to actual events or locales or persons, living or dead, is entirely coincidental.

Library of Congress Cataloging in Publication Data:
Arceneaux, Miles
Ransom Island / Miles Arceneaux
1. Title. 2. Fiction. 3. Mystery. 4 Suspense
-
First Edition: October 2014
978-1-62288-085-0

Printed in the United States of America
Written by Brent Douglass, John T. Davis and James R. Dennis
Designed by Lana Rigsby, Thomas Hull, and Carmen Garza

Stephen F. Austin State University Press
PO Box 13007, SFA Station, Nacogdoches, TX. 75962
sfapress@sfasu.edu sfasu.edu/sfapress

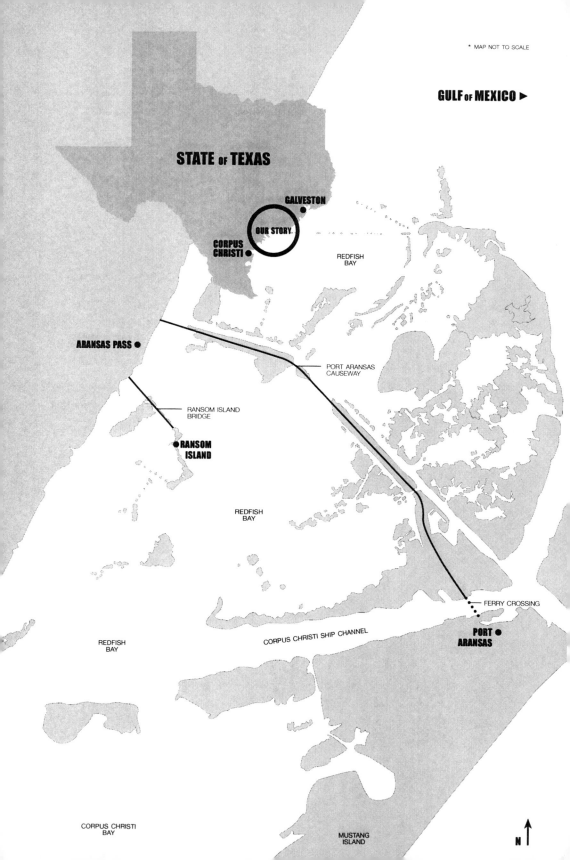

* MAP NOT TO SCALE

GULF OF MEXICO ▶

STATE OF TEXAS

GALVESTON ●

OUR STORY™

CORPUS CHRISTI ●

REDFISH BAY

ARANSAS PASS ●

PORT ARANSAS CAUSEWAY

RANSOM ISLAND BRIDGE

● RANSOM ISLAND

REDFISH BAY

FERRY CROSSING

PORT ● ARANSAS

CORPUS CHRISTI SHIP CHANNEL

REDFISH BAY

CORPUS CHRISTI BAY

MUSTANG ISLAND

N ↑

AUTHOR'S NOTE

Ransom Island is a real place and the inspiration for this book,
but *Ransom Island* is a fictional creation.

In its heyday, you could go there and rent a skiff for a day of fishing on Redfish
Bay and later enjoy a cold beer and a burger in the rustic beer joint. You could come
back later that night and listen to live music, dance, play the slots, or stay in one of the
little guest cabins near the docks. The island was rough-and-ready and had its share
of scandalous characters. In other words, it had all the ingredients for a good story.

A hurricane took out the narrow, one-lane wooden bridge in the
late 1950s and Aransas Pass decided not to rebuild it. So began Ransom
Island's rapid decline. Hurricanes in 1961 and 1970, together with the widening
of the Intracoastal Ship Channel, hastened the process. Today, only shellcrete
foundations, broken water cisterns, and overgrown roads remain, as well as about
a billion rattlesnakes. And this book.

I should note that the "Duke Ellington" in these pages is only a fictional
approximation of the man who might be America's foremost musical genius.
Although I've taken liberties with details, I've tried to reflect the man's
grace and personality. Those wishing a factual look at Ellington and his career
are enthusiastically referred to Terry Teachout's excellent biography,
Duke: A Life of Duke Ellington.

I would once again like to thank Rigsby-Hull for an outstanding cover design,
and also Stephen F. Austin University Press for publishing the book.
Thanks as well to the Texas A&M University Press sales and marketing crew
for their continued support, and finally, thanks to the many pre-publication
readers whose candid feedback helped immensely.

– MILES ARCENEAUX

CHAPTER 01

JUNE 1953

Old Hitler's body washed up on Ransom Island one June morning in 1953, a feathered red-cane lance buried deep in his back. Some insisted it was fate, while others shook their heads and said it was a crying shame. Later on, when all the excitement died down, most everyone agreed it had been a portent of things to come.

Portent or not, it was starting to stink in the hot summer sun.

A young, crew-cut ichthyologist from the Marine Science Institute in nearby Port Aransas stretched a measuring tape the length of the shark and shook his head in wonder.

"Remarkable," he said. "I thought you boys were telling me a fish story when you telephoned this afternoon. This may very well be the largest *Sphyrnidae* ever recorded in the Gulf—twenty feet long, if he's an inch. I could kick myself for not bringing a camera." He glanced up from his notebook where he was recording the hammerhead's measurements. "Mr. Sweetwater, how long has it been lying here on your beach?"

Rupert Sweetwater, the owner, head barkeep, and one-man hospitality committee of Ransom Island, turned to a grizzled figure that stood apart from the group, observing the spectacle from the grassy fringe of the shoreline. "Barefoot?"

Barefoot Nelson lived on the remote south end of the island in a dugout lean-to made of salvaged lumber, driftwood, and tin. He and his devoted but long-suffering wife had been living in the same primitive hovel when Rupert and his brothers bought the island before the war, and they stayed put mostly out of Rupert's good graces. Barefoot kept to himself and approached the rest of the human race with a truculence that made him legendary up and down the Coastal Bend.

Barefoot didn't respond, his eyes fixed on the shark. Its mallet-shaped head spanned almost four feet, and the dorsal fin was so big it flopped over to one side of its own weight.

The old man fished for a living, selling his catch to seafood processors and restaurants in the area, including Rupert's thriving establishment on Ransom Island. He had a creased, leathery face and a wind-blown mop of whitish hair that sprouted from his head like unpicked cotton. Nobody had ever seen Barefoot Nelson in a pair of shoes, not even in winter.

Early that morning, Rupert had encountered Barefoot squatting near the dead hammerhead, the feathers of his rustic lance whipping in the breeze. *Hunting sharks with a homemade pole spear,* thought Rupert in wonderment. *That's crazy even for you, Barefoot.*

"He doesn't say much does he?" said the biologist.

Rupert shrugged. "He's not real chatty."

Numerous scrapes and scars marred the shark's coarse hide, some of them put there by Barefoot himself. For thirteen years Old Hitler had been his nemesis, his white whale. The leviathan had snatched bull redfish off his handlines, swallowing them whole. It had ravaged beds of flounder, methodically rooting them out of the sand by the light of Barefoot's lantern. It had torn holes in his gill nets to get at the mullet he and his wife captured in the channels. Killing the creature had become his obsession.

Fortunately, Barefoot was a patient man.

Several times he'd managed to snag it on heavy test line, but each time the shark managed to bite through the wire leader before he could land it. Occasionally, Barefoot had been close enough to touch the fish, to whack at it with his oar, and one time, to cut a long gash in its hide with a machete. But when he finally managed to herd Old Hitler into a shallow tidal channel and plunge his homemade spear into his black, two-chambered heart, he felt . . . conflicted.

For more than a dozen years he and Old Hitler had competed for fish in the saltwater bays, bayous, and waterways between Fulton and

Corpus Christi. And now that he had vanquished his rival, he felt hollowed out, almost bereaved. Never mind that the marauding hammerhead had cost him thousands of dollars in lost equipment and catch. Barefoot respected the animal purely as a superb fisherman and a worthy adversary—one every bit as relentless and resourceful as himself.

He took a last look at the shark, turned, and disappeared over the sand dune.

"He's an odd sort," said the biologist. "I've heard about him, but that's the first time I've met him. Is it safe to assume that's his Indian lance?"

"Yeah, I'd say that's a safe bet," said Rupert. "Ol' Barefoot's about half-Karankawa, I think."

The biologist wrapped his hand around a knuckle in the bamboo shaft and examined the hawk feathers dangling from the end. "Damned impressive. He must have been standing right on top of the shark to get the tip into him that deep."

He pulled out his tape once more and asked Zachariah Yates, the black man who worked for Rupert, to hold up the tall triangular fin so he could take a final measurement. As he wrote the number in his book, he chuckled softly. "Old Hitler, huh? You know the Coast Watchers Club will be awfully disappointed. I imagine this big fellow was responsible for more than a few false U-boat sightings over the years. All he lacked was a periscope strapped to his first dorsal."

The Coast Watchers Club had christened the giant fish shortly after it began prowling their local waters—about the same time that *Der Führer's* U-boats began ravaging the Atlantic and Gulf Coast waters. Initially, the club had been an active and useful volunteer sub-sighting group, guarding the coast from a genuine threat. But after the war, the Coast Watchers had evolved into a once-a-month old-timers' reunion, dedicated primarily to the consumption of alcohol and distribution of idle gossip. The occasional report of a German U-boat sighting, usually from an inebriated night fisherman, only served to reinforce the club's dedication to its mission.

"I'd appreciate it if you boys would leave the specimen undisturbed until I get back with my camera," said the marine biologist. "After that, I guess you can do with it what you want. Thanks, Mr. Yates. You can let go now."

Zachariah dropped the fin and looked seaward. He'd long ago ceased to be surprised at the random bounties the sea washed up.

Thirty-three years ago, when he was a top hand on the Salt Creek Ranch on nearby Matagorda Island, he rode up on a humpback whale that had beached itself in the swash near Cedar Bayou. Sharks had ripped ragged holes in its massive body and turkey vultures were feasting on the exposed flesh. Two days later a hurricane swept over the island, blowing away the carcass, the bunkhouse, and the corral, drowning twenty of the horses and half the cattle. Hell of a thing for a working cowboy to have to put up with. Zachariah wasn't superstitious, but he didn't like anomalies, and he had a bad feeling about Old Hitler.

Rupert turned to the Mexican man squatting on his haunches on the shore. "Know any good recipes for hammerhead, Gilbert?"

Gilberto Ruiz, Rupert's cook, shrugged. "Sure, but first we'll have to bury it in the sand and let it rot for a few months. Otherwise—"

"Otherwise it'll taste like pee," said the biologist. "The young man is correct. Sharks have a very high concentration of urea in their tissue that tastes and smells like ammonia as it breaks down. Bury the meat and the bacteria will eliminate the urea over time. Old Viking recipe."

"Well then, how 'bout the fin?" asked Rupert. "Don't they eat that across that other ocean?" He cocked his thumb toward Asia. "Some kind of Jap deal?"

"Shark fin soup?" said Gilbert. "It's Chinese. You'd hate it."

"How do you know?"

"Because you won't even eat *menudo*."

"I can't abide tripe, it's true. I just hate to see this creature go to waste."

Gilbert slapped at a mosquito that had landed on his neck. "I guess I could cut out the liver and bottle it for bug repellent . . . you know, like the Indians did."

The biologist looked over at Gilbert and then said to Rupert. "He's a walking encyclopedia isn't he?"

Rupert nodded. "Makes good *menudo,* too. Or so I'm told."

They waded ashore and walked toward the full moon, which rose over the main building of the Shady Palm Fish Camp. Behind them, the sun began to set over Redfish Bay and the mosquitoes were venturing out of the grass to feed.

"I'll be back in the morning to take pictures," said the biologist. "You might want to take some, too. Maybe send them over to the newspaper. This shark is big news . . . and big publicity for your establishment, I would think."

But the magnificent fish was gone before it could be photographed for science, public entertainment, or commercial advertising. Barefoot Nelson returned that night, lashed Old Hitler to his skiff, and hauled him past the jetties into deep water, where he cut him loose and sadly watched him sink into the dark depths of the Gulf of Mexico.

———

CHAPTER 02

Jimmy Glick sat at the bar at the Rainbow Inn eating a bowl of Loser's Gumbo and feeling like the whole world was conspiring to piss him off.

The Rainbow Inn belied its cheery name. It was a ramshackle joint—two joints, actually, joined by a covered walkway at the water's edge of Aransas Pass. The streetside building where Jimmy was sitting and morosely pondering his state of affairs housed the lounge, the restaurant, and a small stage where local country-and-western bands entertained on weekends. The rear half of the establishment was reserved for gambling, cockfights (hence the gumbo), and cribs for the whores who plied their trade with the stoic perseverance of dockworkers.

He looked out the front window at a rickety one-lane bridge that jutted out over the bay and ended on a scrubby crescent-shaped island in the distance. Further to the east, another causeway crossed the bay, transporting cars from Aransas Pass to the ferry that took them the last quarter mile to the tiny fisherman's village of Port Aransas. A grungy shrimp boat with the name *Rebel Yell* painted across the transom motored by in front of the restaurant.

Jimmy really, truly, sincerely did not want to be in this backwater shithole on what was essentially a nursemaid errand. He didn't want to be here at all, out among the redneck fishermen, Polack longshoremen, and coonass roughnecks. He belonged in his natural environment, two hundred miles up the coast in cosmopolitan Galveston, sitting in a corner booth at the swanky Turf Club, in a tailored summer-weight wool suit, drinking iced coffee and basking in the air conditioning while waiting for whatever task, illicit or otherwise, the Ginestra brothers set him to.

The meat in the gumbo was tough and stringy. Fighting roosters didn't make for succulent eating, but Jimmy couldn't stand the thought of another greasy burger or fried fish platter, which pretty much constituted the whole of the local cuisine. Right now he could be enjoying a big plate of Oysters Rockefeller at Gaido's on the seawall promenade, or dining on aged ribeye steak at the Tremont Hotel, but no, he was stuck in the boonies, trying to track down a wayward twenty-two-year-old girl. He shifted the Smith & Wesson automatic under his jacket, where the shoulder holster was chafing his sweaty underarm, and sighed a self-pitying sigh. *This is no way for a badass gangster to spend his time,* he thought.

The trouble was, Primo Ginestra didn't give a hoot in hell what Jimmy Glick thought. And Primo *was,* in fact, a badass gangster. He and his younger brother, Gerardo, didn't run their criminal empire in a democratic fashion or solicit the opinions of their underlings. Mussolini could have taken lessons.

What Primo *did* want was for his number one enforcer to track down the whereabouts of Sally Rose Ginestra, Primo's only daughter. For almost two years, ever since the girl had gone missing from the College and Academy of the Incarnate Word, Jimmy Glick or his colleague, Derek "Deke" Maloney, had been tracking down sightings. One time she showed up in a USO Club on the San Antonio Riverwalk. Another time one of the Ginestras' league of far-flung observers spotted her working in the bar at the Driskill Hotel in Austin. Someone even said she was modeling dresses for awhile for the rich ladies shopping at Neiman-Marcus in Dallas.

Jimmy didn't know where she was, only where she wasn't. Worse yet, he didn't know what to do if he found the little brat.

"You want me to bring her back?" he asked the old man when the whole runaround began. "Tie her to the fender like a deer? From what I remember about her, that might be the only way she'd come."

Primo Ginestra nodded in wry acknowledgment that his daughter had inherited the bullheaded Ginestra temperament.

They both knew the truth was a lot more complicated. Sally Rose was indeed the daughter of Primo's deceased wife, Natalie. But her biological father was just as likely a tenor saxophone player at the Bali Hai Club, the Ginestras' glittering showroom and casino on the Galveston Seawall. Natalie insisted at first that the little girl was Primo's, and he believed her. But Primo was a proud man, and when rumors of his wife's long-running paramour surfaced, he made a point to look into it.

Primo found out the truth, of course—what had Natalie been thinking? He bided his time, patiently, which was out of character for him. When he was sure, he killed Natalie and the sax player both. Jimmy Glick had helped him dump the bodies in the Bolivar Roads ship channel. They'd never spoken of it again.

Primo had never given his unfaithful wife another thought. Still, he felt a lingering guilt towards the little girl—she must have been about three when it happened. She hadn't asked for the life she'd been born into. And he clung to the possibility, remote though it was, that she was his blood daughter after all. Family honor and respect were paramount to Primo, as his two-timing wife should have known. He was decidedly Old World in that way.

As soon as Sally Rose was old enough, he had shipped her off to the nuns in Victoria, where she could grow up and he could keep a distant, paternal eye on her from afar. When she turned eighteen, he consented, with reservations, to send her to the nearest Catholic college where she could study to become a teacher. Now, barely a grown woman, she'd gone missing. Primo couldn't help but wonder what she might have discovered about her papa.

"Just find her," he told Jimmy. "Just let me know where she is, if she's okay. She's running from something, it seems like. I wanna know from what. Or from who." The idea that it might be him never crossed Primo's mind. *She's mine*, he thought. *And she doesn't get to go runnin' off like that.*

So Jimmy Glick packed his grip and went looking for a hundred and twenty-pound skirt who'd busted out of Catholic school. Shit. He, who'd personally handled Frank Nitti when the Chicago mob sent Nitti, their toughest gunsel, south to sniff around the rackets on Galveston Island.

It was the stuff of local bad guy legend. Jimmy had rousted Nitti at gunpoint out of a crib at the Queen of Palms brothel on Post Office

Street at two in the morning. Marching the gangster to his car (Nitti clad only in boxer shorts and undershirt), Jimmy drove him to the West End of the island and dangled him by his ankles over the rail of the San Luis Pass toll bridge.

Then he told him about the sharks.

Frank Nitti caught the first thing smoking back to Houston the next morning and flew straight home. That was the last the Ginestras ever heard from Chicago.

Now look at me, thought Jimmy.

"You about done here, hon?"

Jimmy looked up from his bowl of cockfight gumbo and nodded. "Maybe another Falstaff, how's 'bout?" he said to the wan-looking waitress.

"Sure thing, but do you mind settling up with me for now? We're about to have a shift change and I need to close out my tabs."

"Yeah, sure." Jimmy glanced around as he dug for his wallet: a couple of roughnecks playing for chump change at the shuffleboard table, a local punk touching up his ducktail in the cigarette machine mirror, three hard-worn women with tight skirts and low-cut blouses roosting by the bar, each nursing something brown and cloudy in a highball glass.

The three dames looked like pelicans lined up along a row of pier pilings. The ashtray between them was half-filled with carmine-smudged butts. Their hair was so viciously marcelled in a long out-of-style fashion that merely looking at them made Jimmy's own hair hurt.

Jimmy's waitress, the barmaid, and the other waitress gathered at a serving station and began to ring up their tabs and pool their tips. At that point, the three pelicans (as Jimmy envisioned them) downed their drinks, stubbed out their cigarettes, and migrated to the other side of the bar. One popped the top off Jimmy's Falstaff and the other two tied on aprons and picked up serving trays, while the three off-duty girls took their places on the recently-vacated stools and ordered new drinks.

Shift change? thought Jimmy. *I have got to get the fuck out of here.*

At the same moment Jimmy was watching the floozies play musical barstools, Sally Rose Ginestra came walking up the sidewalk, late, as usual. She was wearing an ankle-length raincoat that covered her outfit, such as it was, of satin cocktail shorts and a halter top—the standard Rainbow Inn uniform for a cigarette girl and hostess in the "cold drink" joint that operated out of the back half of the building.

Sally Rose wasn't at the end of her rope, exactly, but there wasn't enough line left to tie a decent square knot. She didn't have a plan; that was the damned problem. She'd just been operating on instinct ever since she'd learned the truth about her father. Her so-called father.

So she'd bolted, left the school where she was studying, and just lit out. She wasn't sure what she was going to do; she just felt an implacable urge to move and keep moving. And to stay as far away from Galveston as possible. Until she had a plan.

Well, Galveston was only two hundred miles away from Aransas Pass. Too close for comfort. But Sally was out of money and low on options.

She was not, however, short on wits. She'd developed a sort of sixth sense during her time on the run, and it steered her attention to the dust-covered Buick Super parked alongside the restaurant. She noticed it had a dealer frame around the license plate: "Pennington Buick, Galveston."

Just a coincidence, she thought. *Sure.*

But as she edged around the corner and peeked through the plate glass window into the bar, she saw a familiar hawk-nosed silhouette pouring beer into a Pilsner glass.

Jimmy Glick.

Shit.

Primo just never gives up, she thought.

When she was younger and made her school holiday visits back to Galveston, Jimmy Glick had encouraged Sally to think of him as a sort of uncle. One of the fun kind, the sort who would let her drive his Buick along the Seawall when she was twelve and later on give her money for cigarettes, always admonishing her not to let the old man find out. "Or it'll be my ass, get my drift?" he'd say with a wink.

Early on, she'd taken to calling him just "Glick," which annoyed him to no end. Which in turn delighted her, the little wiseass. "Glick, Glick, Glick," she'd chirp.

When she was a teenager and began to get a vague sense of her father's real position in the community—the Sisters occasionally got the Galveston papers and would gossip when they thought she was out of earshot—she came to realize what a life-threatening proposition it could be to tease Jimmy Glick about anything. He ceased being the worldly friend who'd treated her to days at Murdoch's Bath House. She saw him for what he truly was—a hunter.

She was being hunted. And, like prey, she froze.

But her mind was racing. *Whattodowhattodowhattodo* . . . .

Her boarding house was three blocks away, past vacant lots and low-slung bungalows—no concealment if Jimmy looked out the window or finished his beer and began cruising the streets. Anyway, she had no car. He must have known she was in the vicinity. Coincidence was out of the question. She felt like a mouse in the middle of a wide-open field, waiting for the hawk to swoop down out of the sun.

Gottagogottago . . . .

She spun on her heel and walked stiffly to the back of the building, a chill running down her spine.

A refrigerated truck had backed up to the rear door of the Rainbow Inn, and a stocky driver in an undershirt was loading wooden cases of Grand Prize and Pearl beer onto a dolly. He wheeled the load into the building towards the kitchen's walk-in cooler.

Sally didn't think about it. She sprang around the corner of the building and squeezed between cases and kegs of beer until she could crouch down into the smallest recess at the farthest reach of the trailer.

The driver came back outside, stowed his dolly on a rack on the side of the truck, and slammed the reefer door shut. She was trapped. Ten seconds later, she noticed she was freezing her ass off. *Nice going, Sally Rose,* she thought with chagrin. *If the next delivery stop is too far off, it'll be Sally Eskimo-Pie.*

———

CHAPTER 03

"Jesus Christ! Be careful with that!"

Gilbert and Zach paused in their sweaty labors and traded looks. Then they both glanced disapprovingly at Rupert, who stood at the end of a makeshift gangway leading up to the raised porch. He had been fussing at them nonstop since the delivery truck had arrived with the mysterious crate and they'd been called on to help move the bulky cargo into the building. Gilbert muttered something in Spanish under his breath—not a term of endearment.

"You forget I understand them Meskin cusswords, Gilbert," Rupert barked.

"I was just sayin' that this mother scratcher better be a new oven for my kitchen," Gilbert lied, using his sleeve to wipe the sweat from his brow.

"It's better'n that, son. A few more feet and all will be revealed."

At last they trundled the giant crate through the twin doors, across the dancehall, and into position next to the bar. Rupert gave up his supervisory role and the three men attacked the crate with crowbars, tin snips, and pocketknives. When the last of the crate's plywood, excelsior, and other shipping material had been dismantled, what stood revealed was a shiny new Seeburg Select-O-Matic jukebox.

A modern marvel of wood-grained vinyl, red plastic, and softly-glowing black shellac discs, it looked like a piece of abstract sculpture set down in the rustic beer joint.

Zach was impressed despite himself. "It's beautiful, Rupe."

Gilbert, too. "If they'd had a jukebox in the Great Library of Alexandria, I bet it would've looked like this."

"Yep. She can play fifty records back and forth," said Rupert. "That's one hundred songs in the whole shebang. Speaking of which . . . ." He picked up the little cellophane packages of paper titles that would be slipped into the slots keyed to the records. He'd ordered the lineup himself.

He picked one out at random: G-4, "Rockin' In Rhythm" and its flip side, "Creole Rhapsody," by Duke Ellington and His Orchestra. Another (E-7): "Perdido" and its B-side, "Sentimental Lady," by Duke Ellington. A dozen or more titles, all the same—a twenty-year survey of hits by the Ellington band. Rupert nodded in satisfaction.

"Dang, Rupe. That's a lot of songs by one fella," said Zach. "Duke? Is he English?"

Rupert laughed. "Sit down and I'll buy you boys a beer," he said. "Naw, Zeke, he's not English—as a matter of fact, he's colored." Zach looked dubious, and Rupert continued, not sure how to characterize the man. "But he's something more."

Then he told them about the time, a year previously, when he'd been in Houston shopping for a new compressor for the walk-in refrigerator and for some other odds and ends for the kitchen and bar. He had been strolling downtown on Texas Street, past the fancy Rice Hotel, en route to a nearby chili parlor for a late lunch, when he heard, "Yo, Rupe!"

"J.B. Leavitt! I'll be damned," exclaimed Rupert as he turned around to behold a familiar face coming out of the revolving door of the hotel.

Jimmy Boyd Levitt had been in the marching band when Rupert was playing two-platoon football at Aransas Consolidated High School.

J.B. (he insisted the initials stood for "Just Because") derided Rupert as a thickheaded jock, while Rupert teased J.B. for being a band fairy, playing the trombone with his pinky finger sticking out. It had been all in fun, and the two boys did their share of carousing and beer drinking up and down the backroads of San Patricio and Nueces counties. Once, they'd even taken Rupert's old Model-A pickup down the wild reaches of Padre Island to the distant Mansfield Cut, an epic journey in those days. Gradually, as high school boys do, they drifted apart after graduation.

Now, though, Rupert whistled appreciatively. "Damn, Just Because. Did you strike oil or marry a movie star? That suit looks like it costs more than I make in a month of selling beer and bait."

J.B. smiled and rolled a toothpick in the corner of his mouth. "Yeah, I heard you had a little enterprise going out there on the bay."

"You heard right. Biggest dancehall between Corpus and Victoria, just about. We've had Spade Cooley, T-Bone Walker, Hank Thompson and the Brazos Valley Boys play there—got sport-fishin' and duck-huntin', too, if your taste runs to that."

Leavitt worked his toothpick back and forth thoughtfully. "Dancehall, hmmm? Fishin', too . . . ." He seemed to make up his mind about something. "You got anything going on right this second?"

"Just keeping an appointment with a bowl of chili. Maybe some free saltines."

"C'mon in, I want you to meet someone."

He led Rupert back into the wood-and-leather confines of the hotel bar, where several men lounged, each as elegantly attired as Just Because. Rupert was startled to see that all of the men were Negroes. To the best of his knowledge, the restaurant and the bar of Houston's fanciest hotel had never been open to colored people. If they wanted to eat, they entered through the kitchen and were led to a segregated seating area in the hotel cafeteria.

"Where's the boss?" J.B. asked one of them.

"Checking out the ballroom," one of the men said. "Wants to be sure the piano tuner shows up on time. You know him."

"I sure do. C'mere, Rupe. Let me buy you a drink and let's catch up a bit."

The two were debating the merits of two Southwest Conference football powerhouses—TCU vs. SMU—when J.B. glanced abruptly over Rupert's shoulder and straightened up. Rupert put down his highball glass, turned around, and stared into the eyes of the most elegant man he'd ever seen in his life.

Edward Kennedy "Duke" Ellington wasn't royalty by birth, but he carried himself with an effortless ease and grace that made him seem to the manor born. He wore a custom-tailored lightweight double-breasted wool suit as offhandedly as if it were a robe and slippers. But there was nothing foppish or effeminate about him. He projected a natural, streetwise authority.

Ellington's eyes, set off by deep pouches underneath, glittered with intelligence and a shrewd sort of bemusement. His hair rippled back off his long skull, and a pencil-thin moustache set off a generous mouth that, at this moment, was curling into an easy smile.

"Duke," said J.B., "this is an old high-school friend of mine, Rupert Sweetwater."

"Hello, cousin," said Ellington, putting out his hand. Mesmerized, Rupert shook it.

"It's hard to picture my horn-blowin', reefer-smokin' Texas wild man in high school," Ellington said with a twinkle in his eye. "What did you make of your scholarly pursuits, Mr. Sweetwater?"

"I, um, run a dancehall down near Corpus Christi. The, ah, Shady Palm Bar and Grill? Shady's? Perhaps you've heard of it?" Rupert felt like an idiot.

"No, I haven't had the pleasure," Ellington replied as he took a cigarette out of a silver case and lit it. "Who's been fortunate enough to play your establishment?"

For a moment, Rupert drew a horrible blank. He was acutely conscious of his battered khaki slacks and Harry Truman shirt with hula girls all over it—his "city outfit."

"We, ah . . . we had Wilburn Roach and his Westernaire Playboys last month . . . ."

Ellington's eyes narrowed slightly, as though he thought he was being ribbed.

But then (maybe thanks to the big gulp of scotch he ingested) Rupert regained his bearings. "We've also had Teddy Wilson and his orchestra in there. Had a wonderful dance."

Ellington smiled, his big teeth lighting up the dim bar. "Oh, yes. Teddy is the second-best piano player I know. I'd enjoy bringing my boys down to play at, ah, Shady's some fine day."

Rupert couldn't help it. He gawked.

"In the meantime, you'll have to excuse me." He turned to his other band members in the lounge. "Boys . . . rehearsal in 30 minutes. We're going to try to put some legs on the new stuff."

Rupert blinked and managed to say, "My wife and I had our first dance to 'Moonglow' at our wedding."

Ellington smiled and looked genuinely delighted. "It's my honor to have provided a song for the occasion," he said. He motioned for the bar tab for the entire party. "Please have another drink on me."

"And that . . ." Rupert concluded for a rapt Gilbert and Zachariah, "was how I came to have drinks with Duke Ellington."

"Be damned, Rupe," said Gilbert. "You're half-famous. Bet your wife was impressed."

"Darla was as impressed as she ever gets about anything besides Darla," Rupert replied.

"They were in the hotel? Like, *stayin'* there?" said Zach. He couldn't seem to get his mind around it.

"I asked J.B. about that. He said they were playing an invite-only show for the owner of the Rice Hotel, and Ellington told the fellow he'd do it only if his band stayed in the best rooms in the house. Takes a hell of a lot of nerve, especially in Texas, but J.B. said Duke won't even walk in a door unless it's the front door. If some innkeeper makes a fuss, they all just stay in their fancy Pullman cars at the railroad station. He's cancelled big jobs over that kind of peckerwood Jim Crow stuff."

"Did he mean what he said about playing here at Shady's?" asked Gilbert.

"Aw, naw. I reckon he was just being polite. I picked up a copy of *Billboard* at a newsstand in the hotel and found out who his manager was. Jew fella up in New York. I wrote him a letter but never heard back. I expect these records in the new juke are as close as we're gonna get to Duke Ellington. Speaking of which, let's clean up this packing stuff and plug 'er in."

Gilbert squinted out the window as a familiar delivery truck rolled across the bridge.

"I'm gonna leave this with you two, boss. Big 'Un gets aggravated if there's no one around to help him horse those beer crates into the walk-in."

—

Joe "Big 'Un" Mouton drove his beer truck across the rumbling planks of the one-lane bridge en route to his next and last delivery stop on Ransom Island. Despite the chicken fried steak he'd had for lunch at the Rainbow Inn, he was in a foul mood.

He had five bucks on the local Texas League favorite, the Corpus Christi Giants, who at the top of the seventh were being beat like whipped curs by the Beaumont Golden Gators, 9-1. Big 'Un flipped a Chesterfield butt out the window and into the bay. Then he turned off the radio and geared down as he prepared to turn into the parking lot of his last port of call. His mood abruptly lightened. Maybe that cute piece of tail who was married to the guy who ran the place would be tending bar today.

In Big 'Un's eyes, his mirror showed a reflection that was about two-thirds Marlon Brando and one-third Bob Mitchum. (Darla Sweetwater would have called him one-hundred per cent pussel-gutted Wallace Beery gone to seed, and one who smelled like the inside of a beer cooler, to boot.)

Big 'Un's spirits sank once more when he saw the wiry young Mexican come out the back door instead of Darla. Oh well. Help was help. He un-slung his dolly from the side of the truck and ratcheted up the back. A cold cloud of condensation rolled out of the truck as Gilbert and Big 'Un reached in and started pulling out crates of beer.

"Walk-in's open, Big 'Un," said Gilbert as the truck driver lumbered away, his dolly bouncing over the rough oyster shells that paved the parking lot.

Gilbert took a step inside the truck to grab a keg of Jax when he was nearly sideswiped by a cloaked figure who bolted for the daylight.

"*Jesuscristo!*" yelped Gilbert who, for one crazy moment, thought a deer or a kangaroo or some other frantic creature had managed to secret itself inside the beer truck.

He leaned cautiously outside and saw . . . well, it wasn't a kangaroo, but it was a sight nearly as unlikely. A shivering girl in a raincoat, her lips blue with cold, had darted out of the truck and was hiding behind the big water cistern next to the kitchen, out of sight of everyone but Gilbert.

He walked towards her slowly, hands out to his sides, much as he would approach any terrified young animal. His face was scrunched up with curiosity and concern. In spite of the circumstances, he couldn't help noticing she was damned pretty.

"S-sorry to scare you, mister, b-but you've got to help me," she said. "I n-need a p-place to hide." Her teeth were chattering.

"Well, sure. Come inside the restaurant and I'll make you a cup of hot coffee. Damn, *chica*, you almost scared the pants off me."

The girl shook her head emphatically. "I need to get out of sight. Mister—p-please!"

As she reached out to him in entreaty, her raincoat fell open and he saw she was attired in some sort of skimpy shorts and halter outfit.

What the hell? Gilbert thought. The screen door slammed as Big 'Un returned for another load of beer.

"Okay, okay, okay." Gilbert grabbed the girl's elbow and shoved her through another screen door, this one leading to the detached kitchen behind Shady's. "You got a name?"

"It's Sally," she whispered. "Sally Rose."

"Well, Sally Rose. My name's Gilbert, and I sure hope you know what you're doing."

"I do," she said. "T-trust me." Gilbert cocked a skeptical eyebrow as he left. He trotted back to the truck, just in time to grab two cases of Lone Star.

Fifteen minutes later, the beer was safely stowed in the coolers and Gilbert grabbed a longneck and perched himself on a barstool, deliberating over what to do about the pretty girl hiding out in his kitchen. "Moonglow" purred through the speakers of the new jukebox and Rupert and Darla were swaying in the middle of the dance floor, lost in memories.

Looking over their shoulders, Gilbert saw a dusty Buick Super squeeze around the beer truck as it rumbled out of the driveway. The Buick parked and a hawked-nosed man climbed out and began to climb the steps to the front door.

Peeking through a crack in a kitchen shutter, Sally Rose saw the car and its driver, too. *Crapped out,* she thought. *A busted flush.* Then she whispered tiredly, "Jimmy Glick."

CHAPTER 04

Jimmy Glick rolled his Buick slowly across the oyster shell parking lot as he considered his options. That the girl was here seemed logical. He'd overheard the line cook asking Betty Jo, one of the waitresses, if she'd seen the new girl, Sally Rose. A little city charm and misdirection on Jimmy's part (plus a hell of a tip) had elicited that yes, the new girl was living in a nearby rooming house, and no, she didn't have a car. In fact, the waitress could have sworn she'd seen Sally walking up to the building, but wasn't sure where she'd gone to.

The only connecting road inland ran right by the front door of the Rainbow Inn, and the only traffic had been the beer truck returning from the island across the bay. She must have spotted him somehow.

As improbable as it seemed, she had to have stowed away in the truck. Well, she wouldn't stay hidden inside to come back *into* Aransas Pass. So she had to be here on the island. *You've run out of real estate, girlie,* thought Jimmy.

Sally's personal Alamo didn't look like much of a place for a last stand. Jimmy had grown up in Houston, but he'd seen scores of joints like this from the Sabine Pass to the Bolivar Peninsula. A white, tin-roofed clapboard building set up on creosote pilings, with a long, wrap-around covered porch. Except this one was bigger than most.

"Shady Palm Bar & Grill" read a tin sign over the door, bookended by Coca-Cola logos. "Shady Palm Fish Camp" announced another sign beside a turnoff leading to a small complex of bungalow cabins and finger piers. Jimmy saw only one lonely, bedraggled palm tree on the island.

"Skiffs for rent by day or hour" offered a smaller addendum under the fish camp sign. "Fresh bait live and dead." "Shady's Seaside Cabins available for families and groups." "Friendly and expert guides for hire."

Too much goddamn information, Jimmy thought sourly. He didn't like to fish and he didn't like people who did.

He lit a cigarette and flipped the top of the lighter while he considered his next move. *Primo just wants to know where she is,* he thought. *Well, now we know. The question is—do I brace her here or go back into town and take a chance she'll skip on me again?*

While he mulled, Jimmy's mind was running on a parallel track. In spite of the hillbilly bait camp atmosphere, Jimmy could see the place had natural illicit potential. A man who knew the bay's tricky natural and manmade barriers—oyster reefs, shoals, gas pipelines, drilling platforms—and could master its secluded backways could land a handsome amount of tax-free booze on the island.

And there was only one landward route for any law to approach the place—the one-lane causeway, which would expose any oncoming vehicles. The setup reminded him of the Ginestra's Bali Hai showplace, set out in the Gulf on the end of a two-hundred yard T-head pier. The dice tables and roulette wheels were on pivots, and when an alarm was given from the foot of the pier, they could drop through the floor or disappear into built-in alcoves on a moment's notice. Suddenly, a group of degenerate society gamblers were transformed into genteel bridge and gin rummy players.

Once, the Texas Rangers had tried to raid the place only to find a cross-section of Galveston's A-list society sipping pink champagne and competing in friendly matches of Mahjong and Forty-Two. As an added humiliation, when the Rangers finally burst through the door, the band struck up a rousing version of "The Yellow Rose of Texas." Gerry Ginestra, who was presiding over operations that night, placed his hand over his heart as he sang along and shook from head to toe with suppressed laughter.

If you could grease the local tinhorn police and the sheriff, thought Jimmy, *you should be able to run some girls out of those cabins, maybe put some slots and craps tables in the beer joint. God knows the place looks like it could use some action.*

He drummed his fingers on the steering wheel. *Let's get this over with,* he thought.

It was a sorry-assed tableau of humanity that greeted Jimmy Glick when he walked through the double screen door at Shady's. A couple of locals in the universal fisherman's costume of stained white T-shirts and khakis playing dominos in the corner. A brassy featherweight blonde swabbing down the varnished bar with a damp rag. A lean, dark-skinned Mexican kid with a fifty-pound sack of potatoes between his legs, expertly peeling the spuds. An ancient black guy in a cowboy hat waltzing a broom around the dance floor, sweeping up what looked like scraps of packing material and dumping it into a galvanized trashcan. No sign of his quarry.

The flirty blonde looked up and quickly assessed Jimmy's tailored linen suit—big city, for sure. Her eyes quickened with interest. "Beer, mister?"

"No, ma'am, not just this minute. Actually, I just have a question or two. Is the owner available?"

"Rupe!" she hollered over her shoulder. "Gent wants to know if you're available."

Rupert came out of the small office behind the bar, rattling a curtain of Chinese beads. He gave Darla an affectionate swat on the bottom as he squeezed by her. "Available? No, mister, I'm afraid Darla has me spoken for."

Jimmy smiled thinly. "I'm looking for a girl—slender, dark blonde hair. In her early twenties but maybe looks a little younger. Anyway, she was heading this way"

"What's this girl done? Run away?"

Jimmy shrugged apologetically. "It's a little, ah, delicate. I'm doing a skip trace. This girl, she comes from a wealthy society family in Galveston and, well, she has some problems. Black sheep, and all that. She went missing from home with a lot of cash from her father's safe, and a goodly amount of her mama's antique jewelry. The family wants her found and the items returned. Quietly, you know? Wouldn't help things at all if the papers found out."

"Uh-huh. Well, mister, as anyone can plainly see, there's only one road in and out of here. You and the beer truck driver are the only drive-in visitors we've had since noon. Unless your girl grew mermaid fins, I'm afraid you're out of luck."

Jimmy Glick let his face fall into a woebegone expression. "Yeah, shit, I was afraid of that. My employer's gonna have my ass when I go back empty-handed. And me working on a contingency fee for the recovery. Can I at least take a look around, so I can tell him I was thorough? I'd like to see your set-up anyway. Might want to come back and do some fishing one day."

Something about the stranger set off alarm bells at the back of Rupert's brain, but it was nothing he could put his finger on. *Why was he wearing a suit jacket in the middle of June?* He waved his big hand towards the door. "Sure thing, mister. It's a free island. You'll find my two brothers over at the bait house. You can ask them, too."

Jimmy made a show of sauntering slowly out the door and down the steps. He believed the burly bar owner didn't know about any girl, as far as it went. But he was convinced she was hiding around here somewhere, and he was going to find her if he had to scour every inch of this low-rent Tahiti.

He wandered down the sandy path marked by the Shady Palm Fish Camp sign. To Jimmy, who'd accompanied the Ginestra brothers on fishing and hunting trips to the palatial Gun 'n' Reel resort on the Laguna Madre, Shady's piscatorial empire looked like a dump.

Still, who knows, he mused as he strode towards the low-slung structure that housed the bait house and boat rental facilities, fix it up a bit, put some money and polish into the place, get some girl and dice action going, and he really *might* come back to relax a bit. Eat some fresh seafood and knock back a few beers. Judging by the trophy photos he'd seen around the bar, the yokels would seem to have a ready supply of redfish and trout.

A few minutes later, Jimmy Glick was involved in one of the most ridiculous arguments of his life. Over someone's lousy *name*, no less.

He'd wandered into the bait house to see the backs of two men straining over a concrete live bait well. They were muttering to each other, reaching for spanners and lengths of rubber hose and clamps. Something to do with an aerator on the fritz, Jimmy gathered.

Jimmy cleared his throat and the men straightened up and turned around. One of the fellows, he noticed, was a bluff-faced, somewhat stocky man in his early thirties with inordinately large ears. He seemed friendly enough.

His companion looked like something out of a Popeye cartoon. Barely five feet tall, he was built like a fireplug, with solid shoulders, a big shock of red hair, a cigar cocked in the corner of his mouth, and (Jimmy couldn't help but notice) a pugnacious gleam in his eye.

Jimmy launched into his story about the missing heiress while the men cleaned their hands on balls of cotton waste.

As he talked, the Sweetwater brothers regarded him skeptically. Noble, in particular. He had been an MP at Fort Sam in San Antonio during the war, and he recognized the telltale bulge beneath the shoulder of Jimmy Glick's tailored jacket. Moreover, the guy just didn't fit the profile. Noble had done a little skip work for Sheriff Red Burton in the off-season, when fishing was at low ebb. His military law enforcement history had served him well in that capacity. He knew that skip tracers were the blue-collar laborers of the justice system. This gent, with his fine clothes and big-city airs, stood out like a Mardi Gras float in a parade of milk wagons.

"Well," Noble said as Glick wrapped up his spiel, "We haven't seen any young girls out here answering your description. Although Flavius here has soft hands and favors Betty Grable a little, as you can plainly see."

"Fuck you," was all Flavius said. His brothers could rib him. But it stopped there.

Jimmy Glick, of course, didn't know that. Moreover, he wasn't convinced Mutt and Jeff here didn't know about the girl. He decided to push a little harder.

"Flavius?" he said. "Is that Mexican or something? I don't think I've ever seen any red-haired Mexicans."

Flavius' eyes narrowed slightly. Noble stepped back, a smile playing around his lips.

"It's Eye-talian, dickhead. Hell, for that matter it's Latin. Classical deal. Distinguished goddamn name."

"Noblest Roman of 'em all, huh? What the fuck, did your mom watch *Ben-Hur* one too many times when you were a kid?"

Oh, brother, thought Noble. *This is going south in a hurry.* He stepped around behind the counter where he kept an ancient ten-gauge shotgun used for dispatching the occasional rattlesnake that settled under the building.

Flavius' eyes went cold. He took a stance, brought both arms up, cocked at the elbow, and clenched his fists. "Well, since you brought our mother into it . . . ."

Jimmy Glick couldn't believe it. All he'd meant to do was tease the guy a little, and here he was all squared up like a pint-size John L. Fuckin' Sullivan. "You're kidding me, right?" he sneered.

"Do I look like I'm kidding?"

Enough was enough. In the heat of the moment, Glick forgot about the Ginestras' injunction to keep a low profile. The girl was here, goddammit, and he'd find her if he had to wade through any number of jerkwater fishing guides. He was used to bullying people, usually at the point of a gun or a blackjack. He liked it. And he was good at it.

"If you want to go a round, pee-wee, I'll oblige you," said Glick, unbuttoning his jacket. "I'm surprised you even have a mother."

Over in the corner, Noble cleared his throat. The barrel of the shotgun was leveled over the edge of the counter. Noble gestured with it. "Maybe you should lose the iron," he said conversationally. "Just in the interest of a fair fight."

Glick sneered, jerked his pistol out of its holster and slammed it down on the counter. "Like I'd need it. Here's this for good measure," he said, pulling a lead sap out of his back pocket and dropping it beside the gun. "Hell, I'd probably break it on Junior's thick skull anyway."

He turned around. "Awright, you wop Meskin midget mother-fucker, let's go dancing."

Afterward, Jimmy Glick could never quite remember how it all went down. He had the distinct impression he'd been dropped into a thresher. Flavius had charged at him like a miniature bull, slammed him back against a wooden sales counter stacked with lures and reels, and pounded four shots into his midsection in two seconds. Glick tried to land a punch on Flavius's knotty skull or his muscled shoulders, but to no effect. Through it all, Jimmy Glick could swear he heard Flavius *growling*. He never lost the cigar.

Flavius brought his cranium up under Glick's jaw with a force that nearly snapped the gangster's teeth off. He sagged. Another right-left combo, a jab at the nose, one more shot in the brisket for good measure, and it was all over.

Flavius picked up the semi-conscious Glick by the belt and shirt collar and dumped him into the live bait well, where he thrashed like a drowning nutria.

Out of curiosity, Noble picked up Glick's automatic. He'd culti-vated an interest in firearms since his hitch in the Army. He slid the clip out, ejected the cartridges, and took the remaining round out of the chamber. *Huh,* he thought. *Fancy ammo.* He dumped the bullets in an empty Mason jar behind the counter to look at later.

Rupert was nailing up a new wooden shutter under the big covered porch when Flavius and Noble came up the shell path dragging the waterlogged, bell-rung desperado in their wake. One of his fancy Florsheim loafers, Rupe noticed, was missing. He seemed to be wearing an empty pistol holster under his bunched-up jacket, too.

"What happened to our inquisitive friend?" Rupert asked.

"Oh, you know," said Noble as he unlocked the door of the Buick and dumped Jimmy Glick inside. "He disrespected the little emperor."

"Flavius, you took exception, huh? Mother warned you about that."

Flavius took a fresh Roi-Tan cigar out of his side pocket and lit it. "Mama didn't do me no favors when she christened me. And I got tired of that pointy-nose son of a bitch asking questions."

From the cookhouse, Sally Rose watched and worried. Jimmy Glick was not one to forget an ass whipping like that. For a moment, she considered running again. Wait until dark, cross the bridge and stick out her thumb and see where it took her. But the Mexican cook returned to the kitchen and talked her into staying the night. "You can spend the night on the concrete floor in the kitchen supply closet, or you can use the couch in my cabin," he said.

She chose the couch.

Later, Gilbert gave her directions to his cabin while he stayed to clean up. As she slipped out the door into the darkness, he watched her, his eyes narrowed in query and suspicion. He couldn't deny that he was attracted to her, and that concerned him. What kind of woman would stow away in the back of a reefer truck? All he knew about her was that she was running from something and running scared. And it probably had something to do with the stranger Noble and Flavius sent packing.

It was late when Gilbert returned to his cabin. He had hoped she'd be waiting up for him, with a ready smile and a funny story that explained the whole screwy thing. But when he slipped into the dark room, she was sound asleep. Whatever her story was, he'd have to wait until morning to hear it

CHAPTER 05

Before dawn the next day, Gilbert woke from a fitful sleep to behold his improbable roommate lying on the couch reading Thomas Aquinas. She was wearing one of his flannel work shirts, and her long legs rested on the back of the sofa, crossed at the ankles. The light from the kerosene lamp, the only light in the shack, was trimmed low, imparting a golden glow.

Drowsily, he wondered if this was the "beatific vision" the old Dominican was talking about in his *Summa Theologica*, or if it was simply a gorgeous, half-dressed young woman reclining seductively on his couch. He'd be happy with either, he decided. What was it Augustine said? "Give me chastity, but don't give it to me yet"?

She caught him looking at her and returned his gaze. "Interesting library you've got here, Gilberto. I thought you said you were a cook."

"I think there's a Betty Crocker cookbook in there somewhere."

She gazed at the rows and stacks of books that lined the walls of the tiny wooden shack. "Are you some kind of egghead or something?"

"If a GED diploma makes me an egghead then, yeah, I guess I am." Gilbert sat up and rubbed his eyes and then leaned over and lifted the window curtain. A dim glow was beginning to outline the eastern horizon. "Did you sleep?"

"For a little while, I think. Then I got bored and decided to do some light reading."

"You're a big fan of Christian theology? Forgive my saying so, but the way you were dressed last night, I didn't think you ran with many saints."

Sally closed the book and tossed it onto the army green footlocker that served as a coffee table. "The nuns I had for teachers kind of soured me on that stuff."

Gilbert nodded. She stood with her back to him, languidly arching her shoulders and stretching her spine, reminding him of a jaguarundi he'd once seen by the Rio Grande as a child. She was a couple of inches taller than he, and his shirt didn't cover much of her body below the hips.

What was this girl? he wondered. *A hooker? Some big city hustler? A runaway wife ditching her tycoon husband? A femme fatale?*

None of those seemed to fit. Gilbert had seen enough prostitutes to realize how quickly they began to show the mileage. This girl talked and acted worldly, but not with the go-where-I'm-kicked fatalism of a woman who sold herself to strangers. More like a nice girl who'd had to learn some hard lessons in a hurry.

Her self-assurance around him, on such short acquaintance, made him uneasy. Gilbert was no prude, but he had grown up in the chaste, family-centered environment of the Valley. And despite sharing a two-room shack with his father, mother, and four sisters, Gilbert had never seen a woman naked until after he left to join the service.

He had done a good thing on the spur of the moment, but now he was having second thoughts. A damsel in distress was one thing, but a provocative coquette with watchful eyes—yes, he'd seen them, even by lantern light—was something else. What was her agenda? The only thing Gilbert knew for sure was that she had one.

"You seem kinda nervous about me being here," she said. "Aren't girls allowed in the boys' rooms? What's this place called, anyway?"

"Ransom Island," he answered. "And it depends on what kind of girl it is, I suppose."

She furrowed her brow. "What's that supposed to mean?"

"Well, your arrival yesterday was a little . . . unusual. Most visitors don't come here in the back of a beer truck. So it's hard to know exactly what kind of girl you are. The proprietor runs a pretty loose operation, but there are certain types he won't welcome on the island."

"Like prostitutes?"

"Yeah, and grifters. And underage runaways."

"You think I'm a prostitute?"

"I don't know what to think."

She spied a guitar leaning against the wall, picked it up and strummed a chord. "Well, I'm none of those things. I didn't ignore *everything* the nuns tried to teach me."

She paced around the tiny postage stamp of space between the bed and the couch, picking out chords. Gilbert was thinking his domicile never felt so small.

"You play this thing?" she asked.

"A little."

"What kind of music?"

"Most kinds," said Gilbert. "But I prefer classical, jazz, a few boleros."

"Wow. You're pretty cultured for a—"

"For a Mexican?"

Her hands stopped strumming and she looked up, frowning. "For a cook." She put down the guitar. "Look, Gilbert. I really appreciate you letting me stay here last night. And I don't want to get you in trouble. As soon as I can, I'll get out of your hair."

"And go where?"

She started gathering her clothes and when she found her cocktail shorts and halter she held them to her nose. "Ugh, these smell like a waterfront bar."

"Where will you go?" Gilbert repeated.

"I haven't figured that out yet."

"But you can't go back to wherever you came from last night?"

"No, I can't do that. Someone I want to avoid is looking for me."

"The guy with the gun?"

She didn't answer. Just gazed at him without expression. Good poker face.

Gilbert stood up and went to the small kitchenette. He had slept in his clothes and it looked like it. "Can I make you some coffee? It'll just take a minute."

She nodded yes. "Mind if I take a quick shower?"

"I don't mind. The cistern should be full."

She went into the bathroom and Gilbert stood in front of the tiny stove, watching the coffee percolate, listening to the water run in the shower, and thinking about what he should do next. He really should tell Rupert about his secret sharer. Every instinct he possessed told him that this girl was trouble.

His train of thought was derailed a few minutes later when Sally came out of the bathroom. One of his threadbare bath towels was wrapped around her torso; another one was coiled up in a turban on her head. Maybe he wouldn't rat her out just yet. Not before breakfast, anyway. He handed her a cup of coffee.

"Thanks," she said, taking the cup and lifting it to her lips. "Oh God, this tastes so good."

Gilbert watched her sip the coffee, thinking that Maxwell House sales would jump a thousand percent if they made a TV commercial of her drinking their coffee, wrapped in that flimsy towel. *Good to the last drop.*

He forced himself to look away and then sat down on the straight-backed chair that completed his two-piece dinette set. "Are you ready to tell me what's going on?" he asked.

"Not quite yet, Gilbert . . . . Better for you, better for me."

"And I'm supposed to trust you, is that about it?"

"I suppose it is," she said. "I know it's a lot to ask."

Gilbert sighed and drummed his fingers on the table. "That's the second time you've asked me to trust you, you know."

Sally was quiet, giving him a chance to think it over.

"Listen, Sally, in a few minutes I'm going to have to go to the kitchen and start prepping for breakfast. We'll have a load of fishermen going out, and they need to be fed. It's just a suggestion, but maybe you ought to consider coming with me. I can introduce you to Rupert."

"Who's Rupert?"

"He owns the place, and he's a stand-up guy. He's done a lot for me. We can talk it over with him, whatever it is, and work something out." She started shaking her head "no" before he finished the sentence. Gilbert took a deep breath. "Or, I suppose you can stay here in my cabin, at least until you figure out what you want to do next."

"I like that idea better."

"Okay . . . . Have it your way. No one comes around much during the day, but there's a colored guy, an *amigo* of mine named Zach; he has a cabin back thataway." Gilbert gestured to the south. "What he doesn't know yet won't hurt him. But you'll have to keep the door and windows closed if you want to stay out of sight. It's supposed to be a scorcher today, so I'll bring a floor fan over later."

He bent down to put on his canvas deck shoes, and when he raised up Sally was standing directly in front of him. She placed her hands on his shoulders. He never realized Lifebuoy soap smelled so terrific.

"Thank you, Gilberto Ruiz. I appreciate your help more than you know." She tussled his hair.

"How do you know my full name?" he asked.

She pointed to the Army-issue footlocker that had GILBERTO RUIZ and a ten-digit serial number stenciled on the panels. "Hey, you wouldn't happen to have anything in there I could wear today, would you?"

Gilbert rummaged in his footlocker and came up with a pair of paint-spattered GI gabardine pants and a blue denim work shirt. He passed the bundle through the bathroom door. When she came out, he saw that the pants fit her far more pleasingly than they ever had Pfc. Ruiz. The shirt was knotted above her bellybutton. She wasn't Rita Hayworth, exactly, but everything was right where it should be.

"You know what?" she said. "I think I'll do a little reading today . . . to help pass the time. Pick something out for me?"

For a moment Gilbert considered calling in sick and spending the rest of the day with Sally in the steamy little room, maybe introducing her to his collection of erotic French poetry. He felt himself flush at the thought. "Um, how about a good mystery?"

"Ha! Good idea. Life imitates art, right?" she replied. "Or is it the other way around? I can never remember."

Gilbert put his hand on the doorknob. "I'll drop by before lunch and bring the fan. Until then," he looked around his modest bachelor's quarters and smiled, "make yourself at home."

——————

CHAPTER 06

Bob Sweeney, the head salesman and self-described kick-ass stemwinder of the only men's haberdashery in Rockport, was minding his own business when a man with one shoe walked in.

"Well, pilgrim," said Sweeney jovially, "you've come to the right place. Can I interest you in a nice pair of Thom McAns? You look like a moccasin stitch man to me."

"Shut the fuck up," snarled Jimmy Glick as he moved around the store with rancorous efficiency. He jerked a white Van Heusen shirt off the rack, added a pair of too-short gabardine slacks, some dark blue socks with red clocks, a pair of size-9 Florsheim wing-tips and, *God help me,* he thought, a plaid jacket that looked like a horse blanket—the least gaudy of the available offerings. *I'm gonna go back to Galveston looking like a goddamn hobo,* Glick fumed. Small choice— his tailored outfit was a saltwater-logged wreck and he was down to one shoe.

He slammed the items down on the counter and yanked out his Diner's Club card. Bob Sweeney gulped as he rang up the purchase. "Should I, ah, box these items up, sir?" Glick fixed him with an angry glare, scooped up his purchases and marched back to the fitting room.

As he changed, he reviewed the events of an impressively shitty morning.

He'd passed out after being dragged out of the bait tank on Ransom Island and had woken up in the middle of the night in the front seat of his car in front of the Rainbow Inn. His pistol—sans bullets—was lying in his lap. Someone had obviously driven him and his vehicle across the causeway. After staggering out of the car and throwing up in the parking lot, he noticed his back tires had been punctured for good measure. *Bet it was that sawed-off little fucker,* he thought groggily. Jimmy Glick felt as wrung out as an O-Cedar mop. His ribs ached like they'd been beaten with a bat, and there was a crick in his neck that went from the middle of his back to the top of his cranium. He was pretty sure a couple of teeth were loose. An attendant showed up at the Texaco station about the time the sun broke clear of a greasy horizon.

Once his tires were patched, his first impulse, understandably, was to go to the nearest sporting-goods store, buy some ammo and go back and light up every smug sonofabitch on that island.

He'd have done it, too, but he was under orders. And besides, the Ginestras were trying to lower their profile vis-à-vis various law enforcement entities. Mowing down a bunch of civilians over a punch in the nose didn't seem like a good way to accomplish that goal. Besides, he had to admit, it was his own fault. He shouldn't have let the little shrimp get under his skin. *You know better, Jimmy.*

Never mind, though. Once he talked to Gerry and Primo, he had a feeling he'd be seeing the Sweetwater brothers again, on his terms.

Since Jimmy didn't have any clothes in his grip except for a change of shorts and undershirt and a pair of cotton pajamas (it was supposed to be a short errand), the menswear store in Rockport had to be his first stop en route back to Galveston. From there he made a beeline up State Highway 35, stopped at his apartment on 23 ½ St. to shower and change, and by 3 p.m. he was sitting in the anteroom outside of Gerry Ginestra's office on the second floor of the Turf Club.

The inner door to the office swung open and Gerardo "Gerry" Ginestra stood framed in the doorway. He was a short, burly man who exuded a quiet menace, which he nevertheless strove to hide beneath a placid exterior. In this, he was the opposite of his older brother Primo, who was indifferent to the reactions his fierce disposition elicited.

A lot of people told Gerry he looked like Louis Prima, and there was indeed a strong similarity between the "Just a Gigolo" hitmaker and Gerry's swarthy, hail-fellow good looks. Gerry ordinarily favored Churchill-style jumpsuits (the British Prime Minister was a personal hero of the Ginestras; he didn't take any shit from Hitler and he liked a drink or two, as well), but today he was in a short-sleeved tropical shirt and wool trousers. He motioned Jimmy inside.

"Have a seat." He waved offhandedly at a wing chair situated at an angle to the desk. "Drink?"

"Sure, Gerry. Tom Collins, if you got it." Jimmy knew that was Gerry's favorite summertime drink. What the hell. It never hurt to score a point with the boss.

As he fixed the drinks, Gerry asked over his shoulder, "So, Jimmy, did you find Primo's girl?"

"Yeah. That is, I've got a good line on her. She's on a little *strunz* of land called Ransom Island. It's near Aransas Pass, about two hundred miles south of here. Jesus, what a dump."

Gerry handed Jimmy his drink and sat down behind his desk. He hoped Jimmy had tread carefully with the girl. Primo was touchy as hell about her. Gerry had long thought there was something a little unhealthy about it.

"So did you talk to her?"

"Not exactly. Things . . . kind of took a turn."

Gerry set his tall glass down decisively and fixed Jimmy with a grin that was suddenly baleful.

"Get the marbles out of your mouth, Jimmy. Did you see her or not?"

Jimmy sighed and related his tale. How he'd got a line on the girl on the mainland and how she'd given him the slip. How the island was her only possible destination. His encounter with the Sweetwater brothers, and how his attempt at mild-mannered inquiry and diplomatic persuasion was rudely misinterpreted by the psycho runt of the Sweetwater litter.

In Jimmy's re-telling, of course, he gave as good as he got with Flavius, and hostilities only ceased when Noble pulled out the shotgun to save his little brother from certain defeat. Naturally, there was no mention of his bait tank baptism.

In spite of himself, Gerry had to stifle a grin. "Not exactly your usual smooth self, Jimmy." It wasn't a question.

Glick shrugged, palms up. "Yeah, I misjudged the situation. But the girl is there. I'm sure of it."

"How do you know she hasn't left already?"

"There's a junkie daytime manager at this cold drink joint called the Rainbow Inn right by the head of the wooden causeway going to the island. I duked him and his brother, who works the night shift, ten scoots each to keep an eye out and call me if she tries to leave. We've got a guy in Corpus I can call to tail her if need be."

"Did she see you?"

"That's the thing. I dunno. I never saw her. If she was somewhere else on the island and didn't lay eyes on me, maybe she still thinks it's a safe hideout."

"The name Ginestra gonna come up when they talk about your visit?"

"Boss, give me a little credit. As far as they know, I'm just a bondsman with too much attitude looking for some spoiled society bitch named Sally. You and Primo aren't even a rumor."

"Humph." Gerry exhaled forcefully, puffing out his cheeks. "Well, mission accomplished, I guess. Sort of." He chuckled. "I'd like to have seen that fight. You been to see Primo yet?"

Jimmy grinned too. "I was putting it off for a little bit until I talked to you."

"I don't blame you. Primo never got that part about not killing the messenger. He's over at the Bali Hai, auditioning new chorus girls. That brother of mine, he loves show business. Head on over there; he'll be expecting you."

"Will do, Gerry . . . but there's this other thing."

Gerry had thought the meeting concluded and had picked up a *Daily Racing Form*. Looking at the avid gleam in his lieutenant's eye, he put it down slowly. "Spit it out, Jimmy."

So Jimmy laid out the scenario that had been coalescing in his mind ever since he drove over the causeway to Ransom Island. The pieces, he explained, were in place: the limited access, the bayside dockage, the ready-made cabins, the seemingly lax law enforcement (if the Rainbow Inn could run wide open . . .)—the sheer potential of the place.

Jimmy Glick wasn't just hired muscle. On a day-to-day basis, he was responsible for overseeing large chunks of the Ginestras' rackets. When it came to making a dishonest buck, Jimmy Glick knew how the cow ate the cabbage. And Ransom Island had potential dishonest dollar signs all over it.

Gerry nodded thoughtfully. "You sure you don't just want to get back at that little palooka that bounced you around, Jimmy?"

Glick grinned a predatory grin. "That'd just be a bonus."

"Suppose they don't roust?"

Glick spread his hands. "Why roust 'em? Let's just go out as businessmen and make an offer. These Sweetwater boys ain't the Flaglers, and that island sure as hell ain't Miami Beach. Might be they'd welcome a chance to get out from under, with some money in their pockets to boot."

Gerry rubbed his chin as he mulled this over. "This idea of yours comes at a very opportune time, Jimmy. Maybe for all of us." He put his palms down on the desk. "Okay. Roll over and see Primo and take your lumps. Then be back at the Bali Hai at eight tonight. The private room in the back. There's a meeting I want you to sit in on."

━━━

CHAPTER 07

Flavius was thinking the fat lady's sweaty hand felt almost exactly like a chub mackerel, but as he helped her navigate the step-down from the dock to the wooden skiff, he kept his mouth shut. Which was more than he could say for her. She had done nothing but bitch since she'd arrived on Ransom Island less than an hour ago, and presently, her husband was the target of her increasing ire.

"I am going to *roast* out there on the water; there's not a lick of shade. I cannot believe you talked me into this tomfoolery. And just look at this silly boat! Why, it's nothing more than a wooden trough with hard slat seats." She looked up at Flavius. "What kind of chicken outfit do y'all run here anyway?"

Flavius tried his best to ignore her. "Careful ma'am, the boat might be a little unsteady when you step into it." *Especially for a whale like you*, he thought.

A dozen wooden skiffs were lined up along the dock, and Flavius and his brother Noble were helping the guests get into their respective rentals. Each boat came equipped with oars and a small anchor, two life jackets, two rigged baitcasting rods, a bucket full of live shrimp, a lunch sack, and last but not least, a small ice-filled cooler with beer and soda pop. There were no motors in the boats, and they were tied together like a string of packhorses. Once everyone was aboard, Noble would use his inboard runabout to drag them out to various spots on the bay and drop them off one at a time for a half day of fishing.

Flavius was anxious to get them on their way. Then the fat lady's yammering would be her husband's problem. *Well,* thought Flavius, *It's your misfortune and none of my own.*

"Unsteady?" said the lady. "I'll bet it is, tiny rowboat like this. I don't doubt it will sink like a stone when I get in."

Her husband, behind her, sighed.

Flavius off-loaded the hefty guest onto the boat and let her comment slide, much as he hated to. He was hoping the damn boat *would* sink, with Orca and her wimpy husband aboard. Rupert should have known he wasn't any good with customers, yet he still asked him to wait on these yahoos hand and foot. Well, Rupert was the boss.

The woman set one foot on the skiff and listed a bit, trying to find her balance. When she plopped her ass down on the bow seat, it caused twelve inches of freeboard to plunge below the water line. Once settled, she picked up the lunch sack and rummaged around inside. "Two little baloney sandwiches and a few lousy potato chips. I should have guessed." Fanning herself with her hand she added, "I guess we'll be hungry *and* hot today. I should've packed my own lunch."

"Honey, you can have my lunch. I ate a big breakfast this morning," said the husband. She ignored him and looked up at Flavius.

"Where's our umbrella?"

"Ma'am?" He was helping the next guests into their boat, a man and his son. The kid's eyes were shining with anticipation under his ball cap. He couldn't wait to get out on the water.

"Where's our umbrella?" she repeated. "I am not about to broil out there under that murderous sun all day long without protection and with no way to get back."

Flavius looked at the woman and imagined a Thanksgiving turkey basting in an open roasting pan. "We'll be picking you up in four hours. You didn't bring a hat?"

"No. As any fool can plainly see, I didn't bring a hat. Do you need glasses? What was your name again?"

"Flavius."

"Flavius? What kind of silly name is that? Sounds Mexican to me."

"Honey, please," the husband pleaded from the stern.

But the woman continued, undeterred. "In all my days, I've never heard a name as silly as that. Sounds like Pig Latin. And by the way, four hours is simply too long. I want you to pick us up in one hour. Do you hear me? Turn around and listen to me, Mr. . . . Fladiot."

Flavius stopped and began popping his knuckles, one by one. He felt his face redden and he heard a roaring sound inside his head like surf breaking on a reef.

Usually these signs were prelude to a fistfight, as Glick could woefully attest. Flavius had been in a lot of them over the years, mostly on account of people making fun of his name, or his height, or his red hair, but also because he had a wicked bad temper. Could he get away with cold-cocking this woman in front of her husband and the other customers? Did he care?

He turned around to face the Smart-Mouthed Sea Cow From Hell, and instead, found Rupert standing in front of him.

"I'll take it from here, little brother." A knowing smile appeared on Rupert's weathered face, and his blue eyes sparkled below a safari-style pith helmet. He was holding a woman's wide-brimmed sun hat in one hand and an extra sack lunch for his portly guest in the other, compliments of Shady's.

Everyone who worked on Ransom Island followed Rupert's lead when it came to customer relations, even his two younger brothers, who were equal owners in the operation. Guests were to be treated with the utmost courtesy, unless, of course, they turned out to be assholes. So far, there hadn't been anyone in the operation's twenty-year history that Rupert couldn't eighty-six by himself, which he had done more than once. The Shady Palm, or Shady's as the locals called it, attracted all kinds of patrons, and the honky-tonk part of the business could get pretty rowdy on a big night.

But evidently, Rupert had determined that the fat lady was not out of line, so Flavius watched him hand her the sun hat and the food, and then engage her in some friendly conversation. By the time the boat train left the dock a few minutes later, she was thanking him profusely for his manners, his hospitality, and his careful attention to detail. She scowled at Flavius as the boats glided away from the dock.

Flavius scowled back. "Rupe, for the life of me, I don't know how you're able to suck up to people like that."

"'Cause they pay the bills, brother. 'Cause they pay the bills."

"Well, it just ain't in me to do it." Rupert fixed his brother with a sharp look, and Flavius added, "At least not like you, anyway."

"Then how 'bout you give me a hand with the pump on the live bait well? It's been acting funny since you gave that stranger a bath in it. Come on . . . I promise not to make fun of your name."

Rupert and Noble were mere youngsters when Flavius came along—right after their mother had taken a summer class on Great Works of Western Literature at the community college in Corpus Christi. The immersion in the classics was supposed to help Elektra Sweetwater take her mind off a hot, difficult pregnancy, but she had become utterly captivated by Gibbons' *Decline and Fall of the Roman Empire*. And, as Jimmy Glick had unwittingly guessed, she had, in fact, practically memorized Cecil B. DeMille's epic black-and-white production of *Ben-Hur*. There was something about a man in a toga . . . .

In absence of better counsel (the paterfamilias of the Sweetwater clan was drunk in a dockside bar in Aransas Pass when Flavius Octavius Sweetwater made his squalling debut at Charity Hospital), Elektra christened her youngest after two of her classical heroes. Flavius had never heard the last of it.

Sighing wearily, Flavius dutifully followed his brother up the railroad tie steps that led to the bait house. He'd take a faulty pump over a bitchy customer anytime.

The long, rectangular building was built almost entirely of shellcrete, a Gulf Coast concoction made of sand, clay, lime, and crushed oyster shells. Rupert and his brothers had poured the forms themselves when they bought the island in 1934. The structure had proved to be functional and resilient, having survived numerous storms and one hurricane, so far.

Inside the bait house, it was surprisingly cool. Zachariah Yates hunched over a metal table near the back door, trying to untangle a hellish ball of fishing line that completely engulfed the baitcaster reel. Customers were hard on the fishing gear, especially the day-trippers who didn't own their own boat or tackle and generally had no idea how to handle either one. Another dozen rods were leaning against the wall, waiting for deft hands to make them operational again.

"Zach, I wouldn't waste time trying to figure out that tangle," said Rupert. "Just cut the line and re-spool the reel. You could spend all day messing with those knots."

Zachariah nodded and fished some nail clippers from his shirt pocket. His hands were scarred and callused, with two crooked fingers from cowboy roping mishaps years ago, but they moved quickly and efficiently as the old man clipped the line and re-rigged the spool.

The screen door burst open and two shirtless, burr-headed kids rushed in, followed by Lucky, a brindle-colored mutt of a dog. "Uncle Rupert, look!" said the taller boy, holding out two cupped hands. "A horny toad!"

"A horny toad!" repeated the other.

Rupert leaned in toward the boys—they belonged to his younger brother, Dublin "Dubber" Sweetwater, who ran a fleet of shrimp boats out of Fulton—and examined their prize. The spiky, grayish-brown reptile flattened itself in the palm of the older boy, Johnny. "Well, I'll be go-to-hell," said Rupert. "That's one fine horned frog you boys got there."

"Lucky found it under the porch by Cabin Five," said Johnny.

"It spits blood from its eyes," added Charlie, Johnny's little brother.

"It also eats red ants," said Rupert, "which is one thing we got too many of on this island. Whatcha say we let this fella loose out back so it can do its job, which is eat ants, and then you boys can come back in here and do your job, which is sweep the floor. Sound like a plan?"

The boys sighed and moved towards the door, stroking the lizard on the back as they went. As they were leaving, they bumped into Darla.

"We caught a horny toad," Johnny explained, "but Uncle Rupert is making us turn it loose."

"Well, that seems fair," said Darla. "What would you boys do with a horny toad anyway?"

"Rub its belly," said Johnny.

"Watch it shoot blood from its eyes," added Charlie.

"Out," she commanded. "Do what your uncle says." She shooed the boys and dog outside and then stood at the door looking at Rupert expectantly, a huge smile on her face.

"What?" he asked, smiling back at her. He couldn't help himself. Shapely and lithe, today she was dressed in a breezy floral sundress, her mane of lustrous strawberry blond hair cascading over her bare shoulders. Always a vision, that Darla. He still got a little jolt of excitement every time he saw her: part amazement that he was lucky enough to marry a girl so goddamned beautiful; part pride— she always managed to dress the place up, even now, in a shellcrete bait house; and part just plain desire. Their marriage had its share of problems, but none of them were in the bedroom.

"You will never guess who just called," she said.

"Hmm, let's see. Howdy Doody?"

"Nope."

"Joe McCarthy."

"Stop it. It was Sidney Lowenstein, Duke Ellington's booking agent!"

Flavius looked up from the pump he was disassembling. "You mean *the* Duke Ellington, the guy on the jukebox?"

"Yes," said Darla, "*the* Duke Ellington. The agent got your letter and wanted to know if we were interested in booking Duke and his orchestra at the Shady Palm over July Fourth."

Rupert removed his pith helmet and ran his fingers through his sandy hair. "You're not pulling my leg are you, sweetie?"

"No! It's true! Scout's honor."

Even Zachariah looked up. He preferred old-timey cowboy songs to jazz, but Rupert's tale of how he had met the great Negro band-leader had made a profound impression on him.

"Son of a gun," said Rupert. "I mean, I wrote that agent a letter after I met Mr. Ellington at the Rice Hotel. But that was almost a year ago. I figured he'd take one look at the address and use it for birdcage lining." The Shady Palm stationery letterhead featured a palm tree, a topless hula girl and a cocktail glass: not the kind of thing calculated to impress a high-dollar Jewish talent agent in New York City.

"Well, Mr. Lowenstein said they had a show scheduled in Fort Worth later this month and that their next stop, a Fourth of July show in Galveston, I think he said, had been cancelled. So they had an open date . . . and they want to come here!"

"But why here?" asked Rupert incredulously. The biggest act they had booked to date was Spade Cooley and his Western Dance Gang.

"Maybe your old school buddy put in a good word for you," Darla continued. "Who knows? Who cares? And get this. Apparently this is at the tail end of a long tour, and Mr. Ellington wants to do something nice for his band. It turns out some of his orchestra boys like to fish, so Mr. Lowenstein said he did some checking and found out we're famous for fishing *and* have the biggest music hall in San Patricio County—"

"So he decided they could mix some pleasure with business," Rupert finished, "right here on Ransom Island." He shook his head in disbelief.

"Can you believe it, honey? And you know what else?"

"There's more?"

"Yes!" said Darla. "There *is* more. The agent asked if we could find somebody to fill the warm-up slot before the main show." Darla was almost quivering with anticipation as she watched Rupert pretend to mull over possible opening attractions.

"Well, I guess my first choice for the opening act would be the incomparable Darla Lacey Sweetwater."

Darla squealed with delight. "Yes! I am so excited Rupert. I swear I'm about to pee in my panties!"

Rupert had to smile. "Since when did you start wearing panties?" he asked. Behind Darla's back, Flavius and Zach exchanged eye rolls.

Maybe he was wrong to do it, but he continued to encourage his wife's long-deferred dream of stardom, even though he privately doubted her chances. She certainly had the looks, even now, in her mid-thirties, and her voice was plenty good. But it wasn't great.

The main problem was that she had never quite summoned the courage to pick up and move to Los Angeles, New York, or Nashville, where most of the singing acts were finding their fame and fortune. Darla's fears kept her invisibly chained to a thirty-mile radius of "home." The prospect of leaving the Coastal Bend terrified her. That didn't stop her Hollywood fantasies, though.

Rupert knew this, even if Darla wouldn't admit it. So far, the closest she'd come to stardom was singing at the USO Club in Corpus Christi during the war. Rupert half suspected that one of the reasons she had married him three years ago was so she could have her own stage, a friendly local crowd, and the long-shot opportunity to open someday for a big act like Duke Ellington. Right now, Darla was acting like she'd won the Irish Sweepstakes, and Rupert guessed that, in a way, she had.

"Well, hell, I'll call him back and confirm the date and get the details." He smiled at his wife. "You'll knock 'em dead, babe."

"You're damn right I will."

———

CHAPTER 08

The Bali Hai nightclub was everything a top-ranked den of iniquity should be.

The Ginestras' gambling showcase sat on the end of a two hundred-yard long T-head pier sticking out over the gently rolling swells of the Gulf of Mexico. From the Polynesian-decorated porte-cochere anchored on the Seawall to the imposing double doors of the building proper, a covered walkway illuminated by multi-colored light bulbs linked the club to the mainland. As many a frustrated lawman discovered, it was impossible to sneak up on the place unannounced.

The lawmen, it should be noted, did not include among their number the sheriff of Galveston County, who added to his retirement fund every month, courtesy of the Ginestras. When a young reporter, new in town, once inquired why the sheriff didn't raid the joint, when everyone for a hundred mile radius knew what went on inside, the sheriff responded that he was powerless to act. The Bali Hai, he explained, was a private club and he, the sheriff, was not a member.

Those of a certain elastic morality could find just about anything to suit them inside the Bali Hai. The club offered cards, dice, roulette, slots, blackjack, numbers, untaxed hooch, a racetrack wire, reefer, and a high-stakes poker game that had proceeded without respite since Roosevelt's first term.

What there wasn't, were sporting women. The Ginestras, prudently, stayed out of the sex trade. Part of their reasoning was pragmatic—the inventory was fickle, perishable, and not easily controlled.

The other reason was political—the city's power brokers didn't see anything wrong with a friendly wager in attractive surroundings. But they were far less receptive to incidents of whores being beaten with coat hangers, cut with razors, or thrown into the ship channel. Bad for the island's image. The Ginestras owed their position in the community, in large part, to their staying above the messy business of the skin trade.

Primo always said gambling, liquor, and pussy didn't mix under the same roof.

What they *did* do was license the racket. The traditional red light district on Post Office Street was ostensibly run by a madam named Shanghai Lily O'Shaunessy, the Irish/Chinese offspring of a freighter captain from Hong Kong and one of the city's most prominent red-headed colleen prostitutes well before the Depression.

Now in her early forties, Shanghai Lily ran her five-block fiefdom like the Dowager Empress, but she kicked back part of her profits to the Ginestras who, in turn, used Jimmy Glick and his partner, Deke Maloney, as well as lower-echelon family soldiers, to keep the streets safe and the freelance pimps, jack rollers, and Murphy artists in the shadows and under control.

Galveston may have had the only red-light district in the world where a drunken sailor could leave an entire voyage's payday behind the bar in one of Lily's establishments and it would still be waiting when he sobered up the next morning.

Hell, even the Bishop of Galveston weighed in in favor of Shanghai Lily's empire. "We segregate mental and physical diseases," reasoned Bishop Byrne. "Let us do the same for moral sickness . . . . As long as man has free will, some of us will fall into impurity."

"And thank God for that," echoed Gerry.

But it wasn't the usual group of degenerate gamblers and sybarites who gathered behind the locked conference-room doors of the Bali Hai complex that evening.

Gerry and Primo (and Jimmy Glick, by invitation) were joined by Galveston's mayor and its district attorney, the president of the Chamber of Commerce, the manager of the Galveston Downs Turf Club, the principal partner in the city's leading silk stocking law firm, and a handful of hotshots from local business, banking, and insurance concerns. No one who read the society pages in the *Galveston Daily News* (whose publisher was also present) could have failed to recognize most of the faces. All of them had outstanding markers with Primo and Gerry.

Gerry waited until everyone had ordered their drinks and settled in.

"Gents, thanks for coming on such short notice. My brother and I wanted to alert you to a situation that could potentially affect not only our family's enterprises, but the financial stability of the city as a whole.

"Thanks to some well-connected friends of ours"—he nodded to the publisher of the *Daily News* and the district's junior state representative—"we've become aware of a new initiative in the state attorney general's office. As you all know, Will Wilson got himself elected a couple of years back on a 'law and order' platform. Now, we're all big proponents of law and order—hell, my brother and I included. You can walk down any street at midnight in Galveston without having to look over your shoulder, and we want to keep it that way. But all of a sudden, this guy's getting some funny ideas about fixing what's not broken. Probably has to do with the election coming up later this year. We've learned that he plans to 'clean up' Galveston." Gerry made an expression like he'd bitten into a lemon.

"Asshole," growled Primo, who hated politicians as a species. Mealy-mouthed, pious, hypocritical sonsofbitches.

A murmur rippled through the room, and Gerry nodded knowingly. "Says he plans to, ah, 'bust up the rackets'. . . with plenty of reporters and newsreel photographers on hand, of course. He's got the Texas Rangers and even the Feds involved."

Gerry sat down and put up his hands in a "what-the-hell-can-I-do-about-it" gesture.

"Men, you *are* the city. I don't have to tell you about the special relationship all of us have always enjoyed in Galveston. No one who wasn't born on the island could appreciate it properly. Let alone some big shot in Austin.

"Now, my brother and I don't have to apologize for anything. We've built establishments you're not ashamed to take your wives and sisters and even mothers to. We've brought world-class entertainment here, helped make Galveston a national destination and, in our modest way, contributed to the city's way of life. We weren't born here like most of you all, but I think we've put more into Galveston than we've taken out."

"Fuckin'-A," growled Primo, cracking his knuckles beneath the tabletop. He always preferred to let his younger brother do the talking in situations like this.

With a dramatic flourish, Gerry pointed to a painting mounted in a place of honor on the rear wall, beneath a small gallery light. It portrayed a bald eagle, wings flared, clutching an American flag.

"You gentlemen see that picture? Frank Sinatra painted that picture. For me and Primo. He gave it to me after I organized a benefit with Frank and his Hollywood pals after that fertilizer ship blew up half of Texas City in '47."

He paused for effect. "Any of you think Frank Sinatra's gonna paint Will Wilson a picture?"

"No fuckin' wa—" Primo began, but Gerry held up a restraining hand.

"Before this gets too out of hand, I hope you gentlemen will use your connections and your influence to bring this political circus to a halt. Because if the Free State of Galveston—as the newspapers like to call it—ever disappears . . ." his eyes moved from face to face, "all of us may see our way of life disappear with it."

There was a good deal of animated discussion after that, but Gerry's point was well taken. The rackets, for better or worse, had become Galveston's bread and butter, its calling card. Close up the casinos and the nightclubs and the cathouses and what were you left with? A decaying port, some quaint architectural relics on the Strand, and a barrier island not much changed since a shipwrecked Cabeza de Vaca stumbled ashore four hundred years ago. Everyone agreed that would be a sad state of affairs, and the various local power brokers resolved to do something about it.

After a couple more rounds of drinks, the party broke up. Gerry and Primo and Jimmy Glick stayed behind. They had their own business to discuss.

With quick strokes, Jimmy reiterated what he had discussed with Gerry previously. Ransom Island might be a good location for the family to diversify their criminal enterprises, out of the glare of the authorities' spotlight.

It wasn't Galveston, by a long shot, but it wasn't bad. And it was available. The Sweetwater family just didn't know it yet.

The Ginestras had, in effect, been awarded the Galveston franchise by Carlos Marcello, the heavyweight boss of the New Orleans Mafia. Marcello had wanted some kindred *paisano* spirits to shore up his western flank against incursions by Kansas City or, God forbid, Chicago. Those Yankee jamokes, Marcello felt, didn't have any feeling for how things worked below the Mason-Dixon line.

"This thing of ours is different down here," Marcello once told the brothers, as they sipped coffee in Marcello's family social club on Prytania St. in downtown New Orleans. "Different cultures, different rhythms. You all and I, we grew up here. In Chicago, someone don't go along, they put a bullet in his eye the next day and dump him in Lake Michigan. Down here, you can reason with a man. There's no hurry. Sit down, have some oysters and a few drinks, reach an accommodation. People in the South have more larceny in 'em, it seems like. I guess it's the pirate thing.

"Of course," he continued, "with some of these hard-ons, like the mooks at the dockworkers' union, you still wind up having to put a bullet in their eye."

"And dump 'em in Lake Pontchartrain," Primo concluded.

Marcello smiled thinly. "We've found the Atchafalaya Basin works better for that. Lots of bayous. Lots of gators."

He finished his coffee and called for a round of absinthe.

"Your territory stops at the Sabine River. You remember that. And if I was you, I'd leave Houston alone. Nothing but Cajuns and crackers and crazy niggers up there. Tryin' to organize Houston would be like tryin' to teach close-order drill to a riot."

"Galveston is what we're interested in, Mr. Marcello," said Gerry, as Primo nodded agreement. "If we play it right, it could be a bird's nest on the ground."

And so it had proven to be.

In the years since, the rest of the Gulf Coast had become mobbed up. Even Houston, which turned out to be just the kind of cluster fuck Marcello had predicted, was finally organized, as far as gambling was concerned, under "Fat Jack" Halfen, a crime boss with ties to the Chicago and Dallas syndicates.

So expansion presented a real problem. Virgin territory was at a premium. But, as Jimmy Glick pointed out, Ransom Island was on nobody's radar, certainly not the attorney general's or the Texas Rangers'.

"The way I see it, we can run cards, slots, dope, offshore booze, girls, and numbers out of the place," said Jimmy. "And for customers, there's boat loads of flyboys over at the Corpus Christi Naval Air Station right across the bay."

"What about law?" asked Primo.

"There's a sheriff. Couple of deputies. Catching Maggie-and-Jiggs domestic squeals and busting up knife fights between drunk shrimpers is what they specialize in, I'd guess. Little bitty police department. Nobody we can't reason with.

"One interesting thing. There's a stand-alone cold-drink place at the head of the causeway out to the island. Real low-rent—cockfights and a couple of whores that look like they went a few rounds with Jack Dempsey. But it makes me think the sheriff might already be bent, if he lets that place run wide open."

"If not, we'll bend him," said Primo.

Gerry drummed his fingers on the table. "Jimmy, call Deke and fill him in on things. Tell him to round up a couple of guys from his crew—respectable looking guys, not any headbreakers or union goons—and send them down there to feel out the situation. Maybe mention a figure, or least let those guys—the Sweetwaters, is it?— let 'em know one will be coming. Like you say, these hillbillies might just be waiting for the right offer. Maybe we can grease them out of there before they know what happened. No need to strong-arm them . . . at least not yet."

Jimmy was nonplussed. "Okay, Gerry, but . . . Deke? I mean, okay, but I brought this thing to you. I thought I was—"

"It's not your thing, it's *ours*." Primo bit down hard on his words. He wasn't apt to give the help nearly as much elbowroom as Gerry. Then he relaxed. "Yeah, Jimmy, you showed good hustle. But your little dust-up with one of these brothers poisoned the well. You can't very well go back as a respectable businessman. You're damaged goods for now.

"There's the other thing, too," Primo added, almost reluctantly. "Now that we've found her, I need to . . . see her."

"Right," said Gerry. "The girl. Do you think it's a good idea to confront her there? I feel like we're mixing family and business. I know you feel strongly about it—"

"Hell, yes, I feel strongly about it. She's my daughter. I just feel like I gotta, I dunno, be there somehow. Been a long time since I've seen her. I need to talk to her. Straighten some things out."

Gerry sighed. "How about this? How 'bout you and Jimmy take the cabin cruiser down the coast. Anchor away from the island, like you're fishing. With those Coast Guard binoculars Cap'n Mark keeps onboard you can watch everything that happens . . . and look in on the girl, assuming she's still there. And, Jimmy, you'll be around if we need you, but still out of sight."

Neither Jimmy nor Primo were entirely mollified by Gerry's plan, but neither could think of a better one.

"Sure . . . okay," said Primo, giving in, then he grinned (never a pleasant sight) and raised his highball glass. "I always said you were the brains of the outfit, little brother."

Gerry raised his glass in riposte. "It's a goddamn gift."

———

CHAPTER 09

After shutting down the kitchen for the night, Gilbert wrapped some tacos in wax paper and grabbed two beers from the walk-in cooler. It was a slow night, and Rupert and Darla were tending to the remaining customers in the bar.

Walking along the sandy path to his cabin, he was startled by the glow of a cigarette flaring in the dark near the trail. Zachariah was sitting on a driftwood stump puffing on one of his hand-made Bull Durham smokes.

"Evening, Zach. Enjoying the breeze?" Gilbert had to strain his eyes to make out the old cowboy's silhouette.

"First breath of air we've had today," said Zach. "A little earlier it was so still I could hear the mosquito wings flappin'."

"Yeah, these are some dog days, alright," Gilbert agreed. "Where's a hurricane when you need one?" He decided he had better linger a moment to chat. He liked Zach, and they shared an easy friendship. Besides, he didn't want to seem too eager to get back to his own cabin, and to Sally.

"Too hot inside to lie down just yet," said Zach.

"You're right about that."

"Had to open up my own house at lunch today an' let all the hot air escape. I was afraid it might explode."

Zach's cedar-sided cabin sat fifty yards back from Gilbert's and was identical in size and construction. Other than the "Big House," Rupert and Darla's two-story shellcrete bungalow located a stone's throw from the bait house, the one-room shacks occupied by Gilbert and Zachariah were the only permanent residences on Ransom Island. Of course, that didn't include the lean-to used by Barefoot Nelson and his wife, but everyone thought of that makeshift assembly as more of a natural fixture, like driftwood.

"Noticed that your door and shutters were battened down," Zach continued. "I'd sure hate to have been cooped up inside there all day."

He was gigging Gilbert a little, but he was concerned, too. Whatever his friend had got himself involved in, Zach surmised it must have twisted him up pretty good inside.

"A person would be mighty uncomfortable, yes, sir," Zach continued. He glanced down at Gilbert's armload of food and drink. "Would be wantin' more than one cold beer, I'd wager. I sure would."

There was another pause and Gilbert decided to move along. "You have a good evening, Zach."

"Night, Gil. I reckon you'll get 'round to telling Rupert 'bout your houseguest when you think it best. 'Till then, I won't say anything."

Gilbert stopped. "I appreciate that, Zach. I'm working on it."

"Lemme know if I can help."

When Gilbert stepped into the dark cabin, Sally fairly leaped at him, wrapping her sweaty arms around his neck. "We've got to get out of here!" she whispered urgently. "I can't stay in this oven a moment longer."

Gilbert backed onto the porch with her still clinging to him. "Okay, okay. I know a place we can go."

He grabbed her hand and they walked down to the water's edge, following the shore for several hundred yards until they came to a small enclave with a sandy beach. A steady breeze blew in from the Gulf and cooled the perspiration on their skin. Gilbert set the tacos and beer on a driftwood log, peeled off his shirt, and waded into the bay up to his shoulders. He turned to beckon Sally to do the same, but she had already stripped down to her underwear and was splashing in beside him. She submerged and surfaced slowly, the water up to her chin. In the starlight Gilbert could see her blond hair floating around her head like Sargassum.

"Do you want a cold beer?" he managed to ask, flustered by Aphrodite's spectacular dash to the sea.

"Oh, hell yes!" she said. He retrieved a beer and waded out to hand it to her. "Thank you," she said gratefully, reaching up from the water.

"I brought you some food, too, when you're ready. I imagine you're hungry." He returned to the shore and sat down in the sand. In the darkness he could hear Sally sloshing around in the water, cooing contentedly. Before long, she emerged, put her clothes back on, and then plopped down next to Gilbert.

"So . . . dear, how was your day at the office?" she asked, twisting her wet hair into a roll to wring out the water.

Gilbert smiled. "Ah, you know, the rat race. Just trying to move up that corporate ladder. What was yours like, honey?"

"Oh, the usual. Straightened up the house, painted my nails, flipped through a *Ladies Home Journal*, made a fabulous meatloaf, and then baked right along with it in that oven of a shack."

"Did the box fan help much?"

"Lord no. I had it on full blast, but it just shifted the heat from one side of the room to the other. It was torture in there today. And boring. I think I took a dozen showers."

"That bad, huh?"

"Sorry to be a pill, Gilbert. But we've got to come up with something else."

"I can talk to Rupert tomorrow."

Sally was silent and started unwrapping the wax paper. She took out the taco, sniffed it, and then took a big bite, nodding her approval. "A taco with fish in it? Never heard of such a thing."

"Ancient Aztec recipe, stolen from an ancient Mexican fry cook I used to work for."

"It's delicious."

She polished off two tacos and Gilbert opened the second beer for her. She took a drink and then handed the can to him. "We'll share." They drank the beer and listened to the waves gently lapping at the shore. "So, your family's from Mexico, Gilbert?"

"Originally, yeah, from near the border. I was born in Harlingen, but I went to school in Matamoros."

"Why would you do that, if you don't mind me asking?"

"Didn't have much of a choice. They wouldn't let me back across."

"But you're a citizen."

"Didn't seem to matter to the boys at Immigration and Naturalization."

"I don't understand."

"When I was young my family worked the fruit orchards in the Valley, but when jobs got scarce during the Depression, the country rounded up anybody with brown skin they could catch and shipped them back to Mexico. *Gringos* needed work, and all of a sudden, fruit picking looked pretty good to them."

"You were deported?"

Gilbert nodded. "I was just a boy. Then, later, the war broke out, and the country decided they wanted cheap workers again, so we were invited back."

"Back to fruit picking?"

"For my family, yes. Every morning they bused them over, fumigated them like livestock, and sent them to work in the fields. Then, at night, they bused them back to our *pueblito* in Mexico. When the big freeze in '42 killed most of the fruit trees, the Ruiz family packed up the truck and went to the Northwest to pick apples, then down to California to pick vegetables, and then . . . well, I guess they go wherever the work takes them. Last I heard, they were living outside of Bakersfield. Me, I lied about my age and joined the army."

Sally was silent a moment, trying to imagine the life of a migrant worker. She had seen more than one diner hang a sign that said NO DOGS, NEGROS, OR MEXICANS. She'd even worked in a few. "How did you wind up here?"

"After the war, I found a job working the kitchen in the King's Inn restaurant on Baffin Bay. Rupert came in to eat one day and, afterwards, came back to the kitchen to tell me he liked his dinner. He offered me a job at Shady's on the spot, as their one and only cook."

"You a good cook?"

"Best one on Ransom Island."

"Well, I have to say, that was a mighty fine fish taco." She unwound her hair, shook it into a haphazard mop and raked her fingers through it until it made an abstract (though not unpleasing) frame around her fine-boned face.

"So, is it Gilbert or Gilberto?"

"The birth certificate says Gilberto, but everyone on this side of the river uses the Anglicized version. My mom was about half in love with Gilbert Roland, a Mexican movie star with a pencil-thin moustache. My dad put up with it because he had a crush on Ava Gardner. You'll never guess what my oldest sister's name is."

Sally laughed. "I got named after a song. An old Sicilian lullaby my poppa used to hear when he was a kid."

A gibbous moon began to rise above the water. Gilbert turned and looked at Sally. "So I told you my story. Why don't you tell me yours?"

"It's not that interesting."

"Oh, I doubt that."

"You're a smart man," she said playfully. "Let's see what you can *deduce,* you know, like that detective guy from England, the one who smokes a pipe and wears the funny hat."

"Sherlock Holmes? Okay. I'll play along." Gilbert shifted around to face Sally. "You spent your school years under Catholic instruction, but you were rebellious and constantly in trouble with the nuns. Then, you ran away, and eventually became involved in the, um, hospitality business, to make ends meet. Which brought you to the Rainbow Inn. Then something happened. You either saw something you weren't supposed to see, or you came across somebody you didn't want to see you, I don't know which, so the situation forced you to stow away on the first thing rolling through—in this case a beer delivery truck. If it was somebody, my money is on the *pistolero* that came calling yesterday."

Sally smiled nervously. "How did you figure all that out?"

"You told me yourself you had problems with the Sisters, and considering how restless you are—I don't think I've seen you sit still for five minutes—it's easy to imagine you wanting to leave them in the dust. As to your profession, your uh, uniform kind of gave you away. Not exactly school teacher attire. And I know Big 'Un's delivery schedule. The Rainbow Inn is the last stop on his route before Shady's. Has been for three years."

"How'd you know I was a cocktail waitress?"

"Because you said you weren't a . . ." Gilbert didn't finish, but he added, "And I believed you."

"Well, you got the story pretty much right."

"The Catholic school, was it an orphanage? Your parents are dead?"

"Yeah, they died a long time ago." Gilbert could hear the sadness in Sally's voice. "I was attending a Catholic college when I decided to run."

They were quiet for a while and sat listening to the water. Gilbert started to speak, but suddenly Sally leaned over and kissed him on the side of the mouth. "Thank you for helping me," she whispered in his ear. "I really am grateful." She stood up and pulled Gilbert to his feet.

"Sally, what about tonight?" he asked, hoping he didn't sound as flustered as he felt. "You are welcome to stay at my place again."

"You mean to sleep, right?"

Gilbert blushed. "Yes, of course. To sleep. You said earlier you couldn't bear to stay there again."

"The night is fine. It's the daytime that's unbearable."

"But where will you go during the day? Let me talk to Rupert tomorrow. As long as you didn't kill anyone, he'll help you figure something out."

"I didn't kill anyone," she said. "But I don't want to . . ." they both heard a faint splash in the water and could make out two figures near the shoreline, not thirty yards away. One was casting a purse seine into the bay, and the other held a lantern and a long spear and was hunting for flounder in the grassy shallows.

"It's Barefoot Nelson and his wife," said Gilbert. "They're usually somewhere around here most nights." He looked at Sally and smiled. "I have an idea. Hold on a minute."

Gilbert walked over and began speaking with them. Sally couldn't hear what he was saying, but she saw Mrs. Nelson's head lean out several times to scrutinize her in the moonlight.

"Okay, it's all set," Gilbert said when he returned. "You can stay with the Nelsons. They live on the far end of the island. Unless you want to get up before daylight to walk over there, you should probably go with them now."

"Now? Do they a have a house there?"

"It's sort of like a house."

"I don't know, Gilbert."

"Look," he said impatiently. "You have three choices if you want to keep your whereabouts a secret. Spend more days in my inferno of a cabin, take your chances across the bridge in Aransas Pass or wherever, or stay with Barefoot and his wife. You decide."

"Okay," she said. "Them. They won't turn me in?"

"You don't have to worry about that. They are very private people."

"How private?"

He grinned. "You have no idea." Gilbert went back and spoke briefly with the Nelsons and then motioned for her to come over.

"Sally, say hello to the Nelsons."

"Hello Mr. and Mrs. Nelson. Thank you for inviting me to your home."

They stood motionless and stared at Sally like she was covered with green scales and had just dragged herself onto the beach with flippered arms. Abruptly they turned and started walking away. Sally stood there until Mrs. Nelson turned and motioned with her head that she was to follow. As they walked away, Sally looked back and gave Gilbert a feeble wave.

"Sleep tight," he said under his breath. He wondered if she was resilient enough to tough it out with Barefoot and his wife. Staying with them would be a small step up from being shipwrecked on a desolate island with painted savages. If she lasted more than one night, he would figure that she *must* be desperate.

Gilbert went back to his bed and tried his best to sleep. But all he could think about was Sally . . . and about that kiss.

CHAPTER 10

Primo Ginestra picked up the phone, yanked the cord out of the wall, and hurled the entire contraption through an open window and into the Gulf of Mexico (narrowly missing a family of four from Amarillo searching for sea shells below the Bali Hai pier).

"Goddamn sonofabitch Jew bastard!" Primo bellowed, following up that invective with a string of Sicilian curses.

He glared malevolently around the room, looking for another inanimate object on which to vent his wrath. His secretary, long alert to Primo's volatile moods, had gathered her purse and fled for dear life the instant she heard the pitch of his voice start to rise. By the time he deep-sixed the telephone, she was a block down the Seawall, wondering for the hundredth time whether it was time to start looking at the help-wanted ads.

Primo was wrestling a large leather chair towards the window when Gerry stuck his head around the door of his adjoining office. The brothers kept working quarters at the Bali Hai as well as the Turf Club.

"Are you upset with one of our Hebrew brethren?" he asked mildly.

Huffing and puffing with emotion, Primo said, "Guess who I just got off the phone with? That goddamn Sidney Lowenstein in New

York. He regretted to inform me that Duke Ellington was cancelling his Fourth of July dance at guess whose nightclub?"

"What's his beef? We had Ellington here six months ago. Everybody made out."

"It's some nigger bullshit, according to Lowenstein. Said the last time he was here, Ellington overheard the house manager saying how it was a shame we had to book a bunch of coons into the place to make ends meet. Said if he wanted to see that kind of shit, he'd go to Africa or Harlem. Ellington went back to New York and said he was through with the Bali Hai."

Gerry was incredulous. "*Our* house manager said that? Mikey Canera?"

"Mikey ain't renowned for his liberal views."

"Fuck his views. If that little stunt bitched up one of our biggest holiday weekend shows . . . . Ask around, find out if it's true what he said, and if it is, break his legs."

"With pleasure," said Primo. "But that ain't all. You'll never guess where Ellington's playing a make-up date."

"If it's for that rat bastard C.B. Stubblefield across town, I'll burn down his joint."

"No, the Duke Ellington Orchestra is going to be spending the Fourth of July at the Shady Palm Bar & Grill on Ransom Island."

Gerry's blood pressure spiked several points. "You're shitting me."

"Nope. Want to throw something out the window?"

Gerry decided to make a drink instead, helping himself at the sideboard. He was the farthest thing from a superstitious man, but he felt a little tingle up the back of his neck. In all his forty-six years he'd never heard of Ransom Island. And now all of a sudden, it was all he was hearing about. First Jimmy Glick, now this. Some sandspit down in the boonies. Goddammit, he was a busy man, with a criminal empire to run.

He took a long swallow of gin. "Been thinking about what Jimmy was saying last night. About buying the place. Be funny if Duke Ellington showed up and we were holding the keys."

"It'd serve him right, huh?"

"Well, he's all through in Galveston. But when you and Jimmy take the boat down, think about logistics. We got so much coming in from slots and pinball and dice we're having trouble hiding it. Even with our own bank. With all Jimmy says they got going on down there— huntin' and fishin', cabins, the dancehall—there might be plenty of opportunity to mix our hard-earned illegitimate profits with some legitimate ones, to help camouflage the money trail. Deke's on his way down there now," Gerry continued. "Maybe we can turn this whole deal around quick and give Mr. Ellington a warm welcome."

"Might do that anyway," Primo added. "Give that fucker something to remember us by."

"We'll see. In the meantime, you all get rolling. It's a long sail. Take the Intracoastal; it's a straight shot. The skipper will know."

"Will do." Primo paused on his way out the door. He seemed vaguely embarrassed. "Ah, Gerry . . . ?"

"What, big brother?"

"Would you see to getting another phone put in here?"

—

Donald "Deke" Maloney was a smooth piece of work. He had to be. As one of the two top lieutenants in the Ginestra organization, Deke was a necessary counterpoint to Jimmy Glick. Jimmy just naturally put the fear of God in folks. With his bird-of-prey ferocity and ruthless efficiency, Jimmy was the tip of the Ginestra spear. He came off hard and scary. Even his smile left one ill at ease.

Deke didn't scare anybody. At least not at first. He had a round, happy, permanently sunburned face. He looked like any guy next to you fishing off the jetty. The kind of guy who loaned you his special spoon lure and pointed to the spot where the fish were biting. And here, have one of these cold beers out of my cooler while you're at it.

That was Deke. A happy man. He would smile while he extorted your business, sent legbreakers after a degenerate gambler with overdue markers, or burned down a rival's saloon. (The Ginestra brothers called it "building a vacant lot.") Life to Deke was, by and large, a bowl of cherries.

Leo "Big Tiny" Coppola and his cousin L.T. ("Little Tiny") marveled, not for the first time, at their boss's natural equanimity. They moved in the same violent underground world as he, and whatever milk of human kindness resided in their souls had long since curdled. But here Deke sat in the lobby of the Seaman's Bank and Trust in the heart (such as it was) of downtown Aransas Pass, one leg crossed over the other at the ankle, head bobbing to some internal melody, looking for all the world like he had a date with an angel. You'd hardly believe he'd killed at least two people.

And now here came the pigeons.

Deke's face lit up with what seemed to be honest pleasure as Rupert and Noble stepped through the revolving door of the bank. He bounded to his feet and marched across the tiled floor, grabbing Rupert's big paw in both of his and pumping it vigorously.

Big Tiny and Little Tiny kept their seats. They were here as Deke's "assistants" and "secretaries," and they instinctively sensed that the less attention they drew to themselves, the better for everyone's peace of mind.

"Mr. Sweetwater and, ah, Mr. Sweetwater," said Deke. "I'm Don McCullough. Thanks for taking time out of your busy schedules to meet with me this morning. Speaking of morning, have you gents had your coffee? And by the way, call me Don."

Rupert shrugged. "I've been known to have a second cup."

"Outstanding. There's a coffee shop next to my hotel. Let's move this little shindig over there where we'll be more comfortable." Eyeing Rupert's and Noble's fisherman's attire (khakis, deck shoes, and blue denim work shirts buttoned at the neck), Deke sensed they would be more relaxed—and pliable—out of the formal confines of the bank.

He was right. Rupert stretched his legs out of the cafe booth and exhaled as he contemplated a hot cup of coffee and a bearclaw. "Never did care for banks, much," he said.

Deke nodded sympathetically. "It's like that folksinger, Woody Guthrie, said—some men will rob you with a six-gun, and some with a fountain pen."

"Which kind of robber are you, Mr. McCullough?" Noble's tone was light, but his eyes were watchful.

Deke blinked. At an adjoining table, the Coppola cousins stifled grins.

"It's the suit, isn't it?" said Deke, fingering the summer-weight wool lapel of his double-breasted jacket. "I forget things are a little less formal down here than they are in Galveston."

At the word "Galveston," both Rupert's and Noble's ears pricked up.

"Yeah, well, our subscription to *Gentleman's Quarterly* must've run out," said Noble. "And here I was wonderin' if double vents and pleats were gonna be in this fall."

"You'll forgive my brother," Rupert interrupted. "He suffers from an excess of humor. But, well, your telegram did get us wondering. You said something about a 'unique business opportunity'?"

"That's the way my boss phrased it," said Deke. "He and some friends were down this way last winter doing some goose hunting on that big ranch on Saint Joe Island. And, well, you know, there's not much in the way of diversion on that island once the hunting's done for the day." Deke patted his jacket pocket and pulled out a cigar. "Mind if I smoke?"

"Be my guest," said Rupert.

Deke lit the cigar. "Here, have a couple," he said, pushing two Montecristos and a pack of matches across the table.

Rupert took the Cuban cigars and the matches and put them in his pocket. "Thanks. Maybe later."

"So anyway," Deke continued, "one of the big shots of the ranch told my boss about your place on Ransom Island. Dancing, music, fishing and whatnot. Said it was a damn shame it was the dead of winter, or we'd pile in the boat and have a high ol' time."

"Sounds like Al Gieseke," said Rupert. "That old man surely likes to caper. When he turned sixty, he threw a party at Shady's that lasted two days."

"Yeah, Gieseke," said Deke, following Rupert's lead. "Anyway, my boss couldn't get your place out of his head. Sounded like Shangri-La to him, I guess. I made a couple of inquiries to the county commissioner on his behalf and found out a little bit more about the place and about you gentlemen—there's another brother, isn't there? And also your wife, if I'm not mistaken?"

"Yes, Mr. McCullough, there's two other brothers, actually. One's a shrimper in Fulton, not associated with the business, and the other one . . . well, he's part of it but he doesn't have much of a head for business. Also a couple of hired hands. And my wife, of course."

"Exactly. There's a lot for y'all to keep up with out there, isn't there? Cabins and docks and boats and the dancehall and everything . . . to keep it all running. Not to mention the guide business and hiring bands and keeping the books. I'll bet you boys are busier than a cat in a mouse factory."

"You know what they say about idle hands," said Noble.

"I sure do. My boss feels the same way. He had an interest in a couple of shipyards before the war. Well, what with mobilization and some fat defense contracts, he came out with a bunch of extra capital. He wants to put it to work, spread it around. And that's where you men come in.

"If your wife is anything like mine, Rupert, I bet she would like some of the finer things in life, and time to enjoy them. And Noble, you look to me like a man who would probably rather fish than eat, am I right? What if instead of tending to tourists, y'all could take your own boat out to the Florida Keys or down to the Yucatan and really do some championship fishing? Live the high life, ya know?"

Rupert cocked his bushy eyebrows. "Are you making us an offer, Mr. McCullough?"

"Me? Oh, hell no. My boss would be the one to do that. I'm just down here to feel out the situation."

"Hmmm," said Rupert. "I didn't know we had a 'situation.' Your boss runs a shipyard. What does he know about the beer and bait business?"

"Oh, he has an interest in a couple of nightspots in Galveston, too," said Maloney airily. "It's all just business, ain't it?"

"Just by the way of it, what's your boss's name?" asked Noble pointedly.

Maloney paused momentarily. "Uh, Stubblefield. Mr. Christopher B. Stubblefield. But I'd ask you to keep the name to yourself. He's trying to stay under the radar."

Rupert rocked his spoon back and forth beside his empty coffee cup. "Well, you tell Mr. Stubblefield we're not entirely set on closing the books on Shady's. But if he wants to send a dollar figure our way, we'll certainly pay it close attention."

"The boss was hoping you could maybe give me a verbal commitment. A good faith indication that y'all are onboard with the idea. It's a, um, a tax issue. Something about shielding capital gains or something. Time is of the essence, he said."

Rupert shook his head definitively. "No, that's not going to happen. We've got to see a hard offer first, then talk it over, chew on it. We built Ransom Island with our own hands, mister. We're not going to cut it loose over a cup of coffee."

"That's understandable, and good business, too. So, how about this? What if we sent a couple of appraisers down your way to take a look around the property? Take a peek at your books maybe? All in the interest of making you a fair offer, of course."

Rupert didn't feel the need to mention that his "books" were a cigar box full of crumpled receipts. "It's a little early in the game to be opening our books, Mr. McCullough, but you're welcome to send somebody out to look around if you want."

Deke saw he'd pushed as hard as he could for now. "Fair enough, Mr. Sweetwater." He stood up and shook hands with Rupert and Noble. "I thank you gentlemen for your time and attention. I feel certain you'll be hearing from my employer soon."

As Maloney reached for his hat, Noble spoke up.

"Say, I guess this falls into the funny coincidence department. We don't normally get many visitors from Galveston. Y'all have got all the fishing you can handle up there, after all. But you're our second visitor in a week. The last fella, he wasn't nearly as well-mannered as you are."

"What did he want?"

"Claimed to be looking for a missing girl, but his story was awful thin. He left in a hurry."

"What happened to him?"

"We're big on civility on Ransom Island. My younger brother— the one that doesn't have a head for business—educated him in the finer points of etiquette and sent him on his way."

"That *is* a coincidence."

"Yeah," said Noble. "This other bird's name was James Glick, according to his driver's license. Ring a bell at all?"

"No," said Deke Maloney. "Never heard of him."

—

On the short drive back to Ransom Island, Rupert and Noble discussed the meeting.

"You think we'll ever hear from those guys again?" asked Noble.

"It's not the first time somebody's approached us to buy us out," Rupert answered. "And if you remember, not a one of 'em came up with a hard offer."

"This one seems a little different."

Rupert twisted his earlobe thoughtfully as he drove. "Maybe. We'll see." And then he added, "In the meantime, I'd appreciate it if you wouldn't say anything to Darla."

Noble smiled. "Sure thing, Rupe."

CHAPTER 11

While the Sweetwater brothers were in the back room hashing out the logistics of the upcoming Duke Ellington show, Darla was being an inattentive bartender to a group of Shady's regulars. She sometimes helped Rupert work the bar on weekday afternoons, until the dinner staff—composed mostly of students from nearby Del Mar College—arrived to take over. It was a role she tackled infrequently and with a palpable lack of enthusiasm. Did Patti Page tend bar? Did Mary Martin tend bar? Besides, she was preoccupied with the set list she would use on the biggest night of her life.

For twenty years she had been waiting for something like this to happen to her. Other little girls played house. Darla used a mop for a microphone and pretended she was singing for millionaires at the Hollywood Palladium. All the while, as she grew up, something—call it "It"—waited for her, just over the horizon. Whatever "It" was, it was fate, kismet, written in the stars. It was the reason she had practiced all those hours in her room, trying to imitate the songs of Doris Day, Dinah Shore, and her all-time favorite, Judy Garland.

"It" was the reason she practiced tap and ballet until her little painted toes bled. It was the reason her daddy, back when he was flush with oil money and still had some pull in the community, arranged to have her sing a regular afternoon show for the soldiers at the USO Club in Corpus Christi. It was the reason, if she was honest with herself, that she was so attracted to Rupert when he started courting her. After all, he did own the biggest dance hall in the county.

Maybe she would kick off with "Old Devil Moon" to really grab the audience from the get-go. Or would "Tea for Two" be a better choice? Everyone knew the song and it had been a sure-fire crowd-pleaser at the USO Club. *What was killing them this week on* Your Hit Parade? she wondered.

"Darla?" said a squat, ruddy man sitting at a tin-topped table. "Me and Giddyup have been dry for about five minutes now. You didn't forget about us, did'ja?"

Darla sighed. This time it was Cecil Shoat who was intruding on her ruminations. Cecil was an oilfield roustabout who worked offshore and wore his job on his sleeve and on pretty much every other part of his filthy oil-and-grease-stained coveralls. Cecil took pride in his griminess, the hard-earned mark of a workin' man. His battered tin hard hat occupied the seat beside him, and a half dozen empty Grand Prize beer bottles lined his table next to a pack of Camels and a Zippo lighter embossed with the Marine Corps seal. An abandoned domino game took up most of the rest of the tabletop.

Cecil's domino partner was Gideon (Giddyup) Dodson, who, by contrast, dressed the part of a singing cowboy from the movies. Never mind that he'd done nothing more than help city slickers climb onto the geriatric nags at the Dixie Dude Ranch outside of Bandera, and then lead them over the well-worn trail that circled the property. In his mind's eye, he was a cross between Casey Tibbs and the Marlboro Man. The dude ranch went broke after a customer sued them when he fell off an ambulatory oat bucket named Soapsuds, so Gideon drifted down to the coast and found a job selling one-acre ranchettes for an Aransas Pass realty company. As part of his pitch, he wore pointy-toed cowboy boots, a pearl-snapped shirt, and a blinding white Stetson. He encouraged everyone, including adults, to address him as "Giddyup."

Giddyup Dodson and Cecil Shoat were best buddies.

Darla pulled a church key from her pocket and punched triangular holes in a can of Schlitz beer for Giddyup. Then she angled a Grand Prize longneck against the edge of the metal table and popped the cap off with a resounding *thwack*. Cecil and Giddyup might have been Shady's most frequent customers, but they were far from her favorites. Lousy tippers and not above slapping her on the rear if Rupert wasn't looking.

"Thank ya, Darla," said Cecil. "You're a goddamned jewel."

"Much obliged," said Gideon.

"I hope you boys are keeping tabs on the number of beers you're drinking," she said as she walked away, "Because I'm not."

"Oh, yes ma'am," said Cecil, winking at Gideon. "We're keeping a close count." They both snickered like schoolboys.

Darla didn't care. A few beers on the house didn't matter much. What mattered was her gosh-darned set list. What would Connie Francis do?

Darla glanced at the bar and noticed empty bottles in front of the other two customers, and felt obligated to tend to them, too. "Captain Quincy?" she asked. "Gus? Another?"

Captain Quincy was a retired gunnery sergeant and a veteran of WWI. Originally from Michigan, he fell in love with the Gulf Coast, particularly the fishing, after discovering the area at the half-way point of a long Airstream trailer tour. He and his wife arrived one winter day to partake in the bird-watching for which the region was renowned, and decided to stay. Captain Quincy loved fishing, and he loved salt water—so long as he could touch the bottom. He was terrified of boats and was happy to confine his angling adventures to wade fishing and surf casting only. The "Captain" title was strictly self-applied.

"Sure, I'll have another one, Darla," said Captain Quincy. "And I suppose I'm still buying for my Kraut friend over here, since he caught the most *and* the biggest fish this morning."

"*Yah*, you are darn tootin'," said Gus in his thick German accent.

Gustav (Gus) Brauer also came from up north, although they pronounced it "norden" where he came from. Currently, he and his taciturn Czech wife were caretakers of a small dairy farm about twelve miles away, near Taft, Texas. In his halting English, he would tell anyone who asked that he was originally from a little village outside Prague, and that he came to the United States as a refugee in 1938. The story was true, except for the fact that it was his wife's story. Her father, a naturalized American citizen, plucked her from the old country just before Hitler's tanks rolled through their village. She and her father had been milking Jersey cows ever since.

The real time and date of Gus's arrival was zero two hundred on February 17, 1943, and the place was a secluded beach on the outskirts of Galveston. Chief Petty Officer Gustav Brauer was an *Obersteuermann* crewman, responsible for navigation and supplies on U-166, a type IXC German U-boat that prowled the Gulf of Mexico during the war. When the U-boat's Kapitän brazenly (and in retrospect, irresponsibly) allowed a small crew of officers and seamen to go ashore in Galveston for some undercover reconnaissance—the Mardi Gras celebration that raged throughout the city would provide ample cover, he reasoned— Gustav succumbed to the wicked temptations of *Karneval* and awoke the following morning face down on a sandy beach with a debilitating hangover. By then, U-166 was long gone, and there was no telling when it would be coming back.

In his heart of hearts, Gustav was delighted. He was no Nazi. He had never jointed the Party, and he'd been conscripted into the U-boat corps almost arbitrarily. The first night after his unexpected marooning, he stole some civilian clothes from a clothesline and wandered around the town, star-struck. He thought of Germany, with its parsimonious wartime rationing, the nightly bombings and strafings, and the fanatic, idolatrous lunatics who were entangling the whole country in a national suicide pact.

What was that compared to Murdoch's Bath House, the Galveston Pleasure Pier, the allure of the courtesans on Post Office Street, and the warm Gulf breezes? Gus loved his country as a general senti- ment, but so far, Galveston was the most beautiful thing he'd ever seen. Shortly after his abandonment (it wasn't desertion if it was accidental, was it?) he happened upon a wallet and ID papers that had fallen out of a drunk sailor's pocket in front of a whorehouse, whereupon he set about to become that quintessential American— the self-made man.

When he married his fat Czech wife a year later, Gustav settled in for good. And why not? He had an ideal relationship. His hard-working wife and father-in-law handled the milk cows, and Gus made the daily deliveries. That gave him lots of time to pursue his new passion in life, fishing. His tackle was always ready in the truck, and he managed to get in a few hours of angling each day—usually with Captain Quincy, his habitual companion out on the bay. Everybody knew Gus and his refugee story were bogus (his simple-minded wife had spilled the beans), but nobody cared. Not at Shady's.

Darla handed the two men their beers and went back to planning her breakout performance. She hid behind her new copy of *Screen Fan* magazine so the boys wouldn't bother her with small talk. A gauzy photo of Marilyn Monroe graced the cover, along with the banner headline "This Kid Needs a Friend." *Well*, thought Darla. *I don't need a friend. I need a break, and an agent. And a ticket to Hollywood. Or New York. New York would be okay.*

She started humming "I'll Take Manhattan" to herself while she examined the photo of Marilyn to see if it offered any fashion tips. After a quick study she decided no, she'd stick with the classic styling provided by Judy Garland on the '49 *Life* magazine cover. After numerous experimentations with hair color, lipsticks, and eye makeup, Darla had perfected *that* look. It was sure to get the attention of the talent scouts. Maybe Mr. Ellington and his New York agent, as well.

With growing irritation, she tried to ignore the inane conversation coming from the nearby table.

"I don't care how fast on the draw he was," said Cecil. "We're talking about fisticuffs. And Shane would be no match for Marshal Will Kane." Cecil was in an argument with Gideon over which of their favorite Western film stars would win if they got in a fistfight. "I mean, goddamn, Alan Ladd wears lifts in his cowboy boots 'cause he's so little."

"That may be," Gideon countered, "but don't forget that scene at the general store where Shane and his farmer friend opened a can of whip-ass on about a hundred of Ryker's men. He was knockin' 'em down left and right." The movie *Shane* had only been in theaters for two weeks, but Gideon had seen it three times already and considered himself an expert on the subject.

"Ah, bullshit," said Cecil. "Gary Cooper is six foot four inches tall. He'd hold that little man's head with one hand and slap him around with the other. Now, if Shane was to get that gunfighter to help him— what was his name?"

"Jack Palance."

"No, his movie name, you knucklehead."

"Wilson."

"Yeah, Wilson. Now there's a mean sumbitch."

"Well, at least we agree on something."

"Bogart," Captain Quincy interjected.

"What?" asked Cecil, squinting over at the horseshoe-shaped bar where the Captain nursed his beer.

"Humphrey Bogart," Quincy continued. "He could take either of those drugstore cowboys."

"Bogie? Are you kiddin' me? He ain't even in no westerns."

"How about *Treasure of the Sierra Madre?*" Quincy asked.

"Naw." Cecil shook his head. "He was just a crazy man *in* that one. *Loco* in the *cabeza*. Bogart's better at fightin' gangsters and Nazis— no offense, Gus."

Gus lifted his hand to signal that no offense was taken.

Zachariah entered through the back door with a bucket and mop. Part of his job was to swab down the wood plank floor twice a week.

"Well, let's ask Zach what he thinks," Cecil suggested. "He was a real cowboy back in his day. He oughta know. Zach, tell us which cowboy movie star you think is tougher: Marshall Kane from *High Noon*, or Shane, from uh, *Shane?*"

Zachariah put his mop in the bucket and thought about it. He'd only seen one "cowboy" movie in his life: a scratchy Tom Mix film that the ranch owner brought to the bunkhouse as a treat for the hands after a particularly successful roundup. Zach didn't recall seeing much cowboying in the film—mostly just gunfights, fistfights and men in big hats kissing saloon girls. He shook his head slowly. "I don't rightly know. Either one of 'em ever broke a green horse or dug a hunnert post holes in a day?"

"What?" said Cecil. "No, Zach. You're missing the point. We're talking about hand-to-hand combat here. Bare-knuckle fightin'. Who'd be the toughest?"

"Oh," said Zachariah. "In that case, I'd say Jack Johnson."

Cecil turned around in disgust. The rest of the boys laughed. Darla shut her eyes and tried to shut out the incessant gab. A grubby roughneck, a phony cowboy, a pretend American, a fake captain, and a half-lame Negro cowpoke. She should be on Broadway. Not in this room full of rejects. *Would Teresa Brewer put up with this shit?*

But speaking of Gary Cooper . . . the screen swung open and Darla watched the closest real-life thing to the *High Noon* star walk through the door—San Patricio County Sheriff Red Burton, Jr. He was six-four, like the movie star, and had a chiseled, masculine face, similar in many respects to Coop. Marshal Will Kane, indeed.

Darla and Red had been an item once, almost fifteen years ago, when Darla was still in high school and Red was a cadet at Texas A&M. He intended to marry Darla as soon as they graduated from their respective schools, and Darla supposed they would tie the knot, too. Their engagement, although never formalized with a ring or an official announcement, gave her a certain celebrity at Aransas Pass High that elevated her status, she believed, to that of a mature, experienced woman, and not just a flirty teenage girl in flouncy skirts and bobby socks.

But when the war started, Red was drafted and sent off to someplace in Italy she couldn't pronounce, and Darla was left to her own devices, which included cavorting with every available non-draftable young man in a tri-county area. Her parents offered no guidance, having serious financial and marital problems to sort out by that time. So one day, out of boredom mainly, Darla agreed to marry the owner of a bayfront seafood restaurant in the "big" city of Corpus Christi. That was two husbands ago.

Red was disappointed, to say the least. He returned home to Aransas Pass and chose a career in law enforcement, like his father, Red Burton Sr., a former Texas Ranger of considerable renown. Red Jr. was respected in the community and was an effective and (if you were a bad guy) formidable sheriff for the county. He had never married.

"Hi, cowboy," Darla said cheerfully from her perch behind the bar.

"'Lo, Darla," he said, removing his hat. "Boys." He nodded their way and the Shady's regulars greeted the sheriff amiably. He was a familiar sight at Shady's, and Rupert counted him as a best friend. That his wife might still harbor feelings for the lawman was a subject upon which Rupert chose not to dwell. He enjoyed fishing and duck hunting with Red too much.

"Rupe here?" he asked.

"In the back, with Flavius and Noble, discussing some big news." Darla had a wide grin on her face.

"What big news?"

"Go ask him," she said brightly.

Red hoped to God the big news wasn't that Darla was pregnant. He'd be happy for Rupert, sure, but . . . well, he didn't exactly know why he wished it wasn't true. Maybe he still hoped that someday he'd have another shot with her. He shook himself out of that train of thought and went into the small back office behind the bar. He found Flavius and Noble standing over Rupert with their arms crossed, arguing with him about parking for the "show."

"What show?" asked Red.

Flavius looked surprised. "You haven't heard? Shady's is going big time. We've got Duke Ellington comin' to play here on the Fourth of July.

"*The* Duke Ellington, and his orchestra?"

"Damn straight," said Flavius.

"That a fact, Rupert?"

"Yeah, it is, Red. Kind of caught me off guard, too, when Darla told me. But I talked to his manager yesterday and we nailed it down."

Red Burton Jr. whistled. "Well, I'll be dogged. That's a whole 'nuther ballgame for Shady's, isn't it?"

"We've had some pretty big dances here that filled up the house, but nothing like this."

"Biggest thing since FDR went fishing in Port A. I expect you'll need some help with security?"

Rupert smiled. "I was just gettin' ready to call you about that, Red. Got some extra deputies you can spare?"

"I think I can convince a few to put in some overtime. And don't think I'm not comin' too, Rupe. I grew up hearing 'Creole Love Song' on the radio." Then Red's mind started wrestling with the challenges a big event like this would pose. There was parking, and access (on a one-lane bridge, no less), and fire codes he'd have to make sure were followed. And it was the Fourth of July.

Suddenly he remembered a picture he'd seen one time of Duke and his band. Seems like they were mostly all Negroes. That meant that colored folks for miles around would want to come see him, too. "So you'll be doing two shows, of course. It'll be a bear getting everyone in and out."

"Well, that's the thing, Red," said Rupert. "The agent said one of the main reasons Duke chose our place is because he wants to treat his band members to some of our world famous fishing. Their train won't arrive until the Fourth, the day of the show, and the rest of the weekend we'll be taking all of 'em out on the bay and around the jetties."

"Just one show?"

"The nuts and bolts of it just don't work to have two shows, what with them arriving so late, and that skinny ol' bridge. We could never turn the house in time, Red."

"You can't have a mixed crowd; you know that."

"Benny Goodman did it fifteen years ago."

"Yeah, in New York City. It won't fly down here. I suppose you can cordon off the room; set up a place where the black folks can dance, and seat all the white folks up front to listen."

"You know that's not the way we operate."

Red scratched his head. "You're asking for trouble, Rupert."

"That's what I told him," said Flavius.

"Big brother's feeling all democratic all of a sudden," Noble added.

"Boys," growled Rupert. "Shady's has *always* had an open door policy. It's a free gawd-damned country, and we're doin' one gawd-damned show. Anybody that wants to pay their dollar for a ticket is gettin' in—white, black, brown, yeller, or stripedy. That's just the way it's gonna be."

Red sighed. "Why do you want to put my ass in a crack, Rupe? I know you've got the People's Republic of Ransom Island going out here, and I don't personally care who you serve or don't. But there's laws on the books about segregated public events, and I'm in charge of upholding 'em."

Rupert's eyes narrowed. "You gonna wave the 'nigger flag,' Red? Do you some good come the next election?"

Burton looked at him unflinchingly. "You know I don't hold with a lot of that Jim Crow nonsense. My daddy didn't either, but it's still the law of the land, and you know that I'll do my duty, if it comes to it."

Neither of the two men wanted a showdown at that particular moment.

"Well, shit," said Rupert finally. "Maybe we'll all get washed away in a hurricane between now and then."

———

CHAPTER 12

Gilberto Ruiz was in the kitchen before sunrise, rolling out dough for a batch of his famous fruit pies. Cecil Shoat had been known to eat three whole pies at one sitting, rhubarb and blueberry stains overlaying the oil and grease on his face and coveralls. Captain Quincy swore you could bait a hook with one of Gilbert's pies and win the Deep Sea Round-Up every year if they'd allow it.

A rough-planked dog run separated the kitchen from the main dining/dance hall. The workspace was tight and the commercial equipment bordered on vintage (Civil War vintage, that is), but Gilbert utilized it to maximum efficiency. In his domain, Gilbert was the Kingfish, the *Chef de cuisine,* a culinary god among men. It helped that he was also the one and only cook.

After Rupert hired Gilbert to run his kitchen, the Shady Palm menu underwent a dramatic and, most customers would agree, long overdue transformation. Gone were the lunch specials that featured hamburger patties, frozen tater-tots, canned string beans, and Jell-O. Gone was the Manager's Special: Frito pie paired with a canned peach and a dollop of Reddi-wip. Gone were the K-ration Salisbury steaks that Rupert used to buy on the black market from the naval air base in Corpus.

Customers could still get their fried shrimp and hush puppies, but now they could choose from fresh seafood dishes that included Trout Amandine, lump crab cakes, and calamari. ("I'll be dipped in shit, it's a squid!" said Giddyup in amazement after he took his first bite.) Hand-cut T-bones found their way onto the menu, as well as sliced avocado salads, fresh vegetables, and the fruit pies. Gilbert even prepared seasonal dishes like turkey and dressing at Thanksgiving, *posole* at Christmas, and a Cajun jambalaya during Mardi Gras.

For the last two years, in late summer, Gilbert caused a stir when he featured *chiles en nogada*–poblano chiles stuffed with spiced ground pork, covered with a creamy walnut sauce. "You gringos need to know that tacos and burritos aren't the only food in Mexico," he told his boss.

To Rupert's surprise, the traditional Mexican dish was a huge hit. He had been skeptical until he tasted one of the chiles, then devoured two more. But as much as Rupert liked them, he insisted that Gilbert change the name to "stuffed peppers with cream sauce."

"Otherwise you're just perpetuatin' the pepperbelly stereotype, son," he told him. "Anyway, everybody knows chili is spelled with an 'i'." Gilbert never had the heart to tell Rupert that the tri-colored entree was a Mexican Independence Day favorite.

It was peaceful and cool in the kitchen, and Gilbert quietly sang a Lydia Mendoza ballad while he worked. He enjoyed the early mornings. It could get hot and hectic in there at mealtime or when the fishing charters returned from the bays, hungry and thirsty after a day in the sun. After dinner, the menu was limited to the drunks' trifecta of Fritos, corn nuts, and pickled pigs' feet. This left Gilbert plenty of time to read, play his guitar, and pursue his other highbrow hobbies in the privacy of his cabin.

Gilbert was blessed with an innate intelligence and curiosity that bordered on genius. He occasionally wondered if he was squandering his gift on Ransom Island. He would never be able to invent a space rocket in his cramped commercial kitchen, or explore nuclear sub propulsion while he was marooned in the middle of Redfish Bay. And although he was a competent, even creative, cook, Gilbert knew he would never make the cover of *Bon Appetit* as long as he worked at Shady's. But he *did* know that it was better than chopping cotton, humping for the Army, or picking those *pinche* grapefruits in the Rio Grande Valley. All in all, Ransom Island offered him a comfortable and often diverting existence.

He was greasing the pie pans when he felt a presence behind him. He turned around and saw Sally standing in the doorway.

"You look cute in your apron, Gilberto."

He noticed she was still wearing his army trousers and denim work shirt. "Thanks. You look like a poster girl for the WAC—you know, the girl with the star-spangled heart?"

"Well I *feel* like I've been fighting the Japs on a jungle island," she said, tucking a strand of hair back under her bandana. "The Nelsons," she rolled her eyes dramatically, "I mean . . . *hoo-boy*." She grabbed a piece of dough off the table and tasted it. "What are you doing?"

"I'm baking pies."

"What kind?"

"Today, apple."

"Can I help?" She looked at him pleadingly.

"You decided not to stay with the Nelsons anymore?" The poor girl looked like she hadn't slept in a month, and her arms and legs were covered with bug bites. "Beach camping didn't suit you?"

Sally hopped onto a stainless steel counter. "Sure, it's peachy if you don't mind sleeping on a mat in the sand and having crabs crawl across your body. How in God's name do they do it? How does *she* do it?"

Gilbert laughed, imagining the ghost crabs scuttling over Sally's creamy skin during the night. *I should have been a pair of ragged claws . . . .*

"Did you know there are rattlesnakes here? Mrs. Nelson, Emma, found a humongous one under a piece of driftwood near the, um . . . shelter thingy they live in. Without saying a word, she grabbed a machete, whacked its head off, and started peeling the skin—*while the body was still moving*. My God, it was horrifying." Sally closed her eyes as she remembered the ordeal. "She even made me help her."

"A useful skill," said Gilbert.

"And guess what we had for dinner last night?"

"Crepes Suzette and chateaubriand? Maybe a little cognac?"

"Rattlesnake. With beans and cornbread. The other meals were fish, crabs, fish, and more fish."

"Well, fishing *is* what they do for a living," said Gilbert. "You're living off the bounty of the sea."

"Well, this girl is declaring mutiny on the bounty. They hardly say a word, they leave early and disappear in their little boat or wade out into the bay—and they're gone for hours and hours. For two days I sat on the beach scratching mosquito bites and watching the ships and barges pass by, wishing I was on one."

"Sorry you were so lonely. So, are you coming out of hiding now?"

"I was serious about helping you out. You need a woman's touch in this kitchen."

Gilbert had anticipated this. Given Sally's hyperactive and very social tendencies, he knew she wouldn't last long with the Nelsons—he was surprised she had lasted three nights—so he'd devised a plan for her return. Just yesterday, he'd told Rupert that once word of Duke Ellington's visit spread, business would pick up. It wouldn't do to be shorthanded in the kitchen. After all, the restaurant was the most profitable part of the whole Shady Palm enterprise. Rupert should consider letting his head cook hire a helper. And he didn't mean another undergrad from Del Mar College.

Rupert, preoccupied with the big event, distractedly nodded in agreement. So in Gilbert's mind the decision had been made. Piece of cake. *No hay problema.*

Trouble was, Gilbert really *did* need help in the kitchen—skilled help, and now that she was here, he wondered if she even knew how to boil water. No time like the present to find out.

"Can you peel apples?"

"Are you kidding? If I can skin a rattlesnake . . . ."

He handed her a pairing knife and an apron and pointed to a crate of apples on the floor. "The knife's sharp. Don't cut yourself."

Sally smiled. "You won't regret this, Gilbert. I'm a fast learner."

"I hope so. By the way, if you get the job, the pay is 75 cents an hour."

Four hours later, a dozen hot pies were cooling on the counters and on the windowsills. Gilbert was filleting a flounder while Sally cleaned up. He looked over and watched her sweep apple peels and flour into a dustpan. Three of her fingers were wrapped in Band-Aids, but overall, she had performed admirably: watching him work and anticipating how to help, not asking a million questions, doing her job and staying out of his way. She might work out after all.

Gilbert heard Rupert and Darla walking up the path. "I smell pies," said Rupert. "Apple, I think."

"Gilbert's tempting me again," said Darla. "He knows I have a weakness for his pies. Does he want me to get fat?"

"Aw, babe. You look terrific—" Rupert stopped when he opened the screen door and saw Sally. Her blond hair was tied up in a bandana and her shirt, Gilbert's shirt, actually, was tied in a knot around her flat belly. Darla stared at the new girl over her husband's shoulder.

"Hi," said Sally brightly. "You must be Rupert and Darla. I'm Sally, Gilbert's new assistant." She wiped her hand on her pants and held it out to both of them in turn.

"Nice to meet you," Rupert mumbled. He looked at Gilbert. "You found someone right quick, didn't you?"

"Needed to get somebody on board right away so I could train them. And Sally, well—"

"I happened to come by this morning to deliver some produce from the A&P in town," Sally blurted, improvising like crazy. "And Gilbert and I started talking. He mentioned he was looking for kitchen help and I told him I happened to be looking for a full time job, so . . . " she shrugged, "here I am."

Rupert glanced out the window to see if a produce van was parked outside. "You have experience working in a kitchen, Sally?" Rupert asked.

"Oh, yes, sir. I've been working in restaurants for years—full time since I got out of high school. Mostly in Houston," she lied. "But lately I've been doing some part time work locally, at the A&P, making deliveries, not today, of course. I walked over. But before. Anyway, I'm trying to save up some money for, um, nursing school."

Rupert rubbed his earlobe with his thumb and forefinger, something he did when he was trying to work out a riddle in his head. But before he could continue interrogating the camp cook's lovely new assistant, Darla stepped forward.

"Well, sweetie, you are just about the cutest thing I've seen around here in a long time. Welcome to Ransom Island."

Darla moved in front of Rupert and gave her a hug. She didn't care a whit if Sally's story was made up or not, or if she was qualified for the job. The girl was pretty, and that was qualification enough. If there was one thing Darla admired, it was good looks, and this young girl had them in spades. Then an unsettling thought occurred to her. "You aren't a singer are you, honey?"

Sally was momentarily caught off guard. Did this woman recognize her from one of the clubs she had waitressed at in San Antonio or Dallas? "Um, no ma'am. I can't sing a lick. Never could."

"Her talent is in the kitchen," said Gilbert.

"Oh, well," said Darla, visibly relieved. "It's not a job requirement. And we can certainly use some good restaurant help, can't we, Rupert?"

Maybe this fresh face can take over some of my shifts, she thought to herself. *Let the barflies pinch the new girl on the butt for awhile.*

But before Rupert could answer, Gilbert said, "Rupe, I'm going to need more frying oil before dinner tonight. Mind if I take the wagon to town after lunch?"

Rupert blinked and turned his attention away from the girl. "Uh, sure. I won't be needing it this afternoon."

"Great. Thanks," said Gilbert, wanting to wind up the conversation before Rupert had a chance to ask more questions.

Sally stepped forward. "It was terrific meeting you, Mr. and Mrs. Sweetwater. I am so happy to be working at your restaurant. I've wanted to work here for years; I've always heard it's the best—"

Gilbert winced. She was overdoing it. "Okay," he interrupted. "Back to work."

As Rupert and Darla turned to leave, Rupert pointed to the pastries cooling on the windowsill. "By the way, keep an eye on those pies. Dubber is going to be out all month shrimping in the Bay of Campeche, so his two boys will be around for awhile. Those barefoot heathens will steal those pies right out from under you if they can." Johnny and Charlie Sweetwater pretty much ran wild over the island when they visited, but they could be counted on to show up around Gilbert's kitchen or the Big House at mealtimes.

"Thanks for the warning, Rupert," said Gilbert, waving goodbye. He and Sally listened to them walk across the dog run into the main building.

"So I'm in?" Sally asked.

"Looks like you are."

"Oh, goody! What's next?"

"Well, since you've wanted to work here for years, maybe you should tell me what you really *can* do in a kitchen, so I can figure out what I need to teach you. And tell me the truth. I've noticed that making up stories comes very easy to you."

"Fair enough, boss. But first I'm going to have to ask you to give me one of those pies."

"A pie? Are you hungry?"

"No, it's for the Nelsons. They were kind enough to take me into their home, such as it is, and I want to thank them for it. Lord knows they could use some sweetness in their life."

CHAPTER 13

Leroy Stuckey edged his face closer to the telephone pole to study the gaudy letterpress concert poster that was stapled there; maybe he'd missed some fine print at the bottom. He read carefully, his lips moving silently, forming the words. But nope, there was nothing there, either. He scratched absently at the hives that were spreading up his neck in rosy splotches. The doctor said the recurrent rash was stress-induced eczema, but Leroy was convinced he got the condition from a Negro he'd kicked out of the only bunk in county lock-up after his most recent incarceration for public drunkenness. *God knows what a white man could catch in that pesthole,* he thought.

He pulled off his ball cap (*Stuckey's Propane* was stitched on the crown) and ran his hand over a scruffy buzzcut. With increasing disbelief and outrage, he read the poster again, top to bottom.

One Night Only, One Show Only!
DUKE ELLINGTON AND HIS ORCHESTRA
at *The Shady Palm* concert hall on Ransom Island
SATURDAY, JULY 4TH at 8:00 P.M.
COME ONE, COME ALL!
TICKETS: $1.00 at the DOOR

Having listened to nothing more than hillbilly music most of his life, Stuckey had never heard of this band. Below the print was a fuzzy photograph of a man wearing a top hat and a tuxedo. But the fancy dress didn't fool him. The man smiling at him in the photo was unquestionably a Negro. *A duke, my ass,* he thought. *Duke of the Congo, maybe.*

But what about the colored show? Leroy wondered. Generally, when a Negro band played in a white establishment they'd have two separate shows, one for coloreds and one for whites, but the advertisement made no such distinction. *Maybe the coloreds didn't like orchestra music and wouldn't let go of a dollar to hear it,* thought Stuckey. *Come to think of it, why would anybody pay money to see an orchestra, especially in a honky-tonk? Unless it was some kind of African Hottentot symphony, with tom-toms and bone whistles.* Leroy laughed at his own joke. Somebody had to.

But this poster was no laughing matter. Leroy ripped it off the telephone pole and stuck it under the arm of his sweaty work shirt. He vowed to get to the bottom of the matter. In fact, he hoped there *was* just the "one show only," and that "come one, come all" intentionally included whites, Negroes, Mexicans and, hell, even Jews, Communists, Catholics, Indians, and Chinamen. He needed something big to improve his standing with his cronies, and this could be big.

Leroy Stuckey was the long-standing, long-suffering leader of the Koastal Bend Klavern, a provincial branch of the KKK and, as far as he knew, he was the only official card-carrying Klan member in Aransas Pass. As Leroy saw it, he was the foremost defender of Aryan superiority on this stretch of the Gulf Coast. Not that anyone appreciated his efforts.

To attract the attention of the Grand Titan of the Dominion, who oversaw all the klaverns on the Texas Coast from his opulent den in Houston, Leroy had been trying to stir up a bona fide controversy in his hometown for years, but nobody would take him seriously, least of all the upper Klan hierarchy. He understood the deal about being part of an Invisible Empire, but he didn't expect to be invisible inside it, too.

Well, they would take him seriously now. He scratched his neck furiously at the thought of it—races mixing together, eating and drinking off the same dishes, using the same bathroom! Erotic dancing, weed smoking, bootleg hooch. Sweaty black bucks rubbing nether regions with decent Christian white women. Miscegenation! His blotchy skin crawled.

He'd seen a Lena Horne movie one time—*Stormy Weather,* though he couldn't recall the title later—and found himself all at once embarrassed, affronted, and curiously aroused by the dancing, the brassy, jumping music and, not the least, the curvaceous, dusky-colored Miss Horne, who featured in several disturbing erotic dreams in the following nights. Leroy didn't like people who messed with his head. He liked to keep it simple.

Shady's was one of Stuckey's propane customers, and he had already branded the proprietor as a nigger lover—both for the race music he sometimes booked and for his uppity attitude. (The owner had thrown Leroy out on his ear when he'd wittily referred to the Negro who worked at the place as a wooly-headed jigaboo— couldn't anyone take a joke?) And only yesterday, on a gas delivery, he had seen Shady's Mexican cook holding hands with a pretty white girl behind the kitchen. Holding hands! *Bunch of Communistic, race-mixing pirates,* Leroy fumed. Just because the place was built on an island didn't mean it wasn't part of the white man's America.

Nothing like a righteous mob to put things right again, and Leroy Stuckey figured he was just the man to rouse the rabble. He pictured himself in his crisp white hooded robe—his glory suit—presiding as Grand Cyclops over the members of his very own klavern in San Patricio County: Leroy Stuckey, the virile embodiment of robust Anglo-Saxon manhood. His hive-covered neck swelled with pride at the thought of it.

Maybe he wouldn't wait until the big dance. There was still the matter of that Mexican and the white girl. The Klan had eyes everywhere, and certain people needed to learn that. Leroy figured he was just the man to teach them.

———

CHAPTER 14

Captain Marcos "Cap'n Mark" Shorter always thought the boat's owner looked faintly ridiculous in the white ducks and yachting cap he always donned when he came aboard the *Easy Eight*, the 55-foot Chris Craft Constellation Cruiser motor yacht of which Shorter was the master.

Not that Shorter would have ever ventured a comment, humorous or otherwise. He might be the captain, but Primo Ginestra was the boss. On land and on sea.

Setting aside the fact that he was working for a gangster, it was a pretty good gig. Shorter and one mate were expected to keep the twin 700hp diesels tuned up, the galley stocked, the brightwork polished, and the fuel and freshwater tanks topped off. The Ginestra brothers were creatures of impulse, and Shorter had to be ready to raise anchor at any time.

Every once in a great while, Shorter would put the spurs to the *Easy Eight* and they would cruise down to Mexico for some serious billfishing. But most of his trips consisted of easing through the Bolivar Roads channel and taking Primo and Gerry, along with some of their business colleagues (legitimate and otherwise) or occasionally a visiting celebrity or two, out into the Gulf where they could spend the day swilling booze and fishing for bonita, ling, and kingfish.

This trip, though, was a little different. For one thing, Primo and Jimmy Glick were the only passengers, and neither of them mentioned doing any fishing. For another, instead of heading to blue water, Primo instructed the captain to set a course down the Intracoastal Canal, skirting through Galveston's West Bay, past the massive Dow Chemical plant in Oyster Creek, and through the chain of bays that lay behind the barrier islands of Matagorda and San José. They passed by the twin communities of Rockport and Fulton, and through the ferry operation that linked Aransas Pass with Port A and Mustang Island.

Finally, looking over the captain's shoulder, Primo ordered him to drop anchor out in Redfish Bay, roughly halfway between Harbor Island and, as far as Shorter could see, no damn place in particular.

A low island with a few buildings and some small rowboats tied to a series of finger piers lay in the near distance. Otherwise, there was nothing to excite any interest or justify a two-day, two-hundred-mile cruise.

Shorter looked at the charts, checked his position, and cast an experienced eye on the mosaic of grey, green, and tan waters. Unlike the crystal waters of the Florida Keys, the brackish Texas bays didn't reflect the bottoms and relative depths over which they lay. The *Easy Eight* drew just three feet, but Shorter knew it would be all too easy to run the craft aground on a sand bar or oyster reef. And that, by God, he would not do.

Shorter looked around. A tanker chugged down the Intracoastal in the stolid fashion of tankers. A tugboat pushing a barge ran south by southeast down the intersecting Corpus Christi Channel. A few bay shrimpers plied the shallow waters. The Civil War-era Lydia Ann Lighthouse was barely visible in the distance. Why they called this middle section of the coast the Texas Riviera, he'd never know.

Primo sat in a fighting chair at the stern, nursing a beer. Normally a voluble man, he had been keeping his thoughts to himself almost the entire trip. Jimmy Glick had spent his time on the voyage smoking cigarettes, reading *The Daily Racing Form* and taking care of some overdue bookkeeping. *Hell of a way for a serious gangster to spend his time,* he thought, not for the first time.

"Mr. Ginestra," Shorter began. "If you're interested in some fishing, I can tell you this area doesn't hold much promise. Some trout, maybe, and a few redfish in those flats, yonder. If you're interested in something bigger, like tarpon or kingfish, I can steer you to a more likely spot. Better yet, let me call up Port Aransas and hire a local guide. That'd be the way to go."

"No, Cap'n. I'm not here to fish. At least not for tarpon." Primo jerked his chin towards the little island in the distance. "I'm here to keep an eye on that place. There's something there that belongs to me."

"Well, sure, if that's what you want. But . . . ." Shorter spread out his hands to encompass the big white cruising yacht. "We're not exactly gonna hide in plain sight on this. Not many fancy vessels like yours on this part of the coast."

"You let me worry about that. In the meantime, rig a couple of fishing poles off the back. We'll keep 'em fooled for a while anyway. And bring me those big marine binoculars you keep in your office. And a drink."

It's the stern and the wheelhouse, dumbass, Cap'n Mark thought. *And I'm not a goddamn bartender.* But all he said was, "You're the boss."

———

Primo Ginestra never got on a boat without thinking of another boat ride he'd taken almost twenty years earlier. He'd taken that boat ride with Jimmy Glick as well, as it happened.

It hadn't been a bright and balmy day when they set out on that trip, no, and it hadn't been on a millionaire's yacht, either. It had been blackest night, three in the morning, and they were motoring across open water in the face of a bone-chilling wind coming off the bay across from Galveston Island. Both men, bathtub sailors at best, were taking their lives in their hands being out in such weather at such an hour.

Glick was sitting at the back of the boat, steering the small work launch with a wooden tiller. His face was neutral. He'd helped out the Ginestras with some dicey stuff over the years, but this . . . .

Primo sat bareheaded, facing forward into the wind, smoking a cigarette, a play of emotions running across his face. He seemed impervious to the elements.

Between the two men sat two roughly cylindrical bundles, each bound in coarse seamen's blankets and sailcloth, and each weighted down with a hundred pounds of ballast iron. The scrap and winding sheets, like the boat, had come from the Ginestras' small shipyard on neighboring Pelican Island.

Jimmy eased off the throttle and the boat slid to a halt out in the middle of the main shipping channel to Houston, midway between Galveston and the Bolivar Peninsula. The channel was especially deep at this point. At this hour, though, all the shipping was laying up out in the Gulf, waiting for local pilots to guide them through come daylight. Jimmy and Primo were alone on the black, tossing ocean. The silver ray of light from the Bolivar Lighthouse shone over their heads in rhythmic circles, illuminating the tips of the waves when it passed.

"Primo, you ah, want to say anything?" Jimmy Glick felt faintly silly, but it seemed like an appropriate question, under the circumstances.

Ginestra seemed to pause, as if on the edge of reply, then simply shook his head. "Let's do it," he said.

Plumes of vapor erupted from their mouths as the men bent to their labors. They seized hold of each end of the first bundle, and then the second, and muscled them over the side. A quiet splash, an eruption of silvery bubbles, and they were done.

Glick goosed the throttle, shifted the tiller and the small boat headed back towards the lights of Galveston.

What the fuck had Natalie been thinking?

Primo would never understand it. Carrying on behind his back.

He took a long, thoughtful pull on his drink. The warmth of the sunlight on Redfish Bay erased the chill his memories conjured up. But being on a boat always brought it back . . . the strange combination of *thud* and *crunch* that resounded when he brought the Louisville Slugger down on the man's spread-eagled right hand, which Jimmy Glick held in a vise-like grip.

And the screams.

Now the left hand. *Thud/crunch.* Screaming.

Petey Teagarden's saxophone playing days were over.

Not that it mattered. As the man leaned over, cupping his ruined hands in his lap, Primo brought the bat down one last time with all his strength on the back of Petey's head. *Thud/crunch.* Silence.

Now for Natalie.

Primo found her asleep in their bedroom in their two-story Greek Revival mansion on Ave. J ½. Given Primo's nocturnal lifestyle, Natalie had been long accustomed to making her own sleep schedule.

The kid was in there, too, on a daybed in the corner, fast asleep it seemed. Three years old, a little more, she wasn't quite ready for her own bed. She'd sleep where her big, strong daddy could protect her, Natalie had insisted.

Was she his? Primo wondered for the thousandth time since he'd learned about his wife and Petey Teagarden. His emotions swung wildly. She might be a misbegotten little bitch, the living symbol of his wife's infidelity. Or she might be his own darling baby girl.

It had ceased to matter. Jimmy Glick had finally unearthed proof—hotel records, copies of telegrams—that put Natalie and Petey Teagarden together at a resort in Point Clear, Alabama at a time when she'd told Primo she was visiting a sick aunt in Mobile. Nine months after Natalie's sojourn, Sally Rose was born.

Primo eased into the shadowy bedroom, the bloodstained bat clutched in one meaty fist. There was just one small nightlight on, near the daybed that held the sleeping child.

Natalie lay on her stomach, head cocked to the side, a spill of rich auburn hair running across the pillow. She seemed to be smiling in her sleep.

Primo stood over her, suddenly irresolute. They'd had some times. Sure, she'd known what she was getting into, but so did he. Natalie was a good-time girl, that's what he liked about her. And there'd been a lot of good times between them.

What the hell were you thinking, girl?

He raised the bat tentatively. Killing Petey Teagarden had taken the edge off the worst of his rage.

But there was no help for it. He had to finish what he'd started.

He was a man of influence in Galveston, a man of substance. He couldn't be, wouldn't be made a figure of fun, the cuckolded gangster. His pride demanded this. Honor demanded it. If there was one thing Primo Ginestra understood down to the marrow of his bones, it was that pride and honor must be preserved.

He brought the bat down on her head, almost tenderly. None of the piledriving blows he'd dealt the saxophone player. He snapped the bat with his wrists so that it swung in a short arc and impacted against the base of Natalie's skull with a peculiar *tock!* sound. She was out.

Primo picked up the big goosedown pillow from his side of the bed and pressed it over her face for what seemed like an hour. She never awoke, but she seemed to stir, to twitch and finally to lay still.

He replaced the pillow, smoothed her hair back over her forehead—her eyes were closed and he was grateful for that. Then he left the room to go downstairs and call Jimmy Glick, who waited by the phone in the office at the Ginestras' marina.

He never saw the two sleepy eyes peering out from under the down comforter in the shadowy corner of the bedroom.

———

CHAPTER 15

Texas Attorney General Will Wilson didn't allow smoking in his office. That was one reason that Bill "Willie" Dawes—a two-pack a day man—hated to be summoned to the headquarters of the state's top lawyer.

The other reason was that he always felt like a wayward junior high school kid called to the principal's office when he faced Wilson. Though they were not that far apart in age—Wilson was one of the youngest attorneys general in the state's history—he had the kind of doughy, solemn demeanor that put Dawes in mind of every humorless authority figure he'd ever known. Wilson's stolid bulldog personality clashed with Dawes' natural what-the-hell insouciance.

Dawes fidgeted in his chair as Wilson delivered a memo into the Dictabelt machine he kept in the drawer of his impressive hardwood desk. He didn't dare cast a sideways look at his partner, Cliff Hollenbeck, for fear they'd both bust out laughing, from nerves or a mutual tendency towards insubordination or both.

Dawes and Hollenbeck were united in their suspicion that the AG's office, and General Wilson in particular, did not take them seriously. They had graduated in the same Department of Public Safety class with honors and had gone on to become the youngest members of the state's elite Criminal Investigation Division, but neither could shake the feeling that Wilson regarded them as kids dressing up as cops for Halloween.

Well, maybe this is the beginning of a new chapter, thought Dawes. Maybe they were being tapped for something big, finally. Something bigger than flushing numbers runners out of the Negro ghettos in Houston or busting flimflam artists peddling fake oil and gas leases to wealthy widows.

Cliff Hollenbeck was more cynical than his sunny partner. *I bet it's some political bullshit,* he mused sourly. Elections were coming up in the fall and Wilson had drawn an unusually strong challenger in the form of Elmer Leaverton, a retired federal judge from West Texas. With his patrician mane of swept-back white hair and handlebar moustache, Leaverton was the very incarnation of the iconic "Old Man Texas" cartoon that *The Dallas Morning News* had enshrined as the embodiment of the state.

More to the point, he made the young and smooth-faced first-termer Wilson look like a snot-nosed kid by comparison. To the average Texas voter, Leaverton just *looked* like the kind of guy who should be throwing the switch on Old Sparky and personally frying the state's perennial surplus of miscreants and degenerates.

It didn't matter that, in fact, the Texas AG has no law enforcement powers, per se. (His main job is to represent the state in legal matters before the courts.) In the public's mind, the attorney general, with his panoply of DPS troopers and Texas Rangers, was the state's top cop. Wilson was in for the political race of his life.

Hollenbeck figured Wilson's best shot was to portray himself as a reformer—a young, vigorous broom who would sweep away entrenched corruption and intractable crime. Wilson was one of the new postwar generation of public figures and politicians; he wanted to be a crusader.

And where does that leave us? Hollenbeck wondered, not for the first time. He fidgeted impatiently. Cliff was a smoker, too.

At length, the AG switched off the Dictabelt machine and regarded the two young cops impassively.

"Gentlemen, we have a situation down in Galveston County which I believe could benefit from this office's attention," he said in his mock-pompous fashion.

"I spent a few hours yesterday talking to Major Refugio Gonzales, who, as you know, heads up Ranger Company A, which covers the upper section of the Gulf Coast. For years, as you may also know, a licentious and criminal enterprise has taken root on Galveston Island . . . ."

No shit, thought Hollenbeck with amusement. As though every high school kid in Texas didn't know that Galveston was a Mecca for sin, illicit fun, carnal distractions, games of chance, and all the myriad fleshly temptations that kept Baptist preachers up nights.

Cliff had grown up in LaPorte, on the upper arm of Galveston Bay, and he'd heard about the island's fancy casinos and alluring whore ladies from older school chums and layabouts at the local pool hall. He'd never had any problems with the place personally or philosophically, although as a sworn peace officer he supposed he should raise some sort of professional objection. He didn't see any percentage in mentioning to Wilson that he had sampled Galveston's fleshpots a time or two in his younger days.

"What's come to exist over the years is known far and wide as the Free State of Galveston," Wilson continued. "Men, it's a bigger tourist attraction than the Alamo. This state has tolerated the place for too many years. In fact, I'm informed my predecessor had a line of credit at the Bali Hai casino anytime he wanted one." Wilson waved his hand in dismissal.

"More to the point, the Texas Rangers are known personalities down there. They don't have anyone who could successfully infiltrate the Galveston machine to collect evidence on the illegal activities we all know are thriving there."

At this, Cliff and Bill finally glanced at one another, struggling to keep their faces neutral.

Will Wilson withdrew a magazine from his drawer and placed it facedown in front of him.

"The status quo has held for a long time, gentlemen, and we've all been complicit. Obviously, there's a market amongst the public for a certain amount of well-regulated gambling and prostitution. And Galveston is, if nothing else, well-regulated."

He turned the magazine face up and held it towards the two young CID men. It was a recent issue of *Life* magazine. Wilson opened the magazine to a two-page photo spread whose all-caps headline read "WIDE-OPEN GALVESTON MOCKS TEXAS LAWS."

It was a damning indictment, with blurred black-and-white photos taken clandestinely inside bordellos and gambling parlors. The mayor proclaimed, in a caption beneath a headshot that looked remarkably like a police lineup photo, that "gambling and prostitution are here to stay."

"The city of Galveston was founded by pirates in 1817 as a sin camp, and ever since it has made an industry of sin," the story began. "Despite laws and sporadic reform efforts, gambling has thrived and prostitution has been openly tolerated. 'In a seaport town,' said the mayor, 'it's a biological necessity.'"

" . . . Meanwhile," the story concluded, "neither the city nor the State of Texas is taking any effective steps to put an end to Galveston's flagrant violations of the state laws."

Wilson slapped the magazine down in disgust.

"Men, the governor rang me up five minutes after this hit the newsstands and gave me as thorough an ass-chewing as I've ever had the displeasure to experience.

"A couple of local crusading newspaper stories is one thing, but this is *Life* magazine! It makes Texas look like one big hot-pillow joint and dice parlor from Brownsville all the way to Dalhart. You can imagine the going-over the governor's getting from the holy-roller preachers and Chambers of Commerce and fatback political opportunists. It's a major goddamn embarrassment for him, for the state, and now, for me. I don't like embarrassments. They are . . . embarrassing." Hollenbeck stifled a grin.

The attorney general pointed to another picture in the layout, one that showed two well-dressed men lounging at a mahogany bar in a nightclub with a South Seas motif. Both were smoking and laughing, perhaps at something the photographer was saying. One had a sharp aquiline nose and bore a more than passing resemblance to Louis Prima. The other was shorter and darker, and there was an impression of physical power in the wide shoulders that stretched the lapels of his suit.

"I want you to get a good look at these two men," said Wilson. "They're brothers— Gerardo and Primo Ginestra. They look fat and sassy, don't they? Well, they should. The Ginestras control about ninety percent of the vice in Galveston.

"These men, for all intents and purposes, *are* the Free State of Galveston. From the moment *Life* magazine hit the stands they became the governor's targets. And, as of this moment, they're yours too."

Willie Dawes sucked in his breath. A new chapter, indeed. Hell, it was a whole goddamn New Testament.

Cliff Hollenbeck cocked a skeptical eyebrow. "Uh, chief . . . do you mean to say me and Willie here are gonna bust up the Galveston rackets? Isn't that a tall order for two twenty-three-year-old CID men?"

Wilson laughed cynically. "No, Mr. Hollenbeck, you misunderstand. *I'm* going to bust up the rackets. Me and the governor, that is. You may have noticed there's an election coming. If you and Mr. Dawes do your job correctly, your names and faces should never see the light of day."

"General Wilson," Dawes said cautiously, "It seems to me like the voters have already spoken. Galveston's been an open secret all over Texas for years. None of the folks who go down there to roll dice or visit sporting women seem to have a problem with it. The mayor and the sheriff are both on board, it seems like. And everyone says it's one of the safest spots in the state. You can leave your hotel room door unlocked and safely walk the streets blind drunk at midnight."

Wilson narrowed his eyes and looked hard at Dawes, but then he reluctantly nodded in agreement. "The Ginestras run a clean shop, that's a fact. At least the part of it that the public sees. But you talk to Major Gonzalez and he'll show you the Ginestras' true colors. The fact of the matter is, the Ginestras run Galveston like it's a South American banana dictatorship. They've used blackmail, arson, hired muscle, white slavery, threats, and lead to hold onto their little paradise.

"And I don't think there's anything they won't stop at. Major Gonzalez had an informant, a pit boss at the Turf Club, who was trying to pass along some inside dope on the Ginestras' finances—the part they don't share with the IRS. The idea was that the Rangers and this office might be able to find a record of their bribes to state and federal officials.

"The only problem is, our pigeon wound up with half his component parts buried in a dune down by Jamaica Beach and the other half in a trash dumpster over on Pelican Island. Were our friends the Ginestras responsible? I'm convinced."

"Well, sir, why sneak around?" asked Dawes. "Let this Ranger major send in his boys to bust heads and dump every slot machine and craps table into the bay."

"Yes sir," agreed Hollenbeck. "We appreciate the opportunity you're offering us, but a couple of well-publicized raids and a perp walk or two ought to take the starch out of these Ginestra boys."

Suddenly, Will Wilson did something unprecedented. He raised his fist above his head and brought it down with a crash that caused the In and Out baskets as well as the pen and pencil set on his desk to jump into the air.

"Goddammit!" shouted Wilson, his face red, "This isn't an 'opportunity,' it's a fucking order!"

He pointed his finger at each of the two stunned CID men in turn. "You. And you. Who do you think's the boss of this outfit? Y'all are a couple of wet-nosed morons." He paused a moment, regaining his composure.

"Gentlemen, how do you propose we raid the Ginestras' establishments when the Galveston County district attorney has his own table at the nightclub and his own box at their dog race track? Think he's anxious to prosecute? When the sheriff rakes in thousands of dollars of campaign donations from our two friends before every election?

"Half the advertising in the Galveston paper is purchased by the Ginestras' clubs and showrooms. You think the editor is going to cover a perp walk or a raid? The last time Primo and Gerardo were on the front page, they had been elected the Kings of Mardi Gras. They're on the Chamber of Commerce, for God's sake.

"You couldn't get a grand jury to indict them; the Ginestras would probably wind up holding markers on half your jury pool. They may be bootleggers, whoremongers, bookmakers, gangsters, and murderers, but Primo and Gerardo Ginestra are still the toast of the goddamn town. *Life* magazine had it right—Galveston is still a pirate's paradise.

"But," he said with emphasis, "if you two can get enough information to establish probable cause, I can subpoena the Ginestras' books through my office. If we can leverage the information in their records to get an indictment, we can get a change of venue out of Galveston County. (*God*, thought Wilson, *how I'd love to see those guinea sonsofbitches facing one of those hang-'em-high West Texas juries.*) But first we have to get the goods."

Cliff turned to Willie. "Okay, pard?"

Willie shrugged. "I didn't have anything to do this weekend."

They both turned to face Wilson. "Alright, General," said Willie, "We're the men for the job."

Wilson picked up his telephone and told his secretary to get Major Gonzalez in Houston on the line.

After a short pause, the attorney general began speaking; Cliff and Willie were all ears.

"Yes, Major, that matter we talked about the other day . . . . Yeah, undercover is the only way to go . . . . I have two young men here who I think would suit your pistol . . . CID, two years out of the academy . . . . Well, hell, yes, I wish they had more experience" (Hollenbeck and Dawes both frowned) "but nobody knows 'em down there . . . . Yes, I told them about that ill-fated old boy you had an arm on, but hell, he was about half a crook himself. Who knows what else he was into?"

Wilson nodded vigorously. "That's good, Major, I'll send 'em your way and you can give them the layout. Tomorrow at eight at your office should be fine." He hung up and regarded the two young men gravely.

"You two have had training in undercover work. But it's only been training. This is the real deal. You get cocky or careless and you might get worse than a failing grade.

"Report to Major Gonzalez in Houston tomorrow morning. Draw some cash from the bursar's office downstairs. I'll send down a voucher. Keep your badges in your pockets. You aren't CID men on this go-round. You're a couple of sharp young fellas on the make, the kind the Ginestras are always looking for. Talk it over on the car ride down. Pick some new code names you can use in your reports."

Cliff looked at Willie. "Code names, huh? Like secret identities. How about you be Wayne?"

Dawes rolled an unlit cigarette between his fingers. *(Soon, thank God.)* "I guess that would make you Kent, huh, pardner?"

Will Wilson shook his head and looked at his two new racket-busting, straight-shooting undercover men. "You two clowns read too many comic books," he said.

———

CHAPTER 16

Zachariah was applying whitewash to the broad side of a new garage while Rupert tightened the torsion springs on the swinging door. Darla's new Pontiac hadn't been parked on the island two nights before she started pleading with her husband to build a fitting shelter for her shiny Catalina hardtop coupe. It would be unseemly to drive around town with salt scum all over that beautiful mint green body, she said.

The new one-car garage (Rupert's station wagon was still hostage to the elements) was the latest in a series of capital improvements undertaken at Darla's behest. The previous summer, Rupert and Zachariah had built her a screened gazebo with latticework sides and a cedar shingle roof—for afternoon cocktails, she said. As if a cold beer at Shady's wasn't refreshing enough. And prior to that project, she had decided that their living room just wouldn't be complete without Philco's latest combination television, phonograph, and AM/FM radio set.

Darla may not have been the highest-maintenance wife Rupert had brought back to Ransom Island (that would be Erika, the first one), but she was damn sure the most expensive.

Rupert lowered the garage door to test the tension, but the over-torqued spring snapped, whanged off Rupert's funnybone and clattered loudly against the inside of the garage, scaring the piss out of Zachariah and causing him to drop his paint bucket. Rupert unleashed a barrage of obscenities that Zachariah was pretty sure Barefoot Nelson and his wife heard all the way across the island. He peeked around the edge of the garage cautiously. "You okay, Rupe?"

"Yeah, goddammit. I'm okay." He flung a wrench at the door and walked to the back porch of the Big House, plopping down heavily on the steps.

Zachariah ambled over in his stiff-backed, saddle-tramp walk and sat down too, leaning his back against the post. "What's eatin' at you?" he said at length. He'd noticed that his boss had been distracted and tetchy for two days running.

"I don't know, Zach." Rupert glanced toward the half-painted garage. "What the hell do you think she'll be wantin' next year? An Olympic swimming pool? Maybe an ice-skatin' rink with live penguins?"

Zach pulled a tobacco pouch out of his shirt pocket and started rolling a smoke. "Naw, that ain't it. You ain't never been so bothered by her prodigal ways before. 'Fact I think you like buyin' her stuff, just to see her happy. I say it's sump'n else."

"Well how's about you tellin' me what it is, Zach, since you seem to be in the mind-readin' business today."

Zachariah took his time rolling the cigarette, and then he removed a wooden match from his pocket and scraped it against his jeans. The tip flashed, and he cupped the flame in his dark, callused hands before he put it to his smoke.

"I think it's them slick fellas that you and Noble met with the other day. I never seen you get so nervous over a pile of money before."

Rupert rubbed his earlobe for a moment before answering. "That tall fella, Don, he was a smooth talker, alright. But behind that flashy smile I could see him sizin' us up, and sizin' up our place all the while.

"He said his boss has some nightspots in Galveston," Rupert continued. "And that other fella, Flavius' sparring partner, he was from Galveston, too. Lots of big-city strangers coming around all of a sudden."

Cigarette smoke drifted above Zachariah's battered cowboy hat before it was snatched away by the warm humid breeze. "Uh-huh, that skinny one with the pistol that came by last week, he had the look of a curly wolf alright." Another long draw on the cigarette. "Rupe, why you think they're so interested in this here piece of land?"

"Well, I don't think it's because of the fishin'."

The men looked up and saw Dubber's two shirtless boys marching down the path with their dog, Lucky, trotting behind them. The boys stopped when they saw Rupert and Zachariah. Johnny Sweetwater smiled and held up a twenty-four inch red drum. "Look, a redfish!" he yelled.

"A redfish!" echoed his younger brother, Charlie.

Rupert gave them a thumbs-up sign and they skipped down the trail toward the kitchen to present their fish to Gilbert. Dubber Sweetwater, the boys' father, had never really connected emotionally with his brothers' enterprise. He was a shrimper, first and foremost. But his sons thought Ransom Island was Never-Never Land, Narnia, and Treasure Island rolled into one.

Rupert did, too, in a way. He sighed and thought about that other island up the coast. He and Darla had taken a getaway weekend or two at Galveston's nightclubs and casinos, and they'd had a hell of a time. But he read the papers, and he knew the city's fleshpots weren't run by the Baptist Youth Fellowship. He was parochial, but he wasn't stupid.

"I think you know why those bigshots want this place, Zach . . . and what they'd turn it into if they got their hands on it. In no time, they'd have slots and crap tables, back room card games, and probably some Jezebels pullin' back the sheets in the guest cottages."

"Uh-huh. I 'spect you're right about that."

"If it is the Galveston mob sniffing around," Rupert mused. "Do you think they'd let a bunch of hayseeds like us tell 'em 'thanks, but no thanks?'"

"That ain't how they got to be big-time gangsters," Zach replied.

"Nope. What they want, I suspect they take. If they want it bad enough."

Zach puffed on his roll-your-own, taking his time about it. "Unless they decide they don't want it," he said after a pause. "Unless there ain't no value in what they want anymore."

Rupert turned around and eyed his friend dubiously. "The hell you talkin' about?"

Zach stubbed out the tail of the cigarette and began rolling another one, nicotine-yellowed fingers deftly opening the pouch and laying a perfect row of finely chopped tobacco down the middle of the creased paper. Rupert waited patiently until he finished. You couldn't rush Zach.

He grabbed the drawstring of the pouch with his teeth and cinched it closed. "You 'member the Remount Service?"

Rupert rolled his eyes in exasperation and took a deep breath. This would clearly take a while. "Army deal, right? In charge of findin' horses and mules and training 'em to fight in the war?"

"Yeah. That's the bunch."

"What about 'em?"

"Well, 'fore the Great War, when I worked for the Salt Creek outfit on Matagorda Island, we rounded up a sizeable lot of bang-tails that were wild as the dickens. Me and the boys turned 'em inta first-rate cow ponies. Weren't big, but they were tough and quick. Made fine cuttin' horses."

Rupert thought about it for a moment. "But the Army thought they could make better use of 'em pulling howitzers and hauling ammo to the battlefront, right?"

Zachariah nodded. "They sure did. Over there, horses died as fast as the Remount could ship 'em over. 'Round 1917, when 'Merica jumped into the fight, the demand really went up, and them Army boys was gonna buy your horses whether you wanted to sell 'em or not.

"Mr. Hays, the big sugar on the Salt Creek, he told us he didn't see no way around it. Said he guessed we just had to do our part for the war effort."

"Did Uncle Sam take 'em all?" Rupert asked.

Zachariah exhaled a long stream of smoke. "Uh-uh. Those Army boys decided they didn't want nothing to do with our nags."

"Why not?"

"Turned out they were all sick . . . coughing, their noses runnin' a stream, slinging snot everywhere. Them Army men tol' us we better watch out, 'cause there was a chance our horses got the Glanders."

"What the hell are the Glanders?" Rupert knew Zach had a point to make. And maybe he would, someday.

"It's a bad contagious horse ailment. Don't see it in this country no more, but it was plenty bad back in them days, 'specially in Europe. Could kill all a man's livestock, and him too. The Army was scared of it, and they wasn't gonna take no chances with our snotty-nose horses, no sir. Posted a quarantine sign on the barn and at the ferry dock that told folks not to let nary a one off the island."

Rupert pondered for a minute and then looked over at Zachariah, who was sitting with his long arms draped casually over his knees. "The 'Glanders', huh?"

The corner of Zachariah's mouth lifted slightly. "Yep. Turns out that one of the 'gredients in the disinfectant we use to clean our castratin' tools is carbolic acid. An' if you rub a dab of that strong stuff on the inside of a horse's nostrils, well, in no time he'll be lookin' mighty qualmish."

"And after the Army's visit, I bet your horses made a miraculous recovery?"

"Just like Lazarus. It was somethin' to see."

Rupert chuckled. "So what's the moral to your story, Zach? Other than you outsmarted the United States Army?"

"Well, I figure them *pistoleros* want to make more money. But what if they's worried that their Galveston business is gettin' a little *too* successful . . . maybe a little too well-known? Even I know'd they got gamblin' and whorin' in their sportin' houses, and I ain't come nowheres near Galveston."

"So they have a lot of publicity, so what?"

"Well, there's good publicity and there's bad." (Zach had seen Darla's copy of *Life* magazine sitting out in the bar, and he'd read the Galveston article with interest.) "What if Johnny Law decided it was time to shut 'em down? Be like a hurricane hitting the island as far as they're concerned. Maybe they're thinkin' 'bout seedin' a new pasture."

Rupert nodded in agreement. "I guess it makes sense that they'd want to spread their business around in case some of their joints finally did get busted. Kind of like insurance. We'd be perfect for 'em."

"Sure we would . . . unless we weren't anymore," said Zach.

Rupert snorted. "Sure, we'll tell 'em we've all got the Glanders."

"No, not that. But what if that same Austin big shot starts squawkin' about all the illegal and immoral goings on at Ransom Island?"

"What? Cecil and Giddyup's domino game? Zach, you're not makin' any sense."

Zach looked up. "Well, then we'd have to invent some, wouldn't we? All them Galveston fellas need to hear is that Ransom Island has attracted the attention of, I don't know, the sheriff and the 'torney general and the Texas Rangers, and then we don't look like such a smart investment no more."

Rupert sat quietly for a minute, rubbing his ear lobe, a bemused expression on his face. Pretty soon he started chuckling. "By God, Zach, I think you're onto something." He jumped up abruptly and headed for his Woodie station wagon.

"Where you going, Rupe?"

"Goin' to talk to Red Burton."

"You want me to finish paintin' the garage?" Zachariah yelled after him.

"Take the day off, Zach," he laughed. "Go fishin' or something. You earned it."

—

Sheriff Red Burton, Jr. listened patiently to Rupert's proposal, his boots propped up on his office desk, his hands locked behind his head. Finally he'd heard enough.

"Rupe, you are just as crazy as you look!" There was no levity in his voice. Red slammed his feet down on the floor and leaned forward in his swivel chair, scrutinizing Rupert Sweetwater like he'd just attempted to solicit an officer of the law in a premeditated crime. Which is pretty much what his old friend had done. "Why in God's name do you think I'd be a party to such a harebrained idea?"

"Because if we do nothing, Red, I'm convinced the Galveston mob is gonna come here and do what they have to do to muscle in on our island. And me and my brothers will do what we have to do to keep 'em from takin' it. So figure it out. There's bound to be bloodshed—on one side or another. Probably both."

Red Burton sat back and considered Rupert's statement. "But you're asking me to send false reports to the attorney general. Go around behind the county DA's back. You know me better'n that, Rupe. Jesus! My daddy would turn in his grave if he knew I was even *listening* to something like this."

"I'm just asking you to report what you see, Sheriff."

"Report what? A few Saturday night fistfights, some dollar side bets over dominoes? Or you bettin' on Texas Tech over A&M every fall . . . like a dummy? Your place may get rowdy sometimes, but there aren't any whores there, and no illegal gambling goin' on, neither."

"How do you know?"

Red Burton narrowed his eyes. "What do you mean by *that?*"

Rupert shrugged. "I mean, how do you know what goes on over there, day and night, on every part of the island?"

"Ah, bullshit, Rupert. I know because I've been going over there three or four times a week for over fifteen years. And because you and I are friends. The only thing I might be able to bust you for is a building permit violation for Barefoot Nelson's home, which I'm not even sure can be classified as a permanent structure anyway. More like a shipwreck. Hazard to navigation, maybe."

"Well then, how 'bout this? We got a new girl working for us now. Real pretty. Lots of experience in the 'entertainment business,' if you know what I mean."

"Sally? I thought you told me she was a cook, or a cook's helper?"

"Yeah, that's what I told you. But do you know for a fact it's true?" Rupert raised his eyebrows conspiratorially. "And what about the stuff I *haven't* told you? Like about the high-dollar poker games in that back room behind the bar? Or that we might be getting' a big delivery of slots pretty soon, along with some of that fine *untaxed* Jamaican rum."

"You just now made that crap up."

"Red, I'm just askin' you to report what you see and what you hear about. That's all. And then send that information along to the right people. Get their curiosity goin', you know? Maybe they'll make a big deal out of it, maybe they won't—that depends on how convincing you are."

Red Burton sat back heavily in his chair. "And if the attorney general did show some interest, and your Galveston pals heard about it, then maybe they wouldn't be so keen on startin' their own little Rum Row here in Aransas Pass. Is that the play here?"

"Don't ask me, Red. I got my own wildly profitable and highly illegal business to run."

Red Burton, Jr. took a moment to imagine what his job would be like if the Mob moved into his community with their muscle, their guns, and their money. He wondered how soon before the corruption seeped into the machinery of the city, how long before he'd be presented with a fat envelope full of cash for being a team player. Just the notion of it made him feel dirty. He half expected his daddy to walk into the room carrying his wide western belt, slapping it on his open palm. *Son, it may not seem like it now, but this whippin's gonna make you a better man.*

The sheriff looked sharply at Rupert. "Amigo, if we go down this path, and I *do* run across something I should bust you for, then by God, I'll do it. You know I will."

"Shit, Red. Of course you will. You've got your principles and I respect that."

"You're already bustin' my balls by inviting a colored band to play for a desegregated dance. Black folks can't even sit downstairs in the movies around here. You're asking for trouble."

"Well, I got my principles, too, goddammit," said Rupert. "Look, I promise I'll never tell you nothin' or show you nothin' that you'll have to lie about. And I promise that, when push comes to shove, there won't be nothin' you'll have to arrest me for either, okay?"

Red pursed his lips and nodded slowly, almost imperceptibly. "Okay, Rupe. So when should I pay a visit to Ransom Island to begin this vice-bustin' crusade?"

Rupert grinned. "Well, Red, you can come over any time you want to, of course, you being the sheriff and all, but . . . how 'bout tomorrow afternoon? Say, two o'clock?"

CHAPTER 17

Later that evening, Rupert explained the situation to an improbable group of conspirators gathered in his living room. Once they got the picture, they all agreed that the threat was dire. They didn't want Shady's to turn into a glittery, overpriced destination for high rollers and gangsters. They liked it just the way it was: unkempt, under the radar, all theirs.

"Price of a cold beer would prob'ly double," warned Cecil Shoat ominously.

Gideon Dodson laughed. "Shit, Cecil. Even if you washed the pipe dope off yer face, you'd still have to have Howard Hughes on one arm and Hedy Lamarr on the other to get in the door."

"Way you dress, Giddyup, they'd prob'ly think you were some kind of cowboy pimp. Wouldn't let you in, neither."

Rupert tried to keep the conversation from wandering off course. "Look boys . . . and girls," he gave a conciliatory nod to Sally and Darla who were sitting on a bay window sill, "if these hard cases from Galveston have designs on our place—and I think we all pretty much agree they do—then the only way to run 'em off is for *them* to decide it might just be easier to look elsewhere."

"You keep talkin' like this takeover is a done deal," said Flavius. "Like we'll just accept their offer sight unseen and then hand over the keys. But what if we tell 'em to buzz off? Between you, me, and Noble, we can handle those jokers. I took care of that big city shuck the other day all by myself."

"You boxed his ears, brother, that's a fact. But that Galveston bunch won't let one butt-whippin' stop them. And that worries me. Ought to worry you, too."

"I'm not scared of those assholes," Flavius continued. "And neither is Noble."

Noble didn't necessarily agree with his younger brother, but he'd learned it was better to keep his opinion to himself when Flavius had a head of steam up.

Rupert sighed. "Damn it, Flavius. Why is it that every time you get aggravated at somebody you have to make it some kinda OK Corral deal? Let's be smart about this."

"Ya," said Gustav Brauer, "Remember that most of zee brothers at the OK Corral gunfight became shot—on both sides." Gus was an avid student of the Old West, and as an accidental deserter, he also understood that discretion was often the better part of valor.

Gilbert saw Flavius was about to open his mouth again so he jumped in ahead of him. "So, what's next, Rupert?" he asked. "What do you want us to do?"

"What's next is this, Gilbert . . . ." Rupert described the elaborate charade, and after he had finished, everyone agreed to be willing, even enthusiastic participants in the scheme. Darla was especially excited, picturing herself as a woman of intrigue, like Marilyn Monroe in *Niagara* (". . . a raging torrent of emotion that even nature can't control!")

"But it'll only work if people *believe* that Shady's has become a den of iniquity. When the sheriff drops by for a look-see tomorrow, I want it to be convincing. And for it to be convincing, we're going to have to dress the part."

"What do you mean, dress the part?" asked Captain Quincy.

Rupert held up a palm and turned his attention to Sally. "Sally, if it's not too bold to ask, would you mind gussying up a little tomorrow? You know, for show? Maybe dress a little chi-chi? To make yourself look sorta like a, um—"

"Like a hooker?" said Sally brightly, the first words she'd uttered all evening.

Rupert at least had the good grace to blush. "Yeah, like that. Just for pretend, you understand."

"Of course," she answered, with a faint smile. *They all think it's Halloween. They've got no idea.* But some small part of her loved the thought of taunting the Ginestras' bunch. "Anything for the cause," she said, brandishing a Rosie the Riveter thumbs-up. Both Rupert and Gilbert gave a sigh of relief.

"What about me?" asked Darla. "Why can't I be a hooker, too? You don't think I'm pretty enough? Too old maybe?" The men in the room found all manner of inanimate objects to look at, lest they burst out laughing at Rupert's palpable discomfort.

Rupert sighed. "No, baby. You know I don't think that. Hell, there'd be a line from Ransom Island to Corpus Christi if you ever decided to get into that racket."

Everyone in the room muttered their agreement. Darla preened; *Damn right there would!*

"But since it's just Red coming tomorrow . . . well, it's just that he knows you already."

Rupert's backhanded compliment seemed to satisfy Darla, because she turned to Sally and smiled. "I'd love to help you get dressed up for this, Sally, if you'll let me. Remember Barbara Stanwyck in *Double Indemnity?* I've got some things we can put together that will have Red Burton howling like a lobo wolf. We'll hoochie you up good, honey."

"Gotta love show business," Sally replied, trying to put on a brave face.

"The rest of you guys," Rupert said, "We've got some remodeling projects to start on tomorrow. Let's meet up at the cafe in town in the morning and I'll go over the details. Breakfast is on me."

The meeting broke up and the Ransom Island Comedy Players began heading home. Sally grabbed Gilbert by the arm as they walked down the path to Gilbert's cabin where she'd been staying. (He had been bunking at the bait house with Dubber's boys.) He took note of how urgently she gripped his bicep.

"You okay?" he asked. "You were awful quiet in there. Do you think Rupert's scheme is as crazy as I do?"

Sally didn't look at him. All day long she had debated whether or not to tell Gilbert the truth. "I think y'all are biting off more than you can chew, is what I think." It was the best she could do at the moment.

"Well, at least Rupert seems to think we have a handle on it," he said.

"That's partly what worries me."

—

Promptly at two o'clock the next afternoon, Sheriff Red Burton, Jr., feeling distinctly like a fool, drove to the foot of the one-lane, three-quarter mile causeway that connected Ransom Island to the mainland. Thirty yards out, before a gentle hump in the bridge designed for passing boat traffic, a makeshift checkpoint had been erected. A portable camouflage duck blind rested on the turnout, and a trailered jon boat had been positioned across the road, blocking the way. The sheriff rolled to a stop and got out of his car. At the same moment, Cecil Shoat appeared from inside the blind. He was holding a clipboard in his hand.

"Afternoon, Sheriff," he said cheerfully.

"Cecil, why are you blocking the road with that skiff?"

"I'm not blockin' the road, Sheriff. I'm making sure only the *right* people get across't it."

"What the hell does that mean?"

"It means that the Shady Palm Bar & Grill is now a members-only deal. Which means that you got to be a member to get in. In fact, it's called the Shady Boat & Leisure Club now. You a member, Sheriff?"

The hot June sun was already coaxing blooms of sweat from underneath Red Burton's khaki uniform shirt. "I don't know, Cecil," he said with a scowl. "Am I?"

"Well, lemme check, Red." Cecil studied the clipboard for about ten seconds and then he looked up and shook his head. "Nope, I don't see your name here."

"This is ridiculous. What do you think this is, Buckingham Goddamn Palace? Move that boat and let me through."

"'Fraid I can't do that, Sheriff."

Red walked up to Cecil and poked him in the chest. His voice was cold and level. "Cecil, you roll that boat out of the way or I'm gonna push it into the bay, and then I'm gonna send you in after it."

Cecil tucked his clipboard under his arm and raised his hands shoulder high. "Okay, Red, okay. You don't have to get all sheriff-y on me. Just hold on a sec."

Cecil went into the duck blind and came out with a portable Army surplus radio the size of a breadbox, courtesy of his ham radio friend, Captain Quincy. "Shady Base One this is Shady Duck. Come in." There was a screech of static and Cecil shook the radio. "Reception ain't so great out here," he told Red apologetically.

More static and then a muffled voice came over the speaker: "This is Shady Base One. What ya got, Cecil?" Red recognized Quincy's voice on the other end.

"I got the sheriff comin' through, over," said Cecil.

"But he's not a member," came the reply.

"Roger that, Shady Base One. But he's not askin'; he's tellin', over."

Red had had enough. "Ah, for Christ's sake, Cecil. Get the hell out of the way."

"Have it your way, Sheriff." Cecil lifted up the bow of the jon boat and pivoted it around on the trailer's tiny wheels, creating a narrow passage for the patrol car. "There ya go. Officers of the law are always welcome."

Red Burton could hear Cecil jabbering into the radio as he drove away. "Papa Bear comin' through, boys. This is the Shady Duck, over and out."

When Red pulled up to the building, he saw Rupert on the veranda. He was hand lettering a new sign that he had tacked up on the wall next to the entrance. **SHADY BOAT & LIESURE CLUB** read the sign.

"Real clever, Rupert. You misspelled 'leisure.'"

Rupert put down his paintbrush and backed away. "I did? Dammit!"

"Told you," said Noble who was priming a rectangle of wood for another sign.

"Still and all," said Rupert, putting a big slash of white paint through his typo. "You like it, Sheriff? I think it has a nice ring to it."

"What other changes should I expect to see around here?"

"Come on in. I'll tour you around our new enterprise . . . at least the parts that non-members are allowed to see." Rupert winked at his friend and swung open the screen door.

An hour later, Red Burton, Jr. was back in his Aransas Pass office with his hand resting on the telephone receiver, looking at the notes he'd made. Finally, he took a deep breath. "Here goes nothing," he muttered, dialing the phone number.

The other end picked up after the third ring. "This is Sheriff Red Burton of San Patricio County. I need to talk to the attorney general."

—

Later that evening, after Rupert's little matineé performance for the sheriff, Sally was quiet and moody, although inside the tiny kitchen she dispatched her supper-hour duties with brisk and nearly wordless efficiency. Gilbert was quiet, too. He'd been mulling over her remark the night before about them "biting off more than they could chew."

It was part of a bigger secret, he was certain. Even in their most convivial moments, she would scarcely allude to her life before coming to the island. And up until now, that had been just fine.

But the latest encounter with the smooth-talking businessman from Galveston, and the threat he represented, had changed the equation. Gilbert was responsible for Sally's presence on the island, and if she knew something that might have a bearing on the well-being—even the safety—of his friends on Ransom Island, he bore that responsibility, too. Was she playing him for a sucker?

The hell of it was, he wanted her to stay. Even in the face of his growing apprehensions. Not only was she proving to be an exceptional sous-chef in the kitchen, but it dawned on him that he was starting to fall a little bit in love with her.

For five days straight he had worked next to her inside the hot kitchen, and then he had gone back to the bait house and dreamed about her at night. He—crazy, cosmically misplaced Latino romantic that he was—dreamed about the five-star menu the two of them might create together, and the cozy two-story cedar-sided house they could build on the island, with a wrap-around deck and an herb garden to the side; he and his adoring wife sharing a cocktail on the balcony, talking and enjoying the evening breeze. All with Rupert's blessing, of course. He was pretty sure the *jefe's* moral universe was big enough to accept an interracial marriage. They might pull it off . . . just maybe.

And then again, maybe not. That night, when Gilbert walked Sally to the cabin, he found a small, greasy calling card thumbtacked to his door:

YOU HAVE BEEN VISITED BY THE KU KLUX KLAN.
THIS WAS A SOCIAL CALL.
DON'T MAKE THE NEXT VISIT A BUSINESS CALL.

A drawing of a white hooded Klansman pointing his finger in an "Uncle Sam Wants You!" fashion was stamped in the corner of the card. Scrawled in ink on the back of the card was a smeared postscript: *Leave the white girls alone, wetback!*

When Sally saw the expression on Gilbert's face, she plucked the card out of his fingers and read it herself.

"Ignorant hillbilly assholes. Don't let them get to you, Gilberto Ruiz. Never let people like that get to you." Her face was inches from his and he could feel her breath. "Let's forget about the world tonight, Gilbert. All you need to think about right now is me . . . and about you and me. Okay?"

Gilbert nodded and Sally opened the door and pulled him in behind her.

That night, in Gilbert's own swaybacked bed, he and Sally did things to each other that would have caused the self-righteous Knights of the KKK to turn as red as the cherry tomatoes Gilbert's own family was picking that month in the San Joaquin Valley.

———

CHAPTER 18

"Chickenshit," repeated the portly man standing at the back of the room.

Leroy Stuckey was stunned, and mortified. Leroy was a man of substance—the official Klan Kleagle in Aransas Pass—and he'd just been dressed down, in front of all his recruits, by the guest of honor, namely the Grand Titan himself, who had traveled all the way from Houston to observe the Klavern Klonvocation that Leroy had organized in his cousin's automotive garage.

The Grand Titan, one Harold "Dixie" Dixon, the prosperous owner of a midtown Houston plumbing supply company and the sponsor of his son's Little League baseball team, was unimpressed by Leroy Stuckey's Klan efforts up to this point, and he wasn't shy about saying so.

"You'll never get anybody's attention by distributing a bunch of silly calling cards. It's rinky-dink," he said. "Piddly."

Leroy scratched at the rash that was creeping up his neck. He'd thought the meeting was going pretty good up to this point. He'd rounded up a dozen prospective Klansmen for the meeting— drinking buddies, mainly, who he had talked into attending with the promise of free beer afterwards—and he was just beginning to get them good and agitated. He'd started with the story of the white girl and the Mexican on Ransom Island, which drew a few muttered curses and many looks of disapproval. But he'd elicited slack-jawed disbelief and then outrage when he held up the Shady's concert poster and explained the significance of the mixed-race event to his audience.

And then Harold Dixon spoke up from the back of the room and pissed all over his party, asking him what he'd done about these egregious affronts to white, Protestant America. Judging by Dixon's reaction to Leroy's response, what he'd done so far wasn't nearly enough.

"Well, I was also planning on puttin' up a sign out front, out by the road," Leroy explained, "warning that colored orchestra to watch out, ya know? And like I mentioned before, I ripped down every dance poster I could find."

"That's all chickenshit," Harold Dixon said for the third time. "You're nothing but a dog chained to the fence, barking at cars." The crowd listened to the big-city boss with rapt attention. His oratory was powerful, convincing—the voice of authority.

"You boys seem to be slippin' down here on the coast," he continued, shaking his head in disgust. "Things seem to be gettin' out of hand. Let me tell you somethin', fellow Klansmen . . . ." He paused briefly and the men sucked in their breath. "I cannot, and I will not, tolerate these transgressions inside *my* Dominion, which by the way includes your San Patricio County. For some reason, you boys don't appreciate the gravity of the situation. A situation so grave, it could threaten our organization's good reputation."

Dixon regarded the men sternly. A few of them turned around and scowled at Leroy, but they snapped their heads around when the Grand Titan resumed speaking. "These things that are happening, this permissive behavior that I'm hearing about, it's like a virus. Once it takes hold, it can spread . . . all over the state. You let them integrate one dance, like this one that's comin' up—on our nation's birthday, no less!—and next thing you know, there'll be darkies in your schools and churches." He paused for effect. "There'll be zoot-suit-wearing spics asking your daughters to the prom. There'll be Zionist Jews callin' in your bank loans. You may yet witness . . . the end . . . of Christian America . . . in *your* lifetime!"

There were hoots and angry denials from the group.

Emboldened, Leroy spoke up again. "Well, we don't aim to let that happen, Mr. Grand Titan," he said, puffing his scrawny chest out as far as it would go. "Not here. Not on our watch."

Harold "Dixie" Dixon looked hard at Leroy and then cocked his head questioningly. "So, you think you and your boys are up to the task?" It was obviously going to be up to him to light a fire under these bumpkins.

His voice rose and took on the cadences of a Bible-thumping evangelist. "Because it's a *serious* responsibility. Not for the timid or weak of spirit. I'm callin' on you boys to be Christian *soldiers!* I'm callin' on you to take up arms against the *usurpers* and the *agitators* and the *race mongrels* that threaten your community! I'm charging you with defending our Southern way of life! Are you up to it?"

A few of the men mumbled that they were.

"I say, are you UP to it, Klansmen?!"

Leroy Stuckey and his rag-tag band of recruits shouted "yeah!" Hell, yeah, they were up to it! They were the protectors of White Christian America, by God . . . darkies and greasers and Catholics and Jews and Communists and Yankee busybodies beware!

Of course they'd say they were up to it, thought Harold Dixon. They were sheep, and just about as smart and ambitious. He knew he had a weak hand as soon as he walked into the oily auto garage in this podunk town and looked at the assemblage this dimwitted Klan organizer had pulled together. There were no cops or other lawmen in the group, no city councilmen, no business pillars of the community, not anyone, for that matter, who looked like they had a respectable job or could pour piss out of a boot. He had all of those, and more, in his big-city Klavern. But ignorant peckerwoods like this could be useful, and easy to provoke.

Flushed and sweating from his exhortations, Harold "Dixie" Dixon, the Grand Titan of the Dominion, looked at the faces of the men, one by one, and then nodded slowly. "You know what? I think I believe you. I think you boys *are* up to the job."

Everyone nodded back enthusiastically, proclaiming their allegiance to the cause, and vowing to do their part to keep Aransas Pass pure and God-fearing. It reminded Harold of the frenzy he whipped his Little Leaguers into with his pre-game pep talks.

"But drastic situations call for drastic actions," said Dixie. "And I know that you boys have the brains *and the balls* to follow through with this thing."

"Just tell us what to do, Mr. Grand Titan," said Leroy. "We'll damn sure take care of it."

"I know you will, fellow Klansmen. I know you will." Harold Dixon placed his hat on his head and started to make his way to the door. "I'm expecting big things from y'all. This is your chance to make the Aransas Pass Klavern a model for the entire Realm, hell, even for the whole country."

There were more nods as Leroy and his recruits watched their Grand Titan head for the door, but some confused faces as well. Where was their Grand Titan going?

"What is it we're supposed to do?" asked Leroy.

"I know you'll think of something," answered Dixie over his shoulder, then he turned around and added pointedly, "Something *big*."

He'd succeeded in riling these crackers up and, if their hangovers weren't too bad tomorrow, maybe they would actually follow through. If they *did* do something, and fucked it up, or even if they did do something and succeeded (a more dubious possibility), he didn't want any of it coming back on him. Texas wasn't as friendly to the Klan as it used to be, and he sure as hell wouldn't let himself be brought down for the bumblefuck actions of some small-town rednecks on the edge of his territory. From here on out, they were on their own.

Harold Dixon climbed into his Cadillac and drove away slowly, smiling to himself. He'd primed the pump, and he wondered idly what the morons would do next.

Leroy Stuckey stood at the lectern (an oil drum draped with a Klan banner) and wondered, too. The roomful of men in Stuckey's Garage looked up at him expectantly. He had wanted an opportunity to prove his leadership, and now here it was, literally staring him in the face.

"I, uh . . . I do have a plan, men," he lied. A few guys sat forward in their seats, waiting for Stuckey to continue. "I have a helluva plan to stop this immoral dance and put those folks on Ransom Island in their place."

He looked around frantically until his eyes fell on the Shady's poster lying on top of the oil drum. He picked up the poster and pointed to Duke Ellington's cosmopolitan visage.

"Ransom Island is an affront to God and God-fearin' white men," he said. "And it's up to us to stop this unholy attempt to mongrelize America." The men clapped their hands and voiced their wholehearted support for their new leader. *When you need a distraction*, thought Leroy, *always point to a Negro*. "But there's some ah, important research I got to do first," he added. "You know . . . some reconnoiterin'."

The men nodded skeptically. One of them spoke up. "Can't we just find that Meskin and beat him up?" he asked.

"Show that Sambo band they ain't welcome here?" said another.

"Well, sure, we can do that. That would be a start. But the *big* plan," Leroy said, remembering the Grand Titan's word choice, "the *big* plan is way more . . . bigger . . . than that."

"Well, what is it?" someone asked.

"I can't tell you just yet . . . not until the pieces are in place. But it's by-Gawd big, that's for sure."

"What are we supposed to do in the meantime?" asked a recruit.

"What are we supposed to do?" Leroy repeated, pulling the collar away from his inflamed neck and looking around the garage as if the answer would be found in the corrugated tin siding or the racks of Valvoline oil cans.

As it happened, the answer was just beyond the greasy lifts, spare tires, and racks of propane tanks. The answer was right inside the front office. Leroy smiled and looking conspiratorially at his comrades. "What we're supposed to do now, Fellow Knights . . . is drink us some cold beer. I'll be gettin' back to you with your marchin' orders, soon . . . real soon." He picked up a wrench and banged it on the oil drum. "This Klavern meeting is hereby adjourned."

To Leroy's satisfaction, the group clapped enthusiastically and bolted for the hundred-quart marine cooler of beer that waited for them in the front room of the filling station and auto-repair shop. Watching them make their way to the beer—as a group, as a team— Leroy thought, *Maybe I am Grand Cyclops material after all.*

CHAPTER 19

Jacky Jack Vandiver, the owner of the Rainbow Inn, would have been the first to tell you that there was plenty of funny business going on out at Ransom Island lately.

Willie "Wayne" Dawes and Cliff "Kent" Hollenbeck knew that for a lead-pipe cinch because Jacky Jack had been telling them that very thing ever since they ambled into his greasy spoon and ordered a bowl of chili (Cliff), a cheeseburger basket (Willie), and a pair of soda pops.

Four days ago they'd met with Major Refugio Gonzalez of Texas Ranger Company A in Houston and received their orders to begin their undercover assignment—but not in Galveston, as they'd hoped.

Instead, they'd been sent to some backwater dive on the middle Texas coast called the Shady Boat and Leisure Club. Major Gonzalez had apparently decided that the two CID men were not quite ready for the Bali Hai and the big leagues just yet. There was a small gambling operation that had recently surfaced on the AG's radar, thanks to the local sheriff, and it was just the kind of place for the pair to hone their skills. So, per their state-sponsored mandate to snoop around undercover, Dawes and Hollenbeck had asked Vandiver what was up with the offshore fish camp and beer joint.

Jacky Jack turned a chair backwards, crossed his arms on the top brace, and proceeded to give them an earful of colorful gossip, unsubstantiated rumor, malicious innuendo, and paranoid speculation. He told them about mysterious comings and goings of big cars with out-of-county registrations rumbling over the plank causeway at all hours of the night. Checkpoints at the Ransom Island Bridge to screen visitors. He reported canvas-covered flatbed trucks delivering all manner of God-knows-what. A big yacht had been moored just offshore for a couple of days, a fancier rig than anyone in these waters possessed. Strangers sniffing around.

"For all I know, they're building a goddamn opium den out there," said Vandiver. "Maybe a secret headquarters for the Cosa Nostra. Or the Green Hornet."

Cliff crumbled some saltine crackers into his chili and stirred the mixture thoughtfully. "I dunno, Mr. Vandiver. I drove out to the place yesterday for a beer and it looked pretty quiet. Talked to the guy that runs the place, Rupert. Offered to sell me a one-dollar 'lifetime' membership to their private club.

"And, of course, there's the big dance with Duke Ellington that's all over town. Maybe they're laying in supplies for that. Building a special stage, maybe. Bringing in lumber and whatnot."

"Shit, maybe. But there's been strangers going back and forth, too. Not like you boys," Vandiver hastened to add. "But guys in suits. Hard-case lookin' guys. Nobody in Aransas County wears a suit unless they work at the bank or the funeral parlor. I'm tellin' you, something's up."

"You strike me as a man that's pretty well-connected," Willie Dawes said. "If there's something going on anywhere around here, I'd guess you'd know about it."

Jacky Jack Vandiver didn't know dick about the Sweetwaters or their plans, if any, but that didn't stop him from worrying. If, in fact, illegal or immoral doings were afoot on Ransom Island, that meant only one thing—competition.

With Sheriff Red Burton's tacit permission, the Rainbow Inn operated as the sole thriving hub of sin and iniquity in the county. Vandiver didn't run the girls that rotated through the three cribs out back—a tubercular pimp named Frankie Atwood handled that end and paid Jacky Jack a percentage. Vandiver ran the dice and card games, the cockfights, the bootleg hooch, the nickel slots, and a teeny-tiny numbers racket that catered mostly to the local black residents and foreign sailors in port.

Red Burton let the Rainbow Inn operate, within strictly prescribed limits, under the "all the bad eggs in one basket" principle.

"You're a sleazebag, a louse, and a featherweight asshole, Vandiver," Burton had said a few years back when he summoned Jacky Jack to his office for what the sheriff called "a come-to-Jesus meeting."

"But," he continued, "you are incurably small-time. I don't have to worry about you trying to move up into heavy dope or loansharking or extortion.

"So here's the deal. I'd rather know where all the shiftless characters are on any given night than to have to hunt them up all over the county. If you keep your little operation under the radar and don't suffer any delusions of grandeur, and tell me what I need to know when I ask for it, I'll let you roll. But"—he fixed the quaking saloon-keeper with a steely eye—"you let a local high school kid catch the clap in those cribs out back or let a civilian get rolled after he leaves your joint with a pocketful of cash, I will come down on you with the wrath of Jehovah. Say you believe me."

Jacky Jack could scarcely meet the sheriff's grim stare, but he managed to murmur, "I believe you, Sh'rff."

In the years since, he'd never so much as offered the sheriff a cup of coffee on the house, correctly surmising that any gesture on his part that even suggested a kickback would result in Red Burton breaking him like a Popsicle stick.

It was an unorthodox arrangement, as Sheriff Burton would have been the first to admit. It may even have constituted dereliction of duty on his part. But the status quo seemed to work: Aransas' two-bit desperados were effectively corralled, vice was mostly reined in, and public order (a relative notion on the Gulf Coast), was maintained.

Neither "Wayne" nor "Kent," of course, had any idea of this history. All they'd really wanted was some lunch. The two CID men could easily make Vandiver for a small-time hustler; it was practically stenciled on his forehead. But they weren't interested in him, and they saw no reason to drop the Ginestras' name into the conversation.

Which was just as well. Vandiver lived vicariously through the big shots of his criminal fraternity, and if he had thought that Primo and Gerry were within a hundred miles of Aransas Pass, he would have shit a brick.

But just now, Jacky Jack had more prosaic worries. He saw his exclusivity imperiled. By the Sweetwater brothers, of all people. When he'd mentioned his unfounded surmises to the sheriff, all Burton said was that he'd "look into it." That had been a week ago. What, exactly, was going on out on that miserable little island that merited looking into? Burton couldn't or wouldn't say. Vandiver wasn't about to ask twice.

The CID men finished their meal and Vandiver snapped his fingers for the check. Two bits for the chili, which was more than it was worth. Fifty cents for the cheeseburger and fries. Two Dr. Peppers to wash it all down. *Man*, thought Cliff, *this is high cotton, all right.*

"Well, Mr. Vandiver," said Willie. "We thank you for the information. Truth of the matter is, Kent and myself are sort of at loose ends right now. Lookin' for opportunities. We have what you might call real *specific* talents . . . ." he winked at the implication. "And it might be that these honchos on Ransom Island need a couple of hands."

"We might drive over and give these Sweetwater guys' operation the once-over. We'd be happy to mention your recommendation, Mr. Vandiver. By way of thanks, I mean," said Cliff.

Jacky Jack's ratty little eyes narrowed even more. What were these palookas playing at? He hadn't made them for characters, but now that he thought on it, they did look like they could handle themselves. And what was that about "specific talents"?

"Naw, boys. Hell, no. Just shootin' the breeze, you know? I'm sure Rupert and them is just expanding their business. Maybe running up a couple of new cabins or a bait stand. Those boys are go-getters. No need to bring my name up."

—

"Brother Dawes, did you get a load of that little chiseler when we let on we might drop his name with that Sweetwater clan?" said Cliff as they made the drive across the plank causeway towards Ransom Island, shimmering in the heat haze in the distance. "Haw, I think I heard his bunghole slam shut."

Willie lit a cigarette and let the smoke slipstream out the open window. Hot day. "I did indeed, Brother Hollenbeck. 'Specific talents'—I think I saw that in a George Raft movie or something. This could be fun."

"Well, you and I are big city undercover law enforcement agents," bragged Cliff. "I think we can run a shuck on a bunch of locals who can't hardly outthink a sand crab or an alligator gar."

Thirty minutes later, he wasn't so sure. Cliff was staring into the bright blue eyes of Rupert Sweetwater, which seemed to be gleaming with some devilish combination of amusement, insight, and a red-lining bullshit meter.

"So you all would like to do some charter fishing, Kent . . . ?" Rupert looked over at Cliff, who was studiously drawing lines through the ring of condensation left by his bottle of Pearl beer and avoiding his partner's silent entreaty for help. " . . . and Wayne. Say, boys, is Wayne or Kent your all's first or last names? I couldn't quite make it out."

It was a slow day, and Rupert was determined to take his fun where he could find it. Darla was shopping in town, and Flavius and Noble were running fresh bait and beer out to the fishermen's skiffs in the bay. Zach was sweeping up the dance floor, one ear cocked towards the conversation.

Zach had been bored, too. He and Rupert occasionally tired of the sound of each other's voices. Between them, there had evolved a companionable silence over the years, but still, there was such a thing as too much quiet. Now here came these two boys who said they wanted to stalk the wily redfish.

Only thing is, as Zach and Rupert both noticed at once, they didn't exactly fit the mold of Hemingway-esque *pescadores*. One of them was dressed in a tweed sport coat and gabardine trousers. He looked like he might be auditioning for the glee club at the local junior college. His pal had on a crisp new edition of the requisite white T-shirt and khakis of the genus *Anglus Aransas,* but he was wearing the sort of lace-up brogan shoes a West Texas cotton farmer might sport.

And then there was their tackle . . . . Both men had had to outfit themselves as best they could on short notice, the better to blend in with the locals. Willie had grabbed a fly rod from the hall closet of an uncle who was fond of stream-fishing for trout up in Colorado. And Cliff had had to make do with a bamboo pole with a saucy little red-and-white plastic bobber from the TG&Y dime store in Aransas Pass. If these guys were fishermen, Rupert was Joe DiMaggio and Zach was John Wayne. He had half a mind to pass them on to Barney Farley, the king of the fishing guides over on Mustang Island. Barney always appreciated a good laugh.

Cliff felt vaguely ridiculous. They'd never really thought about it. "Wayne and Kent are our, ah, last names, Mr. Sweetwater."

"Hell, call me Rupe. Well, you all look loaded for bear. What's your pleasure—Rainbow trout or steelhead salmon? We can probably scare you up a gafftop or two. Or maybe you'd like to go out on the

salt and hook into a big swordfish or a marlin for the mantelpiece."
He nodded at the fishing poles. "You fellas look like you could give a
marlin a run for his money."

"Marlin'd be nice," murmured Willie, who'd read *The Old Man and
the Sea* just the year before. Behind the CID mens' backs, a smile
appeared on Zach's weathered face. *Fun at last,* he thought to himself.

"Something to put over the mantle," Cliff agreed.

Rupert nodded with solemnity. "Sure, we could do that. Or we
could maybe rig a howitzer on the stern of a converted Liberty Ship
and go lookin' for Moby Dick, if you guys are so inclined. I've got a
Mexican cook out back who could probably steal us a couple of *cabrito*
goats for bait . . . ."

Rupert could usually tell (if Darla wasn't there to remind him) when
he'd pushed a joke too far. Now the young men were just beginning to
look embarrassed. Which wasn't what Rupe had set out to do. Besides,
they had paid good cash money for two of his beers and purchased
"lifetime" memberships to the Shady Boat and Leisure Club.

He held up his hands in mock surrender. "Okay, fellas. I'm sorry.
My wife and brothers—hell, everybody—tells me I can beat a joke
flatter than a truckstop steak. It's not good manners to make fun of
the mainlanders out here while we take their money.

"You boys—pardon my language—clearly don't know shit about
fishing. But if you want a lesson, we'll be happy to oblige you."

Cliff tried to recover his mental equilibrium and made an effort
to look like the cool, calculating guy he saw in the mirror every
morning—the sort of bird with plenty of juice, who dealt the play
and knew all the angles.

"I guess we should have known better than to try to fool a big
operator like you, Mr. Sweetwater. We definitely do not know much
about fishing. Especially young Wayne here."

"Hey!"

"Be that as it may, there are some things we *do* know about. And
some things that maybe we can make an educated guess about.
And maybe we can do something for you besides throw you a
fishing charter."

Rupert rubbed his hand up and down his jaw. Now what was *this*
about?

"Say, Mr. Sweetwater," said Willie suddenly. "What's under the
tarp over yonder?"

"Um, new jukebox. Real nice one, too."

"Um-hum." To Willie, the shrouded mass looked just about the shape and size of a couple of slot machines pushed together. There was the smell of fresh sawdust in the air, too . . . were dice tables and roulette wheels hiding behind the new construction—concealed behind weather-beaten false walls, maybe?

"You like to dance, Mr. Wayne?" said Rupert. Behind the two men, the methodical sound of Zach's broom had ceased.

"Sure, if there's a pretty girl handy."

"Then come to our Duke Ellington show in about eight days. There'll be lots of dancing."

"Someone told us you might have more action going than just dancing," said Cliff. "Said you might be, ah, diversifying your business interests. Maybe even taking on some new partners?"

"How about it, Zach?" said Rupert, raising his voice. "Who was it said they were gonna throw in with us—was it General Motors or U.S. Steel?"

"I thought it was that big shot over in Monaco. Said he was gonna make us a thiefdom," replied Zach.

"Yeah, well, there you have it, boys," said Rupert apologetically. "I'm afraid you boys have come a long way around the barn for nothin'. We are masters of all we survey—a dancehall, a restaurant, and a fishing and boat charter business. I don't think anybody is gonna be making us an offer anytime soon."

"We heard it might be someone else," Cliff persisted. "And that there might be opportunities for a couple of guys who knew their way around and could keep their mouths shut."

Dang, thought Zach, *if you men opened your mouths any wider, you could fill in for the Matagorda foghorn.*

"Nope, I'm afraid we're staffed up at the moment," said Rupert.

"Well, maybe we heard wrong," said Willie mildly. "And we'll surely come back and take you up on that fishing lesson one of these days." He made to get up to leave and shook a cigarette out of his pack of Luckies. "Mr. Sweetwater, have you got a match?"

"Sure. Well, I think. We ran out of Shady's matches the other day, but, hold on . . ." Rupert slapped his pockets and came up with the shiny black book of paper matches that Don McCullough had given him. "Here ya go."

Willie lit his cigarette and took a thoughtful drag as he pushed the matchbook back across the bar to Rupert. He exhaled a long, slow plume of smoke as his eyes met Cliff's, who was also looking at the matchbook. Embossed on the black cover was a distinctive crest and below it, "The Bali Hai—Galveston, Texas."

—

After the two CID men had departed, Zach joined Rupert at the bar. "Well, that beats all I ever saw," said Zach. "And I saw Joe Louis box a kangaroo for charity one time. What the hell were those boys up to?"

"Trying to smoke us out," said Rupert. "They must think they know somethin' about what we're up to."

"Those cockamamie rumors you and Red cooked up are getting around, aren't they? Are we gonna have characters showing up every week along with the beer truck and the produce man?"

Rupert shook his head. "I don't know who that pair were, but they weren't hard-ass criminals. Sure as hell not the kind of talent the Ginestras would recruit."

"Grifters, maybe? But what's the con?"

Rupert's brows squinched down in thought. "Zach, as far as I know, I dunno. But you're right, the pot is starting to boil."

"It's bubblin' alright," agreed Zach. "So why do I feel like a crab at a crab boil all of a sudden?"

Rupert seemed not to hear his friend's comment but was watching the two faux-fishermen back their car out of the drive to turn around. Suddenly, he was hurrying for the door.

"Where you going, Rupe?"

Rupert winked at Zach. "I think I'll invite our new friends back out to the Shady Boat and Leisure Club tonight. It's show time, Mr. Yates."

———

CHAPTER 20

Four months before the siege of Ransom Island began, it had been spring in Galveston. And in the springtime, Primo Ginestra's fancy lightly turned to thoughts of arson.

It was, as is so often the case, a matter of respect.

A young Texas wildcatter named Bob "Bet A Million" Bowman hit a big oil play out in the far reaches of the Permian Basin near the New Mexico line. For forty-eight hours, the gusher rained black riches on his ignorant, incredulous head. When the well was finally capped, Bob Bowman bought the fanciest Cadillac in Midland and bid adieu to West Texas. To be precise, his exact words were "Piss on this God-forsaken shithole. I'll take it up the kazoo from King Kong before I come back."

Bowman headed east, eager for the bright lights, soft women, and easy pickings of civilized society. After eight luckless years in a treeless expanse of dust and drought, "Bet A Million" found himself drawn to the green waters and golden sandy beaches of Galveston.

He came to the Ginestras' attention when he started frequenting their casinos. He didn't bet a million, exactly, but he didn't mind throwing his newfound money around. Bowman liked to make an entrance, flipping shiny silver dollars to the valet parking boys and the coat check girls. Rather than open a line of credit with the cage boss, he liked to slap a thousand dollar bill down on the blackjack or craps table and buy his chips from the dealer. It was a bush-league display; the Born-On-The-Island gentry rolled their eyes. Hillbillies with money . . . what did you expect? They were just glad he didn't ride a horse into the Turf Club. He became a figure of fun and ridicule. He just didn't know it. Or didn't care.

Then, in 1952, THAT book was published. No one in Texas had to elaborate further. *That book* was *Giant*, by Edna Ferber—a carpetbagging Yankee who took a Bolshevistic pleasure in slandering everything and everybody below the Red River. Everybody in her 400-page poison pen letter was a brash, intemperate braggart with the breeding and manners of a feral hog. Or so it seemed to the many thousands of brash, intemperate Texans who swore they would never read the damned thing but had heard all about it. It sold like hotcakes.

Not the least consequence of *Giant's* runaway success was the sudden obsession with every oil tycoon in the state to out-Jett Rink his brethren in excess and ostentatious consumption. A private railroad car wasn't enough; you had to have a plane—preferably a converted DC-3 or Constellation with wet bars, lounges and king-sized beds. A place in the country wasn't enough; the Murchisons and the Richardsons began buying up barrier islands off the Texas coast. A stable of thoroughbred horses wasn't enough; now there were stories of one oilman who rode to get the mail on his pet tiger. Another spent hundreds of thousands of dollars on man-made ice and refrigerated shelters trying to keep penguins alive in Houston's malarial climate. One tasteful and understated fellow made the nightlife rounds in Houston wearing a hundred-dollar bill as a bowtie. As the night wore on and the liquor flowed, he tended to fling his "tie" to appreciative cocktail waitresses and strippers, replacing it each time with a new C-note. "Bet A Million" Bob Bowman fit right in.

But Bowman wasn't just another roughneck yokel with steel-toed work boots underneath his tuxedo. He had a wildcatter's canny, slightly shifty sense of an opportunity and a keenly observant eye. After sizing up the Ginestras' operation for several weeks (without truly realizing what went on behind the scenes), Bowman talked to his bankers in Midland and began making some discrete inquiries among Galveston's commercial real estate agents.

Primo's and Gerry's reaction upon hearing that Bob Bowman was purchasing a foreclosed country club down on Galveston's West End could only be described as pungent. When he announced plans to convert the old clubhouse and golf course into a destination resort, including a hotel, nightclub, casino, and horserace track, the brothers' mood shifted to volcanic.

"Galveston has some amusing nightspots," Bet-A-Million commented loftily to the assembled reporters from Houston who had trekked to the Island for the press conference announcing the grand project. "But hell, most of 'em are just glorified saloons, working off the same ol' business model since before Prohibition.

"You boys seen what's happening out in Las Vegas? Places like the Flamingo and the Sands have got it all in one package—rooms, shows, gambling, fine dining. It's the future of the entertainment and hospitality industry. Galveston needs shaking up, and I'm just the man to do it. Let that damned ol' Glenn McCarthy have his Shamrock Hotel up there in Houston. The new Galveston Empress Resort is gonna put him and everything else in this pissant sandbox in the shade!"

Grimly, the Ginestras watched as Bob Bowman's would-be Xanadu took shape in the distance.

"*Che palle!*" exclaimed Primo. "The balls on that *pezzo di merda.*"

It wasn't the competition that stung so much as Bowman's insistence that Galveston's apex of nightlife and savoir-faire—their joints—were low-class, gin-soaked dinosaurs courting extinction. Respect was not paid.

Ordinarily, the brothers would have squashed an upstart like Bob Bowman with the flick of a wrist. But the oilman's fortune provided wonderful insulation. The Ginestras couldn't fuck with his financing— Bowman still did his banking in West Texas.

They let slip to their tame local union shop stewards that the rank-and-file plumbers and electricians should steer clear of the project. Bowman simply imported his skilled laborers from Houston and San Antonio. Short of blowing up the causeway and the bridge at San Luis Pass, the Ginestras had little hope of stopping Bowman's grand vision, or even slowing it down much. Bowman had money to burn and the single-minded mania of a buzz saw.

And so, an amazing six months after his press conference, the old country club was transformed: a nightclub showroom that covered almost an acre, decorated with Cararra marble, Brazilian hardwood, and French brocade. A six-story hotel tower. An Olympic-plus sized pool (ten feet longer than the behemoth at the Shamrock, as Bowman bragged at every opportunity). A "French" chef from Louisiana. A casino that not only featured the usual games, but also an electronic toteboard posting the odds for ballgames, prize fights, and horse races from across the country. A two-thousand seat quarter-mile racetrack for Bowman's stable of thoroughbreds. A half-mile of manicured beachfront. And, last but not least, a sign—"Bob Bowman's Galveston Empress"—in pink neon scrawl ten feet high and fifty feet long.

And so, Primo Ginestra's thoughts turned to arson.

It so happened that Gerry was in Houston that week, playing golf in the Houston Open with Ben Hogan as his partner.

"Gerry's got enough on his mind right now, trying to impress Hogan. And fat chance of that," said Primo.

Primo spoke to Jimmy Glick as they walked along the seawall. Women's hems were higher this season, he noted approvingly. All was right with the world—or soon would be.

"Call up a couple of your buddies who know how to build a vacant lot," Primo continued. "Don't tell me who and for God's sake, don't tell Gerry. I want this big-shot and his little clubhouse off the Island before Gerry gets back from Houston."

Glick nodded. He knew just the guys.

On the day of the grand opening of the Galveston Empress, Bob Bowman woke early, poured himself a cup of coffee, and read the morning paper approvingly.

The society pages of the Houston papers were full of lavish anticipatory praise for the Island's new showplace: "Isn't 'Bet-A-Million' Bob's new Shangri-La the fanciest Troub-adorable spot to see and be seen this side of fellow oilman Glenn McCarthy's Shamrock Hotel?" gushed one columnist. "It is, it is, and watch the other nightspots on the Island fall into its shadow."

The business sections ladled fulsome accolades on the new venture and its swashbuckling young proprietor: "Bob Bowman's independent go-ahead temperament is the kind of plucky, pro-capitalist spirit that built America and Texas. A self-made man, he is bringing a welcome wildcatter's feisty energy to this sleepy island. Galveston could use half a dozen Bob Bowmans."

On it went: Capacity crowd expected . . . Hollywood stars coming in by train to bring Tinseltown glamour to Galveston . . . Newsreel and radio coverage. (In Galveston's own daily, there was not a line of type about Bowman's new showplace. Both the editor and publisher knew where their bread was buttered.)

Over at the Empress itself, 1500 dry-aged ribeye steaks were cooling in the walk-in refrigerator. Cases of champagne and vintage wine waited to be iced down. Cases of rum, scotch, bourbon, and gin were stacked floor to ceiling in storerooms. A thousand yellow rose corsages had been ordered for the jewel-bedecked female guests. A society band from Philadelphia had been engaged and flown in to provide the soundtrack to the evening.

In the newly purchased mansion on Broadway, within spitting distance of the palatial Ashton Villa, Bowman's Negro servant laid out the lord and master's white tuxedo jacket, yellow cummerbund (to match the rose that would grace his lapel), diamond shirt studs, and his handmade Lucchese cowboy boots.

Bowman himself was sloshing in the Olympic-sized tub in the master bath, singing (off-key) Hank Williams' "Honky-Tonkin'." "Honky-tonkin', honey baby," he rasped, "We'll go honky-tonkin' round this town!"

Bob "Bet-A-Million" Bowman had no way of knowing that he was enjoying the last best day of the rest of his life. The giddy thrill ride that had led him from the Permian Basin oilpatch to a mansion on Texas' Gold Coast was coming to an end.

As best anyone could figure out later, the fire started in a small outside shed attached to the rear of the building where paint, solvents, and lubricating oils were stored. It was two hours before the first guests were due to arrive. Huge rented spotlights lanced through the Galveston dusk. The neon sign sparkled. Inside, the club's multifaceted staff raced to complete a thousand last-minute details. No one noticed the wisp of black smoke that sped away quickly on the breeze.

That was just the first blaze. A second fire, timed ten minutes later, ignited and took hold in a ventilator shaft behind the stage. A third smoldered for a moment and then raced greedily along the crawl space under the pitched pine-shingled roof.

Jimmy Glick's "go-to" guy in such matters liked to keep things simple—foolproof triggers made out of dime-store alarm clocks, phosphorous igniters, and paraffin accelerants. "Burns hot, burns clean," he noted with a professional's attention to details. Gasoline and Molotov cocktails and other fuels that left burn trails for arson detectives to note were for punks and kids. Glick's pal worked off the Boy Scout ethic—leave no trace.

By the time the kitchen staff noticed the smoke pouring out from behind the big commercial Wolf kitchen range, alarms sounded throughout the rest of the sprawling structure. The drapes and curtains and stage sets began to smolder and then catch flame as the second fire found its footing. Overhead, light fixtures popped and sparked as the wiring in the ceiling began to fry and the attic blaze began to race along the joists and beams under the roof.

Bowman's head bartender, a tough German ex-pug named Lucas Kopperl, took charge in the growing panic. He phoned an alarm in to the nearest fire station (some five miles away, near the western edge of the city proper), and ordered his three bar backs to begin evacuating the premises. "For God's sake, get these people out of here," he ordered tersely, but without panic. "Go room by room—the kitchen, the banquet hall, the casino and the pantries and offices. Gott damn, move your arses!"

Back at the Bali Hai, Primo cocked his ear to an open window to catch the rising wail of fire trucks, first one and then many, as they raced towards the western reaches of the Island. He smiled at the pleasing cacophony and poured himself a drink.

Thanks in part to Kopperl's iron reserve, no one died as the fires became committed and began to overlap. When the kitchen blaze reached the propane tanks that fueled the stoves and ovens, the subsequent explosion blew the back half of Bob Bowman's dream halfway across the bay.

Bowman came sliding up to the fire department barricades in a fishtailing screech, his Cadillac slewing sideways. Jumping out of the car, he had to be physically restrained from running into the burning building. Hysterical, eyes popping, he began shouting hoarse, contradictory orders that mostly fell on deaf ears. The Galveston firemen knew a lost cause when they saw one.

Within three hours, Bob Bowman's palatial nightspot was a pile of glowing embers. The beautiful neon sign was a melted slick of pink glass. Even the horse paddocks and the wooden racetrack bleachers had caught fire and gone up. Bowman sat on the curb, clutching a bottle of scotch, his head in his hands. Fire insurance had been near the top of his to-do list, but in the frantic run-up to opening night, it had, he remembered with a sickening lurch, just fallen through the cracks.

The next morning, his car was gone. Two days later, the showroom-new Cadillac would be discovered filled with cement and resting upside down in the mudflats near Offlats Bayou. Some goddamn joyriding kids, taking advantage of the tumult and panic, speculated the police days after the theft.

"It just seemed like a nice touch," Primo told Gerry as they dined on Oysters Bienville and Gulf trout. Gerry had returned from Houston while the ashes of the Galveston Empress were still warm. No one had seen Bob Bowman for days. Rumor had it he was trying to set some sort of all-conference record for whiskey drinking.

"A very nice touch. My compliments. In fact, I can think of a little more lagniappe to bring that goddamn roughneck to heel. Lemme make some calls . . . ."

The next day, a new series of catastrophes began to assail the hapless entrepreneur. A mysterious lien against his Broadway mansion suddenly surfaced, necessitating an expensive title search and extensive court costs. County commissioners met in a midnight executive session in response to an unnamed petitioner and voted to re-zone the land upon which the Galveston Empress had reposed with an agricultural/ranch designation, meaning Bowman couldn't rebuild his nightclub on the same site even if he wanted to.

Finally, Bowman's lawyer received a certified letter from the Texas Railroad Commission's legal office. The TRC, despite its archaic name, was in charge of regulating oil and gas drilling in the state. The letter informed the attorney that his client was under investigation for over-subscribing a package of leases in West Texas. To wit, to raise money for his project, Bowman was alleged to have sold three rounds of investment certificates to hundreds of local investors. One hundred percent being one hundred percent, even in the oilfield boomtowns, the inescapable conclusion of the TRC investigators was that Bowman had sold the same mineral rights to multiple buyers. That he was, in short, a swindler.

In response to the disclosures (initiated, of course, by the Ginestras' capital city lobbyists through third parties), Bowman's accounts were frozen and his Midland bank began a time-consuming audit of his assets. Although the bank's board had been among "Bet-A-Million's" most enthusiastic investors, they were still bankers. Bowman, like every other would-be genius in the oil patch, was hopelessly overextended. When the bank cut off his lines of credit, his house of cards came down with a crash.

Within a month, thanks to the behind-the-scenes machinations of the Ginestras and their minions, the once high-flying handsome young wildcatter was busted, broke, and gutted. The brothers still had a few fillips in reserve, including a young Post Office Street whore who was prepared to masquerade as a 14-year old convent student whom Bowman had supposedly seduced and transported to New Orleans for a weekend of debauchery. And a dewy-eyed young Mexican busboy who was prepared to swear (for a sum of many dollars and a green card) to the same thing. There was even some talk of buying the poor unfortunate a pair of cement cowboy boots and giving him a ride out into the Gulf. But it would have been redundant—Bowman was dead and just didn't know it.

Fun was fun, but in the end, tormenting Bob Bowman was like baiting a crippled bear. The poor bastard never knew what hit him.

But the Ginestras were content. Honor had been satisfied. The natural order had been restored. The food chain was once more intact, with the natural predators at the top.

The last the Ginestras heard of Bob "Bet-A-Million" Bowman, the late millionaire was on a westbound Greyhound, bound for Bumfuck, New Mexico and the hope of catching on as a derrick man on one of the wells he used to own.

CHAPTER 21

Gilbert and Zach were having a laugh about Wayne and Kent as they drove Rupert's battered Woodie wagon into town for supplies.

"Those two fellas never 'spected a thing last night, I'll wager," said Zach, "Even when Rupe came into the room dressed up like a Fancy Dan."

Gilbert grinned. "More like a New Orleans pimp. I thought Cecil Shoat was going to bust a gut when he saw him."

"Know how he felt. And Noble comin' up with that toy slot machine . . . . Where'd he get that, anyway?"

"Borrowed it from the American Legion post."

"Well, it looked like the real thing. Captain Quincy lost five dollars worth of nickels in it."

"At least that much," Gilbert added. "Did you see Darla sashay into the room and take a seat in Giddyup's lap? His eyes almost popped out of his head."

"Outta Rupert's head, too," Zach said with a laugh. "And then them boys, what was their names? Wayne and Kent? They musta asked Rupe four times could they join the card game going on in the back room. 'Specially when Gus came out and borrowed a hunnert dollars from Noble."

It had been an impressive show. After Rupert invited the two guests to "come over and play" later that night and promised to leave their names at the "checkpoint," he assembled his troupe and some other trustworthy extras, and they converted their tavern into a speakeasy out of a Jimmy Cagney gangster epic, complete with tax-free Canadian whiskey, high-rolling card games, and fallen women.

The two CID men were giddy with excitement. First they would conquer Ransom Island, and after that, Galveston. They were already talking about who was going to play them in the movies.

When they talked with the DA the next morning, their jubilation quickly evaporated.

" . . . Let me make sure I've got this straight. You didn't actually see any roulette or blackjack tables. One slot machine. One . . . ." Attorney General Will Wilson repeated, his voice rising. "Or see any bets placed on the numbers boards. You didn't physically sit in on any of those poker games you *suspect* were going on in a back room. And you weren't directly solicited by *even one* of the painted ladies you mentioned. Have I got that about right?"

"We did see a dice table," Willie Dawes (Wayne) offered meekly.

"Anybody playing dice on it?"

"Uh, no, sir.

"It was like the operation was still under construction," Cliff Hollenbeck said over his partner's shoulder. They were both crammed into a phone booth outside the Jackson Hotel in Aransas Pass. Cliff could easily hear the boss's voice booming through the phone receiver.

"I need evidence, you idiots!" Wilson yelled. "Hard evidence. I'm glad you didn't call Major Gonzalez first because he'd have thought I was playing a joke on him, sending you two numbskulls to him for this job."

After they heard the phone disconnect on the other end of the line, Dawes and Hollenbeck lurched out of the phone booth and lit cigarettes. They'd never had an ass-chewing like that before.

"Well," Dawes said after a couple of deep drags on his Pall Mall. "I guess the Christmas bonus is out."

"I don't know about you, Brother Dawes, but I'm gonna be on Shady's like a cheap suit until we get something solid."

"Whatever it takes," Dawes, agreed.

As Gilbert and Zach drove by the phone booth, they didn't notice the two dejected undercover agents standing nearby, grinding out their butts and glumly surveying their prospects.

"You know," Gilbert continued, still reminiscing about the performances from the night before, "I think maybe Gus Brauer gets the Academy Award for best actor."

Zach looked perplexed. "But he didn't act no different than he always does."

"Exactly . . . completely believable," said Gilbert. "Gustav's been playing the part of a Bohunk farmer for so long, it's second nature to him now. He probably believes his U-boat service was just one long fishing charter. God bless America."

"Gilbert, why do you think nobody mentions that?" asked Zach. "About Gus gettin' left here by that U-boat? Everybody seems to know the real story. Even Cap'n Quincy, and he got himself a Purple Heart fightin' *against* the Boche."

"Most people are ready to move on after a war's over, Zach."

Gilbert looked over at his companion, who gazed out the window of the station wagon and puffed on one of his ever-present hand-rolled smokes. The sideburns beneath the rim of his Stetson were shot through with gray, and after years of harsh South Texas weather, Zach's face had attained the patina of an oiled leather rucksack. Zach and Rupert were probably the best friends he'd ever had.

"Hey Zach, did you hear the one about the black cowboy and the Mexican cook that ended up on an island and started their own private supper club? Called it the Bronc and Burro Club."

Zach chuckled appreciatively. "Specializin' in biscuits, *borracho* beans, and horsemeat enchiladas, I reckon." He flipped the cigarette butt out the window. "The truth is, I stay on at Shady's 'cause of Rupe, and 'cause I'm too stove up to punch cattle anymore. And he treats colored people decently.

"But you . . ." he glanced at Gilbert. "You got plenty of smarts—a whole lot more'n most people. I'm not judging, ya understand, but it seems a waste you stayin' a biscuit roller all yer life . . . even in a place as high-toned as Shady's . . . or the Bronc and Burro Club."

Gilbert rolled to a stop in front of Big Todd's Building Supply and replied. "It's like Churchill said, 'It's always wise to look ahead, but difficult to look further than you can see.'"

"That Churchill was a smart rascal," Zach allowed.

After filling their cart with nails, screws, latches, and spring hinges (Rupert wanted to build a couple of not-so-hidden trap doors into the floor to "hide" their non-existent roulette tables), Gilbert tallied the supplies with Big Todd.

"Could you add a dozen twelve-foot 2x4s to the bill, too? And a couple of sheets of 3/4-inch marine-grade plywood?" asked Gilbert.

Big Todd grunted from behind the cash register. His customer service didn't extend to black or brown patrons. He barely tolerated the white ones. After he added the new figures to the Shady Fish Camp account and recorded Gilbert's signature, he cocked a thumb toward the loading dock. "Pull around back if you want your lumber," he said without looking up.

"Much obliged, Todd," said Gilbert.

Just as Gilbert and Zach were exiting through the front door, Leroy Stuckey and three of his buddies were coming in. The men's faces were puffy and pale and two of them had black eyes. They still reeked of the alcohol they'd consumed at the Klan meeting the night before. The Klonvocation after-party had started off well enough, but it degenerated into a melee after a couple of would-be Klan brothers got into a pointless argument that evolved into a drunken free-for-all. (Something about whether an octaroon and a Jew could legally marry, and if so, whether their babies could still be considered American citizens—in retrospect, none of it made much sense.)

After the brawl was all over, Leroy's cousin demanded that the shattered door and plate glass window be replaced straight away, requiring a supply run to Big Todd's the following morning.

Leroy Stuckey and his red-eyed work crew glared at Gilbert and Zach with a sluggish, venomous scrutiny as they crossed paths at the entrance. A few paces inside the store, Leroy Stuckey stopped abruptly and one of his beefy buddies bumped into him. "What the hell, Leroy?"

Leroy held up a hand to signal that they all be quiet. He had to concentrate extra hard to navigate through the shoals of fog in his brain. He recognized those two guys from someplace. Where the hell was it?

Then it hit him.

"Big Todd? Those two boys that just left, the coon and the Meskin . . . they from Ransom Island?"

"Yeah, what of it?" Big Todd looked up. "Hey, what happened to you guys? Looks like somebody took a tire iron to you."

Leroy leaned over the register. "Todd, that Meskin has been keepin' a white girl in his shack over on Ransom Island." Big Todd backed up a step to get out of range of Leroy's rancid breath. "And I think that nigra is in on it, too. Wouldn't be surprised if they're holding that poor girl against her will, doing God knows what to her. White slavery deal, you know?"

Leroy had come across this information third hand, via a beautician in Vera's Gulf Beach Hair Salon, who overheard the wife of the Shady's proprietor discussing it with Vera. It was that tidbit of information that had prompted his nocturnal visit to Gilbert's shack a few days before.

Todd eyed him suspiciously. He didn't like Leroy much— he thought he was a drunk and a loud-mouthed troublemaker— but then he didn't have much regard for blacks or Mexicans either. He decided that even if the little peckerwood was lying, he wasn't one to interfere in somebody else's beef.

"I sent 'em 'round to the alley to pick up their load of lumber," said Big Todd, tilting his big square head toward the warehouse door behind him. "But I ain't in much of a hurry to tend to them."

Leroy rapped his knuckles on the counter. "Oh, I think we can tend to 'em." On his way out the door, he stopped in front of a barrel of axe handles and looked back at the proprietor. "Mind if we borrow a few of these?"

Todd just turned his back and pretended to study an inventory report.

Leroy picked up a wooden handle and slapped it across his palm. "Come on, boys. Let's go dispense some white man's justice."

Gilbert and Zach were sitting on the fold-down door on the rear of the station wagon waiting for Todd, when a rusty one-ton pick-up turned into the alley, huffing exhaust. Four men stepped out. All were carrying axe handles.

Zach looked at Gilbert in alarm, but Gilbert was already on his feet, walking *toward* the men. Zach could have sworn he had a half-smile on his face. His own heart thumped with fear. He'd taken a beating at the hands of white men like these before.

"*Buenos días,* my American friends. *Me alegra encontrarme con vosotros,*" Gilbert said, addressing the men grandly, wishing them a good day and telling them how happy he was to see them.

The small group of hung-over vigilantes blinked in befuddlement as the wiry little man walked up and stood directly in front of them, greeting them like they were his long-lost amigos.

Finally Leroy responded. "You're goddamn right we're Americans," he said. "Not like you. I know you from Shady's . . . Meskin," said Leroy.

Gilbert presented a puzzled expression. "Oh, I am not from Mexico."

"Bullshit," muttered one of the men.

"Where the hell you from, then?" asked Stuckey.

Gilbert puffed out his chest. "From Uruguay. I am Uruguayan." *It was either run a shuck on these guys or take a bad beating,* Gilbert reckoned.

The men looked at each other. "You're a what?"

"Uruguayan," Gilbert repeated.

"I'm a what?" asked one of the men. Was this little half-pint beaner making fun of him?

Stuckey cocked his head back suspiciously. "Your-a-gay-un? Is that like a Meskin?" He waved the ax handle in a small circle and moved closer. "Maybe in Ur-a-gay they let you taco benders run around with white women, but we won't put up with that shit in Texas. I warned you about that."

So this is the son-of-a-bitch that left the Klan card on my door, thought Gilbert. He looked back and noticed that Zach was sitting behind the steering wheel. The car was idling.

"Maybe we should help Heckle and Jeckle on their way," said one of the hungover goons. "Give 'em a little souvenir to remember the fine time they had in Aransas Pass." He walked over to the station wagon, raised his ax handle, and delivered a two-handed blow to the front windshield, creating a web of cracks from one side to the other. Zach didn't know how to drive, but he was prepared to learn in a hell of a hurry.

Leroy smiled maliciously. "You know what I think? I think you made up all that Ur-a-gay crap. You're just a wetback that works in the kitchen over on Ransom Island."

Gilbert resisted an urge to punch Leroy Stuckey in the face and instead tried to think faster. "You've been to the restaurant then! Well I hope you tried the barbecue recipe that I learned to cook there. I am very proud of it."

"What does a Meskin from Uruguay know about barbecue?" asked one of the rednecks, his interest piqued despite himself. Barbecue was a serious subject. Even lynch mobs could be coerced into arguing the finer points of smoked meats.

"In my country we are very serious about our *barbacoa,*" said Gilbert, "And I wanted to measure your famous Texas barbecue against our own."

"Well," asked one of the men, intrigued despite himself. "What's the verdict?"

Gilbert noticed that the men were paying close attention now, and the windshield smasher had rejoined the group, too. Time to throw them one last bone and then scram.

Gilbert lowered his head dispiritedly. "Gentlemen . . . Texas barbecue is the finest that I have tasted anywhere in the world. You Texans—*maestros de la pereza y estupidez*—you should be very proud."

The men looked at each other smugly. "Damn right we got the best," said one man. "I coulda told you that," said another. Every man-jack among them, Leroy included, fancied himself a pitmaster supreme. But it was a good thing for Gilbert that none of them spoke Spanish.

"Beats the hell outta that Kansas City crap."

"Tennessee, too."

"One guy even swore to me they have good barbecue in California," said another incredulously. Everyone shook their heads at such rank heresy.

"The best Texas barbecue is in Lockhart," Leroy proclaimed to the group. "Listen, kid, if you want to try some brisket that melts in your mouth, you need to go to a place called . . . ." But when he turned around, Gilbert and Zach were gone.

Leroy and his gang watched a brown arm wave at them from the window of the wagon as it disappeared around the corner and turned onto Commercial Street.

The men were still discussing how Texas kicked Uruguay's ass in the BBQ meat cook-off when Big Todd opened the single-bay loading dock door.

When Leroy explained what they were talking about, Big Todd laughed. "You dumb fucks. That was Gilberto Ruiz. He's a cook awright, but he's nothing more'n a common border Mexican that Rupert picked up at some restaurant on Baffin Bay. I'd call immigration on the cocky little spic if Shady's wasn't such a good customer." Big Todd grinned sardonically. "Leroy, I'd say you've been danced around and hung out to dry by that pepperbelly."

Big Todd laughed at Leroy Stuckey, and the other men laughed at Leroy Stuckey, too. They might be poor specimens of the breed, but as Texans, they could appreciate a good tall tale when they heard one—no matter who was doing the telling. And Leroy was a miserable little pissant about half the time anyway.

This is the price of leadership, Leroy thought bitterly. His Klavern followers had watched him get shot down twice in two days, first by the Grand Titan and now by Big Todd and that damn Meskin. His dream of Klan ascendency was fading fast. He needed some redemption—something *big,* he reminded himself.

Later, as he sullenly labored alone in his cousin's automotive garage, repairing the broken door and window (his helpers had jumped at the chance to abandon their disgraced leader and retreat to their Barcaloungers and TV sets), Leroy tried to think of a way to get himself back in the game. Late in the afternoon he revisited his original inspiration—putting the quietus on the integrated dance at Shady's. Well, by God, *he* would do something about it. And whatever it was, he'd make sure *this* plan didn't blow up in his face like the others.

Then it came to him. *Blow up in your face.* He dropped his hammer and grinned. There is only one way to get to Shady's and Ransom Island, Leroy remembered—a one-lane wooden bridge over the bay. *And not one nigger or nigger-loving white person will be able to set foot on that dance floor if I blow the Ransom Island Bridge to kingdom come.*

Leroy's eyes sparkled with malicious resolve. "I'm a mother-fuckin' mastermind," he announced to the empty garage.

———

CHAPTER 22

Sheriff Red Burton, Jr. marched into Shady's and tossed a local newspaper down in front of Rupert, who had just sat down for breakfast. The paper landed in his plate of eggs and hash and one corner fell into his coffee cup, wicking coffee into the newsprint.

"I told you you were asking for trouble," said the sheriff.

Rupert picked up the *Aransas Pass Progress* and brushed off a potato that had stuck to the fold. "Good morning to you too, Red."

"That windbag J. Mule at the paper has decided to start tub-thumpin' for integration. And guess what? He thinks your little dance is a great idea."

The headlines above the fold of the diminutive paper asked, "Will City Enforce Race Laws At Concert?"

Editor, publisher, and free-press crusader Jewell "J. Mule" Moncrief was a civic fixture, and had been around as long as the paper itself. He was in the *Progress* office on the morning of September 14, 1929, when a massive hurricane smashed much of Aransas Pass to kindling and drowned scores of people outside his door. Thirty people sought refuge in his second-floor apartment, including a nun leading ten children from the Roman Catholic orphanage, roped together with bed sheets. The presses, on the ground floor, lay utterly submerged, but he and two staffers managed to put out a special Hurricane Edition on the hand-cranked machines by the following morning.

The *Progress* put out its second special edition when Nazi U-Boats were sighted off Mustang Island during the war. By that time, the paper had waged campaigns against the resurgent Ku Klux Klan and on behalf of successive slates of Progressive Party candidates. As J. Mule grew older and crankier, the editorial page would thunder against the perceived excesses of FDR's New Deal. Lately, J. Mule had become stridently anti-union, and thought that fellow Joe McCarthy might really be on to something.

But the paper still took pride in standing up for the little guy, chronicling the changing fortunes of its community, and speaking truth to local power. And Sheriff Burton was the local power J. Mule had singled out in this latest tirade.

"Look, Red," Rupert said cheerfully, "he mentions your name right here."

"You noticed that, huh? Well, it's not particularly flattering."

Rupert shrugged. "I don't know, Sheriff, you *are* kind of 'a throw-back lawman,' like he says. Although I might take issue with you being 'a lackey to the local fat cats.'"

"Goddammit, Rupe, there's probably a line of outraged citizens forming outside my office as we speak, ever' damn one of them set on tellin' me how to do my job."

"You mean the fat cats?"

"Don't push it," Red growled.

Rupert pushed his plate away and interlocked his hands. "When have you ever let a little pressure like this bother you, Red?" Rupert decided now was not a good time to tell the sheriff about the dance-related threats he had received on his home phone. There had been three, so far.

"It's more than a little pressure. Half the town is clamoring for me to shut this show down."

"And the other half is going to be standing in line to buy tickets." Rupert sat back in his chair. "Times are changing, Red. You know those Jim Crow laws are wrong, and you know they're going away."

"The hell they are. The poll tax is alive and well. Miscegenation is a felony, in case you haven't noticed. Colored folks can't sit at the same lunch counter or even use the same washing machines in the washaterias as whites. You know what a liberal in Texas is, right? Someone who doesn't favor lynching on Sunday!"

"I heard your daddy broke up a lynch mob in Waco single-handed one time," said Rupert. "The mob included two city councilmen and a Baptist minister. He called 'em a bunch of curs and cowards and backed 'em down. You got a lot of your daddy in you, Red."

"Lynch mobs are illegal. And so is this dance, dammit! At least in San Patricio County it is."

"In this county it's also against the law to jaywalk, carry fence cutters in your back pocket, or drive a wagon down a public road without a red lantern hanging off the back, but you don't run around enforcing those laws, do you?"

"This is a little different."

"You're missing my point. Your dad faced down the fat cats of the day because he knew it was the right thing to do."

Red shook his head, exasperated. "Rupert, I just want you to understand how much hell I'm going to catch for lettin' this black and white shindig take place."

Rupert smiled broadly. "Your daddy would be proud of you."

"Go to hell, Rupe. You're buying me breakfast this morning." Red motioned to Sally to bring him a cup of coffee and a menu.

Sally took Red's order and waited for a fresh pot of coffee to finish brewing so she could refill some of the empty cups in the restaurant.

Her day had started early, when Gilbert's did. Later, when it got busy inside the restaurant, she pitched in there, too, waiting on customers and bussing tables—basically helping out any way she could.

But she liked the early mornings best, and she found herself looking forward to their time alone in the little setback kitchen. Sometimes they talked while they worked; sometimes they didn't. Mostly, she just enjoyed being with him. Despite her misgivings about keeping Primo and Jimmy Glick in her secret past, her feelings for Gilberto Ruiz were growing.

They had been spending more time outside of the kitchen, too. Between shifts, Gilbert showed her how to rig up her own rod and reel so they could fish off the dock, usually alongside Rupert's two sandy-haired nephews. He played his records for her in the cabin and demonstrated the difference between a bolero and a bossa nova on his guitar. He even taught her how to strum a few chords herself. On occasion, he slept over. It was an island rhythm she enjoyed. For the first time in her rootless life, she begin to imagine a future shared with somebody else—a future with someone she cared about and who cared about her.

Darla walked in and grabbed a clean coffee mug. "How about fixin' me a cup, Sally?"

"You're up early," Sally said as she poured. Darla usually never showed her face until lunchtime.

"I'm going shopping in Corpus today. Lichtenstein's is having a sale and I'm going to be first in line when the doors open." She looked over at Sally. "Want to go with me? Maybe buy yourself a nice dress?"

A new dress would be nice, Sally thought to herself. She'd been wearing Darla's clothes since she arrived on the island; her Rainbow Inn outfit had been torn up and used to clean fishing reels. But unfortunately, one week of kitchen pay didn't buy much of a dress. "Thanks, Darla. But I need to help Gilbert with the lunch special today—something called *chiles rellenos*. Apparently, there are a lot of steps."

"Suit yourself, honey. But remember that a man always likes seeing his girl in a new dress." Darla winked and smiled. "Know what I mean?"

At first, Darla hadn't been so sure about Sally and Gilbert. Sally was such a pretty girl, and Gilbert, well, Gilbert was a Mexican. Mixed-race relationships were frowned upon in South Texas; Darla wasn't even sure they were legal. But she had learned that Ransom Island played by its own rulebook, and it usually wasn't one that the Aransas Pass Women's Club approved of. So she didn't worry about Gilbert and Sally much. Nobody from the Women's Club ever came to Ransom Island, anyway. *Besides,* she thought, *you can't pick who you love. If those two were meant to be together, then so be it.*

As Darla sipped her coffee and mused about Eros on Ransom Island, her eyes landed on the table where Rupert and Red Burton sat. Particularly at Red. *You can't pick who you love,* she repeated to herself. She set down her mug and picked up the coffee pot. "Sally, I think my boys need a refill."

Sally watched Darla make a beeline to Red and Rupert, ignoring the empty cups that other patrons thrust out for a refill. She watched Darla openly flirt with both men as she poured their coffee, all the while resting her hand familiarly on the sheriff's shoulder.

This wasn't the first time Sally had noticed Darla's affection for her old suitor (Gilbert had filled her in on their story), and she couldn't help but wonder, and worry. Rupert and the sheriff were best of friends, but nothing could come between friends like a flirtatious woman.

Darla returned to the bar and leaned against the counter, still gazing at Red. "Here," she said, absentmindedly handing the pot to Sally. "You know, maybe I'll get my hair done while I'm in town. You sure you don't want to come?"

"No, I better not. But thanks for the offer. Have fun, Darla . . . and be careful," she added pointedly.

Darla looked at her curiously and then smiled. "Of course, honey."

———

CHAPTER 23

After the breakfast crowd thinned out, Rupert and his brothers began preparing the skiffs for the handful of customers that had booked fishing charters that day. Despite the mounting problems on Ransom Island, the brothers had a spring in their step as they walked single file to the dock. A new moon, running tides, a slight breeze, falling barometric pressure—all of it pointed to a terrific day of fishing out on the bay.

Noble and Flavius even rigged up a couple of rods for themselves in case they had a break in their duties. At the dock, a ring of customers gathered around Dubber's boys and the mess of trout they had caught earlier that morning. Johnny and Charlie lifted their hefty stringer high for the excited would-be anglers. Everyone was raring to get to it.

Gilbert and Zach were clearing breakfast dishes off the tables when an unfamiliar head appeared around the screen door.

"Is one of you Rupert Sweetwater?" the man began, and then, after looking more closely at Zach and Gilbert, added, "Naw, I guess not."

"He's down at the dock," answered Zach. "Anything we can he'p you with?"

"Take me to him," the man demanded. "I've got a package I was told to hand-deliver to the proprietor, Mr., ah, Sweetwater." He held up a white envelope and slapped it against his palm impatiently.

Zach nodded and studied the man delivering the envelope. He didn't look like any deliveryman he'd ever seen. More like a clerk at a bank or something.

The man cleared his throat. "Right now would be good," he insisted.

Zach shrugged and walked past the messenger, pushing open the screen and turning toward the docks.

The stranger watched him leave and then looked to Gilbert for explanation.

"He's taking you to the docks," said Gilbert. "You're supposed to follow."

When Zach and the courier arrived at the bait stand pier, the brothers were loading the last guests onto a long string of fishing skiffs.

"I'm looking for Rupert Sweetwater," said the man.

"Then I'd say you've found him," Rupert answered.

"I've got a special delivery for you."

He handed over the envelope and Rupert glanced at the markings—it was from a Galveston law firm with five names. The courier continued standing on the dock after Rupert had thanked him.

"I'm supposed to stay until you read it," the man explained.

Rupert nodded. "Sure, mister." He opened the letter and gave it a quick once over. "There," he said. "I've read it."

"There's two copies in that envelope, and ah, they said you were supposed to sign one of 'em. It's just saying that you've acknowledged their proposal, or something like that."

Rupert smiled at the man. "No, I don't think I'm gonna sign anything right now." He stuffed the letter in the hip pocket of his fish-blood-stained khakis.

The courier hesitated. "They said to tell you that it's some kind of mutual confidentiality deal. For the clients' protection, and yours too, of course."

Rupert put his big arm around the man's shoulder and walked him a few steps in the direction of the parking lot. "Look, young fella, you've done what your bosses sent you here to do; you've delivered their message. So now you can go on home."

"What should I tell 'em?" he asked anxiously.

"Tell 'em I got their letter and I read it."

Rupert went back to tending to his guests like nothing had happened. Before they left the dock, Noble and Flavius pulled him aside, curious to know what was going on. Rupert handed them the envelope. "Can't tell if it's a bid or a bribe," he told them as he walked away.

The brothers skipped over the legal mumbo jumbo and the part about "non-disclosure" and "proxy buyers" and went straight to the number at the bottom.

Flavius whistled. "Holy smoke! Are they serious?"

Noble shook his head incredulously. "If this is a bribe, they're really good at it."

—

When Zach returned to the restaurant, he found Gilbert and Sally in the kitchen staring wide-eyed at a massive fish laid out across the cutting board. Or maybe it was half a fish. It wasn't like any creature he'd ever seen.

"What the heck is that?" he asked.

Sally looked up. "Barefoot Nelson and his wife dropped it off. I'm not sure why."

"Didn't you take them a Coleman lantern a couple of days ago?" Gilbert asked her.

"Yeah. Their old one had rusted out, so I gave them a new one."

"Then that explains the Mola mola. Barefoot and Emma always repay a favor, usually in fish."

"You call that a fish?" Sally asked.

"Looks more like they just gave you a fish head," Zach added.

The Mola mola fish was over five feet long with grey, mottled skin and big fins jutting out on top and bottom. It had no tail or tail fin, a small beaked mouth, and tiny eyes that looked like dark, smoky gems.

"Some people call it an ocean sunfish," said Gilbert. "It's in the same family."

Zach marveled at the creature. It did indeed look like a giant sunfish, except cut in half. "Don't that beat all? I reckon you're gonna have a tough time getting this critter in a fryin' pan, Gil."

Gilbert nodded. "I'm not sure it'll fit in a pickup truck bed, let alone a frying pan. I wonder how the Nelsons would cook it?"

"I don't know," said Sally, "but I'm not touching it. It looks like something from a Jules Verne story." Sally picked up a platter of deviled eggs and backed through the kitchen door.

"I'll figure something out," said Gilbert, scratching his head. "Hey, Zach, what did our visitor take to Rupe that was so important?"

"Delivered an offer to buy this place, I reckon . . . from some outfit in Galveston."

"I bet I can guess who that would be."

"Yep. Rupe didn't seem all that excited about it. But his brothers sure did."

—

That night, Noble and Flavius assembled on Rupert's screened back porch to discuss the offer. Rupert found that his brothers' enthusiasm for the deal had not abated, and he was doing his best to temper it.

"First of all, we aren't even sure this deal's on the up and up," said Rupert. "We're not exactly dealing with model citizens, you know. There's bound to be a catch."

"If they pay cash, what's the difference?" said Flavius. "I'll take money from a gangster any day of the week."

"I'm worried about what happens if we *don't* accept their offer," said Noble. "Their next run at our place may not be something we like all that much, and it probably won't involve some silk stocking law firm, either."

"Maybe not," Rupert agreed. "But it's still *our* place—hell, it's our life. What would you two do with yourselves if we sold out?"

Flavius snorted. "I can think of a lot of things to do . . . and a lot a ways I could spend that dough. Yessiree-bob, the world would be my oyster. First thing, I'd maybe buy me a swanky cruiser and take it up to Galveston, spread some of my money around—"

"To Galveston?" Rupert interrupted. "They'd like that wouldn't they? Buy yourself some fancy duds, go pal around with your new Mafia buddies at the club? Stick a big cigar in your mouth and have a pretty lady under each arm? Mr. Big Spender, giving 'em their money back, one drink and one crap game at a time."

Flavius looked away angrily. He hated debating with Rupert.

Rupert raised his big hands pleadingly. "Is that what this is about, boys? A couple of years livin' the high life? What happens when the money runs out? What are you gonna do then? Go back to work for Shady's, as one of their pit bosses or bouncers?"

"I wouldn't mind opening a little restaurant of my own," said Noble. "Maybe an upscale place in Corpus, or Houston, even."

Rupert shook his head, a little stung by this idea. Noble was his right-hand man, and normally wary of easy-money propositions. "Goddamn," he said. "Why are you boys so hot to sell all of a sudden? A week ago y'all were crowing about how we'd never cave in to those goons."

"That was before you opened that envelope," said Noble.

Rupert sighed. "Okay, boys, y'all have spoke your piece, and you've got a vote in this thing, same as me. But keep in mind, it might all fall apart when they find out Shady's is being investigated by the attorney general for gambling and prostitution."

"Shit, I forgot about that," said Flavius. "That could queer the whole deal."

"That was the idea, remember? A way to save Ransom Island from the Galveston mob? You guys act like our place is a lost cause or something. Hell, we've got one of the biggest acts in the country coming to our island one week from today."

Nobody could argue with that, so the three men sat there silently until Noble stood up to go. "Well, it's late, and I guess it's not gonna hurt to sleep on this for a few nights." He gave Rupert a wry smile. "It's not like anybody's holding a gun to our head. Not yet anyway."

After Rupert's brothers drove to their homes in Aransas Pass, he wearily climbed the stairs to his room and found Darla sitting on the edge of the bed, dressed in the pink negligée he had given her on their anniversary. She'd been waiting for him all this time, probably listening through the window to their conversation. It wasn't hard for him to see that she had something on her mind, and he had a pretty good idea what it was.

He'd seen how the Duke Ellington show had rekindled her showbiz fantasies. *Once she knows about the buyout offer,* he thought wearily, *she'll vote to dump Ransom Island like a cheap prom dress.* Well, maybe she still didn't know. He was too tired to talk about it right now.

"You're still up," he said.

"Let's sell this place, Rupert," she said straight away. "We'll never get a better chance."

She knew. Rupert sat down heavily in the easy chair adjacent to the window and shut his eyes. "You too, huh?"

"We could go anywhere," she continued. "Anywhere we wanted." She hopped off the bed and stood behind the chair, massaging his shoulders. "Think of it, honey. We could have us a permanent room at the Shamrock Hotel in Houston, or pick up and move to Miami—get us a place right on the beach. Or . . . " she ran her fingers through his hair, "we could maybe buy a smart little bungalow in Hollywood." Darla drew out the syllables in Hollywood to make it sound, Rupert guessed, more enticing.

But none of her dreamy scenarios appealed to him. A series of images ran through his mind, each one worse than the last. A cramped apartment in the glitzy, three-ring social circus that was the Shamrock Hotel; wandering along a south Florida beach with old retired men in Bermuda shorts and black socks; getting dragged to a hundred different Hollywood film premieres in California, with Darla on his arm—her hoping to get noticed, him wishing he was off fishing. There probably wasn't a shrimp boat within a thousand miles of Hollywood, he thought glumly.

He thought of watching the sun rise over a saltwater marsh on a winter duck hunt, the feel of a having a powerful marlin straining on the line in the blue water off Half Moon Reef. He thought of the way the goat-foot morning glory blossoms looked, uncurling against the sand dunes like purple stars. He thought of himself, and his brothers, and Red, laughing, drunk and telling lies around a midnight driftwood fire far down South Padre at the edge of the known universe, the Milky Way wheeling around them.

"I can't do it, Darla."

Her hands stopped massaging. "Sure you can, baby," she said soothingly, although Rupert could hear an edge in her voice. "You can do anything. It'd be a grand adventure, and you know we'd have a ball. It's . . . it's the chance of lifetime."

Rupert shook his head. "This place is all I ever wanted, babydoll. And I honestly, truly cannot think of anywhere else I'd want to be."

"Phooey," said Darla, walking angrily to the bed. "How can you say that? It's just a scruffy ol' island with a couple of misfit workers and a bunch of goofball customers. We work our butts off, and we barely make enough to live on."

Rupert looked sharply at his wife. She generally didn't leave the house until past noon. And except for an occasional shift at the bar, her "work" consisted of shopping trips to town and reading the movie magazines.

"What have you ever asked for here that I haven't given you?"

"You do your best, honey, I know," she said, softening her tone, "But . . . don't you ever want more? Don't you ever want to meet some *new* people? Maybe a better class of people?"

"Not really."

"But nothing ever happens here! It's . . . boring."

"Duke Ellington is boring?

"No, that's a big deal, but it happened because we got lucky. And apparently, because we've got fishing."

"That's another thing," said Rupert. "Some of the best fishing in the world is right here."

"I hate fishing."

"Darla, you knew exactly what you were getting into when you married me and moved onto this island. And you told me then you wouldn't want to change a thing."

"Humph," she muttered as she burrowed under the covers and switched off the light, her back to him. "I just might have to rethink that."

Rupert sat in the dark by the open window, feeling the Gulf breeze and listening to it rustle the fronds of the island's only palm tree. The lights of Port Aransas twinkled in the distance, and in the bay, marker buoys along the Intracoastal Canal flashed red and green at two-second intervals.

He'd had this conversation with Darla before, and with the wife before her. Ransom Island seemed fun to them at first, and then after awhile the grass looked greener somewhere else. Almost anywhere else. But this time it was different. The money the Galveston bunch was throwing at the place had kicked Darla's itch to leave into overdrive. Even if he convinced his brothers not to sell, he wasn't so sure he'd be able to convince his wife to stay.

Later on, he heard Darla's steady breathing and knew she was asleep. Out in the bait house, lined up on cots, Gilbert and the two boys would be asleep, too. So would Zachariah Yates, bunked up in his wooden cabin a hundred yards down the sandy path. Rupert thought of the leather saddle the old cowboy kept on a saddle-stand in the corner of his tidy little cabin. It was the only thing of value his friend owned. What the hell would happen to Zach if Ransom Island sold?

Sometime before morning Rupert dozed off to sleep.

CHAPTER 24

Primo Ginestra's flinty, criminal heart softened at the sight of his daughter. The Coast Guard surplus binoculars that were part of the *Easy Eight's* inventory brought her almost close enough to grasp.

For the past two days, the yacht had anchored up in the Ransom Point Cut, slightly west of the island. Captain Shorter occupied most of his idle daylight hours fishing the murky green waters for drum and speckled trout.

At night they motored over to the Crab Man Marina on Mustang Island to eat supper and replenish the liquor supply. Emiliano Castro, aka the Crab Man, regarded them with studied neutrality. A native of Havana, he knew American gangsters when he saw them. (Emiliano had a cousin back home, Fidel, who once told him that *los Estados Unidos* was the land of opportunity. Fidel had almost become a professional baseball player in the States before he decided to become a revolutionary. What a pain in the ass.)

Jimmy Glick, bored out of his skull, listened to ballgames on the radio, chain-smoked cigarettes, and spent hours sighting down his index finger, assassinating (in his imagination) sport fishermen, gliding pelicans, and smiling porpoises. By the third day, he was as itchy as a whore in church.

Primo was waiting on word from Ransom Island. Their errand boy had delivered a good-faith offer to purchase the place, lock, stock, and jukebox the day before yesterday. What was the hold up? Deferred gratification wasn't wired into Primo's personality.

And there was the matter of the girl. He chafed with impatience. He wanted to confront her, to possess her, to have her embrace him rightfully as her papa and take her proper place in his life.

In the meantime, Primo knew he had to find his lieutenant something constructive to do. Idle minds were the devil's workshop. (Or was it the devil's playground?) And besides, he was paying him good money. He put the binoculars down and motioned to Marcos Shorter, who reeled in his fishing line and climbed down off the flying bridge.

"Hey, skipper, go up to the front of the boat and get Jimmy, wouldja? I need a word."

Captain Shorter just nodded and stepped away. *It's the bow, you idiot,* he thought sourly, as tired of the stakeout as everyone else.

Jimmy Glick was lying topside, catching some sun in a sleeveless undershirt and Bermuda shorts. Dark glasses concealed his eyes. He was reading a two-month old copy of a *Saturday Evening Post* magazine he'd found somewhere and was absolutely bored shitless.

Maybe some action, he thought as he made his way aft to where Primo sat in his fighting chair, binoculars once again fixed on Ransom Island. *Something, anything. Christ, how did those pirates stand it in the old days?*

It was action, of a sort. Primo had been observing Sally Rose as she went about her busy day, but he'd also observed she didn't spend her spare time doing needlepoint or Bible study. There was a man she was seeing a lot of—slender and dark-complected, from what Primo could see. Sally was fond of him, that was evident—they walked on Ransom Island's meager beach in the evenings when the neon beer signs fizzed into life and the echo of the jukebox stretched across the bay. Sometimes she sat on the tiny porch of what Primo assumed was the kid's cabin, watching him play a guitar. They seemed to laugh a lot. Primo had also seen them kissing behind an outbuilding attached to the dancehall, thinking they were out of sight. *Where do you get off kissing my daughter,* he thought with a murderous flare of emotion.

Primo explained all this to Jimmy Glick, whose eyes widened in surprise behind his Ray-Bans.

"Hell, boss, it must be that Mexican cook she's carryin' on with."
Jimmy was under no illusions that this would come as welcome news.

He was right.

"*Messicano?*" blurted Primo.

"Gotta be. He doesn't fit the description of anyone else on the island."

"Where does that little *figlio di puttana* get off? My daughter!"

Odd as it might have seemed, the Ginestra brothers regarded themselves as social liberals, or at least what passed for such in Texas. They had voted for Roosevelt without hesitation and applauded Truman's initiative to integrate the armed forces. If he had given it any thought—which he hadn't—Primo would have supposed it came from living in a port city, where diverse cultures sailed in and out every day.

Black people didn't gamble in the Bali Hai or the Turf Club—not many Negroes in Galveston had enough loose coin for such swanky joints—and Shanghai Lilly maintained a separate sporting establishment for Latino, black, and Chinese sailors to have their fun.

But on occasions when one of the Ginestras' showrooms hosted, say, Benny Goodman's integrated band or a hot black act from out of town like Ivory Joe Hunter or Ray Charles, Primo and Gerry grudgingly allowed a few of the Island's more prosperous black doctors and attorneys to attend with their wives. But that was as far as they were prepared to go. There never had been—nor would there ever be—a black man, or any other minority, in the upper echelon of the brothers' organization, although they regarded themselves as the progressive *laissez-faire* of Galveston's better nature.

Primo was not so much offended that Gilberto Ruiz was Hispanic as that he was a cook. His one and only daughter was making time with a greasy-spoon flapjack flipper? Like hell. The sight of Ruiz with his arms around his daughter was an outrage. It was intolerable. Parental action was required. Primo took his responsibility as a dutiful father seriously.

He gave Jimmy Glick explicit instructions. "First, no killing. Nothing permanent. Just dance him around, maybe give his dentist a little work . . . a little chin music. Make sure he knows Sally Rose is off limits, even if you have to tattoo it onto his forehead with brass knuckles. Second, don't mix it up with anyone else on the island, especially that apeshit younger brother you told me about." (Jimmy reflexively rubbed his chin on the spot where Flavius had clocked him.)

"Third, for Chrissakes, don't let *her* see you." Primo didn't want his daughter suspecting that any of the Ginestra organization was within two hundred miles of Redfish Bay, at least not yet. She'd been at school when he and Gerry purchased the *Easy Eight*; seeing the vessel anchored out would mean nothing to her.

"How's she gonna take to her boyfriend getting busted up?" Glick asked. He still felt a sort of big-brother regard for the girl.

"She'll feel bad, but she'll get over it. And maybe it'll be an eye-opener for her. Running around with the help isn't for her. And besides, it's probably just a fling. It's hot. She's bored. You know how kids are."

Another thing, Primo pointed out. The cabin where Sally was staying was obviously not hers. Primo had observed Gilbert casually entering and leaving during the daytime like he owned the place— fetching his guitar, or a book or, day before yesterday when a monsoon squall drifted over the bay, a heavy slicker.

But he slept over by the fish camp, in a low-slung building that Jimmy said served as a small store and bait shop.

Things obviously had not progressed much beyond the hand-holding/kissing-behind-the-kitchen stage (though Sally could have informed them otherwise). Better to nip this particular bud early.

"How you do it is up to you," Primo concluded. "Just don't get caught. And don't kill him. Don't kill nobody."

Jimmy went to the cold locker behind the cockpit and grabbed an icy bottle of Jax. He drank his beer and thought about it, rolling a toothpick around in the corner of his mouth. A hawkish smile eventually dawned on his face.

"Boss, I think I got just the thing. I just gotta get a couple of things from below."

"Below what?"

"Below deck, from the, ah, bedroom. Downstairs."

"Why didn't you say so?"

When dusk fell, instead of leaving for the Crab Man Marina, the *Easy Eight* stayed at her anchorage. Jimmy Glick, some items bundled under his arm, had Captain Shorter help him winch the ship's small dinghy down to the bay's surface. He lowered himself in, started the small outboard, and set off for the western shore of Ransom Island.

He beached the dinghy on a small curve of beach, tied its painter to a mangrove, and began to make his way across the narrow neck of the island toward the bait shop a few hundred yards away. A lonely mercury vapor light shed a yellow glow over the gas pump, fish cleaning tables, and the pier with its small flock of skiffs bobbing on the nighttime tide.

He paused out of sight, with just enough backwash from the light to let him see what he was doing, and unrolled his bundle—a sheet and a pillowcase from one of the stateroom bunks, and the boat's fish billy, a wooden bat shaped like an oversized policeman's nightstick. He reached into his pocket and flicked open a switchblade knife and set to work.

Primo had expressly warned Jimmy Glick to stay incognito. If he'd been a Yankee thug up north, he might have chosen to wear a ski mask or balaclava hood. But where the fuck were you gonna find a ski mask in Texas in June?

Then it came to him—who wears masks in Texas except the Lone Ranger and the Ku Klux Klan? Jimmy Glick was no fan of the marauding sheet-heads that infested East and South Texas—they were mostly white trash who preyed on those lower on the social food chain to distract themselves from their own ignorance and poverty. But tonight they'd come in handy.

Glick cut a hole in the sheet and slipped it over his head. He took off his belt and fastened it around the sheet at his waist to gather it in. He carved two rough eyeholes in the pillowcase and slipped it over his head.

The total effect was less nightriding white supremacist and more Casper the Friendly Ghost, but in the shadows cast by the bait shop building, it would do. He would have dearly loved a smoke, but he made himself be patient. Surely, this wouldn't take long.

Surely, it didn't. After Gilbert closed down the kitchen, he walked Sally to the cabin and grabbed a book to take back to the bait shop. Sally had informed him that tonight was "beauty night," and unless he wanted to help her with the application of various hair conditioning products, cold creams, and nail polishes that Darla had given her, he might as well call it a night.

He had declined Rupert's offer to watch TV at the Big House with him and Dubber's boys (even though *Sky King* and *I Love Lucy* were on) and decided he'd turn in early. He was on his way back to his bachelor's cot, thinking about the grocery list for tomorrow's meals, when somebody emerged from the shadows and pile-drove his head halfway to Mustang Island.

It took just eight seconds for Jimmy Glick to ring the fish billy off the side of Gilberto's head, sucker-punch him in the kidneys, jam the end of the club into his solar plexus, and bring the club down again across his kneecaps. He rattled his noggin once more for good measure. Once Gilbert was down, Glick set about kicking a few of his ribs loose.

Gilbert never quite lost consciousness, which was too bad for him. Every blow was a fresh explosion of agony.

At last it ceased. Someone rolled him over. Through blurry eyes, he saw . . . what? A ghost? No, a pointed hood, a white costume. He vaguely recalled the Klan note he'd found tacked to his cabin door a few days ago.

Jimmy Glick reached down and grabbed a handful of blood-soaked hair and jerked Gilbert's head upright.

"*No mas*, greaser," he growled in a guttural voice. "You keep away from that white woman, get my drift? We find out you're sniffing around her any more, and we'll hang your wetback ass."

Those were the last words he heard. Jimmy Glick pulled his lead-weighted sap out of his hip pocket and popped Gilbert expertly behind the ear.

Well, that was diverting, thought Glick as he made his way back to the dinghy. *Wonder if any of the West Coast ballgames are on the radio?*

Back at the beach, Jimmy wadded up his Klansman costume and tossed it into the dinghy, and then pushed the boat into the shallows and hopped aboard.

No one saw him leave except Barefoot Nelson, who was one cove over, seining by the light of the moon for baitfish.

———

CHAPTER 25

A little later, Gilbert's eyes fluttered open to see four young faces staring into his. He wondered for a moment if they were cherubs—the second order of angels, *kerubhim* in Hebrew. But no, they didn't look like those chubby infants the Renaissance painters were so fond of. And their breath smelled like Grape Nehi. Gilbert struggled to unscramble his thoughts.

He blinked his eyes—or eye, as the other seemed to be sealed shut, and the four blurry figures resolved into two. He rolled over and threw up in a patch of sea oats. As he shifted, his broken ribs announced their presence and made the pain in his head seem like a mother's kiss.

"Gilbert, why are you sleeping on the ground?" said a young voice.

"Are you camping out?" said another.

The Sweetwater boys squatted beside their bunkmate, not sure what to do. Their dog sat alongside them, panting contentedly. When Gilbert was on the verge of passing out again, Johnny Sweetwater poked him in the ribs to wake him.

He woke up, alright. *"Puta madre!"* he yelped.

The boys' eyes widened. "I know some dirty words, too," Charlie volunteered.

"Do you need help, Gilbert?" asked Johnny.

Gilbert nodded. "Please." They eased him inside and over to his cot where he sat down heavily. "Go get Rupert."

Rupert didn't say a word as he loaded his cook into the station wagon and rumbled into town. Sally insisted on coming along, as did Zach. Rupert's brothers showed up at the emergency room clinic shortly after.

Two hours later, the Aransas Pass ER doctor had patched Gilbert's head and X-rayed his broken bones. He fastened clips to the end of a long elastic bandage that wrapped around his torso.

"This will help the pain a little bit," said the doc, tucking a prescription into Gilbert's shirt pocket and shaking two blue pills into his hand. "But it won't speed up the healing. You're going to be mighty tender for a a couple of weeks."

"What about that gash and those lumps on his head?" asked Rupert.

The doctor shrugged. "The stitches can come out next week. Regarding the concussion, not too much I can do about that. He'll have a hell of a headache."

"Take two aspirin and call you in the morning, is that it?" asked Noble.

"Best I can do."

"When I got knocked out, I never took nothing for it," said Flavius. He considered himself an expert on the subject. In his amateur boxing career, he had been on the giving, and sometimes the receiving, end of multiple concussions.

"And look what it did for you, Einstein," said Noble.

Flavius shoved past the doctor and planted himself in front of Noble, glaring up at him. The galling fact that somebody had come onto *their* island and roughed up *their* cook had put him in fighting mode, and he was ready to release some steam.

Rupert pried the brothers apart. "Easy, boys. Let's take Gilbert back to the house, before the doc has to stitch up somebody else."

The doctor, a third year resident on loan from Waco, was glad to see the rowdy entourage leave. He hated emergency room duty, especially in coarse little harbor towns like this one. Especially on weekends. Seemed like somebody was getting beat, stabbed, shot, gaffed, or drowned almost every hour. The Mexican kid he'd just patched up had been preceded by two rambunctious sailors who had beaten each other senseless over a dice game, and before that, a commercial fisherman who had staggered into the clinic holding his guts in his hands after a knife fight at Conn Brown Harbor. And it wasn't even midnight yet.

They loaded Gilbert into Rupert's wagon for the short trip back to Ransom Island; Noble and Flavius followed in their cars. Once there, Sally insisted they take him to his own cabin and put him in his own bed. "I'll take care of him tonight," she told them.

After the attack, the Sweetwater brothers discussed ways and means to deal with the peckerwood nightriding sonsofbitches who had busted up their friend. In the absence of any specific plan other than calling Sheriff Burton, Rupert went to bed and Noble and Flavius returned to their homes in town.

Sally tended to her patient and worried about a different adversary, one much more dangerous than anyone from the local KKK.

"Get my drift?" Gilbert's assailant had warned him. (She'd pressed Gilbert to repeat every word the attacker had said.) She knew a man who liked to use that phrase. She'd heard him say it a hundred times when she was a little girl. It was the same man who liked to kick in ribs and crack skulls with a blackjack he carried in his back pocket.

But how did Jimmy Glick know about her relationship with Gilbert? The only people who might have known were Zach, Rupert, and Darla. And times being what they were, she thought she'd been extra careful not to show affection for her lover in public. Not that it mattered now. What mattered now was that they'd found her. Again. And Gilbert had paid the price. Her growing feelings for him compounded the guilt she felt.

As dawn neared, she arrived at a decision—Gilbert and the others wouldn't be safe until she left the island, until she left Gilbert. There wasn't any way around it. She'd wait until he woke up to tell him goodbye. She owed him that, at least.

—

The first thing Gilbert saw the next morning was Sally sleeping in the chair beside him, her chin drooping, almost touching her chest. The second thing he saw was the cheap cardboard suitcase she'd recently picked up in town, no doubt containing the meager wardrobe she'd assembled. The clothes she'd borrowed from Darla sat neatly folded on top.

"You going somewhere?" he asked.

Sally shook herself awake. "Good morning. How are you feeling?"

"I'll live. What's with the suitcase?

"I can't stay here any longer, Gilbert. It's not safe."

"Don't worry about them. They're assholes, but they wouldn't hurt a woman."

"No, I mean it's not safe for you."

"They're just trying to scare me. What was it you said? 'Never let people like that get to you'?"

Sally looked away. "You don't know what kind of people they are, how far they'll go."

"Sure I do. I've had to deal with them all my life. As a matter of fact, I had a run-in with a group only a few days ago. Made them look pretty foolish, too. I expect that last night they were just looking for some payback."

She didn't think she could feel any guiltier. He'd been beaten half to death and didn't even know why. She'd decided it was better he kept thinking it was a brown and white problem, and not a much more complicated *family* problem. She would have to live with that, but Gilbert shouldn't have to.

"Sorry, Gilberto, but I've got to skate. Maybe one day I'll tell you why." She grabbed the handle of her suitcase and came around to kiss him.

Gilbert tried to sit up and winced. "Wait. I want you to stay." But after she kissed him she was already heading for the door. "Sally, damn it. Please stop."

The door closed behind her and Gilbert scooted up into a sitting position and then held his breath while he swung his legs over the bed. What had the doctor told him? That his ribs might be "tender" for a week or so? *Christ*, it felt like someone was trying to yank them off his skeleton. Now if he could just figure out a way to get his pants on.

Gilbert heard voices and then a moment later the door swung open and Zachariah's greying head appeared.

"How we doin' this morning, Gilbert?"

"Not so good, Zach." Beads of sweat covered his forehead from the pain and effort it took to bend over and pick up his pants. "Help me get dressed."

"Settle down, son. I saw that gal toting her grip and heading up to the Big House. Probably to say goodbye to Darla and Rupert. If she's leaving, you're in no shape to catch her."

"I gotta try." He stood up and had to grab onto Zach to keep from falling down.

Zach eased Gilbert back into the bed. "I know all I need to know about horses and cattle," he said. "The only thing I've ever learned about a woman is, they have their reasons."

Gilbert frowned. Reasons be damned. She didn't have the *right* to run off, just like that, without an explanation. Did she? Anyway, like Zach said, at this moment he was dizzy, nauseated, and too weak to catch his own shadow. He closed his eyes and let himself be guided down onto the bed.

"How 'bout you lemme boil up some coffee for you?"

Gilbert rested against the headboard and watched his friend prepare the coffee—cowboy coffee, he called it—a handful of grind into a pot of water: one boil for a normal cup, two boils for a strong cup, and three boils for a brew that would reanimate the dead.

"A broom-tail mare kicked me in the ribs one time," said Zachariah. "And I ain't ashamed to say it made me cry like a little girl." He stood over the pot and waited for the water to heat up.

"Seems like some horses know 'zactly how to hurt a man. Like they *aiming* for your ribs, or your knees, sometimes your noggin. Kinda like that man that worked you over last night."

After the coffee boiled a second time, Zach turned off the gas, let the grounds settle to the bottom, and then poured a cup for himself and one for Gilbert.

"Don't seem like that tin-horn lot we ran into over at Big Todd's would know so much about how to hurt a man."

Gilbert agreed, glad to fret about something besides Sally walking out the door. "The fellow seemed to have had some practice, I'll give you that." He had begun to doubt the Klan story as he replayed the attack in his head. And what was it Sally had just said? *You don't know what kind of people they are.* Perhaps it wasn't the moronic rednecks he'd met behind the building supply store. "Could be they hired a professional."

"Could be, but it seems like a lot of trouble to go to—"

"For a Mexican cook and a runaway white girl?"

Zach shrugged in response. The two men sat and pondered for a few minutes.

Zach topped off Gilbert's coffee cup and sat in a dinette chair. "You can go away with her, you know. I imagine folks would stop chasing if you took her far enough away . . . say, Old Mexico."

"I've lived there before, Zach. It's not exactly the land of opportunity."

"Yeah, not like this here island. Here, we're covered up with opportunity."

They laughed, Gilbert grimacing as the ends of his ribs grated against each other.

"Hell," said Zach. "Rupert might sell this paradise out from under us, anyhow."

They sat together and drank their coffee in silence, lost in their own thoughts. A few minutes later, Zach stood up and dumped the dregs of his cup into the sink. "I'll cover for you in the kitchen today, Gil."

At the door, Zachariah paused, looking at Gilbert as if he were deciding whether to speak again.

"You got something else on your mind, Zach?"

"Long time ago," Zach began, "I had me a gal. Light brown skin, hazel eyes—real pretty. Worked in the kitchen up at the Matagorda ranch headquarters." Zach looked down and smiled to himself, remembering her face.

"But the ranch owner's wife thought she was a mite *too* pretty. I think she was worried about her own man, to tell you the truth. But that gal . . . she only had eyes for me, and me likewise.

"Anyway, the boss's wife sent her packing and off she went, and instead of going with her, I just sat there on my horse and watched the jitney take her to the ferry." He shook his head wistfully, still looking down. "Not a day goes by that I don't regret it."

Zach pushed open the screen and walked outside without saying goodbye.

———

CHAPTER 26

At the Big House, Darla opened the door and found Sally standing on the porch carrying a traveling bag, an armload of borrowed clothes, and a woebegone expression.

"I came to return your things."

"So I see. Come into this house, please." She took the clothes and the bag and escorted Sally to the kitchen table. It was early in the day for Darla, and the kitchen was still dark.

"Sit here, darlin', while I get my robe. I was just fixing to have my coffee." She swished away in silk slippers and a lacy pink gown.

"Where's Rupert?" asked Sally.

"Already at the boathouse," Darla answered over her shoulder.

She returned and opened the venetian blinds and then pulled some cups from the cupboard. "How is our Mr. Ruiz feeling today?"

"He's hurting, but he'll be alright. I don't think he'll be able to work the kitchen today."

"Somebody will cover for him," she said with a flick of her wrist. "Let Rupert figure it out." She poured two cups of coffee and brought them to the table. "I'm guessing you have other plans?"

Sally felt her eyes tearing up. "He got hurt because of me, Darla, and I don't want anything else to happen to him, or to any of y'all.

I mean, everyone's been so wonderful to me these last three weeks, but . . . I think it's time for me to go."

Darla sighed. She liked Sally. And it was nice to have another woman living on the island, especially someone so smart and pretty. Having another woman helped humanize the man-apes of the open-air Ransom Island Zoo. And it gave her someone to talk girl talk with. So what if she had fallen for a Mexican? It was unusual for the time, sure, but Gilbert seemed quite fond of her. And everyone liked a happy cook.

"My opinion? I don't think they'll be back, whoever they were. They just wanted to scare poor Gilbert. You two will just have to be more . . . discreet, that's all."

Sally was shaking her head. "I can't take that chance." *Tell her,* said the voice in her head. *They deserve to know.* But the words backed up in her throat. It was like Jimmy Glick and the Ginestras were in the room, staring down at her.

"Listen, honey. I've talked to Rupert. While Gilbert is healing up in the cabin, we want you to stay in the Big House for a couple of days. You'll have your own bedroom and bathroom."

"But they *know* I'm here. And they know he's here, too."

"So what? It sounds like they don't care that you and Gilbert are on the island together. They just care if, you know . . . ."

"I thought we were being careful," Sally murmured.

"Someone always finds out, honey. Besides, you know what they say, you can't choose who you love." Darla reached across the table and put her hand on Sally's, wondering if she should go on. *Who am I to be giving advice about romance?* she thought wryly. She lit her first cigarette of the day and decided to continue. "And believe me, I know. That little rascal Cupid put two arrows in my heart."

Sally regarded Darla with a questioning look.

"Maybe you heard that Red Burton and I have a little bit of a history. Did you know we almost got hitched a few years back?"

Sally shook her head. "I heard that you dated."

"It was more than that. He asked me to marry him. Before he went into the service. And the thing of it is, those old feelings never quite went away, for me at least." Darla took a puff on her cigarette and watched Sally's expression, which registered only mild surprise. "Don't tell me you haven't suspected for a while. You don't miss much, I've noticed. But that's okay. I've been dying to talk about this with somebody."

"But you still love Rupert, don't you?"

Darla went and grabbed the coffee pot to warm their cups. "Yeah, dang it, I do. And sometimes I wish I didn't. It would be so much easier to leave him if I didn't. How can you not love that big galoot?"

Sally smiled in agreement.

"Anyway," Darla continued. "Everything's going to change if Rupert and his brothers sell this place."

Sally sat up straight. "Sell it to who?" Darla belatedly realized she might have betrayed a confidence. But she plunged ahead. Girl talk.

"Some investors out of Galveston. They've apparently made us an offer we'd be crazy not to take." Darla shrugged and then frowned. "Problem is, my husband might be crazy enough to say no."

"What do you know about these investors, Darla?"

"Hardly anything, but who cares? I'm so ready to move off this scrubby little island."

"When is all this supposed to happen?"

"Who knows if it even will, sweetie. Anyway, nothing's going to happen until the big show next week, that's for sure.

The entire kaleidoscope of Darla's cosmos revolved around the Ellington band's performance at Shady's. As far as she was concerned, the world divided into B.D. (Before Duke) and A.D. (After Duke). She had been working hard on the songs she would sing before the headliner took the stage, and had been delighted to learn that the house band she'd sung with at the USO Club was still playing together. She'd scheduled a rehearsal with them straight away.

Darla reached over and grabbed Sally above the elbow. If she was going to become a star, she needed witnesses. "Stay for the show, Sally. I could really use your help, and your support. This thing with Gilbert, it'll blow over in a few days. In a week you'll wonder why you were thinking about leaving in the first place."

Sally had to admit Darla made sense, even in ways she didn't realize. Primo obviously knew where she was and what she was doing. If her "father" had wanted her home, Jimmy Glick would have come calling a lot earlier, and not under a bedsheet, either. For some reason, Primo was keeping him on a short leash.

And Sally wasn't keen on running again, either, drifting from job to job, bar to bar, in a dozen different towns. The very thought left her numb with fatigue. Of course, if she stayed, she couldn't be with him anymore—that would be the hardest part. Paradoxically, packing her pitiful belongings to leave and turning her back on him made her realize at last how much she loved him. But like Darla said, maybe the thing would just blow over in a few days.

"I don't know, Darla."

"You'll be fine, hon. And if it'll make you feel any safer, I'll loan you a little .22 pistol that Noble gave me for protection. He said it was a training pistol the WACs used in the war."

Darla left the room and came back with the little grey pocket pistol. "I've never shot it before; in fact, I'd forgotten about it until just a minute ago. But Noble assured me it works."

She pushed the pistol across the table and Sally looked at it skeptically. "Where do I keep it?"

Darla laughed. "That's the *real* problem, isn't it? The fashionable handbags are so small and delicate these days. I hardly have room for my lipstick, face powder, car keys, and wallet."

Sally delicately picked up the pistol and examined it.

"Careful, honey. It's loaded."

Sally's eyes widened and she set the gun on the table. "Well, gee, thanks, Darla. If it's good enough for the WACS, I guess it's good enough for me."

CHAPTER 27

Red Burton, Jr. stuck his head out of his office door and growled at his secretary, the unflappable Rosie Pacheco. "The next pain-in-the-ass know-it-all who comes in here and tries to tell me my business is gonna exit through the goddamn window!" The sheriff's office window had metal bars across it, but given Red's mood, Rosie declined to point this out.

"Did you just call the mayor a pain-in-the-ass, Sheriff?" Rosie asked mildly. Hizzonor had just vacated the premises moments earlier.

"Damn straight."

"I thought you liked the man."

Red walked to the water cooler and filled up his Grand Prize beer mug. He hated those little pointy-ended paper cups. He swallowed and shrugged. "Hell, he's alright for a damn politico. But just because he's catching heat from the City Council, the Baptists, the Chamber of Commerce, the Knights of Pythias, and every dingbat on the street about this Duke Ellington thing, it doesn't mean he can unload it all on me. He sat there and cited every damn city statute he could dig up about separate accommodations, public safety, and segregation in commercial establishments and public carriers. Like I don't know the laws I'm supposed to be enforcing."

And now he's venting at me, because I'm the next one down the totem pole, Rosie thought. *Dios mio, this job sometimes . . . .*

"Well, what are you going to do?" she asked. "There was almost a race riot two years ago when you removed the sawhorses between the white and colored sections on Aransas Beach. And that was just a patch of sand."

Red sat down and kicked his cowboy boots up on Rosie's desk—a habit of his that she hated.

"Ah, hell, I expect I'll do my best to keep the peace. Most of the Negroes who are gonna go to this dance are just hard-working local folks. They deserve a chance to cut loose after a long week, just like we do. But I don't know how I feel about the races mixing up. It's not how I grew up. Especially when you add in liquor. It sounds like a recipe for trouble."

Rosie listened patiently. Her boss had another habit of thinking aloud, which she also hated. She'd known he was going to let the dance take place before he did, and she knew she'd have to hear him stomp around the office, ranting and raving until he vented his frustrations. She decided not to mention that she, and just about everyone she knew, was planning on being at Duke Ellington's show. She wouldn't miss it for the world.

"Speaking of Ransom Island, did you see the paper this morning?" asked Rosie, gesturing to the copy of the *Aransas Pass Progress* that lay on the small office couch.

Red slammed his feet down. "That's another goddamn thing! Rupert Sweetwater and his idiot brothers are playing their little shell game out on that glorified oyster reef of theirs, acting like they're the goddamn Cosa Nostra! Rupe's being too smart for his own good if you ask me. I ought to bust his ass just for being such a pain in mine. And, yes, to answer your question, I did see the paper. Thanks for asking."

Specifically, Red had seen the lead editorial. J. "Mule" Moncrief was on his soapbox again, this time railing against all the supposed varieties of sin rumored to be transpiring on Ransom Island, right under the nose of the sheriff, that being Red Burton, Jr.

Bootleg booze! Hot dice games! Roulette wheels! Slot machines! ("Nickel-gulping monsters!"). It was a stain on the community, a threat to The Youth. Somebody ought to put a stop to it. What was this, Galveston?

No one had to wonder where J. Mule Moncrieff stood on gambling in San Patricio County—he was agin' it.

—

At the Sea-Aire Motel, where they headquartered for the duration of their undercover work, Willie Dawes and Cliff Hollenbeck ("Wayne" and "Kent" as far as anyone in Aransas Pass or on Ransom Island were concerned) had also seen the paper and were tickled pink. This case was heating up in a big way. This was the way to rise up the ranks of the CID.

The way they liked to spin it in their own minds, they had followed the Ginestras' trail south from Galveston and discovered they were setting up a local franchise. Then through dogged persistence and daring clandestine investigation, they were able to "bust it up," as their boss liked to phrase it. Maybe the story wasn't as clear-cut as that, but Will Wilson, and that Texas Ranger, Gonzalez, ought to be impressed all the same.

—

Out on Ransom Island, the Sweetwater brothers ignored the hubbub in town. Along with Gilbert, Zach, Darla, and Sally, they worked day and night to transform the Shady Boat and Leisure Club into something fit for the likes of Duke Ellington. They had their work cut out for them.

Even under the best of circumstances, Shady's looked like what it was—a coastal beer joint, with no aspirations to be mistaken for the bar at the Waldorf Astoria. There was nothing pretentious about it, which suited everyone (except Darla) just fine. But that didn't stop them from painting, scraping, scrubbing, straightening, freshening, doing and re-doing until their backs ached and their hands were raw.

The waxed longleaf pine floor gleamed a warm, mellow glow and hurricane lamps swung from the rafters to provide soft and flattering illumination. The battered linoleum-topped tables were covered in crisp white tablecloths and the rented cutlery gleamed. Bamboo-and-wicker screens were placed against the walls to gave the place a luau/island resort/tropical feel (that was Sally's idea). The bar was polished up slicker than a buttered cat and even the neon beer sign lights had been taken down, dusted, and polished.

Rupert and Zach had knocked together a stage out of old dock pilings and salvaged timber. Sally and Gilbert painted it white and strung small white Christmas lights around the edges. Swags of dark material—drapes from Rupert and Darla's living room—hung behind the stage for a theatrical effect.

"Shit," said Noble, leaning back against the bar on his elbows and looking out at the transformed fish camp beerhall, "I almost expect to see ol' Errol Flynn and Rita Hayworth come walkin' through the screen door."

"I'd rather see Dorothy Dandridge myself, but it do look good for a fact," said Zach. Zachariah became a smitten cowboy after he saw a picture of the beautiful movie star on the cover of one of Darla's magazines.

Rupert bought a round of beers for the gang and, under Darla's watchful eye, made sure they placed the bottles squarely on little cardboard coasters.

"Waddaya think, Sally?" asked Gilbert.

"I didn't know I'd signed on for the Labors of Hercules when I washed up here," she said wearily.

"No stables, lucky for you."

"Why would we want stables?" asked Flavius. "We're in the fish camp business, not the dude ranch business. We don't even have any horses."

"It's a classical reference," said Gilbert. "You oughta appreciate that."

Flavius's eyes squinted as he tried to discern if Gilbert was making fun of him in some roundabout fashion. Then he shrugged and took a pull on his beer. "All we got around here is horse's asses."

"And that's the half-assed truth," said Rupert as he looked around proudly. "Boys and girls, I think it's smooth sailing from here on."

CHAPTER 28

Wedge, brace, lash tight with wire.

Leroy Stuckey's tongue protruded from the corner of his mouth, as it always did when he concentrated on an important task. And what could be more important than sabotage? It was dangerous work he was doing, he told himself. Soldier's work. A patriot's work. The Lord's work, even.

At five in the morning, the air was cool under the Ransom Island Bridge. Reflections from channel buoy lights provided scant illumination—probably too scant for Leroy to be handling the dynamite sticks he had stolen from a seismic service trailer the week before. Awkwardly straddling a cross-timber, he reminded himself to focus on the task at hand, but soon his mind wandered again.

Leroy pictured himself as Gary Cooper in that war movie he'd seen at the Rialto Theater in Aransas Pass. *What was it called?* For Whom the Bell Tolls, *that was it.* He remembered there was some pointless dialogue in the movie and a really boring love story, but the action sequences were terrific—Coop and his Spanish buddies kicking the shit out of the Communists, or whoever the bad guys were, blowing up that bridge at the end of the movie and sending the enemy tanks plunging into the river below.

Wedge, brace, lash tight with wire.

Leroy tried to recall how Coop had strapped the dynamite sticks to the bridge in the movie. He thought he was doing it the right way, except, unlike the movie, he didn't have grenades to activate the dynamite. But a good saboteur has to improvise, he told himself, and without the benefit of blasting caps or a long fuse, he'd happened upon a solution at Super Dave's fireworks stand on Highway 35. He'd selected three-dozen M-80 firecrackers and a sack of Big Giant fuses to detonate his explosives. *I'll show you some fireworks, Super Dave*, he thought.

At the target site, he tied a cluster of M-80s to the dynamite sticks, and then connected the packets with long spliced-together fuses he'd assembled on the kitchen table in his house. The bundles of explosives were tucked under the wooden bridge girders about thirty yards from the shore of Aransas Pass—right under the bridge hump, and right after the stupid little check station Shady's had constructed to screen visitors to the island.

During his reconnoitering, Leroy had become convinced there were other shenanigans taking place on the island besides the illegal Fourth of July dance. But these things didn't interest Leroy. His current mission was the only thing that counted. The bridge had to go, or it would only be a matter of time before the island was swarming with Negroes.

Well, not on my watch, he told himself. *Not after the Righteous Hand of Justice sets things straight.* Leroy continued working, steadily, carefully, imagining himself a cool demolitions man—a guerilla fighter behind enemy lines—methodically pulling the weapons of destruction out of his shoulder satchel and fastening them to the bridge.

Wedge, brace, lash tight with wire. It wouldn't be long now.

A hundred yards up the Ransom Island Channel, Gustav Brauer guided his eighteen-foot fishing boat slowly through the water, the inboard motor producing a gentle wake. Seated beside him in the open cockpit was Captain Quincy, encased in an oversized merchant marine life vest, the four straps buckled so tight he could scarcely breathe. The Captain sat stiffly in the pedestal mount seat, his hands gripping the console.

It was a momentous excursion for both fishermen because the Captain was taking his very first motorboat ride—no small thing for a man with aquaphobia. He had consented to the trip after months of gentle coaxing from Gus, and after countless promises that their fishing prospects would expand dramatically once the Captain conquered his fear of deep water. (Deep water, in the Captain's mind, being anything over a depth of five feet.)

Today, they were on their way to a prime spot near Redfish Cut, where the fishing, Gus promised, would be spectacular. Captain Quincy did have his conditions, however. He insisted on wearing a proper flotation vest at all times, and he demanded assurance that they would anchor over water not to exceed waist-deep once they arrived at their destination.

"You are comfortable, Captain?" asked Gustav.

"Sure," the Captain wheezed. In the dim morning light, he resembled an orange Galapagos tortoise seated upright in the chair.

"Soon we arrive. I see the bridge ahead."

Leroy Stuckey saw the lights of the approaching boat and cursed. The explosives had been wedged and secured, the long fuses had been played out along the girders, and all Leroy had to do was light the fire. He twirled a lit punk between his fingers, trying to decide if the fuses would reach the dynamite before the boat reached the bridge.

Too close, he thought. *What if there are white men in that boat?*

Sitting astride a thick timber, his legs dangling beneath him, he waited impatiently for the boat to pass. *Could they possibly go any slower?* He was staring down at the water when he suddenly realized it was getting light enough for them to see him if they happened to look up. He needed to conceal himself better.

Leroy leaned forward on the wooden beam and pulled up his legs. As he maneuvered onto his belly, the gunnysack slipped off his shoulder and he almost lost it, grabbing the strap right before it dropped into the channel. Incriminating evidence was in that bag: a spool of wire, a big handful of leftover M-80s, and unused coils of fuse. Not to mention that STUCKEY'S GARAGE was printed in bold letters on both sides of the sack.

Be smart, Leroy reminded himself. *And be careful!* He glanced down to make sure the punk was still lit. But where was it? *Well, hell.* He must have dropped it. No matter, another punk and a book of matches was somewhere in the satchel. Once the boat passed he'd dig them out, light the fuse and blow the bridge to smithereens. *Yes, Mr. Rupert sumbitch Sweetwater, and Mr. Duke uppity Ellington, in a couple of minutes the earth is most definitely going to move for you.*

The boat approached and the sound of the engine echoed off the underside of the bridge.

Later, Gustav Brauer remembered looking up and wondering why sparks were spraying out from the bridge substructure. Afterwards, if Gus could have asked (he couldn't) and if Leroy would have answered (he wouldn't), Leroy would have told him that his still-smoldering punk didn't drop into the goddamn water, but instead dropped into the goddamn gunnysack. He would have said that when the punk lit the goddamn M-80 fuses, his first thought was that he'd disturbed a rattlesnake nesting in the bridge supports. And when he realized the sound was coming from his bag, he unslung the burden and placed it on the goddamn beam to examine the source of the noise.

The bag of M-80s exploded with such force that Leroy's hand was cleanly severed from his wrist. Gustav could have told Leroy that he actually saw the hand sailing through the air and landing on a sandy bank near the bridge abutment. He could have told him that a flock of seagulls, ever alert for scraps of food, had swooped down and plucked the hand from the sand, squawking and fighting for it as they flapped across the channel toward Ransom Island.

But Gustav and Leroy would never have the opportunity to compare notes. It would be left to Captain Quincy to recount what happened next. After the blast, while Gus was watching Leroy's Righteous Hand of Justice sail through the air, Captain Quincy noticed sparks sizzling down a long fuse toward an unknown destination.

"Hey, Gus?" he remembered saying.

The next explosion was much bigger than the first one. Gus and Captain Quincy crouched down instinctively, shielding their faces from the blast. Splinters, fragments, and hardware rained down from the bridge. Captain Quincy fell to the deck, trying (like a turtle) to retract into his jumbo life jacket. Gustav Brauer was more exposed and not so lucky. A chunk of airborne planking dropped from the sky and landed squarely on his thick German skull. He slumped in his seat.

The third phase of destruction occurred when several massive beams, their bolted joints weakened by the blast, sheared lose and fell into the channel. One creosoted pine girder fell across the fishing boat amidships, breaking the boat in half and launching an unconscious Gus Brauer high into the air. He splashed into the channel fifteen feet from the boat.

When Captain Quincy realized what had happened, he leapt into the water, not with a panicked, abandon-ship reaction, but with a single-minded mission to rescue his friend. He swam toward the spot where he'd seen Gus hit the water and looked around purposefully, calling his name. Without thinking, he shucked his over-buoyant life vest and disappeared under the surface.

Twelve feet. That's how deep Gus said the channel was. Captain Quincy had pushed that number out of his head up until the explosion, but now he used the figure, along with the estimated speed and trajectory of the flying body, the resistance of the water, and the probable strength of the current, to determine the location of his fallen comrade. His gunnery training kicked in and he performed the calculations almost instinctively.

Groping around in the dark water he felt something insubstantial brush across his forearm. When he probed the water with his hand, he grabbed a floating shirttail and pulled it toward him. The Captain could see Gustav's face, inches from his own. Strong kicks to reach the surface, a sixty-foot swim to the bank, mouth-to-mouth, coughing, the expulsion of copious amounts of salt water from Gus's lungs. An eye blinked open.

"*Danke, Kapitän,*" muttered the German.

His eyes closed again and Captain Quincy hoisted his friend over his shoulder and began carrying him toward the lights of Aransas Pass.

CHAPTER 29

Rupert edged to the end of a jagged bridge timber and peered down into the bay. Zach and Gilbert stood a few steps behind and were also looking down at the water.

"Watch it there, Rupe," cautioned Red Burton from across the ten-foot gap. "You don't know how stable that platform is. It's liable to give out with you standing on it."

The sheriff's deputy and a uniformed police officer stood at Red's shoulder, craning their heads to study the damage wrought to the Ransom Island Bridge. Nobody could quite believe the hole was there, Rupert least of all. He had come running when he heard the explosion shortly before dawn, as had Zach and Gilbert. Red had received a phone call from the police station not five minutes after the blast and drove over as fast as he could.

"Anybody have an idea what happened here?" asked the sheriff. The sun had risen behind a low shelf of clouds whose tops were presently rimmed in scarlet.

Rupert shook his head and began tugging at his earlobe. "Hell, no."

The two Sweetwater boys padded up on bare feet. They were shirtless and wearing pajama bottoms printed with cowboys and Indians. They examined the damage wide-eyed.

Next, a car screeched to a stop at the mainland bridge entrance and Noble and Flavius sprinted toward the congregation. "Holy shit," said Flavius, when he reached the gap. "Somebody blew up our bridge!"

"Holy shit," repeated young Charlie Sweetwater, still taking in the scene. Johnny elbowed his little brother in the shoulder.

"Why would somebody blow up our bridge?" continued Flavius, talking more to himself than to anyone else.

Red removed his hat and sighed. "I told you you were asking for trouble, Rupert."

Rupert looked sharply at the sheriff. "You still don't know the why, do you, Red?"

"No, I don't. But can you give me another reason why someone would do this? Other than to stop people from coming onto your island?"

Rupert didn't answer and went back to tugging at this earlobe.

"You're gonna have to cancel the show," said Red.

"The hell I will."

Red looked at Rupert with disbelief. "No? How are you going to transport almost a thousand people on and off your island without a bridge?"

"We'll repair the bridge," said Rupert.

"You're going to repair this? In one day?"

"We have today, tonight and part of tomorrow to get it done."

Red shook his head. "You're crazy."

Noble cleared his throat. "Brother, remember Flap Jackson from Corpus? Comes in for a bite now and again?" Rupert nodded distractedly and Noble continued. "He did lots of work on the Padre Island Causeway a couple of years back. Last month he was over here crying in his beer about how he'd geared up with manpower and equipment for that harbor bridge project over in Corpus and then found out construction would be delayed another two years. Some kind of snafu with the contract. I betcha he might be happy to put some of those assets to work."

Rupert's face brightened. "Yeah, he sure might."

Red Burton swore under his breath. "Boys, I won't allow a bicycle on this bridge if I don't think it's safe."

"It'll be safe," said Noble confidently. "Flap's a real pro."

The sheriff continued to shake his head. "I don't like it."

"Don't like what, Red?" asked Rupert. "Our bridge plan, or the fact that we're still going to have this show?"

"I don't like either," he snapped. "Goddammit, Rupert. Somebody went to a lot of trouble to blow up this bridge, and yes, I think it's because they want to stop you from having an integrated show. If I'm right, and if you somehow manage to fix the bridge in time to get all those people onto the island, I'm going to have a serious security problem to worry about."

"Yeah? Well, here's what *I've* got to worry about: I have to figure out how to repair a broken bridge in thirty-six hours, prepare my joint for the biggest show we've ever had, coordinate transportation, parking, booze, and ticket sales for a shit-load of people, and while I'm at it, I've promised the most famous orchestra in America that I'll take them tarpon fishing after the show."

"You also promised them gourmet meals from our kitchen, Rupert," said Gilbert.

Rupert looked to the heavens. "Yeah, that too, Gilbert."

"I've got a hundred fifty T-bones and four hundred cases of beer scheduled for delivery this afternoon," Gilbert continued, "but I'm sure Gus Brauer will be willing to help me ferry the items over in his boat."

"I'll help you tote that stuff up to the kitchen, Gil," offered Zach.

The police officer whispered something into the sheriff's ear and Red's eyes widened. "Uh, y'all might want to revise that last part. Gus is in the emergency clinic this morning with a concussion and a broken shoulder. Apparently he and Captain Quincy were underneath the bridge when it blew."

Flavius whistled. "Son-of-a-bitch!"

"Is he gonna be alright?" asked Gilbert.

The police office shrugged. "He's still in one piece, but his boat sure as hell ain't. You'll find what's left of it under there," he said, pointing at the water below.

There was a long pause until Rupert broke the silence. "Well, we're burning daylight, boys. Let's get to work. Noble, can you talk to Flap?"

"I'm on it," he answered.

"What do you want me to do, brother?" asked Flavius.

Rupert thought for a moment. "See if you can round-up some of the regulars to give us a hand today and tomorrow. Call Cecil Shoat and Giddyup. Captain Quincy, too if you can convince him to cross the bay in a boat. While you're at it, check on Gus and see if he's okay."

The sheriff instructed his deputy and the policemen to erect a road barrier at the mouth of the bridge. They trotted off obediently.

Gilbert and Zach headed toward the kitchen, the boys trailing behind like little soldiers.

That left Rupert and Red alone on the bridge, glowering at each other across the chasm. Finally Red sighed. "Damn it all, Rupe, I guess I'll call the police chiefs in Portland and Ingleside and see if they'll lend me some bodies to help keep the peace tomorrow."

"So you're gonna—?"

"*I'm* not gonna do anything," Red growled. "I'm sure it has not escaped your notice over the years that this pesthole of yours is about one good spit away from the county line. In fact, you could say Ransom Island is just about carved right down the middle."

"Yeah, okay, but—"

"Shut the hell up. For the next three days, I'm prepared to cede jurisdiction over the Shady Boat and Leisure Club to my esteemed colleague Sheriff Doheney, over in Aransas County. You and your dance hall are his problem now."

"But won't he just—"

"Abner Doheney is 72 years old, set to retire next year and doesn't have to stand for re-election. He's in a good position to tell anybody that don't like it to go piss up a rope. I'll talk to him when I get back to the office, but I don't see a problem. In fact, I think that old man would be tickled by the ruckus."

"Thanks, Red. I—"

Red held up his hand. "After this is over, you're gonna owe me one of them T-bones."

On the way to the Big House, Rupert ran into J.B. Leavitt, Duke Ellington's tenor sax man and Rupert's old buddy, who was leaning against the Shady Palm signpost, puffing on a Lucky Strike. Ellington's road manager had sent him ahead of the band to make sure everything was shaping up satisfactorily. After all, the whole excursion had been his idea from the beginning. He'd spent the night in one of the guest cabins near the boathouse.

"Morning, Rupe."

"Morning, J.B. You sleep okay last night?"

"Sure," he answered. "Until I heard the big boom."

Rupert paused. "Yeah, well, we got that under control. Just a little minor bridge damage to repair."

"Minor damage, huh?"

Rupert took a deep breath. For a moment he debated if he should hold out on his old friend, and not tell him about the sabotage and the threats that preceded it. But he was also well aware that Ellington and his party were coming largely on J.B.'s say-so, and it didn't seem right to keep it from him.

After Rupert explained the situation and what was being done about it, J.B. took a final drag off his cigarette and stubbed it out on the sign. "Well," he said lazily. "I'd say you've got lots of irons in the fire . . . I'll stay out of your way, but keep me posted, okay?"

"Y'all are gonna have a fine time, J.B. Don't you worry. It's just a minor calamity."

"Brother, what you call a calamity is just another day at the office for us. I been working for the man almost twenty years, and we've traveled more miles than Marco Polo, including all over Dixie. We've seen some seriously hillbilly bullshit, but dynamite is kind of upping the ante."

Rupert nodded grimly. "You, uh, gonna tell the boss about this?"

J.B. shrugged casually. "Oh, sure. We don't keep nothing from the man. I'm meeting their train tomorrow morning in Corpus. But I *do* need to tell him if anything more serious is comin' down the tracks. So, like I said, keep me posted."

"You've got my word on that, J.B."

—

Somehow, and against all odds, everything proceeded as planned that day. Noble was able to convince Flap to put his considerable bridge-building assets to work immediately. Flavius managed an eager, if unruly, group of Shady's regulars in the task of erecting ticket booths and signage for the parking areas. And Gilbert and Zach coordinated an armada of food, booze, and equipment shipments across the bay (many of the deliveries being carried out by Captain Quincy, who had successfully conquered his fear of eight-foot deep water). By nightfall, the old walk-in cooler was piled to the ceiling with enough booze to give the entire 101st Airborne a massive hangover.

After the hectic day, Rupert was dragging himself to bed when Red Burton called on the telephone.

"We've captured our bridge vandal, Rupert."

"That's good news, Sheriff. Who was it?"

"It was a local fellow, not very bright, trying to make a name for himself with the Klan big-shots in Houston. Thought that blowing up the bridge would be his claim to fame."

Rupert grunted. "He turn himself in?"

Red Burton chuckled softly. "Sort of. Barefoot Nelson's wife showed up at my office after dark and dropped a severed hand on my desk. Said the old man was fishing near Stedman Reef when he spotted it lying on an oyster bank, covered with fiddler crabs. I called the emergency clinic to see if anyone had come in earlier that day with their hand blown off, and found out that our master criminal had paid them a visit shortly after the blast. Gus Brauer was in the room right next to him, getting his shoulder set and his head stitched up.

"The emergency room doc said that after they patched up the one-handed man he insisted on going home, but he was kind enough to leave his name and address with the nurse when he was released. I paid him a visit. There was some leftover dynamite still sitting on his kitchen table. He said it was for the Fourth of July, can you believe that shit?"

"Was he working with anyone, Red?"

"Don't think so. When he finally fessed up, he admitted that he thought up the stunt all on his own, and I believed him. He's staying at Spohn Hospital in Corpus tonight, but he'll be transferred to county lock-up tomorrow morning."

"I appreciate the news."

"Sure thing. Say, Rupe? Is that bridge going to be ready by tomorrow afternoon?

"I think we're going to make it. Everything's falling into place."

"Well, I wish you luck. Me, too, for that matter."

"Red, I think tomorrow is going to be an unforgettable day."

CHAPTER 30

The next day certainly had an unforgettable start. An hour before dawn, a multi-cell cluster of thunderstorms formed suddenly in the Gulf and spawned a squall line that slammed into Ransom Island like Harvard's infamous flying wedge. Sixty-mile per hour winds blew down signs, submerged fishing skiffs, and tore screen doors off of cabins. J.B. Leavitt woke up to find his bed sheet blown off and pasted to the cabin wall like a playbill. Gilbert and Sally were already up and baking cobbler in the kitchen when the leading edge of the storm hit.

"My books!" shouted Gilbert, and the two of them rushed back to his cabin to shut the windows. They arrived soaked to the skin just as the power went out on the island.

They closed the windows and used bath towels to dry the books and furniture. "Now what do we do?" asked Gilbert.

From the darkness Sally replied. "What do you say we get out of these wet clothes?"

It took them less than ten seconds to strip naked and jump into bed together. The explosive release that followed was as spontaneous and unforeseen as the squall that had abruptly materialized offshore, surged for the better part of an hour, and dissipated as fast as it had formed. After making love, Sally and Gilbert lay together in bed, chatting happily, waiting for dawn.

Their relationship had been tense since the attack on Gilbert the week before. Sally had insisted they limit their contact to the kitchen, and even then had kept it strictly professional. Gilbert sensed her motives and didn't push her for more. He was simply glad she'd decided to stay. All week they had repressed their desires as best they could, but neither of them could deny their smoldering attraction for each other.

So when their impromptu cabin visit presented them with the opportunity, they were only too eager for the relief. Even Gilbert's ribs quit hurting for a time. Sally had insisted on being on top. She was a thoughtful girl.

They lay in bed and listened to the thunder rumbling its way inland. Soon the sky cleared and the eastern horizon began to lighten. After changing into dry clothes, they marched single file down the sandy path to the kitchen, breathing in the glorious morning air, and sharing the same happy thought—how nice it would be to start every day with a quick rain storm, a half hour of spirited sex, and a brisk walk across an island path to a job they both loved.

By noon, the island was back on track. Power was restored, the bridge was patched, and the minor storm damage was quickly repaired.

—

The locomotive engine belonging to the San Antonio & Aransas Pass Railroad, the pride and joy of the line, was christened "The Davy Crockett," and it covered the distance from the Alamo City to the Texas coast at a thundering 24 mph.

Just after dawn, the train pulled into the Southern Pacific station in downtown Corpus Christi and detached a private Pullman coach at a siding away from the main line. Not a crack of light showed from the tightly-closed shades, even as the coach was bumped and jostled into position and the rest of the train departed. Jazz musicians are not early risers. Most of them would put Dracula to shame.

Thanks to the publishing income from a string of hits stretching back decades, Duke Ellington could sometimes avail himself of a chartered railroad car, and he often did so when touring the South. His musicians and road manager could sleep under the same roof every night, eat when they chose and—an important consideration for eighteen bladders—go to the bathroom whenever Nature called. It was a luxury. Eating, sleeping, and tending to basic bodily functions were all highly problematic endeavors for a black person traveling below the Mason-Dixon Line in 1953, let alone nearly twenty of them.

Though he seldom let on in public, it bothered Ellington mightily that he could send records flying up the charts, star in movies, pack auditoriums and dance halls from coast to coast, and enjoy the acclaim of royalty in Europe, but he couldn't take a piss at your average Texaco station in Bumfuck, Arkansas.

Ellington lay awake in his berth, eyes closed, enjoying the stillness after the clattering nightlong ride across the coastal plains. Sometime before dawn, they'd passed through a tremendous storm, but it had blown by quickly and the comforting clackety-clack of the wheels returned. The rhythm of the rails had conjured up a tentative melody in his head, and he was eager to flesh it out. He would compose new music all night after a show, given the opportunity. But now he was tired. *One more gig,* he thought, *then these boys can take a little break. This boy, too.*

The Ellington orchestra (he never thought of them as a jazz or swing band) worked more than 325 days a year. They had to. With the new decade, smaller bebop ensembles and pop singers like Frank Sinatra, Nat King Cole, and Patti Page were getting the A-list bookings. The kids were turning away from the complex arrangements of big bands and tuning in to raw and rocking rhythm and blues outfits. Moreover, wartime rationing, changing tastes, and a ruinous two-year musicians' strike had driven a stake through the heart of many of his big band peers.

Count Basie had been forced to let nearly all his players go. Benny Goodman, Artie Shaw, and Cab Calloway, the same. They performed with small combos or used hired guns to fill out their sound. Many of Duke's players had been with him for decades. If he had to dip into his own pocket to keep it that way, that was what it would take. The music demanded it, and Ellington's relentless perfectionism would permit nothing less. He wanted to keep his band, to use his favorite description, "beyond category."

Meanwhile, he wondered about the next show. *Where was it? Ransom Island? Sounded like a damn Errol Flynn movie.* J.B. Leavitt, his Texas tenor man, had vouched for the venue and the fellow running it. And the fishing was supposed to be outstanding. Not the Savoy or the Cotton Club by a damned stretch, but not a gangster's clubhouse, either. (Oh, yes, he'd cottoned onto the Ginestras' operation five minutes after walking in the Bali Hai door.)

Ellington was no hypocrite. Bad guys had paid large chunks of his salary over the years, going back even to before Prohibition. But the personal insult his guys had sustained the last time the Ellington band played the Bali Hai ensured that Primo and Gerry's little show-place was on his permanent blacklist.

He'd been performing for almost thirty years and his hide, if not bulletproof, was dauntingly thick. He was, as one manager said, "royal in his attitudes." But there was some shit, to paraphrase Winston Churchill, up with which he would not put.

Ellington turned over to try to chase a couple of hours of sleep before Al Celley, his slavedriver of a road manager, came to rap on his berth.

A little sunshine and a fishing trip might be just the thing, he thought as he dozed off.

A few hours later, the orchestra leader emerged from the railroad coach and beads of sweat immediately began to etch the sides of his face. Ellington took off his Panama hat and mopped his brow. No suits for this gig, he told the boys, just keep it casual. He himself was wearing a pair of cream-colored linen slacks and a light cotton guayabera. He'd discovered the comfy, yet oddly formal shirt the last time he'd played Havana. And thank God. Texas summers were hotter than nine kinds of hell.

The band piled into a pair of prewar Chevy limousines that Noble had hired to meet the train, along with two starstruck black taxicab drivers drafted to play chauffeur. Even with four doors on each side of the big vehicles, it was quite a scramble getting everyone situated. An olive-green deuce and a half truck, temporarily absent from Ingleside, courtesy of one of Noble's service buddies, carried the instruments.

The convoy set out but didn't get far. The greasy drawbridge across the channel to Corpus Christi Harbor had to be raised to let a repurposed Liberty Ship sail through towards the chemical plants and refineries upstream. Grimy longshoremen, black, brown, and white labored to unload cargo on the long pier. Hard-hatted laborers swarmed around the smoke-belching refineries that sat back from the ship channel.

"What a dump," said Ray Nance. "Worse than Newark."

"Worse than Calcutta!"

"Worse than the Black Lagoon!"

"The one where that creature was featured?"

"Naw, man, ain't no black lagoon . . . . I'm talkin' about the Tan Strand."

"The Brown Sound . . . . Ebony Estuary." Laughter.

"But still a dump by any other name," Ray concluded.

Ellington turned in the front seat and regarded his cornet player with mild reproof. "Now, brother Ray," he said, gesturing towards the cracking towers of the refineries and the industrial dock cranes shimmering in the early-morning heat, "some of those boys might be our customers. And I wager they have been working hard all week so they can show their fine ladies a good time tonight in . . . where we going?" he asked the driver.

"Uh, Ransom Island, sir."

"Right, in Ransom Island. So, show a little respect."

Eventually the drawbridge pivoted itself back into place and the limos rumbled across. "That's a swingin' bridge," said the trumpeter, Cat Anderson.

"Got the rebop comin' and the bebop goin,'" someone riffed back.

A band on the road was something between a herd of jive-talking gypsies and a troop of reefer-smoking Foreign Legionnaires. But not long across the bridge, there was a sight that killed the good mood deader than Macbeth.

On the outskirts of Aransas Pass, the convoy of musicians passed through an unincorporated blue-collar slum called Jonas Point, which was a little less than a town and a little more than an al fresco cesspool. Shanties, broken-down trailers, tin-roofed tarpaper shacks, and even some discarded metal refinery tanks housed a collection of bottom-rung no-'counts who did the scutwork even the lowest-paid blacks and Cajuns turned their noses up at. Jonas Point was full of the kind of folks who may as well have hung signs reading "Oilfield Trash" around their necks.

And if anyone passing by might wonder where things stood, a hand-painted billboard propped up in front of a cluttered filling station spelled it out:

"NIGGER, DON'T LET THE SON SET ON YOU IN THIS TOWN!"

What had been a bantering group of friends rolling along through a pretty summer day now seemed more like a funeral procession.

"Dumbass shitbirds couldn't even spell 'sun' correctly," said drummer Louie Bellson. "And I'll be kissing your ass on Main Street if this is a town."

"Fuckin' Mississippi with cowboy hats, man."

J.B. Leavitt's face flamed with embarrassment. Aransas Pass was his hometown, for Christ's sake. And, besides the road manager, he was the only white man in the band. He ducked his head.

Someone elbowed him in the ribs.

"Aw, cheer up, Tex," said his seatmate, flashing white teeth in a grin. "Ain't nothin' but bad trick-eration and mendacity by some crackers who can't get laid 'cept at a family reunion."

"Yeah, J.B.," said someone else. "You ain't so damn white."

"'Bout half-khaki by now, since you been runnin' with us."

"Semi-beige. A mellow man with a high-yellow tan."

"Octaroon motherfucker, if you ask me."

J.B. had to smile. These were his brothers, no matter what his redneck daddy might say.

Listening to the ribald back-and-forth among his band members, Ellington had to smile. Keep that sunny side up.

But inside, he was thinking, *Edward Kennedy Ellington, just what exactly have you gotten yourself into?*

CHAPTER 31

"Shit, hurry up, here they come!"

Flavius Sweetwater peered around the new linen curtains that softened the swing-up hurricane shutters. The Ellington entourage was just pulling off the freshly-repaired causeway and approaching the parking lot.

Rupert took a last look around and his heart momentarily sank. Despite the heroic makeover by all hands, Shady's suddenly looked to its owner like an emperor without clothes—a ramshackle, slightly listing beer joint at the ass end of nowhere. What had he been thinking?

His wife, however, thoroughly approved of the improvements, and her upcoming debut had charged her with a nervous, darting energy.

Darla herself looked like the figurative million bucks. Her hair, hanging just below her shoulders, was styled in a dramatic coiffure reminiscent of one she'd seen in a movie with either Dorothy Lamour or Veronica Lake, she couldn't quite recall which. Her silk-screened dress flattered her narrow waist and, thanks to the perfume counter at the Rexall Drugstore in Aransas Pass, she smelled better than a flower-covered parade float.

Sally placed small bud vases of fresh-cut morning glory blossoms and flowering lantana sprigs on the linen-covered tables. Patriotic bunting hung from the rafters in honor of the Independence Day holiday. The piano onstage (borrowed from the USO club band) was waxed and tuned.

Zach regarded it all with silent amazement. He couldn't believe his friends were making all this fuss over a black man. *I bet even President Roosevelt hisself never got this kind of treatment,* he thought.

Rupert held his breath as the two limo coaches and the equipment trucks crossed the newly repaired bridge. They wheeled into the parking lot, the tires crunching loudly over the oyster shell paving. The sound stopped abruptly when the procession slid to a halt in front of Shady's. A light cloud of dust drifted away on the breeze.

Inside the lead vehicle, Duke Ellington blinked his eyes and then looked again.

He'd played the big shoreline ballrooms in Long Island and Atlantic City. He'd packed 'em in for a week every year at the Coconut Grove on the Santa Cruz boardwalk, and sold out luxe hotels on Miami Beach along the blue, sun-kissed ocean. Even the Ginestras' Bali Hai Club in Galveston had a certain raffish offshore elegance about it.

Shady's was not within shouting distance of any of those four-star joints. The square wooden building with its two-story roof, white-washed cedar siding, and wrap-around porch shaded by panels of rust-stained corrugated tin looked like something random hurricanes might have slapped together. The whole place perched uncertainly atop eight-foot pilings. Neon beer signs glowed warmly in the windows. In between were advertisements touting Royal Crown Cola and Jax Beer, and a long painted-over tin sign carefully lettered with the words "Shady's Welcomes Duke Ellington." The crest of the Falstaff Beer logo, imprinted into the metal, was still clearly visible.

The bandleader was taken aback. He wondered, for a moment, if this was the rock bottom that had always haunted him. One of his contemporaries, lamenting the decline of the big bands, had once told him, "Duke, all the white meat's gone off the platter. There ain't nothing but backs and gizzards left."

His fortunes, presently, were as thin as a sheet of wet newspaper. But he was a proud, up-standing man, goddammit—and a bandleader, with a job to do. He squared his shoulders and disembarked.

His bandmembers climbed out of the cars, stretched and looked around. A gull wheeled overhead, laughing its alien laughter. The hot July breeze blowing in off Redfish Bay smelled of tidal flat mud and dead fish. *Christ, where was everybody? Maybe cannibals got 'em all.*

The silence and emptiness of the place were about to become downright ominous when one of the double screen doors crashed open and a big man with gleaming blue eyes and protruding jug ears came shambling hurriedly down the front stairs.

"Duke Ellington! Damn glad to see you again."

Rupert wore his best-pressed khakis and a violently colored shirt bursting with hula girls and hibiscus blossoms. He stuck out a big beefy paw and grinned.

"Jesus, we're glad you and your men are here! Gettin' this place ready for your show has been like rasslin' alligators. But we got her squared away, by God. I promise we'll make you comfortable and get you fed before showtime, and tomorrow I'll show you all a little honey-hole out in the bay where the fish will have fistfights tryin' to get on your hook!" Rupert was nervous and jabbering away like a game show host.

But his enthusiasm was infectious. Ellington smiled a polished smile and put out his own hand and shook. "Mr., ah, Sweetwater. I recall you from Houston. You cut a memorable figure, sir. It's a pleasure to be invited to your establishment."

Rupert's manic grin remained plastered on his sunburnt face. "I don't know how 'established' we are, but we'll do our best to make you and your men feel at home."

He reached around behind him and seized the elbow of a slender, somewhat flashy young woman in a clingy summer dress and thrust her forward like an offering. "This is my wife, Darla, Mr. Ellington. She dabbles . . . ." (The moment he spoke, Rupert realized that wasn't the best choice of words as Darla's eyebrow shot skyward.) "Ah, she's worked her ass off . . . ." *(Damn it, Rupe!)* "That is to say, she's been rehearsing night and day and is honored to be opening the show for you all this evening."

Darla tried to maintain an air of professional hauteur, one artist greeting another, but instead she giggled. "It's a dream come true!" she blurted.

Ellington nodded his head in regal greeting and acknowledgement. It never occurred to him to shake the hand the white woman extended. This was still Texas, after all.

He noticed, in the shadows of the porch, some other denizens of this little seaside asylum: a slim Latino man with curly dark hair wearing a long chef's apron; a slip of a girl, hanging back in the deepest pool of shadow; a pugnacious-looking fireplug of a guy next to a taller, more sallow figure, both of whom bore a family resemblance to the bossman, Rupert. And, most remarkably, an older Negro in a cowboy hat and boots and workaday Levis, standing with one heel cocked against a porch post, smoking a hand-rolled cigarette and looking on.

Real jazz aficionados, the bandleader thought with a touch of cynicism, *a regular passel of connoisseurs,* though his smile remained undisturbed. Ellington almost never displayed his innermost thoughts, especially to paying customers. One thing he'd learned—no matter how bummed, bamboozled or broke-ass busted your own life might be, everyone else was paying you to be *their* Saturday night.

Rupert motioned the men on the porch forward. "Well, hell, let's get your boys unpacked and out of this hot sun," he said.

The Shady's crew tried to lend a hand, but the musicians quickly unloaded the bulky instrument and equipment cases and set up onstage with the alacrity that only three hundred-plus nights on the road every year could impart. (Offshore, aboard the *Easy Eight*, Primo Ginestra regarded all the hubbub with keen curiosity.)

Gilbert and Sally began ginning out hamburgers and sandwiches. Darla, pleased to be playing barmaid for once, dug fistfuls of soda pop and cold beer out of the ice-filled coolers.

As the band began tuning up, Rupert put his head together with Ellington's road manager, who was thinking this was maybe one of the craziest gigs he'd ever wrangled for his star client. But Al Celley also had a feeling that this Sweetwater character was a square dealer—emphasis on "square." And he certainly couldn't quibble with the hospitality so far.

"Me and my brothers have fixed up five of our fishing shacks, err, lodges for you and the fellas in the band to bunk in," Rupert was saying. "And my wife and I have a guest bedroom downstairs that Mr. Ellington would be more than welcome to—"

"We were thinking, the boys and I, that we would all just go back to Corpus and sleep on the train," Celley said, thinking Duke wouldn't much cotton to taking over a white man's house, even for a night.

"Now, you'd be more than welcome," said Rupert, smiling outwardly, but angling to put the hook in Celley like the master fisherman he surely was. "It's gonna be a madhouse trying to get off the island after the dance is over, and hell, you'd just have to turn around and come back early tomorrow for your fishing trip. Early tide's a good time to run some tarpon this time of year."

And besides, thought Rupert to himself, *if some of the local trouble-makers try to make good on the threats they'd been lobbing around, I don't want Ellington and his band to have to run a gauntlet across the narrow causeway and through the town.*

Maybe Celley picked up on Rupert's apprehension. Or maybe he was just looking forward to the fishing. But all he said was, "I'll talk it over with the boss, Mr. Sweetwater. And thank you for your hospitality."

Ellington put his men through a brief forty-five-minute rehearsal, more to check the tuning of the instruments and the placement of the musicians onstage than any need to actually practice the material. It was hot; several of the men stripped down to their undershirts as they played.

Once Ellington nodded his satisfaction with the arrangements, Celley clapped his hands. "Awright, gents, let's break for a siesta. Mr. Sweetwater and his brothers will show you to your digs. Meet back here at five, dressed. Tropical uniforms tonight, it's gonna be hotter than two horny goats in a pepper patch."

As Ransom Island drowsed itself through the early afternoon heat, Cootie Washburn, Ellington's clarinet player, tried and failed to ease into a doze—or cop a nod, as he would put it. Restless, he wandered up the path towards the big dancehall, meandering around back towards the cookhouse and the concrete cistern. He was about to wander back to his guest cottage when a pungent and familiar odor came wafting down the breeze.

He followed the smell until he came to a small cabin. Sitting on the porch was the Negro cowboy he'd noticed earlier that day. The old man was tipped back in a rope-bottomed ladderback chair, his ankles crossed on the porch rail. The man was smoking a hand-rolled cigarette. Definitely not Prince Albert.

The man motioned amiably with his hand and Cootie sauntered over, trying to act cool. The cowpuncher regarded him evenly. "Sit down in the shade, brother and think a cool thought." He put out a callused palm. "Zachariah Yates."

The musician shook it. "Cootie Washburn." He paused, wondering how to put it. "You don't look much like the reefer blowers I know up in Chicago."

Zach smiled. "I reckon not. The Mexican *vaqueros* turned me on to this little treat, lo these many years ago when I was a brush-popper down on the King Ranch. They called it *mota* back then, and I just sort of took to it. It don't quarrel up your blood like whiskey tends to."

Cootie took the pre-offered joint and took a long drag. "No, it do not," he muttered as he held the smoke down. He exhaled a long, blue cloud with satisfaction.

Zachariah regarded the skinny black man with pomaded hair and a go-to-hell pencil-thin moustache with curiosity. "Man, what's it like to be a big-time musician, ride all over the country and make people dance all night?"

"Shit, I don't know. It's all I've ever done. What's it like to be a cowboy?"

"Aw, it's just something to pass the time. Ain't that so?"

Cootie smiled and took another hit. "That it is, brother. That it is."

CHAPTER 32

Rupert was hemming and hawing into the big Shure microphone at center stage, trying to draw the crowd's attention. And doing a piss-poor job of it. As a master of ceremonies, he was a damned good fishing guide.

"Ladies . . ." he said tentatively. "Ah, gentlemen . . ."

No one paid him any attention. Most of the white and black customers were on opposite sides of the room, an unspoken line of demarcation drawn between the tables. The social context was unfamiliar to all parties.

But for all that, there was a jovial ease in the room that put Rupert's private fears (and those of Red Burton as well) to rest. Everybody, but everybody, was out for a Fourth of July good time.

Louis Jordan's "Saturday Night Fish Fry" was playing on the jukebox as the crowd poured in. The white folks were dressed casually, some in seersucker suits and hand-painted ties, more in khakis and sport coats. Their women tended in the direction of cotton summer dresses.

The black couples, on the other hand, were done up to the nines, the women in brightly flowered dresses with billowing skirts, corsages pinned at the shoulder, and big church-going hats, while their men sported their best suits and snazziest fedoras.

The racket was intense. The jukebox boomed. Rupert tried again. "Hello, folks, and welcome . . ." The crowd chattered and hoorawed and generally paid him no attention whatsoever.

Enough was enough. Noble Sweetwater came out from behind the bar, elbowed his way to the stage, pushed his brother aside and bellowed in his best cut-this-shit-out-right-now M.P. voice, "HOWDY FOLKS! WELCOME TO SHADY'S! NOW SHUT THE HELL UP FOR A MOMENT AND LISTEN TO MY BROTHER!"

Shocked silence fell on the crowd, as though a Higher Power had sealed up everyone's voice box like Pharaoh's tomb. Even the jukebox fell mute. The clatter of the cash register as Sally rang up a round of beers echoed in the sudden stillness. Noble looked a little bit abashed. Rupert stepped back up to the mic.

"Thanks, brother," he said and grinned. "Noble Sweetwater, folks. The brains—and the ah, voice—of the outfit. I want to thank y'all for coming out to our little establishment tonight. We could not be more proud to be putting on this show for our friends and neighbors, and we hope you all will relax, have a cool drink, and enjoy yourselves . . ." *And maybe we can get through the night without a race riot or any more dynamite,* he thought.

Rupert sported a white short-sleeved shirt and a broad tie with hula girls painted on it. He tugged the tie's knot loose, suddenly hot and self-conscious under the lights. He looked down and realized he'd forgotten to take off the apron he'd been wearing behind the bar. *Son of a young bitch!*

". . . and we can get this show on the road," he concluded.

He glanced behind him. The borrowed USO musicians were in place, looking bored. They were glad to be off post, but would be gladder still when they were offstage and chatting up the single girls at the bar.

"Now, folks," said Rupert, "some of you all know the young lady who is going to open tonight's show as the prettiest barmaid in San Patricio County. But before this evening is through, you're gonna know her as a singing sensation. You all are in for a rare treat. Please make welcome Shady's resident Patti Page, Miss Darla Lacey Sweetwater!"

Rupert pounded his big mitts together with gusto, and the room erupted in cheers, applause, and wolf whistles as the small follow spot picked up Darla making her way through the crowd at stage left.

Rupert thought his wife's pipe dreams of stardom were a bunch of damn woman's foolishness. Always had. But at this moment, she had never looked more beautiful, and he'd never been more proud of her. This was her night, by God. Nothing was going to spoil that.

Darla made her way onstage and Rupert crushed her to his side in a passionate hug, his brawny arm thrown around her shoulders. She forced a smile. *(My hair! My makeup! My dress!)*

Sally and Darla had spent hours on her coiffure. Her hair was lustrous, swept back in a sculpted wave. A small magnolia blossom gleamed behind her right ear. Her makeup, even in the tropical heat, could not have looked more perfect if she had just stepped out of a Paris salon. Her dress seemed to have been tailored for her by tiny invisible fairy seamstresses. She was every bit as glamorous as the movie stars on the pages of her fan magazines. But inside, a small kernel of apprehension began to gnaw at her.

Rupert was saying, "Ladies and gentlemen, would you please rise in honor of the holiday as Miz Sweetwater renders our national anthem?"

Everyone stood. The men doffed their hats and the ladies put their hands over their hearts. The musicians sat up straight and fingered their instruments. Rupert stepped off the stage and made his way back behind the bar.

The spotlight pinned Darla as she stepped to center stage and fingered the microphone uncertainly. The click of the rotating ceiling fans suddenly sounded like staccato drumbeats. The colored Christmas lights dangling from the ceiling began to pulse in her vision. A hot flash began in her face and chest and then spread throughout her body. All eyes were on her. Behind her, one of the musicians cleared his throat.

Piece of cake, Darla, she thought. *You've been singing this song since grade school.* She squared her shoulders and resolutely faced the microphone and the hushed crowd. *Come on, girl . . . . This is the moment you've been dreaming of.*

She shook her head and her hair fell behind her shoulders. Looking toward the ceiling, trying to disguise her panic, she took a deep breath and opened her mouth.

"Oh, say can you see . . . ."

And then she threw up.

—

Afterwards, when Darla tried to reconstruct her monumental humiliation, she could never quite put the pieces back together. She had vague, disjointed memories of fleeing the stage, hurling herself down the plank steps of Shady's and staggering up the path toward the Big House.

Like a soldier traumatized by battle, she retained fleeting shards of memory, like bits of a broken mosaic.

There was the magnolia blossom she'd torn from her carefully-coiffed hair and then crushed in her hand. There was the stained and stinking gown she'd ripped off in a frenzy of humiliation, buttons torn and seams popped. She threw on the first housedress her hand landed on, grabbed her car keys and purse, and bolted through the front door.

I've gotta get off this fucking island, she thought frantically as she threw her Pontiac in gear, bashed open the swinging garage door Rupert and Zach had worked so hard to install and, spewing fragments of oyster shells, sped down the drive to the bridge. *I'll die if I have to stay in this place one more minute!*

Darla Lacey Sweetwater looked approximately one million miles distant from the sleek chanteuse who had stepped on the bandstand just a short time ago. In her head she heard the voices of Billie Holiday and Julie London, chiding her. *Sister Girl, you better look at doin' something else for a living, 'cause God does not want you to be a singer.*

Inside Shady's, confusion reigned. Darla's hired musicians looked at one another and shrugged. Just when you thought you'd seen it all. They began to pack up their instruments. This gig was clearly over.

The crowd was talking across one another, abuzz at the unexpected theatrics. Some guffawed, though more than a few were silent, feeling awful for the poor girl.

Rupert stood, shocked and dismayed, behind the cash register. He knew, in some distant part of his mind, he should go after his wife, maybe try to offer some comfort, but he just couldn't make himself move. Noble and Flavius were throwing up their hands, trying to answer a dozen questions at once.

Only Gilbert seemed to have a grasp of the necessities. He hustled to the stage with a bucket of sawdust and a mop and swabbed up the mess. He carried the reeking microphone back to the kitchen. Maybe it could be salvaged somehow. Yuck.

Al Celley elbowed his way through the crowd of yammering, sweating customers to Noble's side.

"This is a hell of a wreck, Mr. Sweetwater," he said, not without sympathy. Darla was no more a sultry-voiced vocalist than she was a nuclear physicist. He'd seen that right off. But he liked these Sweetwater brothers and felt a little bad for them. They'd clearly bitten off more than they could chew.

"My boys are still getting ready," he told Noble. "But it'll be forty-five minutes or so before our set starts. You better buy everybody a round of drinks and figure out how to entertain them."

Back at the swinging door that led to the kitchen, Gilbert was thinking the same thing. There had already been more than a little beer and whiskey consumed. The audience, black and white alike, were confused and growing restive. *What the hell kind of dance was this? I paid good money for a show, brother, not to watch the girl singer blow chow.*

Rupert seemed paralyzed.

Gilbert felt a tap on his shoulder. It was Sally. Holding his guitar. *Get up there,* she mouthed, thrusting the rosewood Martin towards him.

He stared at her, incredulous. "Have you been smoking some of Zach's locoweed?" he said. "A Mexican cook with a guitar? They'll boo me back across the river."

"I've heard you play. And Rupert needs your help. Somebody's got to keep this crowd happy for the next half hour. C'mon, Gilberto," she said with a smile and a playful poke in his back. "It's showtime, baby."

Was she making fun of him? This was crazy, even by Ransom Island standards.

"Okay, fine. Just mail my body back to my folks in . . . wherever the hell they are right now," he said. He took off his cook's apron, grabbed the guitar and marched towards the stage. *Hijole, this is a bad idea,* he thought.

At first no one paid him any attention at all. He essayed a little bolero run, stopped to tune, and then essayed "Una Noche En Un Jardin," a ranchera tune he'd picked up in the Rio Grande Valley. Nothing. The acoustic guitar didn't have enough muscle to cut through the din and the smoke. This was a disaster.

He sensed someone moving out of the corner of his eye. He turned. It was Johnny Balfa, Ellington's guitar player, and he was opening an instrument case leaning against the wall.

"Here, *amigo*," Balfa said, handing Gilbert a glistening, tobacco-colored hollow-bodied Gibson Custom. "This here will give you a little more horsepower, 'specially once I plug it in." Balfa took out a coiled cable, slipped one end into a Polytone amp and the other into the input jack on the heel of the guitar.

"I purely hate to see another man of the six-string persuasion hung out to dry," Balfa whispered. "Least now you got a fighting chance."

Gilbert rolled his fingers experimentally over the steel strings and a cascade of silvery notes with beautiful tone came tumbling out of the amplifier. Heads turned towards the stage.

Gilbert tried to pick out a bolero, but he couldn't manipulate the tone knobs properly and he'd never used a guitar pick. He shifted to strumming a border *ranchera*, and within a few bars felt his confidence returning. People began to nod along in time to the warm, romantic melody. *But what the hell am I gonna do next?* he thought with nervous anticipation. *This ain't exactly a "Cielito Lindo" crowd.*

No one was more surprised than he to hear someone behind him riding the cymbal and tapping out a counterpoint on the high hat. Ellington's drummer Louie Belson had slipped onstage and was sitting behind his trap kit. And there was Rupert's buddy, J.B. Leavitt, stepping up, tenor sax in hand, motioning bassist Wendell Marshall to come along.

As the Mexican ballad concluded, Balfa and Marshall leaned over to Gilbert. "Man," said Balfa, who'd picked up Gilbert's acoustic guitar. "We're just gonna start a straight blues. This one's in the key of C and it starts on the four. Go from there. Dig what I'm saying?" Gilbert nodded. This he understood.

"We'll take it out for a walk, see what happens," said Balfa with a smile and nodded at the bassist and drummer.

Thus began the most extraordinary twenty-five minutes of Gilberto Ruiz's young life. Hesitantly at first, and then with growing brio, he flung himself into the impromptu arrangement that evolved, with the nudging of the orchestra members, into "Happy Go Lucky Local," one of Ellington's most vibrant, insouciant 12-bar blues. The dance-floor filled in a heartbeat.

As the band passed the call-and-response choruses around, Gilbert felt immersed in the most intense dialogue of his life. He was *conversing* with these men, explaining to them and having them explain to him in turn about a wonderful something that had never existed just this way before this moment.

The group, augmented now by Cat Anderson and two other horn players, with Gilbert following hard on their heels, segued into a scatting, breathless jazz number. Gilbert played the progression, trying not to step on anyone's toes, making sure to give J.B. plenty of room when he stepped to the front of the room and blew a fiery series of choruses that bridged the segue from "Perdido" to "Caravan."

It was in the latter tune that Gilbert took his first solo, throwing a handful of Django Reinhardt-inspired gypsy jazz licks into a 16-bar vacancy. Ellington's men (and the crowd) cheered mightily at his inspired improvisation. Then it was off to the races again.

There were cheers and shouts and wolf whistles from the happy, sweaty crowd when Gilbert, J.B., Balfa, Marshall and the rest brought the jam session to a shuddering, exhausted conclusion.

Ellington's men looked at each other with delighted surprise. *Hell of a ride, my man,* the expressions said. *Must be the chili peppers that made the brother so hot. Layin' down that Tex-Mex gypsy sound. Shit!*

Gilbert felt himself coming back down to earth, happy, sweating, shaking, and wondering what the hell had just happened. Rupert, Zach, Noble, and even Flavius were clapping, laughing, and behaving in general like thoroughgoing fools. Sally blew him a kiss.

In the back of the room, Gilbert realized with dawning amazement, stood Duke Ellington himself, wreathed in cigarette smoke, his conked hair gleaming in the glow of the Christmas lights in the rafters. Ellington raised his hand and flicked a casually elegant salute in Gilbert's direction.

Gilbert just grinned like a doofus. *It beats picking apples in Oregon all to hell,* he thought.

CHAPTER 33

Darla's eyes opened slightly and she observed the soft furrows of light that filtered through the venetian blinds. The light created pleasing geometric patterns around the bedroom that vaguely reminded her of Morocco, and she drowsily wondered if this was what it would be like waking up in Bogart's apartment, the one he kept above his famous American nightclub in Casablanca. *That would make me Ingrid Bergman,* she thought with pleasure. The window unit droned away, keeping the room cool and comfy. Darla pulled the sheet up to her chin and debated whether or not to drift back to sleep. The bed felt wonderful, luxurious even.

She noticed her shiny new pumps lying on the floor, one shoe upright, its mate tipped on its side. Draped over the back of an upholstered chair was her dress, along with her nylon stockings and slip. Collapsed on a braided rug near the chair was a long pair of khaki pants, girdled by a western belt and a belt buckle the size of a gravy boat. The initials RB were embossed in gold on the buckle. Red Burton. She remembered having this dream before.

Through drooping eyes she took note of Red's cowboy hat hanging on the bedpost, and on the floor below, her panties and bra, carelessly bestrewn as if they'd been flung off in a frenzy of passion. She smiled and closed her eyes. Ah, yes, this was one of *those* dreams. She'd had these before, too.

Her eyes popped open again, wider this time. Where exactly was she, anyway? And whose room was this? It sure didn't look like her bedroom at the Big House on Ransom Island.

Darla sat up and assessed the situation more attentively, casting a sideways glance at the recumbent figure beside her. *Son of a gun.*

Yep, there he was, snoring contentedly by her side—Red Burton, in the flesh. (In her dreams, he didn't snore, so she knew this was real.) She timidly lifted the sheet and examined herself. Yep, there she was too, in his bed, in the all-too-naked flesh. She stepped gingerly onto the floor and dressed with some urgency, but as soon as she finished she slumped into the armchair and just sat there, staring at her sleeping paramour and trying to piece together the chain of events that brought her to her adulterous present.

Today was Sunday, she remembered, July the fifth, the day after the big show. *Oh Lordy, the big show.* It all came back to her in a rush: the huge crowd, the sea of faces staring up at her, waiting, waiting . . . and she had *nothing!* Nothing but the paralyzing freeze up, the spectacular eruption, the utter humiliation! Darla shut her eyes as the ordeal ran through her mind.

She vaguely remembered fleeing the island and rattling over the wooden causeway, wanting nothing more than to get out, get gone, and get off that wretched island. She had almost run down the startled officers who were managing traffic at both ends of the bridge. As she bounced over the terminus and clipped a barricade, she recalled Red Burton turning an astonished face to her before he, too, jumped out of the path of her speeding automobile.

She had driven for hours, first through Corpus, then across the Padre Island Causeway to the Gulf of Mexico, and then back again and on to the town of Mathis, where she abruptly turned around and drove the other direction, back to Corpus. She considered reversing direction once more and heading for the border, but instead, she stopped at the L-Head in front of the USO building. There, she sat on the seawall and sobbed uncontrollably. She realized with crushing certainty that her lifelong ambition had been shattered that night, right there in front of God, Duke Ellington, and almost a thousand onlookers.

Back in her car, she returned to Aransas Pass and somehow, someway, ended up in the driveway of Red Burton's modest little bungalow on Houston Street. It was as if her Pontiac had driven there by itself.

The phone rang and startled Darla out of her brooding funk. Red Burton bolted upright and grabbed the receiver in one swift motion. "Rupert?" he barked. A pause. "No, sorry, I was, um, having a bad dream. What's up, Deputy?"

The sheriff listened with his eyes closed tight. "Um-hum . . . . Yeah . . . . Sure, you do that. I'll be in the office in a little while."

He hung up the phone and turned his head slowly to see if Darla, the love of his life, was still there, in *his* bedroom. She was still there alright, already dressed and sitting stiffly in his easy chair.

"Mornin', Darla."

"Mornin', Red."

He slid out of bed and pulled the sheet with him as he self-consciously tramped into the bathroom and closed the door behind him. He twisted the shower handles and stood under the cold water, hoping it might clear his head and help him make sense of what had happened the night before—also maybe wanting to punish himself for sleeping with his best friend's wife. *Jesus H. Christ, Red. You really ripped it this time.*

He relied on his law enforcement training to methodically reconstruct the incidents leading up to the Great Transgression. After the Ransom Island crowd had dispersed at midnight, he had met with his own deputies and with the men on loan from the surrounding communities, and then he'd thanked them for a job well done and sent them on their way. After that, he drove home and found Darla's car parked in his driveway, with her sitting behind the wheel, crying her eyes out.

He hadn't seen her big debut go up in flames, but he'd heard about it, and he remembered how terrible he felt for her. She'd almost flattened him like an armadillo, but he was prepared to overlook that. And now, lo and behold, there she was, at *his* house, seeking *him* out, wanting him to comfort her.

And boy, did she ever need it. He'd never seen a woman so undone; she was damn near hysterical about what had happened. So, he did what any decent human being would do and invited her inside. He'd offered her coffee but she'd wanted something stronger, and out came the bottle of I.W. Harper.

Red turned off the shower and toweled dry. As he shaved his face, he forced himself to remember what happened next, and that's where it got slippery.

At some point, she'd started crying again, and he'd moved next to her on the couch so he could hug her, in a brotherly fashion, of course. But somehow the hug became more intense, more desperate, and much less brotherly, and when she turned her face up to his, their lips suddenly met. And then they met again. After that, it was as if they'd both been possessed by some kind of horny demon. They kissed and groped and moaned and, the next thing Red knew, he was carrying her into his bedroom, where they flung off their clothes and fell headlong onto the mattress.

Red stopped his razor mid-stroke and stared at himself in the mirror. *Did that really happen?* He wondered. *Did we really do those things to each other in my bed?* But instead of feeling guilty about it, he saw a smile appear on his reflected face, and realized that the memories were pretty goddamn nice. He wiped off the shaving cream and opened the bathroom door. Darla looked up anxiously from the chair.

"Darla, did you mean what you said last night?"

"Um, yeah? I think so. Which part?"

"The part where you said you loved me."

Darla nodded. "I did, Red. God help me, I did. And I do. I think I always have."

"And what about the part where you said you wanted to be with me?"

"I meant that, too."

Red blinked. Things were happening awfully fast. "You mean be with me now, or just every now and again, or be with me, you know . . . forever."

"Forever." Darla was a little surprised how easy it was to say it, but she'd done some candid thinking while she'd been waiting for Red to wake up. She still loved Rupert, she wasn't ashamed to admit it, but the catastrophic meltdown she'd experienced last night at Shady's ended that chapter of her life. In her mind, Rupert, and her marriage to Rupert, were inextricably associated with her botched career as a singer and her unreachable dreams of stardom. When it came right down to it, she had grown tired of herself on Ransom Island, tired of the motley crew that hung out there, and tired of waiting for something exciting to happen to her.

She realized it was time to grow up—not give up, mind you, just grow up . . . and move on. It wasn't only going to be about her anymore, because now she had a new plan, and getting back with Red Burton was just the first step. Darla might have bombed when her Big Break presented itself, but she'd failed mainly because she hadn't had someone to help her learn the ropes. She hadn't been prepared. In short, she hadn't had a mentor.

But Darla could *be* a mentor, and a damn good one at that. She still had the looks, she still had the drive, and Lord knows she still had ambition. She needed someone to share it with, though—a worthy beneficiary for her considerable, albeit, underdeveloped, talent. And sitting in that stuffed chair, appraising Red Burton's movie star good looks, she realized what fine-looking children they could produce together, and she knew that these beautiful children could, over time and with her help, be turned into first-class, grade-A star material. If she couldn't become a star, then, by golly, she would raise she would raise some offspring that would. She would make it her mission to do so.

"I want to be with you forever, Red. And I want to start a family."

Red Burton sighed deeply. "Okay, Darla. Then I'm your man. But this next part is not gonna be much fun for either of us."

———

CHAPTER 34

Galveston Island looked a little the worse for wear after the Independence Day holiday weekend. Red, white, and blue bunting still hung limply from storefronts and light poles up and down the seawall. A few hungover patriots, freshly released from police chief O.W. Miller's drunk tank, wandered morosely up and down the derelict harborside stretch known as the Strand. Discarded picnic debris, beer bottles, and spent fireworks littered Stewart Beach. Someone had driven a car out onto the Pleasure Pier and, God knows how, collided with the Ferris Wheel. The island looked less like the queen of the coast and more like a frazzled dowager who'd been tossed into a burlap sack with a mess of alley cats.

Gerry Ginestra considered himself a flag-waving American, but he pledged his allegiance to the Almighty Dollar. He had a dishonest living to make, and the Fourth of July always made him feel like a true patriot. As he sat in his office at the back of the Bali Hai tallying up the weekend's receipts, he couldn't help but smile at the banded stacks of hundred-dollar bills, each of which bore a vaguely dyspeptic portrait of Benjamin Franklin. Now there was a by-God Founding Father for you.

Though he'd never been much of a sentimentalist when it came to his native land, Gerry proudly bore the stamp of a true-blue American: he was a taxpayer.

And a scrupulous one at that. It was a lot cheaper to pony up to the penny than to keep a gang of cannibal lawyers on retainer fighting off a phony tax beef.

Well, the taxman ought to be happy with his cut from this take, Gerry reflected. He'd lucked out and managed to snag Louis Prima and Keely Smith at the last minute for the holiday slot vacated by Duke Ellington. Though he felt a certain kinship with the New Orleans-born Italian singer, Prima's irreverent, sweaty, swaggering take on mock-wop hits like "Just A Gigolo," "Buona Sera," and "Please No Squeeza Da Banana," jazzed up with a hot-sauce mixture of jump blues, Crescent City R&B, and pounding drums, left Gerry with a headache.

He lit a cigarette and looked out the window at the Gulf. He wondered how Ellington had made out at that swampy island hideaway down the coast. And speaking of Ransom Island, what was taking Primo and Jimmy Glick so long to lock that deal down?

"Marie!" he hollered down the hall to summon the latest new secretary who'd yet to experience one of Primo's existential fits of temper. Gerry hoped this one had more staying power.

Marie Crowell, a trim black woman the employment agency had sent around, stuck her head in the door. "Yes, Mr. Ginestra?"

"See if you can raise my brother on the ship-to-shore radio or telephone or whatever the hell you call it."

"Yes, sir."

Directly, his phone buzzed. There was Primo's voice, sounding like it was crunching its way through a box of saltine crackers.

"How's it going, *paisan?*" Gerry asked.

Primo gave him an earful. For a sleepy tropical backwater, Ransom Island was seeing more action than Iwo fuckin' Jima. Explosions, gambling intrigue, the Klan, assorted crazy shit. It was a hairball, alright. But the fishing was excellent.

"How was the Ellington show?" Gerry asked.

"Goddamn gangbusters," Primo replied. "I never thought these hayseeds could pull it off. I got one of our guys running some interference for me. He was at the show; said the place was packed and the band played its ass off. Ellington and his crew are still sticking around and doing some guided fishing. I thought the coloreds couldn't swim, but they seem to be having a ball."

"Huh," said Gerry. "I'm still pissed at him, but maybe Ellington did us a favor. Kind of put the spot on the map, makes it more of a draw for the new management . . . . Speaking of which, what's the hold-up? You've been down there over a week. You coulda merged General Motors and Ford by now."

Primo paused. Uncharacteristic for him. "It's . . . complicated," he explained. Meaning the girl, but not saying so. "These guys are attached to the place. Three brothers named Sweetwater, and they look at this shithole like it's Camelot or something. Deke tried to money-whip 'em, and Jimmy roughed up one of their hands, a Mexican. Good cop/bad cop kind of deal. They wouldn't budge. I can't believe it's about the money or whatever little racket they're running. It's all tied up with . . . family, seems like."

Gerry drummed his fingers on the desk. That he understood. The few unfortunates who had the bad judgment to try to move in on the Ginestras over the years didn't understand they weren't just dealing with cutthroat gangsters. They were putting the squeeze on *brothers*. It was invariably a fatal miscalculation.

"Okay. But it's time to quit fucking around. We've got a business to run here, in case you haven't noticed. These rubes here aren't going to fleece themselves. I need you back here in Galveston, and with the deed to this Ransom Island gin mill in your hand. And you have to make up your mind what you're gonna do about the girl. I think she's twistin' your head like a pretzel."

"I know," said Primo, his voice seething with frustration. "I know, goddammit. But," he repeated, "it's complicated."

"Well, de-complicate things. That's something you *used* to be good at."

"Alright. Jesus." Primo struggled mightily not to hurl the ship-to-shore receiver into the bay. Being dressed down by his younger brother always put him in a foul mood.

"Make it happen," said Gerry, and hung up.

Primo stomped off to his bedroom (his *cabin,* Cap'n Mark could have told him) and sat down on his bed (his *berth*), and waited for his blood to cool.

After a time, he went forward and found Jimmy Glick in his customary spot at the bow of the vessel. His nose was slathered with zinc oxide and he was doing what he'd been doing all week long: smoking, reading magazines, and not giving a shit.

That last item changed straight away.

"Jimmy, I've got a job for you. I'm tired of fucking around. I want to be in my own bed, in my own house, and not having my own brother pissed at me."

"Things around here moving a little slow for Gerry?" Glick asked.

"And for me, too. Listen, we've tried grease, and we've tried muscle. But the more we lean on the Sweetwaters, the more they close ranks. It's time to lean on somebody else, show we're fucking serious."

"How serious?"

"Dead-fucking serious."

"You got somebody in mind, boss?"

"Not for certain. I want you to go into Aransas Pass, sniff around; I'll have somebody bring you your car. Find a Ransom Island regular, someone the Sweetwaters are sure to know. Someone without any local family, but a regular citizen who likes to frequent a certain beer joint on a certain island."

"What would you like to happen to this certain someone?"

"Something definitive."

Jimmy took a last puff of his smoke and flipped the butt over the rail.

"I'll get right on it."

CHAPTER 35

The two-day break following the show was just the sort of downtime J.B. Leavitt had hoped for. After it was all over, thirty-six tarpon were landed, the bass player hooked a twelve-foot sawfish and then lost it near the jetties and, on the last day, six astonished members of the horn section were watching their guide, Barney Farley, trying to board a large king mackerel when a massive bull shark swam up and bit the fish in half. Only Louie Bellson, the seasick drummer, found the excursion less than satisfying, having spent most of the outing throwing up over the boat rail.

Duke Ellington spent most of his downtime inside his Pullman car, putting the finishing touches on a new composition that he and his co-composer, Billy Strayhorn, had titled "Satin Doll," but he asked J.B. Leavitt to drop by to report on the band's Ransom Island vacation. He was pleased to hear that everyone was having a grand time, even Al Celley, who (thanks to Cecil and Giddyup) had become a born-again domino hustler.

"I'm glad to hear it," said the bandleader. "After the tour we've had, the boys needed either a fishing trip or a ticket to the asylum. Although," he added with a smile, "Ransom Island seems to fit both bills."

Nor were there any complaints about the food at Shady's. The first evening after the gig, Gilbert and Sally prepared twenty-four T-Bone steak dinners, which garnered raves from the musicians, accustomed to backstage sandwiches and greasy diner fare. Ellington himself showed up for supper, talking and laughing amiably with his orchestra, and enjoying the tales of misspent youth that J.B. and Rupert swapped at the table. On the second evening, the crew feasted on the very trout and redfish they had pulled out of the bay earlier that afternoon. Fish stories were being traded right and left, stretching a little with each telling. The only person conspicuously absent was Darla Sweetwater who, according to Rupert, had taken to bed with a migraine.

After dinner, Duke and his eighteen band members thanked their hosts, climbed into their limousines, and rolled across the patched-up Ransom Island Bridge for the last time, heading for the train and their first gig of a new tour, 1,500 miles away in Los Angeles. When the wheels of the last vehicle touched ground on the far shore, Rupert sighed a sigh of relief. He put his hands on his hips and appraised the crew of misfits that comprised the island's body politic.

"Lady and gents," he said. "I cannot *believe* we pulled that off."

"I thought for sure we'd have to break up a fight or two at the dance," Flavius remarked with mild disappointment.

Noble nodded in accord. "But there wasn't even a scuffle."

"Nary a discouraging word," Zach agreed.

"It's like everyone went color blind once Mr. Ellington struck up the band," said Rupert.

"Like all anybody could do was move to the beat," Noble added.

Zachariah finished rolling a cigarette and put a match to it. "Mr. Duke said it all when he played that song—what was the name of it?"

"'It Don't Mean a Thing (If it Ain't Got that Swing)?'" asked Noble.

"'Black and Tan Fantasy?'" Gilbert suggested.

"No," Sally said. "I bet Zach's thinking of 'All God's Chillun Got Rhythm.'"

"That's it," Zach agreed. "That's the one brought to mind, 'All God's Chillun Got Rhythm,' yessir."

Even the normally recalcitrant Dubber Sweetwater was impressed. He'd come and brought his boys, Johnny and Charlie, with him for the show, and afterwards they'd stayed for the fishing. He was proud of his brothers' accomplishments, but still thought they were crazy to have come up with the idea in the first place.

"I believe I'll stick to shrimping," he said. "Show business looks too nerve-wracking for me."

The group disbanded and began the task of changing Shady's back to normal. But each of them had a different vision of what the new "normal" might be. Noble and Flavius were imagining what their lives would be like if they sold the whole kit and caboodle to their disreputable suitors from Galveston. Zach wondered the same thing, but at his age, he had trouble picturing any life other than the one he had. He might could buy a car with the money he'd saved. But then he'd have to learn to drive.

Rupert's concerns were more localized and immediate. His wife had barely spoken to him or to anybody else since she'd returned from God knows where and taken to bed. Something was up, and he had a bad feeling about it.

Sally, for her part, had been apprehensive and watchful when people began pouring over the bridge for the show. She wondered if Primo and his brother had sent spies to check up on her and on their prospective investment. (They had.)

Now that the show was over, she worried anew about Gilbert and about her eclectic Ransom Island friends. What if their faux casino scheme didn't work? It was all her fault, she thought guiltily. The Ginestras would never have heard of Shady's if she hadn't stowed away on that beer truck. For the hundredth time, she fretted that her decision not to confide in her new friends would have grave repercussions.

Gilbert worried about Sally's downbeat demeanor and wondered if there was another shoe left to drop.

Inside the kitchen, the two began cleaning up after the Ellington farewell fish fry. They worked silently, side-by-side, scrubbing pans and washing dishes, hoping their chores would distract them from the foreboding they both felt, until Sally proposed a solution.

"Gilbert, let's run away together," she declared impulsively.

She was leaning against the butcher block, legs apart, arms akimbo, striking a defiant pose. *God Almighty she's beautiful,* he thought. Gilbert wasn't surprised by the proposal and was happy to hear her say it, ecstatic even, but that didn't mean he was ready to drop everything and run away.

"Where would we go?"

"Los Angeles," she said confidently, even though the destination had just that instant occurred to her.

"Why L.A.?"

"Because I heard it's pretty there. Because it's a long way from here."

Gilbert smiled. "Aye, there's the rub, isn't it? It's also a long way from our friends here."

Sally pulled the soapy gloves off her hands and threw them onto the counter in frustration. "Your friends . . . I mean *our* friends, would be smart to pick up and leave as well."

"Sell out, and move on. Is that the idea?"

"Why not? It's not such a bad idea. It's certainly the most sensible one. Things will get ugly in a hurry if those Galveston mobsters decide to move in. And besides, Zach and Rupert, and his brothers, they can take care of themselves."

Gilbert watched her quietly, evaluating the options, calculating everyone's risk individually. Despite his strong feelings for Sally, he could barely contemplate walking out on the only real friends he'd ever had.

"We can start new lives out West," Sally continued. "You and me, together. They say California is the land of milk and honey, don't they?"

"That's what they say," Gilbert answered, although in his mind's eye he pictured his parents and siblings hunched over in a California field, picking strawberries for twenty dollars an acre, twelve hours a day.

Gilbert was an optimist by nature, but he realized that Sally was right about the trouble that lay in store for Ransom Island if their gambling ruse didn't dissuade the Galveston mob. Someone was likely to get hurt, maybe killed. And on top of that, there was the trouble he'd brought to the island by becoming intimate with her. His busted ribs reminded him of that every time he coughed or tried to reach for something. Leroy Stuckey wasn't the only Neanderthal in area.

But on the other hand, he and Sally made a good team, and he was confident they could make a go of it on the West Coast. Follow his heart and abandon his friends? Or make a last stand on Ransom Island and risk watching his girl ride off into the sunset like Zach's hazel-eyed mulatto?

"I suppose you'll go with or without me."

Sally blinked. "I'm going, Gilbert. I've brought enough trouble to you all. But I want you to go with me."

"Why? Why do you want me go with you? You could have your pick of movie stars out West."

She cocked her head and looked at him like he'd lost his mind. "Because I love you, you idiot." She threw a rubber glove at him. "You may know French poetry, but sometimes you're a real nincompoop when it comes to women."

Gilbert felt a warm rush. There, she'd said it. She said that she loved him, and that was what he wanted to hear. Of course, she'd also called him a nincompoop, but still . . . . Right then he made up his mind.

"Okay, Sally. California here we come, but can you please give me a few days to put things right with Rupe and Zach? I'm not going to light out like a thief in the night."

Sally smiled. "Fair enough, Gilberto. We'll be happy out West, I just know it. But right now, I want you to come over here and hold me." She opened her arms wide and waited for his embrace.

Even with Sally in his arms, Gilbert pondered the wisdom of his decision. What if it didn't work out in California? What if she left him after they arrived? What if her secret, whatever it was, followed them to the West Coast? *What the hell,* he decided, *I'm willing to chance it. I love her, for better or for worse.* One of Ellington's songs began playing in his head: "I Got It Bad and That Ain't Good."

Over Sally's shoulder, Gilbert saw Red Burton's car through the window, lurching down the narrow road toward Rupert and Darla's house. Probably going to congratulate Rupert on the success of the first integrated dance in San Patricio County, he supposed. Good. Let Rupe enjoy that victory before the next battle begins, whatever it turns out to be.

—

Rupert knew who was driving up to the house even before he glanced out his bedroom window and saw the official vehicle. He cast a long, melancholy look at his wife, who was still in bed, facing the wall and curled up in fetal position under a sheet. He wasn't even sure if she was asleep. If she didn't want to talk about it, fine. He was pretty sure he already knew the score.

He'd experienced the same matrimonial roller coaster with his last wife: the initial excitement when he brought her home (*"Honey, your very own island!"*), then a smooth phase where she yielded to Ransom's unique tropical rhythms and enjoyed, for a while at least, the entertaining parade of characters that frequented their little paradise on the bay. And then came the slow turn as the novelty wore off and the responsibility of managing a bar, a restaurant, and a fishing charter business became a daily grind. Gradually, the island transmuted from a paradise into a prison, and she began looking for a way to escape.

Rupert had seen it coming with Darla for months, though he tried to tell himself that things would be different this time. But then, night before last, he'd watched her last flame of hope snuffed out on the makeshift stage at Shady's.

And of course, there was the matter of her whereabouts after the show. She had wandered home the next morning, announced that she had a splitting headache, and crawled into bed, still dressed. She'd been there ever since.

But there was something oblique and awkward about her manner that made him suspect she'd been up to the devil's business. When he saw Red Burton's car driving up the gravel road, it all but confirmed his suspicion.

Rupert walked downstairs and opened the door to find his friend standing in the front drive. The sheriff held his Stetson in his hands, tentatively fingering the brim of the hat.

"'Lo, Red."

"Rupe."

"You looking for Darla?"

Red Burton's jaw tensed. "She okay?"

"Don't know. She's been in bed for two days."

"Y'all had a chance to . . . talk yet?"

"Talk about what, Red?" asked Rupert, his eyes narrowing.

The sheriff cleared his throat and kicked at a shell with the toe of his boot. "Rupert, I um . . . I need to fess up to something."

"I was wondering if you'd be man enough to come out here and do it face to face."

"Well, here I am."

The two men stood there, bowed up and glaring at each other in the waning summer light, when suddenly, a rush of wings directed their eyes upward. A flock of roseate spoonbills was flying over-head, and the last rays of the sun seemed to electrify their bright plumage, accentuating the pink and salmon of their wings and the brilliant carmine at their shoulders. Rigid legs, straight as arrows, trailed behind bright orange tails. The intense color of the birds was arresting, and the two men on the ground could not take their eyes off them—it was like they were witnessing a fantastic aberration of nature, or perhaps a mysterious sign from above. The birds briefly dipped their spatula-shaped bills at the figures below and then winged away, seaward.

Rupert sighed and looked at his old friend. "If we have to talk about this, I'm gonna need a drink," he began walking toward Red's sedan, "in a proper bar."

Red fell in step behind him. "It looked closed up when I drove past," he said, placing his hat on the dashboard and climbing behind the wheel.

"We shut down early tonight. It's been a long weekend. But I'm fixin' to open it up again."

Driving to the main building, they passed Zach first and then Gilbert and Sally walking down the path toward their cabins. Each of them stopped and waved at the car as it drove by, but the two men didn't wave back, both of them focused on what lay ahead.

Rupert unlocked the front door and turned on the interior lights. "What'll ya have, Red?"

"Beer's fine."

Rupert shook his head. "No, this isn't a beer kind of situation." He rooted around beneath the bar and came up with a bottle of Bushmill's. He grabbed two rocks glasses and filled them almost to the brim with the Irish whiskey.

"What do we drink to?" asked Rupert, holding up his glass.

Red raised his drink and hesitated. "Hell, I don't know, Rupe. To life, I guess."

Rupert clinked glasses with Red and took a gulp. "To life, she's a funny ol' dog."

Red nodded. "Sure is."

"So . . . Red, to make this part go quicker, I'm gonna come right out and tell you I think you slept with my wife."

Red's face darkened a shade, and he straightened on his barstool. "I'm afraid I did, Rupert."

Rupert shook his head. "Well, I can't say that I didn't expect it. She's had a flame burnin' for you since she was a teenager. If she wadn't so damn impulsive, she would have waited for you to get back from overseas and married you straight away. Then we wouldn't be in this bind we're in."

"I'm sorry I put us in this bind, Rupe. She was all unwound when she came to my door. I should have brought her home. But I didn't." He saw his friend wince and tried to fix it. "I mean, it was me that was being forward about it. She never would have—"

"Yeah she would've," Rupert interrupted. "I know Darla. In fact, I usually know what she's going to do before she does." He smiled and shook his head. "Although I sure didn't expect her to choke like she did at the show the other night."

"Was it bad?"

"Oh, goddamn, was it ever. Thank goodness Gilbert jumped up there and kept the crowd from throwing beer bottles at the stage." He took a big swig of whiskey. "I'm going to miss her, Red, that's a fact." Rupert paused and stared at his drink, his big hands wrapped around the glass.

The sheriff stared at his drink, too.

"Do you love her?" asked Rupert.

"I do, Rupe. I guess I always have."

Rupert sighed. "You know, to make matters worse, I suspect Gilbert's thinking about running off with Sally. And now that the idea of selling the place has taken hold with Noble and Flavius, they're both itchin' to get out and do something else, too." He tugged at his earlobe. "It's gonna end up being just me, Zach, and the Nelsons left on this island. Ain't that a hell of a crew?"

"I ain't going nowhere, Rupe," Red offered sympathetically.

"No? Don't be surprised if Darla starts talking to you about moving to Hollywood pretty soon. She'd never do it on her own, but she'll damn sure make you think it was your idea."

Red Burton was amazed that Rupert was taking the whole thing so easy, and it gave him a little thrill to hear himself and Darla talked about as a couple. But even so, he felt guilty about getting off so easy, and he felt compelled to mention it.

"Dang it, Rupert. I wish you'd stop being such a swell guy about this whole thing. I almost wish you'd punch me or something."

Without warning, Rupert reared back and popped Red right between the brows, knocking him off his barstool and onto the floor. When the sheriff opened his eyes, Rupert was standing over him, holding out his hand to help him up.

"That's for cheatin' on your best friend," he said.

The sheriff let himself be pulled up and tamped down a surge of anger at being sucker-punched by his "best friend." As soon as he was upright again, Rupert let go of his hand and belted him again, this time square on the nose.

"And that's for sleeping with my wife."

After that, Red was unable to put a lid on it. He picked himself up off the floor and planted his fist in Rupert's midsection, and then followed that with an uppercut to his chin. Rupert flew backwards over a table and scrambled up amidst the upturned chairs.

"I was wondering how many times I was gonna get to hit you before you finally hit me back," he said, putting up his dukes for what was apparently going to be an extended fight.

Red wiped off the blood that had bubbled out of his nostril. "You're a crazy sonofabitch, Rupe."

The two men met and went at it with all the gusto and ferocity of a bull and bear fight—the tall, rangy sheriff and the thick-necked, thick-headed proprietor of Shady's. Whenever Red began having success with his long jabs and crosses, Rupert would charge him and the two of them would crash over another table and scramble around on the floor. At one point in the brawl, Red knocked Rupert to the floor three consecutive times, whereupon Rupert taunted the sheriff to "get down on the floor and fight like a man."

But Rupert kept getting up. After ten minutes, the two men were battered, bloodied, and worn out. Bent over, with their hands on their knees, they decided that the battle was over; they'd both had enough. Whatever pent-up grudges they had carried into the fight had been punched out.

"What do you say we finish that bottle of Bushmill's?" Rupert suggested.

Red found his Stetson and dusted it off. "I say that's a good idea."

The two men sat at the bar drinking, talking, and laughing late into the night.

At one point, Rupert asked out of the blue, "Was she worth it?"

And the sheriff replied, "I reckon they're all worth it."

When Zachariah Yates came in early the next morning to sweep the floor, he wondered for a second if someone had routed a cattle stampede through the dance hall. No less than a dozen tables and chairs were scattered around the room, a neon sign and a clock had been knocked off the wall, and was that a tooth on the floor? But when he saw the empty bottle of whiskey and the two blood-rimmed glasses resting on the bar, he surmised that Rupert and the sheriff had worked things out, in their own way.

CHAPTER 36

Jimmy Glick was sitting at what he had come to regard as his own personal corner of Purgatory, namely the window booth at the Rainbow Inn. He'd been there for six hours, smoking cigarettes, working the crossword puzzle in the Corpus Christi daily, and letting his eyes wander occasionally to the railroad-tie bridge that led to Ransom Island. He noticed that the dipshi⁺ duck blind still guarded its entrance.

For lunch, he'd foregone the usual Fisherman's Platter and decided, in a fit of wild abandon, to order a chicken-fried steak. It would be awhile before he could stand the sight of another fish, either swimming free in the bay or fried and resting in a basket with hush puppies and tartar sauce.

Through the pass-through window that gave a view to the kitchen, Jimmy could see the Chinese cook, Jim Bob (the closest the locals could get to his given name of Jin Bao) Qui, beating the living shit out of the innocent piece of round steak that was destined for Jimmy's blue plate special.

Jim Bob was flailing away with a meat tenderizer, swearing in Cantonese and sweating into the pot of bubbling cream gravy that would accompany the culinary masterpiece, once it was properly subdued and flattened. Jimmy had put less effort into breaking the legs of deadbeats and freelancers back in Galveston.

He figured this was as good a place as any in Aransas Pass to perch while considering how to carry out Primo's directive. It was a straightforward and unambiguous assignment, but Jimmy thought of himself as a painstaking craftsman. Any punk kid could squeeze lead into a citizen with a rusty Saturday-Night Special. Jimmy was in charge of sending a message.

Five minutes after he arrived, he'd braced the Rainbow Inn's ratty-looking proprietor, Jacky Jack Vandiver. He described to him the sort of fellow he was looking for though not, of course, why. Someone who took a special interest in Ransom Island and the Sweetwaters, he explained. Someone who lately had spent a lot of time on the island. Someone who, frankly, couldn't shut up about the place.

"I'm trying to get an angle on those brothers," said Glick. "My boss is trying to sweet-talk them into selling out, but we just can't find the right handle. I can't go nosing around myself—they already know me and why I'm here. But if I could talk to someone with a, ah . . . with an affinity for them and the place, then maybe I could find a play we've overlooked. Get my drift?"

Jacky Jack Vandiver nodded. When it came to the Sweetwaters and that over-rated fish camp they ran, he'd be happy to dime out some random somebody if it meant that Shady's might be out of the picture. (Never the brightest bulb in the chandelier, Vandiver didn't realize what would be in store for him if Jimmy's "associates" did indeed move in next door.)

Those Sweetwater sonsofbitches had already cost him plenty of dough. He'd heard talk of big-pot poker games on the island that made his little dice-and-cards operation look like a round of "Go Fish." And compared to the dishes that Mexican cook was preparing over there, his food tasted like fried tarantulas. To top it off, not only did Darla Sweetwater make his own waitresses seem like the offspring of the Wicked Witch of the West, they'd stole his best-looking cigarette girl and had *her* working there, too. It wasn't fair. The brazen, outrageous success of the Duke Ellington show was the last straw.

Jacky Jack thought he had just the patsies this character was looking for. "There's a couple of guys that's come in here a few times.

Young fellas. They's name was 'Kent' and 'Wayne,' though I couldn't tell you which was which. They seemed a little confused theyselves.

"Anyways, they was always talkin' about Shady's. They couldn't stop goin' on about it, Jesus on a sidecar they sounded like a broken record. They sort of let on they might be some hard-case boys theyselves, but they didn't look like they had much bark on 'em."

Jacky Jack fancied himself a connoisseur of desperados.

"They'd stop in here for a hamburger or a pack of smokes, but then they'd make a beeline acrost that causeway, pretty near every day. You want the inside dope about what's going on over at Sweetwater's place, I'd say they might oblige you. They act like the place is some damned old Taj Mahal."

Jimmy Glick thanked him and set up shop in his booth.

Now, he was waiting.

Focused, immobile, patient. Like the red-tailed hawks that perched on the crosspieces of the telephone poles along the highway, waiting for some little varmit to flush and run. Then, dinnertime.

Speaking of which . . . . With a sour expression, Jimmy stubbed his cigarette out in the congealed puddle of cream gravy on his plate. He used the nail of his little finger to fish out the last wad of gristle from between two molars. His meal sat in his belly like a chunk of concrete. At least the iced tea was fresh-brewed.

What Jimmy Glick wouldn't have given to be sitting in Galatoire's in New Orleans, eagerly anticipating a piping hot plate of Shrimp Creole and a second icy-cold Sazerac cocktail. Or shooting the shit with some old boys he knew up in Fort Worth, swapping lies in a juke joint roadhouse on the Jacksboro Highway while waiting for his blood-red 16-oz. ribeye to make its way from the grill to his table. Shit, even a hamburger at the little seawall stand by Murdoch's Bathhouse in Galveston would have tasted like a four-star Michelin meal compared to the Rainbow Inn's bill of fare. As far as Jimmy was concerned, Primo Ginestra owed him some serious digestive restitution after this gig.

Jimmy gave neither Wayne or Kent—which ever one was which— a second thought. That individual was just a speed bump between Jimmy Glick and a decent meal.

It wasn't in Jimmy's nature to question the Ginestras' business decisions; self-preservation discouraged it, for one thing, and Glick enjoyed the perks that came with the job. But this current obsession of Primo's with the girl, who might or might not have been his daughter, was a sideways sort of deal. It had a weird, off-kilter feel about it that made Jimmy vaguely uncomfortable. It was personal mixed up in business, for one thing, and it was intimately personal to Primo, which was quite another. Jimmy could usually count on Gerry to keep a relatively cool head and focus on the dollars and cents of a matter at hand. But Primo walked around every day of his life like a lit fuse. Jimmy didn't want to be collateral damage when the bomb went off one day.

Ah, well. Nobody ever said being a gangster was a bowl of cherries.

Glick was interrupted in his reverie by the ding of the bell over the front door of the café. He didn't turn around, but he saw Jacky Jack Vandiver jerk his chin towards the new arrival.

Showtime.

Glick waited until the young man ordered his shrimp basket and cold beer at the counter before he approached and tapped him on the shoulder.

"Hey, podnah," he said amiably. "You mind if I borrow that sports section?" He nodded towards a discarded newspaper some previous patron had abandoned.

"It's all yours," said Cliff "Kent" Hollenbeck. He was flying solo today. His partner, Willie "Wayne" Dawes, had driven back to Austin to give Attorney General Wilson an update about the general state of iniquity on and around Ransom Island. They'd flipped a coin, and Willie had won and opted for Austin. He had a girl there he hadn't seen in nearly three weeks.

Glick turned to the baseball scores and pretended to scan the agate type. "You following the Yankees this year?" Kent asked.

"No, I'm a Texas League man," Glick replied. "I keep trying to give the Fort Worth Cats a chance, but those dogasses traded away every decent fielder they had. A wheelchair cripple could score on a pop-up fly against those turkeys. I guess I'm gonna have to go with those Shreveport Swamp Dragons this year."

"Cooler name, anyhow," said Kent.

"There's that, too," said Jimmy with an easy laugh.

"But hell, I know what you mean. I went and saw the Austin Senators play Fort Worth, and our guys beat the Cats like a ratty old rug."

They bantered about sports for a few minutes, and then Glick eased the conversation around to his real area of interest. "Hey, I'm just passing through, but you look like a guy who might know his way around here. Where can I get a decent line on a fishing guide? I finished up a job in Corpus and I've got a day or two to kill before I've got to get back to the home office. Any chance you'd know someone who could show me where to get a line wet around here?"

Hollenbeck's face lit up with enthusiasm. "Oh, shit yeah," he said. "Just follow that causeway down at the end of the block. You'll wind up at a place called Shady's. Hell of a great place. The brothers that run it, they'll hook you into all the fish you want. Trout or redfish, even tarpon if you want a real thrill. Great guys."

"Shady's? I thought that was just a dancehall. Didn't they have some big shindig out there a couple of nights ago?"

That really got "Kent's" motor running. "Oh, yeah, hell of a dance. Never seen a blowout like it. White folks and coloreds mixing it up, everyone dancing and having a ball. Just like being in Harlem. Or so I've heard."

Glick looked sly for a moment and said he'd heard there might be some other action going on as well.

Kent lowered his voice and glanced around conspiratorially, even though there was just one bored waitress and two oblivious patrons studying menus in the room. The lunch rush was over before it began.

"Well, it seems like it," he murmured. "I been out there almost every night this past week or so and it sure seems like they've got some action going. Heard about some big card games. Even saw a couple of roulette wheels and slots in a back room . . . . " (Noble had bought the two defunct slot machines second-hand from a failed North Beach penny arcade in Corpus Christi to go with the one he borrowed from the American Legion, and Zach had cobbled together the "roulette wheels" from old washing machine parts.)

Kent enjoyed giving the impression of a man with an inside track on things. A guy who was in on the action. He glanced around again for effect, "I even heard there's some mobbed-up guys from Galveston sniffing around, maybe looking to move in."

"These, ah, brothers—Sweetwater brothers, you said—you on good terms with 'em?"

"Aw, yeah," said Cliff, full of innocent self-importance. "They're real standup guys. Well, one of 'em, named Flavius, if you can believe that, has got a temper on him. But yeah, I get along plenty well with those old boys."

"Kent" and Jimmy Glick talked on pleasantly, and the former told Glick everything he knew, or guessed he knew about the Sweetwaters and Ransom Island. Glick listened avidly. He'd found his man.

"Hey," Glick said when the opportunity arose. "I got extra tickets to see the Beaumont Golden Gators take on the Tulsa Oilers over in Corpus this afternoon. They're doing a barnstorming tour or somethin'. My client laid 'em on me, and I was gonna run over and catch the game. Too late to do any serious fishing today, anyhow. What do you say? You wanna watch the ballgame, maybe get on the outside of a couple of cold ones?"

Hollenbeck didn't have anything pressing to do until his partner returned the next day from Austin.

"Why the hell not?" he said, standing up.

No one paid any attention.

And no one, except Jacky Jack Vandiver, saw them leave.

▬▬▬

CHAPTER 37

Cecil Shoat wondered aloud if a hand could be reattached after being blown clean off.

Giddyup Dodson interrupted his pull of beer mid-swig to offer an opinion on the subject. "A fingertip maybe, but not a whole hand. Especially after it's been picked at by crabs and birds and such."

"Very true," added Captain Quincy. "I lost a fingertip in the loading assembly of a howitzer one time. I glued it back on and it was good as new." He stuck out a crooked pinky as proof.

Cecil snorted. "A fingertip? That ain't shit." He presented his scarred and misshapen hand to the patrons at the bar. "Y'all see this?" He waggled a ring finger that was stubbed off at the first knuckle. "And this?" He pointed to a truncated digit capped with a misshapen fingernail the color of antique ivory. "I've seen more dismember-ments in my line of work than an autopsy guy. Comes with the job," he declared proudly. "Roughnecking ain't for pansies."

"Anyway," Giddyup continued, "the sheriff didn't find Leroy Stuckey's hand until the next morning. It wouldn't have been good for anything by then."

"Except bait," Cecil agreed.

"I thought Barefoot Nelson found the hand," said Captain Quincy.

"He did," said Cecil. "He found it on Steadman Reef; that's a long way from the bridge."

"It couldn't have flown that far in the explosion," Giddyup replied. He turned to Captain Quincy and Gus Brauer for amplification. "Y'all were there. What did you see?"

Gus looked down at his glass of beer. The head bandage he wore covered most of his scalp and one ear, and his arm was still in a sling on account of his broken shoulder. "I saw nothing," he replied. The image of the seagull flying off with Stuckey's severed hand dangling from its orange beak was too disturbing to discuss. He wasn't even sure the memory was real.

Captain Quincy shrugged. "I only remember seeing Gustav fly through the air."

The bar regulars laughed at this and then knocked back their beers. The Ransom Island Bridge explosion story was shaping up to be a classic.

"Hey, Sally, how 'bout another round of brews?" Cecil bellowed. "This round's on me."

"You haven't paid for the last round you bought for the house," she answered.

"Well, put it on my tab."

"You know Rupert doesn't allow tabs."

Cecil was well aware of the "no-tabs" sign above the bar, but he also knew it was haphazardly enforced. He counted on Shady's lax accounting to stretch his drinking budget. He'd been getting away with it for years. He nudged Gideon Dodson with his shoulder. "Hey, Giddyup, loan me a ten, will ya?"

Giddyup pushed his cowboy hat back on his head and sighed, just like he'd seen John Wayne do in the movie *Hondo*. "This is the last time, Cecil." He reached into the back pocket of his Wranglers like he was surrendering the deed to the ranch. "Sally, darlin', since Cecil is being so generous with my wallet, could you be an angel and see what Gilbert's got cooking today? I'm starving."

"Sure thing, cowboy," she said. But before she went, Sally pulled each patron's preferred beer out of the fridge and set it on a fresh napkin in front them. She'd spent enough time in saloons to know what services produced the biggest tips, although Shady's played host to a pretty cheap bunch. The tip jar usually contained about as much coin as a gumball machine.

She walked to the screen door and called out to Gilbert, inquiring about the snack selections. He'd probably heard the request already, loud as everyone was talking. With all the drama surrounding the bogus casino, the bridge explosion, Duke Ellington's triumph, and Darla's disaster, there was much to talk about, and the regulars were plenty amped up for the occasion. It was the first time they'd really had a chance to hash over the details and compare notes.

When Gilbert answered from the kitchen, Sally smiled and walked back inside.

"So," asked Cecil, "what'd the chef say was on the snack menu this fine afternoon?"

Sally paused for dramatic effect. "He said, 'Finger sandwiches.'"

The bar burst into laughter, a raucous, over-the-top laughter that shook the glassware on the shelves. Gideon stood up and whacked his cowboy hat on his thigh, and Cecil actually banged the bar top with his fists. Even the reticent German, Gustav Brauer, rolled his head back and brayed like a donkey.

Sally folded her arms and watched with amusement. *I'm going to miss this place,* she thought.

Suddenly, Rupert Sweetwater came through the front door and the laughter trailed off. He walked by the crowd with his head down, his expression inward. Everyone in the bar knew what had happened between Red and Darla. The divorce papers had been quickly filed and now Darla was in the process of moving her things into the sheriff's house in Aransas Pass. It was a hard thing to watch, and the regulars were embarrassed for Rupert.

Perhaps sensing the solicitous attention of the customers, Rupert stopped and glared at them. "What the hell are y'all looking at?"

Eyes averted and heads turned away. What could they say? The man was a train wreck, and he had a right to be. Cecil wanted to ask him when they were going to resume their casino gambit, but he decided to wait for a more opportune moment. And Gideon was dying to know why Rupert's face was bruised up, but he held his tongue as well. At present, the man was inconsolable.

"Drink your goddamn beers," Rupert bellowed.

After he exited through the back door, there was a momentary silence in deference to the proprietor's misfortune, but before long, the beer bottles began tipping back anew and the bar banter ratcheted up to its previous decibel level.

Rupert marched across the wooden gangway and stuck his head in the kitchen. "Gilbert? Soon as Darla is finished using my wagon, I want you to swing by Big Todd's and get some tubes of marine sealant. One of the skiffs is leaking like a sieve." He shut the screen door and then, seeming to remember something else, opened it again. "While you're at it, pick me up a new toaster, too."

Gilbert looked up from the pile of potatoes he was peeling. "I don't think Big Todd carries toasters."

"Then go by the five-and-dime," he snapped, "or wherever the hell it is that they sell toasters." With that, he slammed the screen door and stomped off in the direction of the bait house.

She took his toaster, too, Gilbert realized. *Man, oh, man.*

Watching his boss lumber down the sandy path, he felt sympathy for him, but he also knew that a divorce was probably for the best. In the long run, her leaving would be good for him. But in the short run, having your wife run off with your best friend was a bitter pill to swallow.

Meanwhile, Rupert was being an insufferable grouch. Hanging around the island while Darla drove back and forth to Red's house with carloads of her things (and some of Rupert's), all the while enduring the pitying looks of his friends and family, was just too much, and he was taking his misery out on anyone who crossed his path. Rupert needed to get away for awhile, reassess his situation, change the station . . . and somebody needed to tell him so. Gilbert figured it might as well be him. Besides, he hadn't helped matters when he informed Rupert about his own plans to leave Ransom Island with Sally Rose.

Gilbert untied his apron and threw it on the counter. *No time like the present,* he decided.

When Gilbert went into the bait house, he found Zachariah Yates sitting on a folding chair, repairing a fishing reel. Rupert stood at the doorway, facing the bay, his back to the room and his hands jammed into his pockets like a petulant boy.

"Howdy, Gilbert," said Zachariah.

"Howdy, Zach."

"I was just suggesting to Rupe here that he consider a little vacation, maybe get out of town for a spell. But he seems to think we aren't capable of lookin' after things while he's gone."

Gilbert smiled. Zach was a step ahead of him. "You would think he'd have more confidence in us, wouldn't you?" said Gilbert. "I mean, after all, he's the one trained us."

"Uh huh. If I didn't have such a tough hide, I'd feel downright affronted."

"It does sting a little, for a fact."

Rupert turned around and narrowed his eyes at them. "You two are tryin' my patience."

Zach set down the reel he was working on. "You hear that, Gilbert? He says we're trying *his* patience."

Gilbert shook his head. "Like my mom used to say, '*El comal le dijo a la olla, que tiznada estas.*'"

Zach nodded his head in agreement, like he knew what Gilbert had said.

"What the hell does that mean?" Rupert asked with irritation.

"It's the Mexican version of the pot calling the kettle black," Gilbert explained.

Rupert waved his hand as if he were shooing away a fly. "Ganging up on me, huh? Well, let me tell you—"

As if on cue, Noble walked through the door. "Hey there, sports fans." It didn't take him long to realize that he'd interrupted something. "What's up, fellas?"

"Rupert was just fixin' to tell me and Gilbert why he thought it was a good idea for him to go on a vacation," said Zach.

"That's a hell of an idea, Rupe," said Noble, his eyes widening. "I was coming over here to suggest that very thing. In fact, I checked the train schedule this morning, and there's a sleeper that leaves the Corpus Christi station at seven this evening. It'll get you to New Orleans about breakfast time."

Rupert looked at the three men suspiciously. "Who's the leader of this little mutiny? Is it you, brother?"

Noble looked surprised. "I didn't put 'em up to it, if that's what you mean. I thought I came up with the idea on my own."

"Same here," said Zach.

Gilbert nodded in accordance. "Me three. Spooky, huh?"

Rupert began shaking his head and pacing. "There's too much to do 'round here. The bridge still needs to be shored up in a few spots, we've got some leaky boats need patching and, unless you boys have forgotten, we've got a fake casino to run."

"I say we shut the place down for a few days," Noble suggested. "Let things rest a little. After the Ellington event, you know we've got the scratch to tide us over."

"Shut down Shady's?"

"Not 'shut down,'" Noble continued. "Just . . . take a break. Hang a sign on the door that says 'Gone Fishin'. Everybody deserves a breather, anyhow."

Rupert stopped pacing and pulled on his earlobe. "Why is everybody so anxious to get rid of me? What else is going on?"

Zach looked up. "Rupert, you wanna hear the truth? We think it'll do you some good. Nobody likes seeing you walkin' around here being such a sad-sack."

"Some jambalaya and a good dose of Dixieland jazz will be just the thing to cheer you up," Gilbert offered.

"He's right," said Noble. "You haven't taken a vacation since . . . ." He thought about it and then looked away sheepishly. His brother's last vacation had been his honeymoon with Darla, three years ago.

Rupert winced and then took a deep breath. "I suppose you boys are right. I guess maybe I've been a little difficult to be around these last two days."

The other three men exchanged glances. He'd been a perfect pain in the ass, and if he'd have said no, they were prepared to hogtie him and put him on the train by force.

Noble opened his hands as if the matter had been decided. "Great. I'll come by the house at six and run you to the station. That still gives you a couple of hours to pack."

Rupert nodded wearily. "Aw, what the hell, I've always wanted to drink a beer at that merry-go-round bar at the Monteleone Hotel."

———

CHAPTER 38

Even though the cardboard sign on Shady's door announced that the establishment was officially "closed for repairs," Gilbert woke up early and wandered to the kitchen out of habit. A gentle breeze moved over the island, smelling of mud, salt water, and a hint of something sweet. Rupert said the sweet scent came from oily slicks created by feeding schools of fish, which he swore smelled like Big Red soda pop. Bullbats swooped above the scrub, dive-bombing mosquitos and flying ants, and nearby, a Great Egret perched majestically in the bowl of a thatch palm, the bird's long mating plumage floating on the wind.

Do I really want to leave this place? Gilbert asked himself again. Zach was absolutely right that it was a dead-end job, slinging hash in a fringe restaurant set in the middle of a shallow bay. But was that so bad? Did he really have an obligation to make something of himself? To make his mark in the world, as Zach had said? What was wrong with just being happy on Ransom Island? He doubted Rupert would ever bring himself to sell the place, so why not stay where he was and keep eating the lotus?

Well, for one thing, Sally was leaving, and she had *asked* him to go with her, to start a life with her on the West Coast. Him. With her. And he'd told her yes. That's what it came down to. He wasn't going because some half-witted rednecks roughed him up, and he wasn't particularly worried about the avaricious goombahs in Galveston. He just wanted to be with Sally. And Sally was bound for California.

When Gilbert walked to the front of the building to make sure the cardboard "closed for repairs" sign was still up, he learned just how mistaken a man could be.

He climbed the stairs and discovered someone slumped against the front doors. Gilbert approached the figure cautiously, unsure whether he was passed out drunk or just asleep and waiting for the bar to open. On closer inspection, he realized the man was dead, funeral parlor dead, with a dark hole the size of a dime in the middle of his forehead. The sign that the Sweetwater brothers had hung on the door had been flipped over. UNDER NEW MANGEMENT had been scrawled on the backside with a piece of charcoal.

Gilbert stepped back and looked around, feeling light-headed. The face of the dead man looked familiar, but for the moment, Gilbert couldn't place him. He backed slowly down the steps, eyeing the corpse warily, as if it might spring up and chase after him. When he looked around again, he saw Zach approaching from his cabin. He whistled and waved him over.

Zach had the same reaction as Gilbert when he climbed the steps. "Lord have mercy!" he whispered. "That man's been shot, Gilbert!"

"Do you recognize him?"

Zach edged closer and peered at the face. "It's one of those fellas that came in here looking for work awhile back. Wayne or Kent, I believe his name was.

"Kent," said Gilbert. "You're right, his last name was Kent."

Zach walked to the edge of the porch and grasped the rail, muttering to himself.

Gilbert watched him with concern. "You okay, Zach?"

Zachariah looked to the west and shook his head. "I been knowing something bad like this was gonna happen . . . ever since I laid eyes on that dead shark. I just felt it, you know?"

Gilbert didn't say it, but he'd been troubled by memories of the dead hammerhead as well . . . and by the fact that Old Hitler's ghastly end coincided with Sally's appearance on the island. He had tried to block it out.

"I'm gonna go call Noble," said Zach, wanting to get away from the body.

Noble and Flavius got there a few minutes later. Gilbert sat on the bottom step while the two brothers examined the body and discussed the situation.

"Those sons-of-bitches wanna go to war? We'll go to war," Flavius declared.

"Which sons-of-bitches would you be going to war with, brother?"

Flavius hesitated before answering. "You don't think it was the Klan that did this?"

Noble shook his head. "No. I think it's a message from our friends up the coast."

"Well, then we'll go to war with *those* sons-of-bitches!"

"Uh huh, and see what it got this poor bastard?"

Noble's quiet observation sobered his brother considerably. Fistfights were one thing, but this . . . .

Flavius stepped forward to take a closer look at the dead man. "Should I try and get aholt of Rupert?"

"No. He'll be back in a couple of days. Besides, we don't even know where he's staying. All we can do right now is notify Red and let him do his job." Noble rose from his squatting position and rubbed his temples. "Damn, what a way to start the day."

Gilbert moved to the stoop behind the kitchen and sat alone, sipping on a cup of coffee, trying not to think about the dead man. He could hear the commotion going on out front: multiple vehicles rattling over the bridge, car doors opening and closing, voices, footsteps on the porch as the authorities photographed and then removed the body.

A little later, Sally rounded the corner of the building, walking quickly toward him. He could see that she was upset.

"We have to leave now," she said breathlessly. "Today."

Gilbert looked up at her. "Today?"

"Like right now, Gilbert." She looked around nervously.

Gilbert was taken aback at her urgency. "Somebody's sending a message. But it's got nothing to do with you and me."

She shook her head forcefully. "No, you don't understand. It's got everything to do with me. They'll be back, and these men will kill more people if they have to: Rupert, his brothers. You and Zach. Believe me, I know."

Sally's conviction alarmed Gilbert, and also made him suspicious. "How do you *know?*" he asked.

"I've heard what they do to people who stand in their way or to people who cross them."

"You seem to know a lot about them."

Sally's eyes darted away from his. "Trust me, Gilbert, I—"

"*No.* I'm tired of you telling me to trust you." And he was tired of being patient. For a month he'd been waiting for her to open up to him, and he still didn't know any more about her past than when she'd hopped off the back of the beer truck. He needed to know what she was mixed up in. "Talk to me, Sally."

She looked at him with teary eyes. "I'm afraid you won't love me if I tell you."

"I doubt that."

Sally wiped her eyes and opened her mouth to speak, but then stopped and stared at the ground.

"Let's start with an easy question," said Gilbert, "like, what is your real name?"

"It's Sally Rose. Sally Rose Ginestra."

Gilbert gulped and tried to respond calmly. "Any, uh, relation to—?"

"Primo Ginestra is my father."

"*Santo cielo!*" he muttered.

"I've been running from him for more than two years. Him or his people."

"Does he know you're here?"

She nodded slowly. "Remember the guy that beat you up?"

How could he forget? "That was Primo's guy?"

She nodded again. "His name is Jimmy Glick." It was hard for her even to say his name.

"How could you know it was him?"

"It's something he said to you—a catch phrase. I'd heard him use it when I was younger."

Gilbert let this sink in. Primo was Sally's dad—a ruthless mobster and killer—and daddy strongly disapproved of his daughter's boyfriend. Swell.

Sally began crying. "I'm sorry I didn't tell you this before. I thought not telling you wasn't the same as lying. I'm so sorry."

Gilbert stood up and looked at her. He wanted to slap her, and kiss her—he wanted to do both. "You should have told me before."

"I know. I know. But . . ." she paused, her voice catching, "I was afraid you would make me leave."

He took a deep breath and put his hands on her shoulders. "Sally, if we're going to be together, you have to promise to be honest with me from here on out."

She put her forehead to his, tears streaming down her face. "I promise."

"Okay," he said. "Thank you."

"There's more."

Gilbert stepped back and looked at her. *Oh boy.* He grabbed her hand and pulled her behind him. "Let's walk."

But where could they go on the tiny little island that was safe from a guy like Primo Ginestra? He had *watched* them, had seen them together on the island, then he'd sent one of his thugs to bust his ribs. He also seemed to know that Rupert was crawfishing on selling the place, so he'd killed one of Shady's customers and planted him on the front porch to remind them it was time to close the deal.

Gilbert took Sally to the little cove on the west side of the island, where he sat her down on the sandy beach. She talked at length, working backwards, from her narrow escape from Jimmy Glick at the Rainbow Inn, all the way back to her first, and most disturbing, memory as a child, watching her father murder her mother.

"For years I wouldn't admit to myself that I saw it," she concluded. It felt good to unburden herself at last. "I thought it was a bad dream. Later, I tried to talk to the nuns about it but they wouldn't listen. They said I was too young to remember something like that or that I made up the story to get attention. One even tried to convince me the memory was planted there by the Devil." She laughed bitterly. "Well, they were right about that last one; that about sums up my dad."

"What was the *official* story on your mother?"

"They said she ran away with a horn player."

"Never to be seen again."

Sally sighed and let a handful of sand run through her fingers. "Never to be seen again. All I have is a picture of her. One picture."

"Was she beautiful, like you?"

Sally smiled. "She was lovely. I'll show you her photograph when we get back to the cabin. But we need to start packing."

Gilbert took a deep breath. "Sally, I understand why you want to pack up and leave right now, but I really want to wait until Rupert gets back. He's like family to me, and it wouldn't be right to run away, especially at a time like this."

Sally was thinking that *a time like this* was precisely the right time to run away, but she reluctantly acquiesced. "Okay. I understand, I think."

CHAPTER 39

Life was funny sometimes. By virtue of rank, maritime law, and experience, Capt. Marcos Shorter was the master of the *M/V Easy Eight* and he was accustomed to being regarded as such.

But as the volume, accusations, and invective rose between Primo Ginestra and his brother back in Galveston, Cap'n Mark felt compelled to remove himself from the bridge of his own vessel. It wasn't just the volcanic tone of the back-and-forth, but the *substance* of what they were discussing. Of course, as "discussions" went, this was right up there with the one between the Nazis and the Russians at Stalingrad.

So Cap'n Mark, an easy-going soul by nature, abandoned his bridge and went back to the stern where he sat in one of the fighting chairs, lit a cigarette, and wondered if he'd one day be compelled to repeat what he'd overheard to a grand jury.

". . . He was a *cop*, Primo!" Gerry roared over the ship-to-shore. "It was just on the radio! That's what I can't seem to get through that fucking thick skull of yours! Of all the people you could've clipped. Jesus and Santa Maria. What were you thinking?"

"I was thinking I wanted to get the job done! The one you sent me down here to do, you asshole! Jimmy didn't know he was a CID man! He picked him up in a café. He was just trying to make a point, to get things settled. He was just supposed to be some yokel fisherman we could use to push these Sweetwater bastards off high center."

"Why didn't you just have Jimmy plug J. Edgar Hoover and be done with it? Jesus, you stupid . . . ." Gerry broke down into spluttering Sicilian curses, which surprised Primo. His younger brother had never really taken to the mother tongue, and he wasn't aware he knew so many foul words.

The Ginestras were furious with one another's perceived shortcomings. And as far as Primo was concerned, it went back a long way; his younger brother never had the stomach for the rough stuff. Gerry would have countered that Primo couldn't have found finesse with a six-man scouting party, and was paranoid and hair-triggered, to boot.

But underneath, fueling the anger, was the realization that everything they had strived to build was suddenly in terrible danger.

Nothing, absolutely nothing, made cops in Texas so batshit crazy and dangerous as the slaying of one of their own. All the gloves came off, all give-and-take "understandings" canceled. The rule of the day was a whirlwind dragnet for every snitch and lowlife in sight, followed by backroom interrogations and the righteous black-flag fury of an Old Testament God. Nothing, not even the Ginestras' machine, could stand in the face of it.

The bomb went off when Red Burton found Cliff Hollenbeck's real I.D. in his room at the Sea-Aire Motel and called the attorney general's office in Austin. Will Wilson's face faded to white ten seconds after he picked up the phone. He asked a few short questions, listened, and then replied quietly, "Whatever you need, Sheriff. And I mean whatever."

As it happened, Willie Dawes was seated in the A.G.'s outer office, waiting to have a last word with his boss before heading back to the coast. Wilson sent for him, but then sat silently, head bowed, absorbed in some profound mood. Finally, he reached in his desk drawer, pulled out a pack of Pall Malls and offered his young officer a cigarette. Willie was nothing short of floored—Will Wilson thought tobacco was the eighth deadly sin. They lit up together and smoked for a moment in silence.

"Ah, sir," Dawes mentioned after a minute, "is there something you wanted to tell me?"

Finally, Wilson raised his head and met his young officer's eyes. "Yeah, son . . . . There is."

There had been a scene, of course. Dawes' face crumpled in grief, confusion and anger at the news. He howled, stomped his feet, vowed he was gonna go back to Aransas Pass and burn down the sonofabitch who killed his friend.

Wilson understood completely. He'd been there himself, long ago and more than once.

He got up and put his arm around the young man's shoulders. "Officer Dawes, I need you to stand down," he said, not unkindly. "I need you here, not running off with blood in your eye. I need you to find out who was closest to Dawes—girlfriend, parents, kin. We'll go talk to them together, and we need to do it soon, before they see it in the paper or hear it on the radio. That's the best way to help your friend right now. Can you do that for me?"

Eyes glistening with unshed tears (CID guys don't cry), Willie replied, "Yes, sir. I'll see to it."

Wilson ushered him out and then picked up the phone once more. "Get me Ranger Refugio Gonzalez over at Company A. And then get me the governor. But first, get me the sheriff down in San Patricio County that identified our man."

—

Two hours later, in Galveston, Marie Crowell stuck her head around the jamb of Gerry Ginestra's office at the Turf Club. She looked like she'd swallowed a thumbtack.

"Mr. Ginestra . . . ." Gerry broke off in the midst of one of Primo's tirades and put his hand over the telephone mouthpiece. *"What?"* he snarled at his secretary.

She gulped. "There's a whole mess of law enforcement outside in the lobby. They're here to see you and Primo, an' Mr. Glick. There's Texas Rangers, the state patrol, and those men from the attorney general's office."

Gerry sighed. "Call one of our lawyers, Miss Crowell. Shit, call all of 'em. And get me the sheriff."

Maybe we can get a little "professional courtesy" going between our sheriff and the crew outside, Gerry thought fleetingly. *Maybe slow down this shitstorm avalanche.*

"Offer them some coffee. Tell them our attorney's on the way. Tell 'em I'm on an important business call."

Marie looked dubious, but she backed out and closed the door.

At that moment, although Gerry had no way of knowing it, everyone in his outfit was getting a roust, courtesy of Will Wilson and the Department of Public Safety. It was a general roundup, designed to throw the fear of God into every lowlife the troopers could get their hands on. Deke Maloney, to name but one, was enjoying a show-up at the behest of Texas Ranger Refugio Gonzalez, personally. He'd wanted to put the arm on Deke for a long time.

Maloney, as ordered, paraded back and forth in a pool of light under an unshaded overhead bulb in a borrowed interrogation room at the Galveston P.D. Behind a smoked glass pane, Ranger Gonzalez was explaining to his fellow officers what an upright citizen Maloney represented. He made certain the intercom switch was open so Deke could hear his glowing testimonial.

"Men, take a good look at this one. He's a dan-ger-ous gangster," said Gonzales mockingly. "A real gunslinger. Though personally, I think he spends most of his time diddling little girls behind the Tastee-Freeze out by the junior high.

"What he's known for most, though, is being a bad driver. Always has a taillight out or an expired license plate. A menace on the highways. If I was you men, I'd keep an eye out for him and pull him over ever' chance you get. Just for the sake of the driving public's safety, you understand. Then you might consider kicking his ass, maybe laying your nightstick upside his head and then escorting this piece of shit to the nearest county line. Your fellow motorists will thank you."

Other Ginestra associates were receiving similar treatment, courtesy of the few cops and sheriff deputies who had neglected to sign onto the brothers' gravy train.

Back in his office, Gerry returned to the telephone. He sensed he'd better cut the conversation short. Something told him his leisure time was about to be seriously compromised for the foreseeable future.

"I'll come back there as quick as I can," Primo said contritely. His temper had cooled a trifle. And he knew he'd fucked up, in Technicolor. "I can help you square this beef."

Gerry thought quickly. "No, Primo, I don't want you anywhere near Galveston. It's too hot right now." He grabbed a Texas highway map out of his desk drawer and scanned the coast quickly. "Take the boat and go to . . . shit . . . ." South of Aransas Pass and Corpus Christi, the coastline curled through the vast emptiness of the King Ranch countryside, down to where the Rio Grande met the sea at Boca Chica—a goddamn desert island, all the way to Mexico.

"... Maybe haul ass north, to New Orleans. Even just Morgan City, if that's as far as you can get. Keep off the Intracoastal. The important thing is to get out of Texas, and damned fast. If they're looking for you, it's a cinch they know about the *Easy Eight*. Gotta do it now."

"I'm supposed to rendezvous with Jimmy in forty-five minutes," Primo reminded him. "Soon as we pick him up, I'll—"

"No, Primo," Gerry cut him off. "*Now*. The cops are gonna put out an APB on you and the boat any minute, if they haven't already."

"But Jimmy's family."

He's family, but he's not "family," Gerry thought. But all he said was, "Jimmy's the most resourceful guy we know, brother. He's a big boy; he can take care of himself. He'll understand. He'll be pissed, but he'll understand."

"Okay, but I'm not leaving without Sally. And that's not up for debate."

Gerry's temper spiked instantly. "God *damn* it! Will you give up on her and that fucking island!? You know you've queered that pitch, don't you? Everything we thought made Ransom Island such a bird's nest on the ground—it was out of the way, under the radar, we could slip in quiet-like and make a killing—all that shit's as dead as Lindberg's baby.

"I don't give a damn about Ransom Island anymore, and I sure as hell don't give a damn about that little bitch *who may not even be yours!*"

Gerry had more to say on the subject, but he suddenly realized he was talking to an empty line.

He replaced the phone gently in the cradle and pinched the bridge of his nose between two fingers. *Christ, I'm tired,* he thought.

There was a timid tap on the door and Marie ushered in the Galveston County sheriff, a portly, sweating redneck named Joe Don Luling. Joe Don had been on the Ginestras' pad since his days as a rookie beat cop. Moving over from the police to the sheriff's department hadn't changed a thing.

Gerry got right to the point. "Joe Don, can you maybe intercede with your law enforcement brethren outside? Tell 'em you've got everything on this end under control? Express our condolences and all? Promise cooperation?"

Luling shook his head, his expression hangdog sad. "Mr. Ginestra, I gotta tell you there ain't enough juice in the world to sidetrack this thing. They say they've got a make on Jimmy down south, and all the law south of Beaumont knows Jimmy's tied in with you and Primo. At least they do by now. This ain't some whorehouse stabbing. Jimmy—or someone—capped one of their *compadres.*"

There was another tap at the door and Marie tipped her head around the jamb. Clearly this wasn't an errand she relished.

"Dammit, Marie, I'm meeting with the sheriff, as any fool can plainly see . . . ."

Two suited figures slipped around the quickly-retiring Marie and stood smiling blandly at Gerry and Joe Don.

"Aw, hell, she was just doing her job, Mr. Ginestra," said one. "As are we." He produced a business card.

"My name is Landry, from the state comptroller's office? And my colleague, Mr. Hazard. He works in the Austin office of the Internal Revenue Service, I think?"

"'Deed I do, Mr. Landry. Mr. Ginestra, thanks for seeing us. We had the dickens of a time scaring up a cooperative judge in your little fiefdom down here, but we managed. Now comes the fun part." He reached into the inside pocket of his suit jacket and took out a folded document.

As he handed the search warrant to a disbelieving Gerry Ginestra, he smiled and said, "You see, Mr. Ginestra, things are never so bad that they can't get worse."

———

CHAPTER 40

And here, he'd always thought it was just an expression.

But it was true. He really and truly could not believe his eyes. Primo was gone.

Hell, the whole *boat* was gone. From where he stood on the finger pier at the Crab Man Marina on Mustang Island, where they had agreed to meet, he could see the spot out in Redfish Bay where the *Easy Eight* had anchored for the past week. Nothing.

This wasn't like being late for league night at the Pelican Bowl, for Christ's sake. He'd very recently dumped a dead body in a very public place. It was time to make tracks, lay up, and, maybe, the next day, make a discreet call to those asshole Sweetwater brothers and ask how business was going now that customers were afraid to set foot on their island.

But of Primo, there was no sign.

He paced. He swore. For a hoodlum, Jimmy Glick had a fastidious streak. He took pride in doing things a certain way and he put a high value on punctuality. Particularly when it came to getaways.

What could have happened?

His end had gone off with typical Glick-ian efficiency. He'd pulled over on an empty stretch of highway between Aransas Pass and the edge of Corpus Christi and asked Kent to go into the cooler in the trunk and fetch a couple of cold beers. Something to cut the dust on the way to the ballgame.

As Kent opened the trunk and leaned in (where there was in fact a cooler with a six-pack of Pearl iced down), Glick thumped him behind the ear with his lead sap and tumbled the limp body into the trunk.

And there the CID man lay, unconscious, for the balance of the evening and most of the night while Jimmy ate his supper at a greasy-spoon drive-in, sat in his car, smoked cigarettes and waited. Once, he thought he heard stirring from the trunk, whereupon he opened the compartment and sapped his victim once more for good measure.

Finally, at four in the morning, before even the fishermen were stirring, Glick drove around behind the back of a boarded-up gas station near the Ransom Island Bridge, removed his gun from under his arm, and shot the unconscious Cliff Hollenbeck in the forehead.

Glick had come to favor the old Smith & Wesson revolver that a gun collector friend had introduced him to. The .35 caliber round had enough charge to get the job done and tended to make a nice sized hole and rattle around inside some, seldom leaving an exit wound. Less gore for Glick to deal with afterwards. He was a tidy man.

He wiped his hands, lit a cigarette, and drove slowly, without lights, across the rumbling planks of the causeway that led to Ransom Island. Watching for any sign of lights or movement, he hauled Hollenbeck's body up the stairs to the porch, flipped over the cardboard CLOSED FOR REPAIRS sign, scribbled his provocative note, and then crept away.

Now the sun was freshly up and he was at the arranged meeting place at the right time and . . . nothing. What the fuck?

Worried now, Glick went storming back through the marina's retail operation and slammed the screen door as he exited to the parking lot. His Buick threw up a small tornado of caliche dust as he spun around and headed back towards the ferry that would take him to the mainland and Aransas Pass.

Hell, thought Glick, *I'll drive to Galveston if I have to. And Primo better be there to explain about this merry goddamn mix-up.*

But first . . . .

He wheeled into the parking lot of a tiny drugstore in Port Aransas and walked in, spotting—as he'd hoped—a wooden phone booth in the rear. He pulled a handful of change out of his pants pocket and started pumping in dimes. No answer at any of the Ginestras' numbers, not even the unlisted ones. Jimmy's little germ of apprehension was turning into a full-blown epidemic of alarm. *What in the hell was going on here?*

The phone booth was stifling. As he pondered his next move, Jimmy cracked the door in time to hear a departing customer say something to the young female cashier along the lines of ". . . catch the sonofabitch that shot that fella."

Glick swallowed. He had to roll the dice.

He exited the phone booth, kept his head down, extended a dollar bill and asked the girl behind the cash register for a pack of smokes. Luckies would do just fine, thanks.

The girl, who was painting her fingernails a particularly aggressive shade of tangerine and reading a movie magazine at the same time, didn't look up while she made his change.

"What was that the guy was saying? Someone got shot?"

The girl stretched out her fingers to admire her handiwork. "It was just on the radio, he said. Some poor guy over on Ransom Island, looks like. Turned out to be an undercover po-lice man. I think the radio said it was some gun-thug from Galveston what done it."

Jimmy feigned only mild interest. "I'll be damned," he said with a shrug.

Once he was outside the door, he staggered to his car, his mind racing. *Kent was a cop? Jesus, I'm fucked.*

Glick had no reason to mistrust the information. It wasn't the kind of detail the dimwit behind the counter or the yokel customer would dream up. And it would explain Primo's absence. Jimmy realized he'd suddenly become not just hot, but radioactive.

He was under no illusions about how Texas lawmen regarded cop killers. Not many of them survived long enough in custody to finally ride the lightning at the penitentiary in Huntsville.

And how in the name of God did they know it was me?

—

Less than four hours earlier, the sheriff stood over the cooling body of Cliff Hollenbeck. Noble, Flavius, and Zach kept him company while they waited for the coroner.

"Anybody know who he is?" Red asked. "Or where he was from?"

"Kent was his name, I think," said Noble. "He was in here a lot lately. I think he said he was living in a motel over on Wheeler Street in Aransas. Jesus, he was just a kid."

Zach bent down and looked in the dead man's face. "Hard to believe someone would shoot a man that way. Like puttin' down a horse. Who would do such a thing?"

Noble immediately thought of the gun-toting gangster that had tangled with his brother weeks ago. Suddenly he perked up. "I might have something that'll help you, Red." He told the sheriff about the dust-up between Flavius and the man whose name (according to his driver's license) turned out to be James Glick.

"I took a gun off the fella before he mixed it up with my brother, and I got the feeling he would've used it without blinking an eye—he had that kind of brass to him. Anyway, I've always been interested in firearms since I was in the Army, and the gun this guy was packing was a a Smith & Wesson automatic, Model 1913. They didn't make very many of them that year, and not a one after that.

"Anyway, I took the trouble to relieve the gent of his ammunition . . . and I'd never seen cartridges quite like 'em. So I saved them. What with the bombing and the dance and all, the whole thing slipped my mind. In fact . . . . Wait right here, Red. I'll be right back."

Noble loped over to the bait house and returned, out of breath, with a Mason jar with six cartridges inside. "Here you go, Sheriff,"

Red dumped the rounds in his hand and examined the flat-fronted bullets. "Hmmm, wadcutters."

"If those belong to your killer," Noble continued, "maybe he'll still have his fancy pistol with him. Be easy to match those bullets with the one they take out of this poor fellow."

That would be handy, agreed Red, pocketing the rounds. "By the way, you didn't happen to note the make of our suspect's car, did you?"

"It was a late model Buick Super," Noble answered, "with a Galveston dealer frame around the plates."

Red nodded appreciatively and scribbled the information onto a note pad. "Listen, y'all stay here and wait for the coroner. I guess I don't have to tell you not to touch anything."

Ten minutes later, Red Burton was standing in "Kent's" rented room at the Sea Aire Motel, staring in anger and disbelief at the shield and identification of Cliff Hollenbeck, duly sworn officer of the state's Criminal Investigation Division.

He had to move quickly. He picked up the phone on the night-stand table and asked for an operator. The attorney general's office in Austin, please. And yes, it was an emergency.

—

Now, Jimmy Glick was not only on the run, but he'd assassinated a policeman—and apparently, it was already on the radio, and he'd somehow been identified as the killer. Time, he knew, was the last thing on his side.

He gunned his car up Cotter Avenue through the light Port A traffic, heading for the ferry landing that would take him from Mustang Island to the mainland. Once he was inland, there were a million little back roads he could lose himself on before the alarm became too general. He still had a chance.

He skidded up to the ferry landing. Only a couple of cars ahead of him, thank Christ. And here, chugging along, came the little Highway Department ferryboat, heading his way.

Then Jimmy's eyes shifted beyond the approaching ferry to the opposite landing, across two hundred yards of open water.

There was the ferryman's shack, there the big railroad arm that could be raised or lowered to control traffic, there the wood-plank causeway that stretched across a chain of muddy islands to Aransas Pass, the mainland, and freedom. And there . . . Jimmy nodded to himself in resigned, fatalistic acceptance . . . there was the police barricade at the causeway's entrance.

Time had run out.

———

CHAPTER 41

Jimmy Glick had lived on an island, namely Galveston, for most of his adult life, but he was just now coming to terms with the downside of being completely surrounded by water. In other words, he was stuck in Port Aransas, jammed up like a crab in a trap, like one of those stupid ships-in-a-bottle the boardwalk souvenir stores sold.

Jimmy knew there were only two ways for a man in an automobile to exit Mustang Island—the Port Aransas car ferry, where he sat looking at cops checking every vehicle approaching the ferry dock, or the new concrete causeway at the southern end of the island, leading over to Corpus Christi. He had no doubt another roadblock awaited him there (and one, in fact, did, thanks to a quick call from Red Burton to his colleague in neighboring Nueces County).

Glick wheeled around in a three-point turn and eased away from the ferry landing, his mind racing. Cut off from access to the mainland, he was marooned as surely as Robinson Crusoe. The cops could take their sweet time combing the island until they netted him.

Like an over-caffeinated rat bouncing around in a cage, one frantic thought kept ricocheting through his brainpan: *How did they make me so damn fast?*

And then, the unthinkable: *Did Primo give me up?*

That was unimaginable. Over the years, the Ginestras had trusted him with their secrets, their fortunes, and even their lives. In their service he'd broken every commandment in the book, and probably a few God hadn't thought of yet. He prided himself on being a stand-up guy, and it went without saying that Primo and Gerry were stand-up guys, too.

Except Primo hadn't exactly been his typical criminal mastermind self lately. It was the girl. She'd gotten inside Primo's head, twisted his priorities all out of whack. Jimmy thought of the hours Primo had spent on the deck of the *Easy Eight*, glued to his binoculars, staring fixedly at Ransom Island, hoping for a glimpse of . . . what? Some unattainable ideal of a loving daughter? Something maddeningly intractable that he was unable to subdue, buy off, or bludgeon into submission?

Jimmy didn't know or care. It was enough that she'd fucked up Primo's focus which, in turn, left Jimmy Glick up the proverbial creek.

I'm gonna kill that bitch and tell God she died, he thought savagely.

But first there was the little matter of escaping a police dragnet.

Glick spied a tidy little bungalow a few blocks inland from the ferry landing, on a deserted little side street. It had an empty look about it. Curtains drawn, grass overgrown. No empty milk bottles for pickup, no paper on the lawn. A detached wooden two-car garage rested at the end of a shell driveway.

A northern snowbird's winter cottage, he thought—hoped—empty for the summer, while the owners did whatever the fuck Yankees did up North in July.

He had to get the car out of sight. He felt like he was driving a circus wagon. He wheeled into the driveway, rummaged through the burglar's tools in his trunk, came up with a short pry bar and popped the padlock off the garage's latch. Empty, sure enough. He eased the car inside and closed the garage doors.

With a shaking hand, he lit a cigarette and cracked a small sliding window to let in some air. He opened the rear door of the car and stretched out on the back seat, smoking and thinking. It was dark and cool and still, but Glick wasn't the least bit soothed. *C'mon, you're a stone-cold desperado and all-around dangerous man,* he thought. *What would a real outlaw do in this situation? Where's John Dillinger when you need him?*

As soon as Red Burton, Jr. learned that "Kent" was in fact a CID cop, the sheriff knew time was of the essence.

Earlier, after Red had hung up with the attorney general, his first call was to the ferryman's office. Just one car had crossed over from the mainland that morning—a fancy Buick with a single male driver. Red was betting the killer was still on Mustang Island. If he could confine the killer to the island, catching him might be slow, it might be dangerous, but it would be inevitable. If the bad guy made it across the causeway to Aransas Pass, he could light out for the territories and be halfway to Amarillo by nightfall.

He hung up and dialed the Aransas Pass P.D. Get a roadblock up at the ferry landing. Yes, he'd square it with the chief later. Now, in the interest of interdepartmental cooperation, please move your ass. A similar call to the Nueces County sheriff's office secured a second checkpoint at the southern end of the island.

His next stop after the rooming house was to drive a few blocks to the Rainbow Inn and grab Jacky Jack Vandiver by the scruff of the neck under the shocked gaze of the customers who'd come in for an early breakfast. Burton ran Vandiver headlong through the twin swinging doors that led into the grimy kitchen.

"Git," the sheriff growled to Jim Bob Qui, the Chinese fry cook, who prudently hauled ass.

Red backed Jacky Jack over the stove, uncomfortably close to the broiling hot steel griddle on which Jim Bob scrambled eggs and grilled burgers and, in so many words, threatened to charbroil the little weasel's face on the grill if Jacky Jack didn't spill everything he knew about the man named Kent. He flashed the picture on Hollenbeck's ID card.

"This man's car is sitting in your parking lot. When was he in here last?" The sheriff inclined Vandiver's head a trifle closer to the griddle. A drop of sweat fell off Jacky's forehead onto the hot stainless steel surface, sizzled and instantly evaporated.

In very short order, Jacky Jack dimed out Jimmy Glick. Yeah, a guy answering the description the Sweetwaters had given the sheriff—a stranger from Galveston named James Glick—was eating lunch with the kid just yesterday. No, he couldn't hear what they were talking about. They seemed friendly enough, they even left the café together and climbed into the stranger's Buick. That had been the last he'd seen of 'em. Jesus, Sheriff, this thing is hot!

Red released Jacky Jack, but promised he would come back and make a tuna melt out of his face if Vandiver was stringing him along.

But instinct told him he had his man.

Red radioed his office and the Aransas cops and conveyed Glick's name, description, and the make of his car. He called the local AM radio station and told the station manager to spread the word on the air: a law enforcement officer had been killed; a man from Galveston was wanted for questioning. The news would go statewide. By the time he gave the attorney general's office an update, it was almost lunchtime. He drove past the roadblock and took the ferry over to Port Aransas.

Stomach growling, he walked into Shorty's Place near Port A's commercial wharf and ordered a sandwich and an iced tea. He sat at the counter and chewed thoughtfully, trying to put himself in the mind of his quarry—he couldn't drive off the island, he couldn't sprout wings and fly, and unless he grew gills like Aquaman in the comics, he couldn't swim away.

What would you *do, Red?* he heard his father asking. He swallowed the last bite of his sandwich and stood up. *Shit, Dad, it's simple when there's only one play left. I'd steal a boat.*

You're brighter than you look, son. But don't swear.

A half mile away, lighting the latest in a chain-smoking succession of cigarettes, Jimmy Glick came to the same conclusion.

—

Juan Estrada loved to fish. He'd taken it up in Hawaii while he was stationed there during his stint in the Navy. The problem was, he loved fishing on the open water, which required a boat. So when he'd finally saved enough money, he purchased a little 12-foot open cockpit runabout that had foundered during the last hurricane. He'd fixed it up and attached to the rear, Frankenstein-like, a converted motor from an old milking machine. Connected by shafts and bearings to the propeller, it was an unholy-looking device, but it would have to do until he was able to pull together the dough to buy a proper sporting yacht.

Juan toddled down the dock just after dusk with his gear, including his nine-foot light rod and free-spool casting reel. He figured he'd try his luck fishing under the lights out by South Pier. At least, that's what he had been figuring before Jimmy Glick stepped out of the shadows behind the wharfside fisheries warehouse and sapped him down from behind.

Twenty-five feet away, observing events from inside Barney's charter operation, Red Burton got ready to move. It was suppertime and the docks were empty. But Red had been staking out the marina since early afternoon. Barney Farley, the pre-eminent fishing guide and boat builder in this part of the world, kept him company for a time, talking quietly about this and that.

"Think of him like a jewfish," Farley said when Red told him about his quarry. "A jewfish will hide out under the offshore rigs or in rock crevices along the jetties. He'll wait in his hole, all day long. But dangle a live crab or cutbait in front of him and you can flush him out."

Red felt certain his game would flush. The sport fishing boats lined up alongside the commercial fishing vessels in Port A's small marina were too tempting a bait to resist.

And now, sure enough . . . . The sheriff winced when Glick silently clocked the civilian, whom Red recognized as a sometimes customer at Shady's. While Jimmy was going through the unconscious man's pockets, looking for boat keys and cash, Red slipped out and took up position on the other side of a wharf piling, behind and to the left of Glick's crouching form. Red drew his sidearm.

"Howdy do, Mr. Glick," he announced.

Jimmy spun on his heels. He was in a bad position, stooped over Juan's prone body, and he knew it. Without a word or a moment's hesitation, he changed plans. It was part of what made the hawk-faced gunman so deadly.

He picked up the insensible fisherman, jammed his revolver in his ear and began dragging him down to the finger pier where Juan's boat was tied up.

Red followed. "Leave the citizen out of it, Jimmy. You're done."

Glick smiled tightly. "I'm done alright. You gonna save me from an appointment with Old Sparky up there in Huntsville? Maybe hold court on me yourself? Far as I can see, that's the only two options on my dance card."

"That's up to you, Glick. This is your party. But I'm telling you, turn that fellow loose."

Jimmy continued to drag his hostage down the finger pier. "Can't see my way clear to do it, Sheriff. But I tell you what I will do.

Let me get to this man's boat, and I'll make you a present. I'll tell you everything I know about the Ginestras."

"Not interested," said Red coldly. "You've got that boy you shot this morning to answer for."

"I see your point," said Glick, and as he spoke, he dropped Juan Estrada and began to turn, bringing his revolver to bear on the sheriff. But Jimmy was standing on a two-foot-wide finger pier with no freedom of movement. And Red had positioned himself so that the gunman had to bring his weapon all the way across his body to put the sheriff in his sights. Once more, and forever, Jimmy Glick had run out of time.

Red's first shot was a poor one. He hit Glick in the side and knocked him down. Glick raised his weapon again.

Center mass, son, Red heard his father saying. *Deep breath. Steady hands. Put him down.*

And, with his second shot, Red did.

━━━

CHAPTER 42

Zachariah Yates tapped a cigarette ash into an empty Maxwell House coffee can and resumed watching Gilbert sort through his multitude of books.

"If you're hopin' to put all them books in that trunk, I can tell you right now, they're not gonna fit."

Gilbert sat cross-legged on the floor next to his open Army footlocker. "You see any books you want, Zach?"

Zach grabbed four books from a column near his chair and read the titles aloud. "Albert Einstein, *Essays in Physics.*" He set the book back on the pile without comment. "Adam Smith, *The Wealth of Nations.*" He shook his head and discarded that one too. "*Beginning Latin.* Uh huh, *that* sounds interesting." He examined the fourth book and thumbed through some of the pages. "Why, there's not a word of English in this one, Gilbert."

"*Don Quixote,* by Cervantes," said Gilbert without looking up. "He's Castilian."

"Now, what would I do with a book written in Castilian?"

"What kind of books do you like?"

Zach shrugged. "Can't say I've read many. Lemme think on it a minute." He pondered the question while he puffed on his cigarette, sending lazy smoke rings upwards to the ceiling. "I suppose I like adventure tales."

Gilbert leaned back and scanned a long row of books that rested against the wall, ultimately selecting three titles. "You might like these," he said, handing him Robert Louis Stevenson's *Treasure Island,* Edgar Rice Burroughs' *Tarzan of the Apes,* and Jack London's *The Call of the Wild.* "Guaranteed to pass the time quickly."

Zach took the books. "At my age, I'm not sure I *want* the time to pass quickly." He studied the colorful artwork on the book covers and sniffed at the pages inside. "But I b'lieve I might enjoy these."

"I think you will, too. Those pages will take you to tropical islands, to jungles in darkest Africa, and even to Klondike gold country in the far north."

"I'm much obliged, Gilbert."

The screen door creaked and Sally Rose walked into the room. "Holy Moly! Unless we're driving a moving van to California, you're going to have to lose most of those books, baby."

"I'm working on it," Gilbert answered. "What I can't fit in this . . ." he held up the trunk's removable cardboard tray, "is going to Dubber's two boys or else to the Aransas Pass library."

"That town has a library?" Sally looked surprised. "Well, I expect they'll have to build a new wing, then. And they'll probably put your name on it: The Gilberto Ruiz Collection of Random Subjects."

Zach nodded his head in agreement. "Some of those books aren't even in English."

"I hate to part with 'em, but . . . ." He looked at Zach, who was already rolling another cigarette, "maybe if someone volunteered to help me haul them to California? What do you say, Zach? You want to go with us?"

Zach collected his three books and stood up. "Naw, I reckon I'll stay here and take care of Rupert and the rest of them Sweetwater boys. It's a full-time job."

"We're serious, Zach," said Sally. "We'd be happy for you to come along. They say there's lots to see out there."

Zach raised the books he held in his hand. "Who needs California when I'm going to darkest Africa and to some other place called Klondike."

After Zachariah left, Sally sat on the edge of the couch and watched Gilbert halfheartedly sort through his books. She put her hand on his shoulder and squeezed. "Zach'll be fine. Rupert will be fine. Everybody will be fine." When he didn't respond, she hopped down on the floor next to him. "Gilbert, we already talked about this."

They *had* talked about it, the night before. With Jimmy Glick dead and the attorney general making a public show of "busting up" the illegal gambling enterprise at Shady's, the situation had changed substantially. (In his press conference, Will Wilson paid tribute to his slain CID recruit, but neglected to mention that since no real evidence of illicit gambling was found on the island, no formal charges were filed.) The phony casino plan had worked, sort of, the mob threat had been deflected and disarmed, and Ransom Island, for all intents and purposes, was out of danger.

But Sally had convinced Gilbert that their future was in California. Besides, she had too many bad memories associated with Texas. And although they had only talked about it obliquely, they agreed that Ransom Island would be no place to raise a family, unless maybe it was a family of rattlesnakes.

They continued packing and putting the cabin in order while the sun sank slowly into Redfish Bay. The light in the room softened and then dimmed until Gilbert lit the kerosene lamp. Before long, Gilbert's footlocker and Sally's suitcase were packed and ready to go—they would leave as soon as Rupert returned from New Orleans, which, they agreed, should be any day now.

A sudden breeze blew in off the bay, and the lantern flame flickered out, so they covered up with a blanket and made love on the sofa. Afterwards, they talked until midnight, speculating on the future and reminiscing about their short but eventful time together on Ransom Island. Eventually, Gilbert drifted off to sleep, his head resting on her lap.

When the wind died, Sally listened to the sounds of the island—crickets, toads, the muted trill of a screech owl—and tried to imagine what their life would be like out West.

Whatever awaited them, Sally was confident they could handle it. She had survived two rootless years as a runaway. California didn't scare her at all. As for Gilbert, she knew he'd do fine; he was the smartest man she'd ever met. Maybe they wouldn't strike gold out there, but she figured they had a better than even chance of finding happiness. And that was good enough for her.

Sally thought she heard a footfall on the porch. She listened closely and concluded she must have imagined the sound. Even so, she continued to stare at the screen door, sensing that something was not quite right, sensing a presence. Was that a figure behind the screen? Standing there, looking in? Was she imagining that, too?

She quietly slipped off the couch, careful not to wake Gilbert, and approached the door warily.

"Hello, Sally Rose." The voice from her nightmares was hushed and moderated, intimate. It froze her in place.

"It's me. It's your father."

She put her hand on the kitchen table to steady herself and stared at the burly silhouette.

"It's been such a long time," said the voice. "You're all grown up now."

"What do you want?" she whispered.

"I've come for you, *mia figlia.* I've come to take you home."

She turned on the porch light and Primo squinted at the sudden burst of yellow light. She looked upon the rough peasant features she'd come to hate: the wide nose, the heavy eyebrows, and the slicked-back hair. She even recognized the smell of his cologne. She hated that, too.

"Kill the light," he growled, and she involuntarily flipped off the switch. "You've been a hard one to track down," he continued in a gentler tone. "I still don't understand why you ran."

Sally was silent, gathering her wits, trying to think of a way to get away from him.

Primo sighed. "I guess it runs in the family. And then of course, there was your mother . . . ."

"What about my mother?"

"Let me in and we'll talk about it."

Sally grabbed the screen handle and held it when he tried to open the door. "What about my mother?" she repeated.

Primo hesitated. "Well, she left me, you know? God only knows where she is."

"You know where she is."

He shook his head. "You don't understand."

"I *do* understand, you bastard. *You* killed her. You killed my mother."

Primo blinked, his face registering pain and regret for just an instant, but then his expression hardened. She was *his;* she didn't get to talk to him that way. He struggled to find the right tone, the one that would make her see things his way, forever.

"*Mia piccola bambina* . . . You don't know what you're talking about. Your mother . . . she left me."

"No, you murdered her. I *saw* you do it."

"You were only three. You couldn't have . . ." he stopped short.

Sally's eyebrows shot skyward. Part of her had still hoped, somehow, she had dreamt it all.

"With a baseball bat and a pillow," she said, her voice rising.

Gilbert roused from his sleep when he heard the voices. "Sally? Is someone there? Who are you talking to?"

"It's nobody," she said. She tried to slam shut the door but it burst open when Primo threw his shoulder into it. Sally flew backwards into the room.

When Primo turned on the light he saw a shirtless Mexican kneeling on the floor, holding Sally in his arms. He scowled at Gilbert and then addressed his daughter. "Let me take you home, Sally Rose. The family must stick together."

"We haven't been family for a long time," she said, anger fighting with fear inside her. "Get the hell out of my cabin."

Primo set his jaw and watched the Mexican help Sally to her feet. "You're just confused, Sally Rose," he continued. "Let's forget the past and start over, *d'accordo?* Everything will be good. You'll see." Primo held out his arms, almost pleadingly and then seized her by the bicep. "Come. *Vieni.* It's okay."

"No!" she screamed.

Gilbert stepped in front of Sally and grabbed Primo's wrist. "Let her go."

Without thinking about it, Primo threw a roundhouse punch that sent Gilbert to the floor. It happened so suddenly and violently that Sally instinctively jumped backwards and put her hands up to shield her face. When she removed them, she saw Primo pointing a gun at Gilbert's head.

"Stop, Poppa! Don't hurt him."

Primo looked up, surprised, a smile forming on his face. "You called me poppa."

"I'll go with you, Poppa," she said, thinking fast. "He's only tried to help me since I came here. Let's go home."

Primo returned the gun to a waistband holster under his shirt. "Now you're talking sense, baby girl."

Sally took a deep breath. "I'll just get my purse and make-up bag from the bathroom."

He nodded.

Out of Primo's sight, she reached up and felt behind the medicine cabinet that hung over the sink, searching for the gun Darla had given her. There it was, behind the mirror, resting on top of the cabinet. She held the training pistol in her hand—hadn't Darla said it was loaded?—and then tossed it into her purse.

"All set," she said as she walked back into the room.

She went straight to the door, trying to keep from looking at Gilbert. Keep it simple, she told herself. Keep Gilbert out of it. She hoped he was smart enough to see what she was doing. His life depended on it.

Primo took a step toward the door and then paused, as if he'd forgotten his keys. He looked back at Gilbert. "Get up, you. You're going with us."

The last thing he wanted was to have this Mexican making trouble, like maybe running to the cops or some other foolish thing. He could tell the kid was hot for his daughter, and he figured he was probably dumb enough to try and be a hero for her. Once they were on the *Easy Eight* and headed for Galveston, he'd put a bullet in the boy's temple and toss him overboard.

"Please Poppa. Let him stay."

"He's going." Primo pulled out his gun and motioned for Gilbert to pick up Sally's suitcase. "Somebody's gotta carry your luggage."

As they filed out the door he leaned into Gilbert's ear. "Don't get any ideas, *messicani*."

By the light of a full moon, they marched in silence down the sandy trail: Sally in front, followed by Gilbert and Primo, gun in hand.

Gilbert realized they were heading for the sandy beach on the western shore of the island, the same beach where he and Sally picnicked and swam. The same place she had kissed him for the first time, almost a month ago. Then an image of the dead hammerhead flashed into his head and Gilbert had a premonition: *I'm going to die there.*

They arrived at the cove and Primo Ginestra waved them toward a dinghy bobbing in the water. He was in a hurry, and the sooner they were out to sea, the better. He'd already taken a huge chance by laying over an extra day, the Easy Eight nosed up into a mosquito-infested dredge channel, waiting for nightfall. But he had figured, correctly, that the vicinity would be crawling with cops after the dead body was discovered.

They stopped at the shoreline and Primo holstered his gun, ordering Gilbert to get into the boat first. "After you get in, you help her, *capisce?*"

He heard Sally's voice behind him, full of iron. "Don't get in the boat, Gilbert." Turning, he saw her unsteadily holding a small pistol.

"I'll shoot you, Primo, I swear to God I will."

"Why are you doing this?" He spoke to her like a father speaks to a stubborn little girl, more exasperated than angry.

"I love him, and I'm not going to let you kill him, too."

"Give me the gun, Sally," he said more forcefully.

"No."

Gilbert still had one foot in the dinghy, and he searched inside for something to use as a weapon. But Primo acted first, taking three aggressive steps toward Sally, who fumbled with the safety, unable to fire in time.

Primo snatched the pistol from her hands. "Gimme that goddamn gun." He raised his hand to strike her but Gilbert charged him and tackled him to the ground. They scuffled for a brief moment before Primo stood up, took a step back, and shot Gilbert three times. *Pop pop pop.* The gunshots from the .22 sounded like firecrackers.

Gilbert staggered backwards and fell.

He moaned and looked down at his wounds: one in the shoulder and one in the thigh—the third bullet had ricocheted off the side of his skull, leaving a deep crease in his scalp. Sally rushed to him and cried out when she touched his head and felt his blood-soaked hair.

Primo looked at the .22 and sighed. "Fucking toy pistol," he muttered, hurling the gun into the bay. "Come on," he repeated. "Help him up and let's go."

When she didn't move, Primo turned and looked down at her. "What are you waiting for? *Sprigarsi!* Hurry up! The sooner we get him onboard, the sooner the captain can patch him up."

"No one will patch him up," she screamed. "You'll kill him on the way to Galveston."

Primo was impressed with the girl's intuition. "Who cares?" he said offhandedly. "He's no good for you anyway." He grabbed her by the arm. "I'm your father, Sally. You belong to me."

Sally jerked her arm away. "You are not my father!" She wiped her tears away and looked at him with hate in her eyes. "I hope you burn in hell for what you did."

Primo's face darkened, a fury boiling within him that he was unable to control. He pulled out his .38 and pointed the gun at Gilbert. Maybe this would teach her not to talk back. After he killed her boyfriend, he'd figure out a way to make it up to her later. She'd come around, eventually. She'd have to. She was his daughter, and she would love her father.

She would, goddamm it. She would.

Primo cocked the trigger of his .38. "Get out of the way."

Sally held on to Gilbert even tighter. "No!"

She closed her eyes and waited for the gunshot, but instead she heard a whooshing sound and then a loud smack. When she looked up, Primo's eyes were bulging and his arms hung limply by his side. He was staring down at the sharp metal point that poked out of his breastbone. He lurched forward, dropped to his knees and fell face forward in the sand. The ground pushed the spear upwards but it remained pinned to his back. Bird feathers fluttered around the shaft of the lance.

Sally wiped the tears from her eyes and looked again, trying to comprehend what she saw. A figure materialized and stood over the body, and two strong arms removed the spear. The man paused and looked down at them. He didn't speak a word.

"*Gracias,*" Gilbert whispered.

Sally glanced down at Gilbert, and when she looked up again she saw the man walking away, carrying the deadly spear in his hand, like an ancient warrior. He was barefoot, she noticed, and on his head was a glowing, untamed thatch of white hair that seemed to be dancing with the breeze.

▬▬▬▬

CHAPTER 43

Zach had to use a ladder to reach the half-dozen ceiling fans that hung from the rafters. He jerked the pull chains until the blades were spinning as fast and as dangerously as airplane propellers. Not that it did any good; it was still over ninety degrees inside Shady's and so humid that the entire building seemed to sag like a melting Popsicle. The total effect of Zach's efforts was to move waves of hot air from one corner of the bar to the next.

Outside, it was even hotter. The breeze had petered out before noon, and Ransom Island had been baking under a hot July sun ever since—the kind of day Rupert referred to as a weather breeder. The hardcore Shady's regulars slumped on their barstools in a soporific daze, hanging their heads and sweating through their shirts. The heat stifled the usual bar banter, and energy was conserved for essential activities like beer drinking. Even the tunes on the jukebox were dragging. Hank Williams labored through "Lost Highway" sounding like he just might be too hot and tired to finish the song. When it finally ended, nobody bothered to punch in another one.

Zach left the ladder in the middle of the room, meaning to stow it away once the heat wave passed, if it ever did. For five days a high-pressure system had been squatting over the Gulf Coast like an obsessive hen, discouraging any agreeable change in weather. The old cowboy grabbed a chair by its top rail and slowly dragged it across the floor to the wall, feeling as spent as a used matchstick.

He wasn't the only one that felt that way. After last week, it was inevitable everyone would fall into a slump. How could they not? A murder, a manhunt, and then a shootout—followed by an abduction, another shootout, and finally the skewering of one of the country's most notorious gangsters.

Zach sat in the chair and tilted it back, leaning his head against the wall. He had intended to roll a cigarette, but instead, he closed his eyes and let his mind idle.

Over in Aransas Pass, Red was tired, too. Since Hollenbeck's murder, Wilson's men had been swarming all over his office. Rosie was having to brew a new pot of coffee every half hour. And on the home front, Darla was already making noise about them moving to Hollywood, just as Rupert forewarned. He wanted this case tied up and put away, for good.

Although Red wouldn't, and couldn't, say it, he saw no need to complicate things by involving a certain recluse who only wanted to be left alone on Ransom Island. But no one on the law enforcement side of things seemed overly interested in how an infamous crime boss had come to be shish-kabobed in the course of committing a felonious assault. The common sentiment was that Primo Ginestra got what he deserved. "Don't overthink it" seemed to be the order of the day.

Zach leaned forward and pulled out his tobacco. As he rolled his cigarette, he reflected on the future. Everything was changing. Gilbert and Sally were leaving for California. Noble had decided to open his own beer joint in Corpus Christi, and Flavius was talking about taking a welding job at the Lazarro shipyard. Once the prospect of selling Shady's had been introduced—along with Rupert's adamant refusal to consider it—the brothers' commitment to the family business seemed to flag, prompting them to act on plans long held dormant.

So now, there was nothing to do but wait for Rupert. He'd sent a telegram that said he'd be extending his trip for a few days. That was almost a week ago.

Cecil Shoat poured the last of a Grand Prize beer down his throat and turned to Gideon Dodson. "I musta drunk ten beers already, and I still don't need to pee. What does that mean, Giddyup?"

Gideon mopped his brow with a bar napkin and shrugged irritably. "How the hell should I know, Cecil?

Gustav Brauer and Captain Quincy, both originating from cooler latitudes, were particularly affected by the heat wave. They had fished that morning until the breeze died and the fish stopped biting, and then they watched the bay become so completely still that it seemed like an extension of the bright sky it reflected. Standing chest deep in the water, the two men had the dizzying sensation that they were floating free in space. They decided to retreat to the safety of Shady's, where they moored themselves to their barstools and waited for the doldrums to lift.

"Maybe you should switch to water," said Captain Quincy, belatedly responding to Cecil's comment.

Cecil grunted, not even bothering to acknowledge such an idiotic notion.

Noble noticed that Gustav's beer was empty, so he reluctantly rose to retrieve another, lingering in front of the open icebox as long as he could. Gustav took the beer and held the sweating can to his forehead, rolling it from one side to the other. The good German's head bandage had been replaced by a butterfly Band-Aid, which hung limply from his scalp, unstuck on one end.

The small group of patrons clustered at one end of the bar, crowding around an oscillating desk fan that Noble had placed on the bar top. Flavius was nearest to the fan, leaning forward on his stool so that his head was directly in the airflow.

"Your hair's gonna get caught in them blades and snatch you bald-headed," said Zachariah, looking up from his chair.

"Mind your own business," said Flavius, his red hair swirling in the air currents.

Sure enough, a moment later the fan snagged a big hank of hair. Flavius grabbed at his scalp and yapped. "Turn it off! Somebody turn this sumbitch off!"

Noble unplugged the fan and tried to help his brother untangle himself. "God dang it, Flavius, there's a bunch of hair wrapped around the shaft. I'm going to have to cut it off."

"The hell you are!"

For some reason, Flavius was vain about his hair, although to most people it looked like an outcrop of red coral had attached itself to his head.

"I tried to tell ya," said Zachariah.

"Please don't provoke him, Zach," said Noble, tugging on his brother's hair.

Flavius grimaced. "Stop it, goddammit! You're gonna rip it out."

"I can rip it out or cut it out. Or you can wear that fan like a hat. You tell me which."

The regulars watched with poorly-disguised amusement as Noble took a pair of scissors and snipped at the tangle of hair. Watching Flavius' misery helped expiate their own discomfort, if only just a little. By the time Noble freed him, Flavius' hair looked like a tangled ball of fishing line.

A few heads turned at the sound of car doors closing out front, followed by heavy footsteps as someone clumped up the steps. Suddenly the double screen doors burst open and Rupert Sweetwater barged into the room.

"Howdy, everyone!"

A huge smile stretched across Rupert's face, and the men smiled back, glad to see that the two-week sabbatical had brightened his attitude. Then their jaws dropped open when a gorgeous, raven-haired woman stepped out from behind him.

"Boys, let me introduce you to Victoria Sweetwater . . . Vita . . . my new wife!" Rupert opened his arms wide, and said dramatically, "Honey, welcome to the Shady Boat and Leisure Club . . . and your very own private island!"

The men sat stock-still on their barstools, speechless, the clacking ceiling fans the only sound in the room.

Rupert cocked his head at his dumbstruck friends. "Hey! How 'bout we show some manners and say hello to Vita, huh? What the hell are y'all thinking?"

What they were thinking was that this woman was a dead ringer for Jane Russell, from the jet-black hair that tumbled to her shoulders, to the impressive bust that strained the buttons on her summer dress. Did Rupert just say she was his new *wife?*

Noble was the first to break out of the collective trance. He came around the bar and gave her a big hug. "I am pleased to meet you, Vita. I'm Rupert's brother, Noble."

Next, Zach Yates walked over to introduce himself, and soon the entire gang had Rupert's bride surrounded, eager to make a favorable first impression.

Vita greeted the men amiably, already forming her own impressions. Shady's wasn't quite how she had imagined it. And it was certainly different from the way Rupert had described it. Duke Ellington played *here?*

"Give her some air, fellows. Give her some air." Rupert stepped in to rescue his wife from her new admirers. "I'll tell you what," he said, "let's go sit down at the bar, and I'll tell you boys the true story about how me and this beautiful lady fell in love and got married."

The men dutifully took their places, and Rupert began. "So there I was . . ." he said grandly, "at the famous Sazerac Bar in the Roosevelt Hotel. It was my first day in town and probably a little bit early for a cocktail—"

"It was ten in the morning," said Vita.

". . . but hey, you guys know what kind of funk I was in."

Everyone nodded. They knew.

"And who do I see behind the bar?" Rupert put his arm around Vita, "I see this beautiful woman right here. We talked for a long time. In fact, I stayed there through the evening rush and until her shift ended. Came back the next night, too. In fact, I came back every night that week, until she finally agreed to go out with me."

Rupert pulled a round a beers out of the cooler and passed them around. "Now I guess y'all are wondering why Vita would pick me outta all those Creole swells in New Orleans."

Everyone in the room had been wondering that exact thing, even before he mentioned it.

"Well, I'll tell you . . . ." Rupert nodded sagaciously and looked at their expectant faces. "I don't have a goddamn clue."

Everyone laughed, and Vita laughed, too. She wasn't quite sure either. She had never been one to act impulsively, but by the end of the first week, she had fallen in love with the bigger-than-life Texan, and by the end of the second week, she had married him and agreed to return to Shady's to help him run his business. On her own private island. Her friends thought she'd lost her mind.

By the time Rupert brought them up to the present, a breeze had picked up and the temperature had dropped fifteen degrees. So involved was everyone in the tale that it took a rumble of thunder for them to realize that the debilitating heat wave had finally lifted.

Gideon Dodson proposed a toast to the marriage, and then Noble followed up with another one. Beers were produced, bottles were clinked, and everyone cheered enthusiastically.

After the toasts, Rupert swiveled his head and wistfully surveyed the interior of his tavern. "You know, while I was away, I actually missed this place a little bit. Anything interesting happen while I was gone?

Rupert was confused when everyone exchanged knowing glances and grinned at each other. Finally they broke into laughter.

Noble slapped his brother on the back and cast a quick glance at Vita. "Rupe, how 'bout you follow me and Flavius out back so we can fill you in. It's our turn to tell *you* a story."

Rupert hesitated and glanced at his wife, but Noble tilted his head insistently toward the back door. (Kent, Jimmy, Primo . . . too much too soon for Rupert's new bride, Noble figured. A little discretion was in order.)

As his brothers escorted him out of the room, Rupert looked over his shoulder. "Vita? . . . Um, would you mind rustling up some beers for these heathens while we're away?"

"Sure thing," said Vita, sliding around behind the counter. Out of habit, she began picking up empties and cleaning around the bar. Moments later, a pretty blond girl pushed through the kitchen door and came around to help.

"Hi, my name's Sally Rose," she said, extending her hand.

Vita smiled and shook. "I'm Vita Dautrieve, ah, make that, Vita Sweetwater."

"Sweetwater?" Sally looked confused, so Vita gave her the short version of her whirlwind courtship and marriage to the Sweetwater paterfamilias.

"Gee," said Sally. "Congratulations," and then added, "Well, I should warn you, you'll meet some real characters in this place."

"I'm from New Orleans, honey. We don't hide our characters there; we parade 'em around on floats and give 'em free cocktails."

Cecil Shoat cleared his throat. "Uh, Mrs. Sweetwater? You mind hittin' me with another cold one?"

Vita glanced at his empty to ascertain his brand, put a cold replacement and a fresh napkin in front of him, and whisked the empty can into the trash—all in one fluid motion.

"Thanks, bartender." He looked at Gideon and winked. "You can just put it on my tab."

Vita glanced at Sally, who shifted her eyes to the NO TABS sign posted over the bar. Vita nodded and planted herself in front of Cecil's barstool, arms folded.

"Who here can tell me how much a beer costs at Shady's?" she asked the roomful of men.

Cecil opened his mouth to answer, but Vita spoke first.

"Gus?" She had already committed the regulars' names to memory. The one named Gus seemed to have the most honest face.

"Thirty cents, *ya.*"

Cecil had been ready to tell her they were a quarter.

Vita held out her hand and Cecil fished thirty cents out of his pocket, dropping the coins in her hand like they were precious heirlooms.

"And for the beer before," Vita added.

Cecil looked aggrieved. "That round was for your wedding toast."

"Then let's consider your payment a wedding gift."

Cecil reached in his pocket once again, and the other customers did the same. There was a new boss in town, but damn, wasn't she easy on the eyes?

A flash of lightning preceded a loud thunderclap, and then a few seconds later, raindrops could be heard hitting the metal rooftop. The popping sound increased until it began to pour outside.

Captain Quincy perked up. "Rain!"

The men grabbed their beers and went out to the deck to enjoy the cool breeze and watch the summer monsoon wash over the island. Giddyup Dodson and Cecil Shoat loped out to the parking lot and raised their arms and faces to the rain. Sally and Vita came outside and watched as the two men locked arms and danced a jig around a spreading pool of rainwater.

"That's prob'ly the cleanest Cecil's ever been," said Zach. "Another ten minutes out there and you won't even reco'nize him."

Soon Gus Brauer and Captain Quincy were splashing around in the puddles, too.

Vita couldn't help it. She had to laugh. *This could be fun,* she thought.

At the sound of thunder, Gilbert came hobbling around the corner and stood next to Sally on the porch, his arm around her waist. Sally made the introductions. "We're off to California," she added, turning to Gilbert and brushing a wet lock of dark hair off his forehead.

"You sure you can tear yourself away from this place?" Gilbert asked. "The wild West might seem boring next to Ransom Island."

Sally looked around—at the four nitwits dancing in the rain, at the elderly black cowboy who had taken both of them in, at the bemused new bride, shaking her head and laughing. She turned her head to watch the rain drumming on the bay. A wave of cool air, smelling of the sea, washed over her. She could stop running. Right here, right now. She had only to choose.

So she chose. She held Gilbert's face between her hands and looked at him joyously, burning this moment and these people into her memory.

"Now's the perfect time to go," she said.

———

FINITO

ABOUT THE AUTHOR

Miles Arceneaux is the *nom de plume* of Texas-based writers Brent Douglass, John T. Davis, and James R. Dennis. Miles was born many years ago as this group of friends began a collectively-written story that ultimately became the popular mystery novel, *Thin Slice of Life* (2012), followed by *LaSalle's Ghost* (2013). *Ransom Island* is the third in this series of salty Gulf Coast thrillers.